Under the Harmony

Roxie Holland

First published in Great Britain by Roxie Holland

ISBN (paperback): 978-1-918175-02-8

ISBN (ePub ebook): 978-1-918175-03-5

ISBN (hardback): 978-1-918175-42-4

Book Cover Design 100 Covers

Editing: Kaitlin Slowik

Internal Formatting: Atticus

1st edition 2026

About Roxie

Roxie Holland grew up in the UK. Born into a large family, she spent half of her time with her nose in a book, and the other half writing her own stories.

Now, Roxie lives in the Midlands with her husband, two children, and a couple of energetic dogs. She spends her day in the world of spreadsheets and rules, but her evenings are spent creating heartache and angst in new stories.

You can find Roxie lurking on Instagram as RoxieHolland_Author or you can find more details by visiting her website roxieholland.com

Also by Roxie Holland

The Love She Forgot

Protecting Her Heart

One Night Only

<u>The Love Blooms Series:</u>

Under The Heartbreak

Under The Stars

To my parents, simply for being nothing like most of the parents in this book.

To anybody who has found themselves in a situation like Rose before she ran away:

You are worth a *million* of them.

Content Warnings

Coercive relationships

Unplanned pregnancy

Assault, including dubious consent

Parental neglect

Family issues / illness

Opening Quote

"Cry for me, Princess, watch what it does to me," he growls.

No. No. No.

Chapter One

Blake

NOW

The late morning sunlight streams through the bedroom window, rousing me from sleep. Damn, I wish I remembered to close the curtains when I finally made it to bed last night. One additional minute before sliding under the covers would have avoided me being woken by the harsh light, and I'm pissed off because all I want to do right now is sleep.

I roll over and throw the covers over my head, trying to block out the light. All that does is leave me feeling suffocated, hot, and sweaty. I groan in frustration. I've no other choice but to get up. I take a deep breath, throw back the covers, and get out of bed, stretching before I head to the bathroom. I shower and shave, dress in jeans and a T-shirt, then grab my mobile from the bedside table.

I walk through to the kitchen-diner in the flat I'm renting, flicking the kettle on so I can make a coffee. I potter through to the living room, turning on the radio just to break the silence in the flat.

I sit on the sofa, looking out at the panoramic views across the river as I drink my coffee, crossing my fingers that either the coffee or the view will improve my mood. Maeve—my personal assistant—outdid herself when she found this place for me. It might be a relatively small flat compared to other places I've stayed, but everything is stylish and comfortable, and the views are incredible. It's mine for a four-month rental while I take a break from touring. The plan is to have some much-needed personal time before I'm due back in the studio to record another album.

Four months to get my head together. Four months to plan some tracks. Four months to find some inspiration. Four months to get myself out of the rut I've apparently fallen into.

I've been here two days so far, and inspiration has not been as forthcoming as I had hoped. I thought that by getting out of the madness that tends to surround my daily life, the lyrics would find me, but all I have currently is silence. If there was a cartoon drawn of what's going on in my head when I try to think of some lyrics, it would be one of those giant tumbleweeds blowing in the wind as it rolls over a figure that looks suspiciously like me.

I finish my coffee and go back to the kitchen, looking into the fridge. I know the contents are scarce because I've got through most of the food items Maeve organised for when I arrived. I told her I didn't need any shopping brought in, but she's still arranged coffee, tea, sugar, milk, bread, chocolate spread, a bottle of Jack, and a giant bowl of Granny Smith apples. The apples have always been our inside joke. When I interviewed her, I made a joke about demanding bowls full of one shade of sweets in my hotel rooms, and she told me I needed to grow up and eat something healthy. I hired her on the spot, and since then, she's arranged a bowl of green apples in any room she's booked for me. I have long understood she uses the apple brands as a coding for her mood. Crisp green Granny Smiths means everything is good, given they're the ones I love. I know she's pissed about something when the bowl is crisp red ones. Tolerable apples, but not the best. It's usually a schedule issue that she's not happy about—typically something beyond my control—but the apples keep me in the loop to her thoughts. She's never done a bowl of those hideously soft red apples before, but I think that would be my cue to beg her not to quit.

I'm busy staring into the fridge when my phone beeps. I unlock it to see a message from Maeve.

Maeve: Are you up? Run out of chocolate spread yet? Been to see your dad?

I type a message back.

Me: I'm up. Half the chocolate spread is gone, of course. Chocolate spread on toast for breakfast, chocolate spread sandwiches for dinner. Granny Smith apples for tea.

Maeve: You eat like a child when you're on your own. Get some real food. Though I guess I should be glad you're eating the apples.

Me: Yes, Mum.

Maeve: What about seeing your dad?

Me: I'm heading there now. Stop worrying about me. Go enjoy the sunshine with Libby.

Maeve: I do worry about you, Blake.

Me: No need, sweetheart. I'm fine.

I put my phone back in my pocket. I'll know she'll message me later, but I hope she doesn't get distracted. Maeve and her wife, Libby, are on a long overdue holiday. Maeve has been with me on tour for the last six months and Libby has been on tour for months as well, working as a personal stylist for another artist. I don't know how they manage to keep their relationship going when their schedules are like that—moving around from place to place, rarely overlapping to get some quality time together.

Maeve's leave has always been planned for the end of the tour. It just ended up being exceptionally bad timing when my dad announced on the night of my last concert that he has cancer. Instead of my planned overseas holiday, one where

I expected to enjoy fancy hotel rooms and picture-perfect tranquil beaches, I'm back in Nottingham—my hometown—trying to convince my dad to let me ferry him to his appointments at the hospital. I insisted Maeve still went away, even though she told me she wanted to support me. She deserves the break. More than that, she needs it. I reassured her I was fine, telling her that staying near my dad for a while would be good for me.

I haven't been home much since my career took off. The media attention is sometimes crazy, and it always feels worse when it's on my home turf. Then, it feels like more of an invasion of privacy. Somehow, being pictured having a drink with old friends is worse than being pictured by myself on some random beach. Due to the media attention that tends to surround me when I least want it, Dad is reluctant to let me help. We've had a bumpy relationship since I was a kid, but he also doesn't want me to get spotted while I'm ferrying him around to appointments.

It feels weird to be home. I wasn't expecting that spending time in my hometown would stir up so many memories. Last night, I nursed a couple of glasses of Jack and took a trip down memory lane, thinking about everything from my childhood to my twenties—the people I knew and everything I've done. This morning, those memories are still in my head, compounding what should be a minor hangover into a much bigger headache.

I shut the fridge and chide myself for procrastinating. I should do some shopping, get some real food, and then go to see my dad. I should do everything I've told Maeve I'm going to do today. I grab my baseball cap and wallet from the kitchen counter, pulling the cap on and pretending that it's like a cloak of invisibility. I'd wear sunglasses if it weren't for the overcast, late September weather. Got to love the UK. Blink and you miss the summer.

I walk down the stairs of the flat and let myself out into the little alleyway that leads to the main street. The main street is bustling with people. I take a deep breath, feeling like I'm trying to summon enough strength to join the crowd. I cross my fingers and hope that I'll be able to blend in and be just another person in the rush rather than anything for anybody to pay attention to.

I look out at the crowd, and somebody crosses my line of vision.

It can't be her.

The woman on the street looks like Olive, my ex, but there is no way it is really her. It would be too much of a coincidence for her to be on the street where I'm staying, right at the same moment I step outside. I'm imagining things because I was thinking about her last night. I should speak with Maeve and ask her to arrange for me to stay somewhere tranquil—tell her I'm clearly losing it given I'm conjuring up images of people.

I take a couple of steps towards the main street. The woman is almost out my line of vision. If she takes a few more steps, and I head in the direction I planned, she'll be gone from my view, and I won't know if it's really her or not. I can chalk this up to a moment of temporary madness, but curiosity gets the better of me.

"Olive?" I call out. I don't expect her to turn around because surely it is not really her, but she turns. I get a better look. It is Olive. I wasn't dreaming her into existence. I'm relieved, and surprised.

She gives me a wide smile. She walks towards me, up the little alleyway, and she throws her arms around me to give me a big hug.

"Oh my God, Blake! How are you doing?" she asks in a tone which portrays nothing but warmth and enthusiasm.

"Evidently, not as good as you." I smile and gesture at her stomach when I pull away from her embrace. Her hand rises, rubbing across her high baby bump. She wears a serene smile.

"Three months to go," she says.

"I'm happy for you," I reply.

I'm not sure whether it's the pregnancy or married life, but it suits her. She has a glow to her. She looks peaceful, rested. She looked peaceful the last time I saw her, too, not long after her first child was born. She and her husband Tyler both had that slightly exhausted but totally serene new-parent look about them.

"Thanks. I reckon I'll be convincing Ty to have a vasectomy after this one. Two is enough, I think, and this pregnancy is playing havoc on my bladder. It's much worse than it was with Mia. I think this one thinks my organs are footballs to kick," she says with a slight grimace.

"Is that why you looked like you were walking at one hundred miles an hour?"

"Yes, I figure there will be a café on the high street that'll take sympathy and let me use the bathroom without making me order something."

"I'm staying on this street. You could pop up and use the bathroom if you like," I offer.

"Oh, I couldn't. You look like you have places to go."

"Of course you can. Come on, go to the bathroom, and we can have a catch-up over a cup of tea."

She laughs. "If you give me a cup of tea, I will just have to pee again."

"So, pee, tea, pee again, and off you go on your merry way." I laugh along with her.

"Okay, if you are sure you don't mind."

"It's an offer to use the bathroom, Olive, I'm not offering you my firstborn child," I joke.

"Fine. You can tell me all about your showbiz, jet-setter lifestyle."

"It's just up here." I point towards my rental. I start to walk towards the entrance with her following me.

"So, come on, what are the parties like in superstar land?"

"As you'd imagine, full of people with big egos." I unlock the door and let her into the shared hallway. There's another flat that shares the main front door, but as far as I can tell, it's empty. I haven't seen anybody going in there, and I haven't heard anything from that flat, either.

I shut the door and gesture at the stairs to the upper flat.

"Do you own this place?" She looks curious as we walk up the stairs together.

"No, it's a short-term rental. Well, I say short term, but it's mine until some point in January. I wanted to come home for a bit and see my dad. He isn't one for the limelight or attention, so staying with him isn't an option," I explain as I open the door to the flat. She steps inside and whistles when she sees the view of the river.

"Nice," she says.

"Much better than the last flat I took you to, right?" I joke.

The flat I'd lived in when we'd been going out had been the absolute worst. It was tiny, damp, and cold, but she was always happy to stay there with me. She preferred to stay with me there than at her own place.

She smiles at me. "You've done well, Blake."

"The bathroom is just down the hall." I point in the direction she needs to go in.

Olive wanders down the hallway so I head to the kitchen, putting the kettle on. I busy myself making the cups of tea, debating whether I should put sugar in hers or not. She always took a spoon and a half in hers. I wonder if she changed in the years since we were together.

I wonder if it makes me presumptuous to assume it's the same or a sad loser because I remember.

Olive walks into the kitchen as I'm reaching for the sugar bowl.

"One and a half for me, please," she says, and I laugh as I relax a little.

"Still not weaned yourself off that half spoon?"

"Better than having gone up to two."

"So, how's Tyler? Is he still in sales?" I ask as I stir in the sugar. She shakes her head.

"He changed jobs last year. He works for a charity now. It's a bit of marketing, a bit of PR, a bit of management."

"What is the charity?" I ask. I know it will be something saintly and honourable. The guy has always been too good to be true.

"They're mostly known for their support for people getting out of domestic violence situations, but they do a lot of work with other homelessness charities as well," she explains as she takes her cup of tea from the counter.

"Good for him." I smile. I walk through to the living room. She follows and sits in the armchair across from where I sit on the sofa. "He won't mind you being here?"

"Ty? No, of course not. I already texted him. I asked him to guess which superstar bathroom I was currently peeing in." Olive flashes a cheeky grin.

I always loved that grin. It was what had first caught my attention about her. She had grinned at me as she threw some change into my guitar case when I was busking in the street. I stopped playing and rushed after her, asking for her number. I was over the moon when she grinned again and wrote her number on my hand.

"Did he get it right?" I ask.

"You were his first guess. I think because you're the only superstar I know, and we were talking about you this week."

"Seriously? Should I be worried?" I ask. I wager if I come up in discussion, I'm referred to as *that awful bloke Olive used to date.*

"No, of course not." She rolls her eyes. "His sister, Jen, and her husband, Jack, went to your concert, the one on Saturday. It was the only place they could get tickets, so maybe you should consider them as super fans who followed you halfway across the country."

"I hope they enjoyed themselves."

"They did. Jen said they had a great time, and that it was the best concert she'd been to. She told me you didn't sing 'Freefall.' " Olive cocks her head slightly.

"Yeah, I don't sing that now." I shrug. My debut song was a massive hit. I used to close my shows with it. The crowds always went wild from the second the music started.

"I always loved that song," she muses.

"Me, too, the crowd usually does, too. I just haven't sung it in a while."

"You should. It's one of my favourites."

"Mine, too," I say, tentatively.

She sounds genuine and as supportive as she had been the day that I went to her house to ask permission to include the song on my album. "Freefall" was a song I wrote thinking about my relationship with Olive when we were still together—when I knew a future between us was unlikely. I wrote it when I wondered if I would ever be able to compete with the memory of her dead fiancé.

It was long before I truly comprehended that it wasn't just him in her heart, but Tyler, her best friend, too.

Olive never asked if the song was about her, but she must know. She must know who the yearning in the song was about.

The media attention on my first album was insane, and there were multiple articles published running my picture and my lyrics, asking "who broke his heart." My promotions team lapped it up. They instructed me to never commit to an answer about who the song was about. Even without their instruction, I never would have said it was about Olive. We never spoke about it when we were together, and we certainly never spoke about it after she started her relationship with Tyler.

"My favourite song on the second album is 'Repercussions,'" Olive says with a wry smile.

I'm surprised she's bringing this song up. My second album was just as popular as my first. It included some older songs I wrote that hadn't fit into the first album, becoming songs the media assumed to be written about women I dated since my first album launched. There were wild speculations in the articles published, trying to guess which celebrity had broken my heart. Instead, I wrote "Repercussions" the day Olive broke up with me. I used sentences we said to each other in the lyrics.

She may doubt that "Freefall" is about her, but she must know "Repercussions" is.

"Have you ever been to one of my concerts?" I deflect the comment.

She shakes her head. "No, but only because you didn't start touring until after Mia was born, and then there is this one." She rubs her stomach again. "I want to go next time you're touring. Ty wants to go, too."

"I'll sort you some tickets, I promise. Some fancy all-access passes, too. Anything you like."

"So long as you promise to sign our chests like we're a bunch of groupies." Olive giggles, and it's like a gut punch. How many times when we were together would she tease me and say she was like my groupie?

How many times did I treat her as if she were one?

I laugh like I'm not thinking these memories, pretend that the sentence doesn't hit hard and she hasn't made me think of what a terrible boyfriend I was.

"I'm sure Tyler would love to have his chest signed by me," I tease.

"He might elbow me out of the way to get in there first."

I want to laugh because I'm sure Tyler would not bat an eyelid if I fell off the face of the earth. Maybe I'm being unkind. Tyler was her best friend, somebody who always struck me as a solid, stand-up guy, even if he intimidated the fuck out of me. It was just a shame he loved the same woman I had, a shame that when Olive finally decided to open her heart again, it was to him, not me. Olive and I broke up before she took that step with Tyler, though I wasn't surprised to hear they got together. Even I could see how well they fit together, despite wishing it was me she let in.

"Can I ask you an awkward question?" I ask.

"Sure." Despite the agreement, she sounds hesitant.

"Do you ever wonder what things would have been like if I had been better for you?"

"Better for me, how?" Olive looks at me quizzically.

"If I had been a better man. If I hadn't dicked about, made you think I didn't care. I did, you know, even if I acted like I didn't."

"If you recall, I was a bit of a mess when we were together, Blake. I didn't know it at the time, but I was. I wasn't the right person for you. And in the nicest possible way, you weren't the right person for me because you're not Ty. You and I were exactly what we needed at that time of our lives. We weren't right for each other long-term, but there wasn't anything that you did wrong. To be honest, I'm a little sad that you think it was. It might not have been a perfect relationship with the happily ever after between us, but I do treasure the time we had together."

"I'm just trying to write songs for a new album, and I've been thinking a lot about my past relationships, that's all. Don't get me wrong, I haven't been pining for you for four years or anything." I force myself to laugh.

"Oh, I know you haven't been pining. I've heard the gossip." Olive smirks. She sips some of her tea.

"You know that's all bullshit, right?" I scoff.

"So, you weren't on a yacht with supermodels Petra and Hélène?"

"Maybe, but nothing like what the magazines would have reported."

"You weren't on the cusp of proposing to Celine?"

"Absolutely not."

"No hot and heavy love affair with Jacelyn?"

"Nope. I'd never have picked you for reading the gossip rags, Olive." I grin.

"I have a bunch of younger people working in the office. They like to tell me the gossip of all the hot celebrities, trying to keep me hip and trendy," she says, but she rolls her eyes as she talks.

"Ha, did you tell them we dated? That would automatically make you hip and trendy, surely?" I joke.

"They would never shut up about it, and ask inappropriate questions, so no," she replies with a laugh.

"Tell them it's all bullshit. Celine and I collaborated on a song for her upcoming album. There were never any feelings between us—no dates, no romance, despite what was reported at the time. Petra and I met when she was in one of my music videos and she introduced me to Hélène. They were having a party and invited me. The papers turned it into some innuendo that we were having a threesome or some shit like that. Jacelyn and I had something like three dates. It was nothing serious, but the gossip mags made it seem like we were in love until we stopped being pictured together, and they labelled her my rebound girl, which is just disgusting."

"I feel like I've offended you now."

"No, it's just the papers and gossip sites are a lot to deal with. It gets a bit tedious sometimes. I mean, I'm renting this place because my dad doesn't want photographers near his house. It sucks, sometimes, to not be just another face in the crowd," I explain.

I know she probably thinks I sound like I'm complaining and that I'm ungrateful for the life I have. I know I'm lucky. I wanted this, and she has enough right to tell me how much I wanted this and remind me what I was willing to pay for it. My desire to become a successful artist was something I put before her. When we dated, I skipped our dates last minute, like the time I was chasing a lead with the band because we heard a record agent was at a club, or the time I left her behind because there was a band we could link up with on their small tour.

Not only was I inattentive to important things, but I also acted in ways I'm not proud of. When I was in the band, we all adopted personas. The dangerous one. The tortured soul. The talented one. Me, I played the flirty bad boy. We all enjoyed how fans reacted to those personas. I found it hard to know when to switch that off and to go back to being just Blake. Multiple times, I carried on flirting with women in front of Olive. I thought it didn't matter because I would never cross the line, but it was just another way of how my blind focus and desire to be successful made me act in ways that I don't feel proud about. I naively thought I only needed to be like that until I had my big break, except Olive got tired of it long before then.

I spent so long chasing this life, doing what I thought was needed to help move things along. I just didn't understand the implications when I was dreaming about it. I didn't realise what the true price was going to be.

I wanted my music heard. I wanted people to hear my lyrics. I wanted people to tell me that my lyrics helped them get through something. I just didn't expect all the other noise that seems to come with my life now. I wanted to be a successful artist without accepting that fame was an expected by product. I can't even take my dad to chemo because if the news gets out, it isn't just my life that is on display and under scrutiny, but his, and he doesn't want that. He doesn't want cameras being thrust into his face when he is sick, nor should anybody deserve that.

Olive clears her throat. "If you ever want to be just another face, you are always welcome around at my house for tea," she offers.

"I'm sure Tyler can help me feel like my feet are on the ground," I reply.

"Oh, no, not Ty. Mia will do that for you. There's nothing like a two-and-a-half-year-old to make you feel grounded." Olive laughs.

"Do you know what you're having this time?" I wonder, glancing at her baby bump.

"Another girl. Ty is going to be so outnumbered." She says this with a grin.

"Thoughts on names yet?"

"I did try to get Ty to agree to something crazy, something out there, but I was only joking. Occasionally I like to suggest something outrageous, just to see his reaction. When we eventually get around to a name, it'll probably be a short name to go with Mia's. He likes Ava, and I like Ivy. I'm sure after labour, he'll let me go with Ivy."

"Maybe I'll take you up on the offer of tea, once you've recovered after the baby arrives. I wouldn't want to impose."

"Any time, Blake. I mean it. Even if it's just as a thank you for letting me go to the bathroom. Which, if you don't mind, I will do again. Pregnancy is a bitch."

Olive grins at me as she hauls herself out of the armchair. Her baby bump isn't huge, but it's probably much more weight than she's used to carrying. She's got one of those pregnant figures where she is all bump. Everything else about her is still tiny.

"Well, you make it look good," I say. She flushes slightly and then heads back towards the bathroom. I finish my cup of tea while she is gone.

"I really should get going. I'm supposed to be meeting Becky," Olive announces as she comes back into the living room.

"It was good to see you, Olive."

"I meant what I said about being welcome at ours. Let me give you my number." She picks up her bag from the floor. I assume she's going to rummage around for a pen to write down her number, so I take my phone out of my pocket, unlock it, and hand it to her.

"Put your number in," I suggest. She takes the phone from me and inputs her number into the contacts then hands me the phone. I smile when I see she has input her name as *Olive Who Inspired Repercussions Saunders*.

She grins back at me. "I'm still waiting for my royalty cheque. I'm pretty sure some of those words were *mine*. I reckon it would be enough to put Mia through university."

I compose a text back to her so she can have my number. *Ivy/Ava, too. I'll get the cheque raised.*

"There you go." I smile. She laughs when she reads my text.

"Okay, I was joking, but I'm now storing you in my contacts as 'the dude who owes me money.' I promise not to leak your phone number to crazy fans."

"Much appreciated." I laugh.

She throws her phone back into her bag. "Right, it was great to see you. Weird and unexpected, but great."

"I'll see you out." I walk with her towards the door and down the stairs. I open the door for her, and she steps into the alleyway.

"Bye, Blake."

"See you, Olive," I say, and she turns to give me another hug.

I watch her walk down the little pathway towards the main road. She doesn't give me another glance and then she disappears into the crowd. I wait at the doorway for a moment before sighing and turning back towards the house, going up the stairs to the main door.

I shut the door behind me. All thoughts of heading out to see my father are gone for now. I need a moment to collect my thoughts. I won't focus on anything Dad has to say right now.

I pick up the empty cups and take them into the kitchen to wash them. The radio is still playing in the background, and I hear the familiar lyrics, hear my voice over the airwaves. "Freefall."

"And I hit that wall every goddamn time. Wondering if my girl will ever truly be mine. Fighting every goddamn day to scale her wall. Knowing that I'm always going to be in freefall. Loving the woman who is always out of reach. With walls so high that I'll never breach."

I switch the radio off, and now the silence seems to echo around the room.

Somehow, now feels worse than when I was drowning my sorrows in half a bottle of Jack last night, having an impromptu walk down the proverbial memory lane. I blame being home, being in town. It's making me feel worse, making me think of all my failings.

I know I made a lot of dick choices in my past, some about family, some about my former bandmates, some about Olive. Most of the mistakes that have kept me up over the last couple of nights have been about her because she was the last woman I loved. She was the last person I felt like I had a genuine connection with, even if it wasn't reciprocated in the way I hoped.

Not telling her I loved her when we were together? Dick move.

Too scared to tell her about my feelings because I was afraid of what she'd say? Dick move.

Standing her up, treating her with indifference, and acting like she was a fucking groupie? Dick move.

Letting her think I was only in it for sex, like screwing her at any opportunity in places like makeshift dressing rooms? Dick move—just a different type. More a move led by the dick, I guess.

I know the past can't be undone. It isn't an outcome I really want to change, either. I'm smart enough to know that what Olive said was right. We were never destined to walk off into the sunset together, holding hands and living happily ever after. Despite that, the way I felt about her has certainly been a yardstick I've used to measure relationships up against since. I want to find somebody who I can feel the same way about as I had with Olive, but to have the person feel the same about me in return. I want to find somebody I know I can skip off into that mythical perfect sunset with, holding their hand and knowing we can fight any battles together.

I won't make the same mistakes again. The next time I have feelings for somebody, I don't want there to be any doubt about how I feel for them, and I want to know they love me in return. I'm going to put my heart on the table and risk it, because I know it can give me the greatest reward.

I don't want to be left broken-hearted again, especially if I'm the reason for it.

Finding somebody, though, feels like an impossible task. The dating world is hard enough. I remember the shitshow of dating I had in my early twenties, and that was when it was easier to find somebody. Dating as a celebrity, it's fucking brutal. There is no such thing as a quiet, non-pressured date. There's no option of taking leisurely strolls around the country parks, hand in hand, kissing under blossoming trees because the moment feels so perfect. Not without some enthusiastic fan taking a photograph they can whip up online in an instant, tagging with names and practically giving directions to your location. One kiss and the gossip sites have you married off and having kids before you've even decided if you want a second date.

Even finding dates feels like a minefield. Somebody famous? Paparazzi wet dream. Cue the endless obsession of dragging up dating histories, matching you by your star signs or various other idiotic titbits they've got on record about you. It's even worse if your names can be combined for a cute nickname, reducing you to one person in print. No thank you. The alternative, though, is somebody not from the showbiz lifestyle, which is a baptism by fire and something I'd hate to inflict on somebody. It's bad enough my private life is often splayed out in the gossip mags. Asking somebody who isn't in the industry to join me is too much. They'd never survive it, and the ones who are keen to do so are clearly the ones desperate for their own slice of fame. The idea of finding somebody to put up with that crap, only for them to sell stories to the gossip rags turns my stomach.

I shake my head. My love life is not on my radar right now. It wasn't the driver behind my break from the world. I've more important things to worry about than my love life. My dad's health. Getting him through treatment. Finding a miracle fix. Then, when all of that is better, working out my next step in my career. I've a management team expecting a third album, but I have a severe case of writer's block and I've no idea how to fix it.

Right now, I should get back out there, get some shopping done, go see my dad. Instead, I flick the kettle back on to boil.

Another drink, and I'll get my life back on track.

Chapter Two

Blake

NOW

The sound of my phone blaring startles me awake. I scramble around on the bed for the phone, just so I can silence the god-awful noise. It's still dark but that could be because it's still nighttime or because I remembered to close the blackout blinds last night.

My phone screen lights up, telling me it is six in the morning, and that Maeve is calling.

"This better be a genuine, life-or-death, fucking emergency," I growl as I answer. I love her to death, but fuck, I've never been a fan of the morning, especially when I have the opportunity and plans to sleep in until mid-morning.

"It is. Sorry, Blake, I know it's early there, but I didn't want to wait." Maeve sounds fretful, and I'm immediately more alert.

"What is it?" I sit up and rub the sleep out of my eyes. "Why aren't you and Libby slathering sunscreen on each other, or skinny-dipping in some heavenly looking cove?"

"Well, we were about to start with the skinny-dipping, but I checked my phone before we could get started."

"I can't decide if I should call you a tease about the skinny-dipping idea or call you a loser for checking your phone when you're supposed to be on a romantic getaway."

"You can joke later. You need to check your phone. I'm sending you a link now."

"Yeah, okay, hang on," I say.

I switch her to hands-free. I open the messaging app and click on the link that she's sent me, scowling a little when I see the address is for a run of the mill gossip website. By run of the mill, I mean a site run by people with no scruples, with baseless articles that are full of shit. It's the type of site where you find accusations and innuendo, and exactly the type of page I hate being featured on.

As the page loads, I wonder if it will be about my dad. I saw him yesterday afternoon, and I took him to an appointment. I waited in the car for him to get back rather than going in with him to see the doctor as well. It was what he asked of me. I hid behind the heavily tinted windows of my hire car, but somebody could have still seen. He'll be angry if there are pictures of him looking sick, his face looking sunken. As the page refreshes, I'm annoyed that they used my dad as clickbait, but then I see it.

It isn't an article about my dad and his illness. Instead, this somehow feels like it is worse. I suck in my breath as I read the headline and the article.

LOVER-BOY BLAKE AND HIS MYSTERY LADY

Pop heartthrob Blake Daniels was seen canoodling with a mystery young woman on Thursday. The dark-haired hunk entered a private residence with his mystery companion, and they were out of sight for some time. One can only speculate what they were doing.

When they emerged, Blake, who was wearing his trademark dark jeans and a stylish T-shirt, embraced the mystery woman, who was wearing a red dress. Both looked relaxed with each other and wore wide smiles. The woman appeared heavily pregnant.

Is this the woman who has finally tamed the wild loner? Has the "Repercussion" singer met his match, somebody to stop his "Freefall"?

Scroll to see our exclusive pictures!

Well, shit.

I scroll down to look at the photographs. They're grainy and clearly taken from a camera phone rather than some press camera. Despite the low quality, it is clear they're pictures of me and of Olive. Anybody who knows her will see these are photographs of her.

"Who is she, Blake?" Maeve asks.

"She's an ex-girlfriend."

"Please tell me she's only an ex-girlfriend. You're not—"

"You know how I feel about cheaters, Maeve. I don't cheat, and I wouldn't be 'the other guy' for somebody, especially somebody who is pregnant."

"I know that, but it doesn't look good. Anybody who doesn't know you could read more into this than is really there."

"Olive is an ex from way back when. I ran into her yesterday. She still lives in town, with her husband, their kid, and another on the way."

"I can tell she has another on the way," Maeve comments. I look at the pictures again. A nice, unexpected reunion looks like it's going to bite me in the ass.

"She isn't going to be happy about this," I murmur.

"Tell me more about this relationship," Maeve suggests, and I laugh.

"There isn't much to tell. I met Olive when I was busking. We dated for seven months or so. She didn't feel the same for me as I felt for her. I wasn't the most attentive boyfriend, a bit too focused on trying to get my big break. She broke up with me. It was an amicable breakup. End of story."

"Is there anything you want me to release?"

"No. First, you are supposed to be on holiday. You need this downtime. Don't make me send you for some therapy to understand how to enjoy some relaxation. Second, it's nothing. It's a picture of me hugging a friend. Not canoodling, for God's sake. Olive might be a bit pissed off when she sees this, but it'll blow over."

"You're not going to see her again?"

"No, not likely. She offered for me to go to tea with her and her husband, I said I'd hook her up with concert tickets, but nothing more."

"Okay. If you are going to see her again, it might be better to get ahead of this," Maeve muses.

"Like I said, it is unlikely I'll see her again."

"Are you sure?" She sounds fretful again. Part of it is her job, and part of it is her nature. Maeve is always on the lookout for threats and things that could be harmful for my career. She's a bloody amazing PA and I love her for it.

"Absolutely. Now, go enjoy your holiday."

"Have you done your shopping yet?" she teases after a moment of quiet.

"Goodbye, Maeve. Go skinny-dipping with your wife." I laugh and hang up.

I'm sure it won't be long until Olive sees this article. I wonder if she will find it amusing or if it won't even register with her. Maybe she'll laugh and make a joke about it with her friends. Maybe she'll text me to retract the invite for tea and tell me I've ruined her week. Whatever her reaction, I'm pretty sure I'll be hearing from her at some point today.

I swing my legs over the side of the bed, sighing to myself. Might as well get the day started.

***

I'm surprised that it takes until seven thirty in the evening for my phone to ring, the caller display flashing Olive's name.

"Well, if it isn't my mystery woman, to what do I owe this pleasure?" I joke, but even in the small silence, I can hear her frustration.

"Blake, tell me you're going to handle this," she says with a sigh.

"There isn't anything that needs to be handled," I reply. I walk across to the kitchen so I can flick the kettle on.

"Seriously? Headlines that you're *canoodling* somebody doesn't need to be handled?"

"You can clearly see from the photographs that we were not canoodling, and anybody who gets their news from a site that even uses the word canoodling needs to get their head checked. It's just trash, Olive," I reply.

"Come on, Blake, just issue a statement."

"It would only add fuel to the fire, trust me." I sigh.

I've dealt with the media since my first album launched. It's been nothing but conjecture, misquotes, heavy editing of words said, and misinterpretation of facts. Olive hasn't had that kind of experience though, so I understand her frustration. She probably assumes a quick "hey, you got the wrong end of the stick," statement would be enough to make everything disappear. She lives in a world where when something is untrue, an apology and a retraction is forthcoming.

"Well, I don't think it is possible to make this worse. At least, not for me. How do you think I felt when I was dropping Mia off at nursery this morning and all the mothers were looking at me like I'm some sort of cheating, lying bitch who is stepping out on her husband?" Olive's voice drips with annoyance. I forgot how pissed off she could get.

"They don't think that, and if they do, I'd be questioning their intelligence." I try to appease her. Anybody salivating over the headlines and a fairly innocent picture needs to get themselves a life.

"One woman asked me how Tyler feels, knowing I'm carrying your baby," she snaps.

"Who are these women?" I laugh.

"It doesn't matter who they are. All you need to know is they're talking about me and making incorrect assumptions about my life. It's my picture online. I'm the one being talked about."

"I'm sure if I refresh the page, there will be a few comments about me and my morals. It'll die down," I soothe.

"My direct reports at work couldn't wait for me to arrive so they could gossip."

"Ignore them, Olive."

"Sort it out, Blake." It sounds like she says this with her teeth gritted together.

"It'll die down, I promise."

"Blake, please."

Now there's a desperation in her tone that I've never heard before. It makes me feel bad for her, but desperation doesn't go well with the media. Any weakness and it's like a feeding frenzy.

I sigh and pinch the bridge of my nose to help me focus. "What do you want me to say?"

"Anything has got to be better than this innuendo, surely?"

"If I tell them that it isn't true, they won't believe me anyway. Of the people I've been linked to, how many do you think I've dated? I told you yesterday how misconstrued things can be. If even a tenth of what was written about me was true, I'd have broken more hearts than I can count."

"You could just say, hey, Olive is an old friend. We dated, eons ago. She and her husband are looking forward to their second child arriving. You could just tell them I desperately needed the loo, and you were a chivalrous gentleman, I don't care!"

"You'd rather the world was discussing your bladder?"

"Better than thinking I'm cheating, or, no offense, some harlot you have knocked up."

I haven't looked online to see any more articles, not since the one this morning that Maeve sent me, but I'm not stupid enough to think there aren't going to be more. Media articles are like a Hydra. One pops up, then more. Sometimes it's just a copy and paste, a rehash as to what has previously been published, and sometimes it is further innuendo. It isn't too much stretch of the imagination to assume a lowbrow site might have alluded that Olive is pregnant with my child, and it won't just be idiots she knows in real life reading it, but worldwide for people to see at a click of a button.

This is what will be upsetting Olive.

I sigh. "How's Tyler reacting to this?"

"Well, he's not exactly impressed by it."

"Oh, come on, he can't be mad with you about this," I scoff. I hear the tut she gives before she takes a deep breath, and I know she's about to put me in my place. "I'm joking. I know Tyler wouldn't be mad at you."

"No, he isn't mad with me, but he's fended off a few calls today from fake friends with their bullshit curiosity. It's amazing who comes out of the woodwork when there is a hint of drama, people you haven't heard from in years. He's had half a dozen random text messages from people he hasn't heard from in months, wondering how he is."

"Tell them to fuck off," I suggest. There is a pause between us.

"Is this what your life is really like, all the time?" Her voice is slightly softer now. Whatever fuel she had for her anger is dimming.

"Yeah, pretty much. In my experience, it is better to just say nothing. Keep your head down and it blows over."

"It sucks, Blake. I thought maybe it couldn't be that bad, but this seems shitty. Now I see why you might want to be just another face in the crowd."

"I'm assuming your tea invite is rescinded after this crap?"

"No, whenever you want to come, you just let us know."

"You're very kind, Olive. Tyler, too."

She chuckles. "Well, we're trusting you that this will be the last of it in the gossip columns."

"I'm sorry that this has happened. I hope those idiots at the nursery get a bit smarter. It's worrying they're in charge of the next generation when they lack the ability to think clearly."

"Yeah, I agree with you. Have a good evening, Blake."

"Good night," I say, and then she's gone from the line.

I put my phone down and look around the kitchen. The bag of shopping I got earlier is still on the countertop, waiting to be unpacked. I unpack the contents, throw my ready meal into the microwave, and prepare myself for a long, quiet evening, wondering if I'll find any inspiration tonight.

***

I wake up on the sofa. It takes a moment for me to realise what has woken me up. It's my mobile phone, blaring an alert that my name has been linked in an article. I'm starting to feel like my mobile is cursed and needs to be thrown away, but this time I only have myself to blame for the disturbance. I felt stupid last night setting up the alert, but apparently it was warranted. My mobile phone display states NEW NEWS ARTICLE ABOUT BLAKE DANIELS.

I feel a wave of stress washing over me. I'm sure this is not going to be good news given the article yesterday. This is either a rehash of the article yesterday, or it's a follow-up. A follow-up is always worse. I cross my fingers that it's just another site repeating the same story, a bit behind the times of the million sites that seem to have run with the pictures yesterday.

I sit up on the sofa and open the link so I can read it.

BLAKE'S BROKEN HEART

We can exclusively reveal that Blake Daniels's mystery woman is none other than the woman who inspired his greatest hits. The woman who inspired "Freefall," "Repercussions," and several other tracks is the woman who broke his heart by betraying him with his best friend. It is understood her deceit resulted in a violent showdown between the involved parties.

An anonymous source exclusively revealed that Daniels "lost his mind" after discovering the betrayal, and his muse moved on "surprisingly quickly," leaving Daniels stunned and "lashing out" in his heartbreak, following reckless paths.

Keep scrolling to see our exclusive pictures.

Holy shit.

I scroll and I'm shocked to see the photograph. It's an old, grainy image. I squint at it and wonder when it was taken. In the picture, I'm walking next to Olive. The image is blurry, but it is clear she has marks on her face and a swollen cheek. Tyler is in the picture, looking uncharacteristically pissed off. The image is accompanied by several comments and bullet points from the writer.

Pictures emerge of Blake Daniels and his battered companion!
Woman looks downcast and injured!
Blake's former best friend's disapproving stare!
We will exclusively reveal the shocking reasons for her injuries!
The heartbreak she suffered before inflicting heartbreak on Daniels!
The reckless path Daniels followed when his heart was broken!

What the fuck.

I read the rest of the article. There isn't any more depth, no further pictures, just heavy innuendo. There isn't enough explicitly written to say I beat my girlfriend, but enough not said that it is the only interpretation the reader can make as a conclusion. Unfortunately, most of the people who read sites like this are idiots with terrible minds. The site typically caters to the public who are outraged when two co-stars who are married to other people walk next to one another because clearly, they must be having an affair.

I'm sure this site relies on a splattering of exclamation points just to keep their readers salivating.

The article reveals Olive's full name and contains links to articles about how her fiancé had been stabbed to death not long before their planned wedding, years before I met her. I know she will hate having this dragged up again. She was never able to talk to me properly about what happened to her fiancé, and the one time she told me the full story, she looked like her heart was breaking the whole time.

I look back at the photograph that has been published with the article. I have no idea where they got this, or who gave it to them, but I do have an idea of why she looks like she does. The only explanation for this picture is that it was taken after she had fallen off her bike. She had an accident where she nearly collided with a car, had hit a barrier and taken a bad fall. She looked battered for a while. We had a couple of nights out with Tyler after she was injured, one where the two of them came to see me and the band, another where we went out with Harriet, Tyler's girlfriend at the time. I don't know what night this was taken, who took it, who released it, but I do know that Olive is going to be furious.

I take a deep breath and close the article, pulling up my contacts list. I'm going to get ahead of the game this time. I'm not going to wait until her anger boils over and she calls me.

I dial Olive's number, crossing my fingers that she will answer. It's only seven, but I'm sure she will be awake. Either her daughter will have woken her, or somebody will have spoken to her about this article.

There's a chance she has blocked my number if she has read this article. There's a chance she'll make Tyler answer the phone. I'm not sure which option is worse.

The line stops ringing. I wonder if it has timed out, but then I hear her give a little sigh. I'm not entirely sure, but it sounds like she may have been crying. I thought reading the article was bad, but apparently, I'm still not well-equipped to handle tears. It feels a little like my windpipe has been crushed.

"Are you okay?" I ask, once I've got a grip of myself.

"It's been a stressful start to the morning, Blake."

"I can imagine. I'm sorry. At least it cannot get any worse," I joke, but when I hear her sharp intake of breath, I know I've made a grave error in judgement. Phoning her was a good step, but joking about the situation, that was stupid.

"Do not talk to me about worse," she snaps. "This *is* worse. You told me that if you made a statement, it would make things worse, but you said nothing and now there are pictures being published like I'm some cheating woman, again, and you're an abuser!" She sounds furious.

"I know, I know, it's shit."

"Get in touch with the site and get these taken down."

"I'll sort it."

"Do it, or I will. This is... God, this is so intrusive. I feel so violated, and I didn't even think it was possible to feel violated when it's just words online. This is my life, Blake. This is my history on display, albeit some of it is a lie."

"I said I'll do it."

"You should have done what I asked before. Now my parents worry I was in some abusive relationship and that's why I never introduced you to them. My mum was on the phone as soon as she saw the article. She's really upset. She was crying, Blake. It isn't fun trying to calm down my mother when I've also got Mia just waking up and Tyler stumbling out of bed and wondering what the hell is going on."

"Surely you told your parents the truth behind these pictures. They're from when you fell off your bike, right?"

"Yeah, but you don't always think rationally when it comes to your kids. When you eventually grow up and have some, maybe you'll see what I mean."

"Hey, I am grown up. I turn thirty this year," I point out.

"Old enough to get this shit sorted out then, right?"

"I will sort it out, I promise," I vow.

"Funny that you seem ready to act on something when it's your life being prodded at like this, now there is a risk to you, but not when the risk was with me."

"Me sorting it out has nothing to do with the damage to my reputation, I swear. I'm so sorry that you were dragged into all of this. I thought if we kept our head down, it would go away, but I was wrong. I'll put it right."

"Whilst you're at it with the site and wanting to make things right, tell them they should make a sizeable donation to a women's shelter, to help people who need it, rather than making up shit. They should be fucking ashamed of themselves for making these baseless accusations."

"Maybe I'll suggest they donate to the charity where Tyler works."

"Try to keep Ty out of this, if you can." Olive sighs.

"I assume he is not finding this very amusing?"

"He found the idea that you two were besties the only hilarious part of the article."

"To be fair, that is the only thing from that article that made me smile."

"I'll bet," she says, and there is a hint of a laugh in her tone. She never could stay mad for too long. She's like a firework sometimes, a burst and flash of anger and then back to normal.

"Do you have any idea who released the picture?" I ask.

"The only people that spring to mind would either be your old bandmates or Harriet," Olive replies. "When I fell off the bike, they were the only people I saw socially with you."

"Well, my former bandmates hate me enough to do something like this."

"Harriet probably hates me more than they hate you, and it's the kind of stunt that she would pull. She was always angry about how quickly I got with Ty after he broke up with her."

"Weirdly, I saw her not long after I heard you and Tyler were together. She didn't hold back on her opinion. I tried to calm her down. She was having none of it, telling me you and Tyler had been together behind our backs," I tell her, remembering now how furious Harriet had been. I forgot all about it until now.

"I hope you know that wasn't true. I know it wasn't long after we split up that I got together with Ty, but I never—"

"I know you didn't cheat, Olive. I know you."

"Yeah, but still, I know what it's like to be on the receiving end of Harriet's anger. She's very determined to get her point across when she thinks she's been wronged," Olive growls.

"She always did have a stick up her ass."

She laughs at my assessment.

"It's out of the blue though, we haven't heard from Harriet in years. Why would she do something so vindictive?"

"Money is a big motivator. I'm sure the site would have paid well for that photograph, and a little bit of gossip," I point out.

She sighs. "Do you promise to sort this?"

"I promise. I'll draft something up on my socials right now, and I'll get on my management company to release a formal statement and contact the website."

"Thank you." Her voice still sounds a little tight.

"Do you want to read a statement before I post it?"

"No, I trust you."

"I'm sorry you're going through this. I bet you wish you'd peed at the café now," I joke.

"I think I'd even take peeing myself in the street over this," she mutters.

"Oh, come on, don't make me feel bad. I swear, nobody else in the world makes me feel guilt like you do. It's like a special skill you have," I groan.

There is a small huff of laughter, followed by a pause. "I'm sorry that this is your life, that nothing innocent can remain like that, that it is all twisted."

"Well, price of fame, and all that," I say. There is another silence between us. I clear my throat. "Can you, please, tell Tyler that I'm really sorry."

"He doesn't really need an apology, but I will tell him anyway."

"Try and have a happy Saturday," I add. She tells me she hopes I have a good weekend, too, and then she is gone.

I contemplate phoning Maeve, but I don't want to interrupt her holiday. My fingers hover over the dial option against her name in my contact list. Maeve is more than my assistant; she's a good friend, somebody I regularly turn to. She's always pragmatic and honest, always willing to calm me down or formulate a plan. I'm torn between my desire for her to have a good break versus my need to talk to somebody who can keep me settled. I can tell Olive I'm sorting things, but it doesn't mean this article hasn't upset me, too. I don't think there are many people who would be happy reading articles suggesting they beat women.

I lock my phone screen, but then it rings. I pick it up, only partly surprised that it is Maeve.

"Blake, are you okay?" She sounds fretful.

"I'm fine, apart from being pissed off."

"What the hell happened, where have these pictures come from? I swear, Blake, you've been home for less than a week and the world seems to be going to shit. I'm starting to think you should have gatecrashed my getaway. You clearly can't be trusted without me," Maeve scolds.

The fact she isn't immediately talking damage control reassures me that she knows me well enough to know the article is complete bullshit. I'm sure though, for every person like Maeve who believes me, there will be a million others who thinks there is no smoke without fire and will believe I would hurt somebody like that.

"Olive and I both think the picture can only have come from one of two sources, as they're the only overlaps in the time. It's either the guys from the band, or it's the woman who was dating Tyler at the time," I explain.

"Who is this so-called best friend, the one in the article? He couldn't have released this?"

"No, that's Tyler in the picture. He was Olive's best friend at the time. They got together after Olive broke up with me. He's her husband now," I add.

"You're both sure he wouldn't have released a picture?"

"Absolutely sure. Tyler wouldn't do anything to upset Olive," I tell her. Even when they were just friends, I'd have staked money that Tyler would lay down his life for Olive, if required.

"The picture…." Maeve's voice trails off.

"She had a bad accident on her bike."

"Okay, look, do you want me to come—"

"If you carry that sentence on with the word 'home,' I might have to consider firing you," I joke, cutting off the rest of her sentence.

"You'd never find anybody better than me," she retorts, and I smile to myself. She's right, as usual. She's worth her weight in gold, as well as Granny Smith apples.

"I'm going to put a statement out on my socials. I'll ask the rest of the team to contact the website to get the article removed."

"I'll pick everything up with the team, you do your statement," Maeve offers.

"You'll do nothing of the sort. You're on holiday," I point out and she sighs.

"It's fine. Libby has some work to do today as well. Besides, do you even know the right people to contact in the team about this?" Maeve challenges. She takes my silence as acknowledgement of how useless I am.

"Okay, but then go enjoy your holiday, Maeve."

She promises to update me later and says goodbye before hanging up.

I head to the kitchen to grab my laptop. I sit at the table, waking the screen, closing the notes I'd been making yesterday, scowling at my pathetic attempts at lyrics. I open a new document and start typing.

STATEMENT FROM BLAKE DANIELS

As many people will be aware, it is very rare for me to talk about my personal life. However, there have been articles posted on several media sites that I cannot let go without providing a response.

This response is not for me. It is for a friend whose life is being turned upside down by baseless and hurtful reporting.

Here are the facts. Here is the truth.

Olive Saunders and I dated several years ago. I cared deeply for her, but I was also young with a desire to make my big break. This desire for fame was something I prioritised over everything, including our relationship. With regards to that, I could have been a better man for her, but I still wouldn't have been the right man for her. Inevitably, we split.

Olive and I were together for several months. In that time, she helped me see things clearly. She encouraged me, she was the one who gave me the confidence to write the music how I wanted to. She made me realise my own self-worth as an artist. For these reasons, I will always cherish the time we had together. Whilst our relationship was short, it was special. I'm a better man because of our relationship, because of her.

Olive and I ended amicably. There were no other parties involved. Our relationship just ran out of steam. There was never any violence during our relationship or after—between us, or us and anybody else.

There have been two photographs released and posted this week. To address the first: This is an innocent photograph of two friends hugging goodbye. I'd seen Olive by chance, and we caught up over a cup of tea. I hadn't seen her since before the first album was released, when I'd spent the afternoon with her, her husband, and their baby daughter. It was nice to catch up this week and to see a friendly face. However, to know that this innocent catch-up led to people speculating Olive is pregnant with my baby, or suggesting that she is cheating on her husband is hurtful. Not just for me, but for her and her family.

To address the second picture and to correct the errors in the reporting:

When we dated, Olive had an accident on her bike. She swerved to avoid a car and went over the handlebars. It was an accident. Her injuries in the photograph were sustained in that accident.

The man in the picture who was described as my best friend was actually Olive's best friend. The disapproving stare was probably because I'd been late turning up, or something equally as benign.

To the person who released this picture—what was your aim here? To manipulate the facts and suggest I'm violent? To tarnish my reputation, or to tarnish Olive's by suggesting she was a cheater? Either way, I hope you feel ashamed of yourself, about your false assumptions and the lies told. Domestic violence has no place in our society. False accusations should have no place in our society, either.

Furthermore, the writers of the articles dug up Olive's history, which has forced her to relive a painful part of her past, the senseless murder of her fiancé nine years ago. To force somebody to relive something so painful in the media is nothing short of despicable.

The speculation on Olive and her family after these two articles has been disgusting. She's not a celebrity who accepted intense media speculation would be part of her life, some bullshit she would have to accept as the counterbalance to the fame. She is a private woman who loves her husband and their daughter and is looking forward to the arrival of their second child. As a family, they live a quiet, private life. They do not deserve for their lives to be splashed over the front page of gossip sites or for anybody to pick at her history.

To the websites running the story: My team will be in touch. Your article is baseless, unfounded speculation. You did not reach out to anybody to fact-check. I can only assume you were busy salivating at a potential scandal to do proper research, or maybe you are comfortable hiding behind false statements from "a close source."

If you feel any guilt in your part of misreporting, donate to a charity caring for people escaping domestic violence, or to an anti–knife crime charity.

I do not want, nor need, your apology.

I need you to do better.

Blake Daniels

I re-read the statement before posting on all my socials and website. I send a link to Olive. I look up the charity where Tyler works and email a link to Maeve to ask her to arrange an anonymous annual donation, matching the one I already send to an anti–knife crime charity. I've donated to the same charity since my first album sales went crazy, something I felt was an attempt to give gratitude to Olive and how much she helped me. I donate to a charity she felt important after she lost her fiancé, even if I've never told her I donate and always kept private, like charity donations should be.

My phone buzzes.

Olive Who Inspired Repercussions Saunders: Thank you, Blake. That means a lot. Any time you want tea with me and Ty, you're welcome, if only to give you some time away from the bullshit.

I fire back a response, telling her I'll keep it in mind. I put my phone back down and then head to the bathroom. Might as well get the day started.

Chapter Three

Rose

NOW

I slowly drive my car down the little street, whispering a little prayer of thanks that Libby arranged a small and inconspicuous car for me to drive. If she arranged anything flashy—like I usually drive around in when I'm on some downtime—I would stick out like a sore thumb based on the cars I saw when driving through the surrounding town to get into the village. Given I'm aiming to be inconspicuous, fancy sports cars are off the menu for a while, and I'm glad at her foresight to make me fit in.

According to my research, Whistlethorpe is a tiny village. Tiny enough that it doesn't even have a large supermarket, just some small shops, a post office, an infant school, a small pub, two cafés, and a couple of takeaways. It is apparently home to five thousand residents. Five thousand and one, now including me. Driving through it confirms that yes, the village is tiny.

The navigation programme tells me I've arrived at my destination. I look out to the little cottage that stands on Sea View. This is my supposed refuge for the foreseeable future. It's quaint—the exact type of place you'd see in advertisements for a secluded retreat, littered with words like peaceful, tranquil, and the perfect escape.

In front of the cottage, there is a neat, well-maintained little garden and a driveway for two cars, with a little fence providing a barrier between the gravel of the driveway and the flowers in the garden. There is a cared-for looking wisteria plant growing up one side of the cottage, cut neatly around the side windows. It makes the house look like it should be in a storybook, the type a hero would take sanctuary in through their hour of need.

The cottage is in a set of four. The other three all have their front shutters closed and they look like they're closed down for the winter. Two of the gardens are in state of disarray, with dead flowers, piles of leaves, and overgrown hedges. It reassures me that I'm not going to be bothered by well-meaning neighbours.

In front of the cottage that I'm supposed to be staying at, a man stands next to the front door. He is wearing a suit and a slightly stressed expression on his face. He was checking his watch as I drove up the street, but he looks across at my car now, his expression relaxing slightly when he sees me.

I get out of the car, open the backseat, and grab my suitcase. I pull the case down the little path towards the cottage and plaster a bright smile on my face, the type that hurts the cheeks because it's so forced and fake.

"Mr Sharp?" I ask. He smiles warmly, the stressed expression completely gone.

"Miss Smith?"

"Yes, I'm so sorry I'm late," I apologise, trying to act like the name he is using is really mine rather than something Libby created to keep my identity a secret. I smile like this is the name I've used my whole life, not something I had to remind myself a hundred times on the drive, repeating Elodie Smith, Elodie Smith like a mantra.

I offer my hand to the man to shake. His handshake is one of those only given by somebody who shakes hands regularly; it isn't limp or too forceful. I've shaken a lot of hands before, and it is surprising how people can get something so basic so wrong. I learnt from an early age how to keep my expressions neutral when faced with clammy and clingy hands, so I'm grateful to avoid that now.

"It's fine, I was worried you'd gotten lost. Here's your key, let me show you in and around," he offers.

I wonder if I should tell him I'm all set—just take the keys and tell him to get on his merry way—but that would be rude. He seems like a nice guy, and Libby has vouched for him. She said he helped her with some legal stuff in the past and called him a "genuinely nice guy." Coming from Libby, it is high praise indeed.

I'm just not sure I believe much in the concept of a genuinely nice guy anymore.

"Sure, that would be great, but I wouldn't want to keep you, given I'm so late," I settle upon.

"It's fine. It won't take long. The main thing is just to show you about the heating and thermostat, so you don't freeze when the poor weather hits." Another warm smile. I notice he wears a wedding ring.

"Your wife won't be annoyed at you being home late?" I ask.

"Annabeth is on the beach at the back, with the kids. I'm going to join them when I'm done here."

I look at his suit, which looks expensive, and his shoes, which do not scream beach attire. Then I look at the weather, which even by the usual standards of September in the UK looks dark and gloomy, on the cusp of rain or maybe even a thunderstorm set to arrive.

"Your kids are out in this, and you're off to the beach looking like that?" I can't help but laugh.

"I was in the office today, but I'm never going to miss a chance to be on the beach with my family. Faith, our youngest, she will be wearing about twenty layers, and Willow, the oldest, she loves the beach this time of year. All year round, really. She doesn't care about the cold. In fact, I think she prefers it. We always spend Monday evenings on the beach. It's a perfect antidote to the start of the week."

"Okay, let's see this place, so you can round up your family, Mr Sharp."

"Call me Nathaniel," he suggests.

"Elodie," I tell him.

It's not entirely a lie given it is my middle name. Most people know me by my stage name. It's the one the papers use. They've never published my full, real name, and I'm convinced most people assume my stage name is my real name.

Even my parents seem to have forgotten what they put on my birth certificate. Regardless, using my true first name feels like it could be risky, when I've gone so far to maintain privacy, when Libby has tried to protect me, too. I've cut my trademark long blonde hair and dyed it brown. My natural blue eyes are hidden behind brown contacts. I'm wearing an outfit that is so far removed from my usual clothes, it's laughable. I feel like a kid wearing their mother's outfit and shoes for dressing up and just hope I don't look like it as well.

"Come on in, Elodie." Nathaniel opens the door to the cottage. "We used to live here, before we accepted that we needed more space as the family grew. We live across the village now, so we are not far away if there is a problem with the house."

"Okay. What's the village like?"

"It's nice, a little quiet, especially now it is the off-season. If you're here for peace and quiet, you're going to find nothing but that. I know when I first moved here, it was a culture shock."

"Are the houses on the street also for rent?"

"Usually, but they close up at the end of September. They used to be owned by families but sold in the last year or so as summer rentals, so you're on your own on the street."

"Sounds good," I reply, and I feel like a weight has been lifted from me.

"Okay, so the thermostat is here; it's on a set cycle but it's easy enough to boost it if you need a bit of extra heat. It can get cold here, given it's so close to the sea, so feel free to adjust the timers if you want it warmer. All the utilities are included in the rent. The main bedrooms both have electric blankets as well, should you need them," Nathaniel explains. He gives me a quick explanation of the thermostat, somehow managing to not sound like he's mansplaining, though I'm sure I zone out in parts.

"Thanks for showing me around," I say after he gives me the details of everything to do with the house.

"If you need anything, our contact numbers are in the documentation shared with your assistant. You can call either of us, but Annabeth works at the school, so she isn't available until after five," Nathaniel apologises.

"Thank you for taking the time to meet me and show me around. I hope you have fun at the beach." I smile. He gestures to the back door.

"That leads you straight to the beach, down the side path," he explains.

"Go see your family, Nathaniel. I'll be in touch if there are any issues."

Nathaniel gives me another smile and then he heads towards the front door, leaving the second key on the side table near the front door. I watch him leave, shutting the door behind him, leaving me in the silence.

I leave my suitcase in the hallway, put the deadbolt on the front door, and then head upstairs to check out the rest of the property. There are three bedrooms—two large double rooms and a small box room. The double bedrooms both have double beds and nice functional furniture. The box bedroom has a small single bed, a wardrobe, and a small desk. The bathroom is nicely laid out—fully tiled in a black and white design with a shower and separate slipper bath. Everything looks neat and tidy and a perfect place to stay and relax.

I go back downstairs, looking around again, listening to the silence, which seems more on the deafening side rather than peaceful and relaxing. I open my new phone, put on the app for one of the national radio stations, catching the end of a Blake Daniels track.

I pick up the little note that is next to the kettle. It's handwritten, in swooping cursive lettering.

Dear Guest,

Welcome to your holiday stay. We hope you enjoy your time here. We have left you some essentials to get you started. You'll find coffee, tea, creamer, bread and other items in the cupboard, and a few items in the fridge. There are takeout menus in the top drawer. Most places take online orders. The shop on the high street is well-stocked but only open until seven, so please plan accordingly, otherwise you'll have to drive to one of the larger towns. There are some lovely cafés nearby, though check the hours as they're seasonal.

If you have any queries or issues, please feel free to contact us.

Best, Annabeth and Nathaniel

I look in the cupboards and find them stocked with more than what is mentioned in the note. I'll give Libby something, she knows how to find good hosts.

The song on the radio ends and then the familiar strings come out of the radio. I take a deep breath as my own vocals fill the room. Trying to distract myself, I go and get my suitcase, taking it up the stairs to the bedrooms, carrying my phone with me to keep the music on. I head into the single room. It's painted with a shade of warm yellow. It feels almost like a cocoon, so I plonk my mobile phone onto the little desk, haul my suitcase onto the bed, and open it. I unpack, trying not to be distracted by the track playing on my phone.

I focus on my clothes as I pull them all out of the case. They're not the usual clothes I wear. They're clothes Libby organised for me, clothes she packed into the suitcase that she hid away in the car she secured for me.

I hang up pairs of jeggings, skinny jeans, leggings, oversized tops, shirts, and jumpers. I put the small case of toiletries onto the table, next to my laptop. I throw the underwear into the drawers at the bottom section of the wardrobe. Libby appears to have arranged for several pairs of thick socks as well as pairs of thermal pyjamas. The final items in the case are a pair of trainers, a pair of walking shoes, and a pair of slippers. God knows what Libby thinks I'll be doing while I'm here. Hiking seems unlikely. I think it is more likely I'll be in some of the jeggings and thick socks as I hide under my duvet and escape from the world.

I zip the case up, stowing it at the bottom of the bed. The track on the radio finishes.

"In line with our throwback theme, that was Briar Rose's debut track. Can you believe it is ten years old? Briar Rose was in the news this weekend as it was announced she has been fired from her first film lead role. Briar Rose has reportedly been replaced by Bess Leoni. Briar Rose's management team denied she was fired because she is in rehab for addiction to drugs and alcohol, but she has been notably absent from the media since she finished her last concert. Such a mystery for one of our most famous pop stars. Where are you, Briar Rose? How are you doing?"

The voice of the radio presenter is light, jovial, discussing things as she fills the gap between the tracks. I wonder if she ever thinks there's a possibility the person that she's talking about might be listening and might not feel so light and jovial.

In frustration, I switch off the app and the silence—whilst still oppressive—feels like a relief to hearing my name on people's lips.

I look at myself in the mirror that is attached to the front of the wardrobe. I'm still not used to the dark hair, and my contacts are starting to irritate me. I look at the unfamiliar reflection and sigh to myself.

Where are you, Briar Rose? How are you doing?

I hear the echo of the radio presenter—her jovial question—and I have no idea how I would answer her, if I were able to.

***

Twenty minutes later, the sound of the silence in the house is too much for me to bear. I double check the front door is locked and then head out of the house via the backdoor. I follow the path towards the back of the property and find myself on the sandy walkway that leads towards the beach.

Stepping onto the beach makes me feel like I'm in a different world. The weather still looks on the cusp of turning nasty and the sound of the waves roaring across the sand is almost deafening, but for the first time in a long time, I feel like my problems are not the biggest thing in the world. I used to feel like this as a child. Whenever I found the world too overwhelming, I'd go outside and look up at the moon and I'd feel insignificant, like my problems were not going to crush me.

For months, problems have felt like they'd crush me.

I look around the beach. It is unsurprising given the weather, but the area is mostly deserted. The only people I can see are a little further up the beach. Despite the distance, I recognise Nathaniel. I watch him and his family for a moment. He is at the edge of the waves, his shoes discarded further up on the sand, and the waves hit his trousers, but he looks like he doesn't have a care in the world. He's laughing with a young girl who is jumping in the waves. Her delighted shrieks travel on the wind towards me. She sounds like a child who is having the best day of her life, as if nothing could dim her happiness. The woman with Nathaniel holds a little girl who doesn't look much older than one. The woman is wearing a stylish dress and jacket and a bright scarf around her neck. Like Nathaniel had said, the young child she is holding appears to be dressed in several layers to shield her from the cold wind.

They look like a family who do not have a care in the world. The woman holds on to the youngest child like she is the most precious gift.

Watching them feels like I'm intruding, so I kick off my shoes, turn on my heels and head in the opposite direction, carrying my shoes with me as I march through the sand—determined and fast—even if I have nowhere to go, aside from running away from my thoughts.

To distract myself, I focus on the sound of the waves rushing up the sand, the sound of the wind howling, the feel of the sand against my bare feet and the taste of the sea salt spray as it hits my face when I get too close to the water. Every time my mind starts to wander, I refocus myself. I hold my shoulders back and pretend like I don't have a care in the world.

***

I wake up the following day in the small bed in the little box room of the cottage. I know there are two larger, nicer, rooms I could sleep in—rooms that have electric blankets on the beds—but I'm finding the smallness of this room reassuring. Even being in a small single bed seems preferable to being alone in a double bed.

I check my watch, and I'm surprised that it is gone one in the afternoon. Given I've had weeks of not sleeping well, I feel a little victorious that I managed to have a solid sixteen hours of sleep, even if I feel stiff and still like I could sleep for another sixteen.

I get out of bed and head to the bathroom so I can shower. I dry my hair, and I'm surprised again by how short it is compared to my usual length, wondering how long it'll take me to get used to it.

I dress in a pair of the soft leggings, thick socks, and oversized jumper. All the clothing feels like a hug, and it makes me think Libby chose clothes like this so I wouldn't feel so alone.

I potter downstairs so I can make breakfast, helping myself to the cereal left in the house for me and some milk from the fridge. I make a cup of coffee and then sit at the table, wondering what I'm supposed to do with my time.

The silence is stifling again but I force myself to sit still. I'm here for peace and quiet—to get away from everything. I'm going to have to become comfortable with silence. After a while, I drum my fingers on the tabletop, making patterns with my tapping. I'm too afraid I'll hear my own songs on the radio to risk turning it on again.

Libby phones at four. Last week, she phoned me every day, even though I told her she didn't need to. She gave excuses, telling me things like she was checking everything in the house was okay given I stayed at hers before driving here.

"Hey, sweetie, you didn't reply to my message last night, I assume you were fast asleep," she says.

"I was, I had a good night. I'm sorry I didn't get back to you. I hope you weren't worrying. You are on holiday, after all," I point out.

"Well, Maeve had a few bits and pieces to do today so I thought I would give my favourite person a call."

"Your favourite person is on holiday with you," I say with a laugh.

"Okay, well, you're a very close second," she replies. I can hear the warmth in her voice.

Libby has been my personal stylist for the last year and during that time we became good friends. I know a lot of famous people who suddenly realise the people they call friends are all people on their payroll—where they're unsure if it is a genuine friendship or just part of the package of what else is being paid for—but Libby is different. Our friendship is genuine. Sometimes I feel like she's the only genuine friend I have left. It was surprisingly difficult to maintain friendships I had when I was fourteen, given I was suddenly no longer in school but being taught by private tutors as I toured the country.

Libby, however, has been with me through thick and thin since the day we met. She's the reason I'm here. She knew what was going on in my life, knew how far off track I was. She was the one who arranged the car, the incognito outfits, and this place for me to stay. She organised a new mobile phone, a new number, the haircut, and colour. She is the one who is lying to the rest of my team, telling them she knows nothing of my whereabouts. I owe her everything. At a very minimum, my sanity.

"Thank you for organising this place. It's nice. Peaceful. Speaking of peaceful, I'm hoping you haven't had any calls from people wondering where I am?"

"Harry called," she says, naming my manager. "He says if I know where you are, I should pass on the message that you need to sort your shit out. I told him that I'm sure you're fine, and that if you believed you needed to sort your shit out, you would be doing that, and we should leave you be to work through the alleged shit."

Despite everything, I laugh. "I appreciate that."

"So, how are you holding up?"

"I went for a walk on the beach last night."

"That sounds nice."

"It was. Though, it was cold and damp, I got caught in the rain on my way home. I had a lukewarm shower when I got back and then climbed into bed."

"Okay, so not as nice," she says, laughing.

"Then I had a long sleep. Got up late, had breakfast, watched a bit of television. Caught up on some of the rubbish in the newspapers. It was boring as hell. In fact, the only excitement I had was a power cut a little earlier, but it at least saved me from a really shitty show on the television." I finish giving her a running commentary of my day.

"To be fair, I wasn't expecting you to find this an easy transition. You've never really had any relaxation before, Rose, you've been full on since you were fourteen, so of course you're finding this difficult, but you know it's necessary," Libby soothes. "If you didn't take this break, you know it would have been worse. You were at a tipping point. I wasn't going to let you push yourself to the edge. You need this time."

"I know," I whisper.

Libby isn't wrong. I was discovered at the age of thirteen. I was young, keen on music, posting videos of me singing songs, my songs and others, on social media sites. My parents were contacted by a music label, and I was offered a record deal. It was an opportunity to make a record and capitalise on my social media following. My parents were supportive; they told me they wanted me to see my dreams become a reality, but now, as an adult, I wonder if they were more motivated by the financial offering or whether they were just too naïve about what it all really meant—for me and for us as a family.

Dad quit his job to become my manager to start with, until the obscene values of money came in and he hired Harry as a replacement so he could sit back and enjoy the lavish lifestyle. He now enjoys the lavish lifestyle with a twenty-five-year-old model he met on one of my video shoots. My mother—who had also quit her job when I got my record deal so she could be my chaperone—spent some time in a haze and a lot of time flirting with younger men to massage her ego before disappearing to a wellness retreat, leaving me behind.

Sometimes, I wonder what it would be like if I didn't accept the record deal, what my life would have been like, who I would have become instead.

My first album was released on my fourteenth birthday. The next ten years turned into album after album, guest stints on UK soap shows, celebrity guest spots on comedy shows, interviews on the radio and television, interview after interview, more music released. There were auditions for films alongside long, sold-out concert tours, promotions, and a never-ending marketing campaign.

My image was strictly controlled by my team, trying to keep me as the bouncy, innocent, full-of-smiles person I had been at fourteen, regardless of my older age. Dating was frowned upon, my team keen to maintain the image of innocence I had when I first started. All my relationships started with a non-disclosure agreement being thrust into my love interests' faces, and dating was expected to be done incognito.

I was even stopped being able to control my own social media pages and interacting directly with my fans, something I'd loved before my first album. Everything posted on my social media pages is created by one team, vetted by another, assessed to ensure that the words are unproblematic, that the messaging is correct. It's always checked with me before they post, so they don't post something I don't want to say, but they never post what I'd really *want* to say. Any endorsement I allegedly make on the pages are assessed to ensure they "fit the brand."

It is always light and fluffy content, upbeat and happy.

The last six months though, I rebelled. I decided I was done being controlled or being the person people assumed me to be, so I pushed back. I was desperate to be my own person—to be me—even if that version of me couldn't be seen by everybody. In the end, I was the one who got burnt. So far, the only people who know everything that happened are Libby, me, and the man who did his best to destroy me, but it's always there, hanging over me like the sword of Damocles. One day, it will become public. One day, one of the carefully constructed threads I've put in place to hold all the secrets together will be tugged upon and unravel, destroying everything.

"You there, Rose?" Libby cuts into my thinking.

"Yeah. I was just thinking. I need to start working on some new music. The media is starting to get a bit brutal. They're circling, and I need to get ahead of this. I heard speculation on the radio yesterday. I need to pull out something spectacular, enough to help me ride out any storm that is coming my way."

"You need to *rest*, Rose. It's only been two weeks since your last concert, hardly the rest you were planning on."

"I will do that. I'll stay here. I'll take the downtime, but I need to do something to help me bounce back. I also need something to do other than watching daytime television."

"Leave everything for now. Take a couple more weeks to rest and recuperate, please," she urges.

"Okay," I say after a moment.

"Are you okay for money, do you need anything else?"

"Libby, you stuffed two grand into the glovebox of my car so that I had cash and gave me a prepaid credit card. Where on earth do you think I've spent that?" I laugh.

I do have to hand it to her; she knows how to close the gaps when somebody wants to run away from their life. She insisted on the cash and the prepaid credit card because using my bank cards will be traceable by my management team when they get frustrated by my silence and start digging into my whereabouts.

"Yeah, okay, I just wanted to check."

"I'm going to cook some tea in a bit," I tell her.

"Man, I wish I could be there to see this." Libby giggles.

"Rude," I shoot back, but I'm smiling to myself.

"Have you ever actually cooked? Do you know how to use the hob? Wait, do you even know what one is?" she teases.

"On that note, I'll see you later." I laugh.

"I'll call you tomorrow," she promises.

I put the phone down and then head to the kitchen. I look in the cupboards and the fridge at the food that Annabeth and Nathaniel organised. There is a loaf of bread and a block of cheese, and I get a wave of desire for some hot, greasy cheese on toast. My parents used to make me cheese on toast as a treat—back before life went crazy. Mum would make it when I had a bad day. Dad would make it when I was sick, telling me if I could stomach it, I must be better. I wonder if making it for myself will feel like I did as a kid, that somebody cared about me.

I slice the block of cheese and put two slices of bread onto the tray for the grill. I turn the knob to preheat the grill and frown when it won't light. I tell myself that it is not acceptable to fall at the first hurdle. I might not know how to use the grill, but I can make it into a toastie, cooking it on the hob instead. It's close enough to what I intended. Except, I can't get the electric hob to work, either. I press button after button, but nothing happens.

I groan to myself and then get my mobile phone, looking up Annabeth's number on the note. I remember Nathaniel said she wouldn't be available until after five, but it's not far from the time. I send a text that I cannot get the oven or the hob to work.

I'm surprised to get an answer from Annabeth almost straight away, telling me she is free and that she is on her way over. Five minutes later, there is a knock on the front door.

I open the door and see Annabeth. She is dressed in a similar outfit to yesterday on the beach, except today she doesn't have the children with her. I'm immediately relieved.

"Hi, Elodie, right?" She smiles at me, a big wide smile. I get the impression she's the type of woman who has never had a problem in her whole life.

"Nice to meet you, I'm sorry to drag you away from your plans."

"It's okay, come on, let's get this sorted."

"Thank you."

I open the door wider so she can step inside. She kicks off her shoes in the hallway and then walks through the house towards the kitchen. I follow behind her.

She busies herself in the kitchen. She hums along to the song playing on the radio.

"Did you have a power cut today?" she asks.

"Yeah, how did you know?"

"I thought the power cut was only at the school, but it must have been across the village. Anyway, that's the problem. The oven and hob don't work without the clock being set. The power cut knocked it out," she explains as she resets the clock.

"Well, I feel like a dumbass," I reply, hoping my forced laughter is the right sound. I feel like a failure.

"Ah, don't worry about it. The first time I cooked here for Nathaniel, I couldn't work out how to take the child lock off the hob. I had to Google it, not that I would admit that to him. My search history that day was the make and model of the oven, desperately trying to work out how to use it without having to admit defeat." She gives me a grin as she sets the time on the microwave as well. I assume that also doesn't work without the clock being set; either that or she's just very particular about things being set properly.

"I'm so sorry for wasting your time."

"No biggie. Everyone needs a bit of help every now and again." She shrugs.

I'm still disappointed in myself. I'm twenty-four, almost twenty-five. I should be perfectly capable of working this stuff out, but I've never had to. I've always been surrounded by people, or teams of people, taking care of what must seem like a hundred mundane activities in my day-to-day life. Need something from the shop? There's somebody to do that for me. Fancy something particular for my breakfast, lunch, or dinner? There's somebody to make that for me. My car needs cleaning? Servicing? Fixing? Already taken care of for me. Before my record deal, my parents took care of everything for me. I've been taken care of my whole life.

In what feels like a personal jibe, the radio song changes, and a track of mine starts playing. Annabeth sighs.

"Are you okay?" I ask.

"I love this song. We danced to this on our wedding day," she explains. They can't have been married long—a year at most, based on when I released the track.

"How long have you two been together?" I ask, curiously.

"Two years. Married for one," she replies. My thoughts jump to the older girl on the beach. I wonder if she is Annabeth's or Nathaniel's, given she is much older than two.

"Nathaniel said you have two children," I comment, hoping she won't think I'm being nosy. Truthfully, my day-to-day interactions are usually limited to my team. I don't think I've ever had the whole girl-chat experience that is so exaggerated in books and movies. She probably thinks I'm a nosy bitch, but her expression doesn't change.

"Yeah, we do. Willow is nearly seven, and Faith is just over one. We finalised Willow's adoption about a year ago. Her parents died. Her mother was Nathaniel's sister."

"I'm sorry about her parents." I bite my lip. "I saw you on the beach yesterday, you all look very happy together."

"Oh, sickeningly so." Annabeth laughs. "I'd introduce you to Willow, but she's a huge fan of yours, and I'm assuming you've a reason to be here inconspicuously."

"I'm sorry, what?"

"No offense, you can cut and dye your hair, but you can't get away from that face. You're Briar Rose, right?" She cocks her head and stares at me. "Don't worry, I'm not going to out you. I can get Nathaniel to draft a non-disclosure agreement if you like. He's a lawyer," she adds when I don't immediately respond to her comments about my identity. I detect only pride in her voice as she talks about her husband, rather than excitement about who I am.

"Well, that's depressing if my perfect disguise didn't even last twenty-four hours."

"I'm just astute with attention to detail. I have to be, what with teaching a class of year one students. Plus, I'm a big fan, too. Your secret is safe with me, though."

"You're not going to tell anybody?" I ask, my surprise evident.

"No, of course not. Though, I will question if this was your plan for tea." She gestures at my cheese and bread.

I laugh. "I fancied something hot and greasy."

Annabeth gives me a smile. "If you're up for company, I'd happily run to the chip shop for some fish and chips," she offers.

"You don't have to do that," I protest.

"I'd love to. Nathaniel took the afternoon off for a Daddy-girls afternoon. I'm at a loose end, and after the day I have had at school, some greasy chips sounds like heaven right now. What do you think? Care to join me?"

I have no idea why she's not immediately on the phone, calling the press, telling them she knows the whereabouts of Briar Rose. The warning not to trust somebody echoes in my head, but they're the words of my parents, my manager.

Libby would tell me to let somebody in, let somebody look after me.

"I would love that," I reply with a smile.

Chapter Four

Blake

NOW

"Blake, are you going to sue..."

"Blake, are you based here permanently..."

"Blake, who do you think released the photograph..."

"Blake, when is the next album out..."

"Blake, what did your management team have to say..."

"Blake..."

The noise of the photographers is intense, both from the bombardment of questions and the never-ending clicking of the camera shutters. I hadn't expected them to be waiting on the street. I assumed as the alley was quiet that my location must still be unknown but, clearly, I was wrong.

"Blake, accusations about you..."

"Blake, how do you respond to..."

I stop trying to find a route around the photographers. I square my shoulders and take a breath. I'm not going to get away from this with silence.

"I know you're all doing your job, but you all know me well enough to know I don't speak about things on the street. Everything I wanted to say about the situation, I said in my statement. Any questions about my work can be directed to the label. Have a great day."

I force a bright smile, trying to come across as friendly and nice. It's been my default position with reporters since the day anybody started taking interest in me. It's something I find jarring—something I never anticipated when I got my record deal. It's exhausting and some days—like today—it's more exhausting than others.

I duck my way around the cameras that are still being pointed at me, trying to get another photograph. I'm sure half of the photographers just want a candid shot that they can use of me in the future, and the other half are holding their breath, hoping they'll get a shot of me losing my shit.

I keep my expression neutral as I move away from them. I'm not stupid enough to get caught looking sullen. I put my hand in my pocket, feeling for the car keys, squeezing my palm around them like they're a talisman.

I continue my walk to my car, aware some of the photographers have followed me. I'm sure, when I return, some will still be waiting outside my flat, hoping I'll return soon and in a better mood and be more agreeable to give an impromptu soundbite. They are the ones who obviously don't know me and don't believe what I've just said. I don't like to answer questions in the street, and I keep my interviews strictly to business.

I ignore them as they continue to shout behind me. I tap the key to unlock the car and get in, driving away as quickly as I can without breaking any rules. The last thing I need is a headline that I was so stressed about being asked questions that I endangered road users or pedestrians in my desperate attempts to get away.

The first time I found reporters outside my place, I was surprised. I was told by my management team to be prepared for life to get a little crazy, but I hadn't expected to see a flock of photographers, camped out and waiting for me. When the first question they screamed at me was *"Blake, how do you respond to your band's claims you stole their shot at stardom?"* I realised the media can be vicious. They took some photographs of me looking surprised, so over the following months, I trained myself to look impassive whenever reporters were around.

I can go months without seeing a photographer or reporter in the street. I give interviews between concerts—in hotel rooms when I'm surrounded by my team and friendly faces—and it's all very civil, so the only time I'm hounded is when something has caught their attention like the story with Olive. I know it'll die down because it always does. It takes a true scandal to keep them occupied for longer than a few days.

I just need to ride it out until life goes back to normal.

***

I drive a long, convoluted route to my dad's house. I'm still ahead of schedule so I feel relieved I'm not adding to the stress of Dad's day by being late to pick him up.

I park up on the quiet street and I head down the pathway towards his front door. On my keychain is the key to the front door of his house. He gave it to me yesterday, which felt weird as I've never had a key to my dad's house before. It feels like a momentous step for us, even if neither of us want to admit it. He handed it over with a gruff comment about how a key might be useful, and I nodded and remained silent as I put it in my pocket.

"Dad, are you ready?" I call as I let myself into the house like he suggested before he gave me the key. I shut the door behind me.

It feels a little weird to be in his house. This place has never been my home, and I've barely spent time here. Now, as Dad needs help, I'm determined to push past our slightly stilted relationship to make sure he has everything he needs. Him giving me the key feels like he also wants to push past to make a proper relationship between us. I doubt we'll ever get to the great father-son relationship I wished for as a kid, but we're at least trying to get somewhere, and it's much better than when I was younger.

"Blake?" Dad sounds surprised as he walks out of the kitchen.

"Your appointment is today, isn't it?" I frown. He looks like he's surprised to see me, like I hadn't arranged to come around today.

I'm sure I've got the day right, that today is his follow-up appointment with the consultant. I wonder if I have been relying on Maeve too much, that my brain has stopped functioning since she went on holiday, or maybe the idea of sitting in a cancer consultant's office to hear their plan to fix Dad is messing with my mind more than I'd like to admit. Maybe the seriousness of the appointment is messing with his mind, too.

"Yeah, I thought I sent a message though, telling you that you didn't need to put yourself out," Dad explains. I haven't had a message, but I probably would have put it down to him not wanting to be a burden rather than something for me to take seriously.

"It's not putting me out at all, Dad. I said I'd be here for the appointments," I remind him. I agreed to take him to the consultant appointments, the blood tests, the chemotherapy sessions—anything he needs.

He makes a gruff noise. "Do you want a coffee?" he asks.

I nod to be polite given I've already had a couple of coffees today. The multiple cups of coffee and the photographers have made me feel like I have the jitters. Additional caffeine might be a terrible idea, but it might also be enough to steady me through his appointment.

I follow him back into the kitchen. He works in silence to put the kettle on to boil. He pours the water into the cups and looks at me.

"I see there are more articles about you in the papers," he comments.

"They're all bullshit," I reply.

"A reporter came here last night," he adds. He pours the milk into the cups and then hands me a drink without adding any sugar. I don't correct him.

"I'm sorry they came here. I know you didn't want that."

"They were quite friendly," Dad replies.

Both his words and his tone make my ears prick in attention, and I start to feel a fleeting panic that this story is not going to end well. A friendly reporter is somebody desperate for their story—asking questions in a way to make it seem like an innocent chat when all they're trying to do is dig until they get some dirt they can print. Anything can make you sound like a piece of shit if it is taken out of context. More than one person has fallen victim to this, thinking they're chatting with a friend, saying something that has derailed their career, even if it was misconstrued and taken out of context, twisted to fit a narrative.

"What did they ask?" I sigh. I take a sip of the coffee, just for something to do. It's steaming hot and bitter tasting.

"They asked me if you were violent as a kid or as a young man." Dad puts his own coffee cup down on the countertop and he frowns at me.

"I hope you told them it was all bullshit." I laugh. I can think of a hundred words to describe how I was when I was younger. Immature. Childish. Unfocused. Drifting. Lost. Alone.

I would never describe myself as violent; it's just not my nature. I've never even been in a scuffle before.

"I didn't tell them it was bullshit." Dad shrugs. That icy feeling of dread makes its way through me again.

"What did you tell them?"

"I told them I wasn't going to talk to them on my doorstep when they've turned up unannounced."

"You could have led with that, Dad." I laugh. The dread gives way to a feeling of relief, but then I see the expression on his face.

"They're coming back another day."

"Just tell them to go away," I advise. Dad shakes his head.

"I invited them. They're coming to do a proper interview."

"A proper interview about what?" I can feel a headache brewing.

"They just want to know your life story, Blake."

"What kind of story do you think you're going to tell them about my life?" I snap, frustrated. I take a breath.

Getting annoyed with my dad isn't going to help anything, but he wasn't there for most of my childhood. He walked out, turned his back on me and Mum. We didn't have the type of relationship where he picked me up every other weekend and on alternate holidays, nor were there messages sent to say he missed seeing me. We didn't spend our Saturday visitations fishing with each other, chatting by the riverside about big important topics and getting excited about the weight of our catches. We barely even had Saturday visitations. If I got my hopes up and expected him to turn up, I ended up disappointed when he let me down and cancelled. I learnt early to accept I'd be left behind. He just wasn't there for me like that. I barely saw Dad when I was a teenager either, and I saw even less of him when I was an adult, staying in touch with brief messages and updates.

Before his cancer diagnosis, Dad had been in touch to tell me he thought he needed a kidney transplant. Although we hadn't spoken much in the previous year, I didn't hesitate to offer to get checked to see if I could be a donor. I did all the tests—willingly—only for the doctors to realise they made a mistake about my dad—that it wasn't a kidney he needed but chemotherapy to try to tackle the cancer that apparently is in more places than my dad can count.

It's only now that I've been trying to build bridges to see one another, but there is something about knowing one of your relatives could die to make you think you should at least give a last try to fix things.

Despite the tentative forging of a new relationship now, Dad has no insight to offer on what my life was like. I don't even think my mother could offer insights, if somebody convinced her to do an interview. I wasn't close to my mum either when I was growing up, but at least I lived with her. She saw me, even if it was only briefly before she rushed off to her night job after I got back from school.

"Why are you mad with me for doing an interview? They're going to pay good money." Dad cuts into my thinking.

"What do you need money for?" I ask. I pinch the bridge of my nose.

"I can use the money for some help around here. I need some help with the bills because I won't be earning when I'm having treatment," Dad points out.

"I already told you I would give you the money you needed. I can transfer it this week, how much do you want?" I ask.

We've had this conversation before. When we first spoke about what he is facing—after we knew the true diagnosis—my first reaction was to ask what he needed me to be there for. My second had been to ask if he needed money.

"They're paying handsomely." Dad shrugs. "I can pay for a home helper."

"I told you I would pay for you to have full-time carers if you wanted that. Tell me what you want, and I'll pay it." I stare at him.

I wonder why he's ignoring that I've already offered him everything. Once he told me he had cancer, I said I'd do anything he needed. I even offered to pay for private medical treatment, so he didn't have to wait for appointments with consultants who are already snowed under with work. He told me no.

"I don't want to take your money," Dad snaps. He didn't have the same stance when my first album skyrocketed. He let me pay off his mortgage and his debts, as had my mother.

"I'd rather you took my money than sold a story about me," I reply, quietly.

"What's the harm if I do?" Dad asks.

I can't believe he's asking this, like he doesn't see the devastation that he could push into my life. There's harm, even if it wouldn't be intended. I've done my best to keep my private life private. Stories about alleged romances are one thing. Stories about my less than stellar relationships with my parents is entirely another.

"What time is your appointment?" I sigh, changing the subject.

I know I could list the reasons I think an article would do harm, but I don't think it would make a difference to Dad. When he has his mind set on something, there is no swaying him.

"I don't think you should come. I am going to go by myself. I did message you to tell you that," he argues.

"Well, I didn't get the message, and I'm already here, Dad."

"Well, I don't want you to come." Dad's response is almost a shout.

"I should at least drive you there and back. You shouldn't be on your own after an appointment like this one," I coax.

I stare at him, wondering if he just doesn't like the idea of being upset in front of me in the appointment. I understand, Dad's not exactly known for showing his emotional side—not for anything other than what he'd consider to be "manly" reactions. He doesn't mind showing frustration, anger, annoyance, but showing vulnerability, I'm not sure he is shaped like that. When I was a little kid, probably about four or five, I cried when I was out with him one day, and he told me that real men don't cry. Sometimes, I think if he'd stayed with my mother, my life would have taken a different path, pushed into that bullshit toxic masculinity. Being mostly raised by my grandmother made me who I am today, but I understand why this might be a struggle for my dad.

"I'm fine. I'll be fine by myself at all my appointments, or I'll pay the carer to take me. You don't need to put yourself out."

"You don't want me at any appointment?" I ask.

"I think that's for the best, don't you?" Dad asks.

I put my coffee cup down. It tasted bitter before; it'll probably taste like acid now. I take the key he'd given me and place it on the countertop.

"Yeah, I think that's for the best, too," I reply. I stand up.

"I'll keep you updated with how I am getting on."

"What, via an article in the papers?" I mutter.

"Don't be like that, Blake, it doesn't suit you."

"I hope the appointment goes well."

I don't wait for him to answer me. Instead, I head out of the house and resist the urge to slam the door behind me.

I get back to my car. Once inside, I let out a string of curse words. I've had people give interviews about me before. My former bandmates weren't exactly complimentary when I first hit the music scene, but their interviews were always more slanted to how they felt cheated by my big break. A few ex-girlfriends made some cheeky references, but it was more along the lines of "Blake, call me," than "Blake, burn in hell." There isn't anything Dad can say that will mean anything, I have no skeletons in the closet, but the fact he is willing to talk to the media and make money from telling stories, that is what stings.

I shove the key into the car and drive away, refusing to look back at my dad's house.

***

"Blake, where have you been today?"

"Blake, tell us more about the reaction to the statement you issued..."

"Blake..."

The photographers are still there as I walk up the main street. Of course they are. All I want to do is get into the flat and shut the door to the world. I walk around the photographers. I learnt early on in my career that this is easier than pushing through them. I let myself into the building and I don't look in their direction as I shut the door behind me.

I head up to my flat and step inside, throwing my keys on the sideboard. I pick my phone out of my pocket and call Maeve.

"Hey, Blake, what's up?" she asks as she answers.

"It's a friendly call. Call me soppy but I just wanted to hear a friendly voice," I say. She sighs. She knows I have other friends to call, but nobody I trust more than her.

"What's happened today? Was it bad news for your dad?"

"I don't know, he told me I don't need to go to his appointments with him. Right after he told me he is giving an interview about me." I sit down on the sofa as I talk. The panoramic view doesn't do anything today to raise my spirits. It's started to rain outside, and the skies look grey.

"What on earth does he think he can say in an interview that is going to be newsworthy? Hi, I'm Blake's dad and I skipped out when he was a kid? Hi, I'm Blake's dad and I did my best to avoid paying child maintenance? Hi, I'm Blake's dad and my son somehow managed to turn out pretty damn awesome, despite his shitty parents?"

"Maybe." I manage a laugh.

"I'm sorry, Blake. Do you want me to ring around and find out who has the interview, try to get it cancelled?"

"No, I want you to tell me what you and Libby have been getting up to."

"Ah, you want a distraction?" Maeve catches on to the main reason for my call.

"Yes, please provide a distraction for me. A distraction from my dad, whatever interview he's going to give, and the photographers who are camped out on the street in front of the flat."

"Do you want me to tell you all about the hot night Libby and I had? We had a threesome with a woman we met at the beach. I felt like I was in a woman sandwich. Is that enough of a distraction for you?"

I burst out laughing. "You are a terrible fucking liar, Maeve. No, I don't need you to make up shit. Tell me about the beach. Is it as beautiful as it looked in the photographs on the website?"

"Hey, we're capable of having a threesome, you know," she protests. I don't believe her. I've never met Libby or seen them together in person, but when Maeve talks about her it's like she's witnessed a miracle.

"I'm sure you are, but I don't think either of you like to share."

"Yeah, you're right. I'm only joking. Nice to hear you laugh, though."

"So, come on, the beach, tell me about it," I suggest.

"Hang on, let me call you back," Maeve says and then she hangs up. She calls back a second later, this time on video call.

"I thought you abandoned me for a second." I laugh.

"Never. I just thought this was easier." Maeve laughs with me and then she turns the phone so I can see the view from her location.

She's stopping in a luxury hut on the beach. She takes a couple of steps, the view looking shaky as she walks, but then I see the decking of their place, the pristine white sand, and the clear blue sea ahead of her. It's the definition of paradise—the type of view that gets printed on postcards for people to sigh over and wish they were there.

Right now, I wish I was there too. Not with them but whisked away to somewhere peaceful and quiet. There's nothing to stop me hopping on a plane and jetting to somewhere beautiful. I am only here to take my dad to appointments. If that isn't happening, there's no reason to stay. I can write—or not write—anywhere.

As Maeve moves the camera around, I see Libby lying in a hammock, wearing a bikini and talking on the phone.

"It looks amazing, Maeve. Looks like Libby is busy, so I feel less guilty about calling you."

"Yeah, there's nothing we wouldn't do for our bosses," Maeve jokes. I see Libby put her phone away.

"Thanks for that chat. You two go enjoy that sea. I'll see you soon, okay?"

"Blake, I'm being serious. If you need me for anything, you know I'm only a phone call away. Don't worry about your dad's interview. It'll just be fish and chip wrapping."

I laugh. "I don't think fish and chip shops use actual newspapers now."

"Well, to be fair, who buys an actual paper when the news is always at our fingertips? But the sentiment still stands. It'll blow over. Just hang tight, things will get better, I promise. You focus on writing."

"Yeah," I reply. Now I wish we weren't on a video call as she can see my facial expression.

"Is the writing not going well?"

"It's not really going at all. Don't worry about it though. Right, I'm hungry. I'm going to make myself a sandwich."

"Look after yourself, Blake," Maeve says, and I spot the frown on her face.

"I'm sure if anything else goes wrong, you can try to tell me some group sex story as a distraction. I mean, I know it would be total bullshit, but hey, if you want to get creative, I'll let you try." I laugh.

"Deal." Maeve grins. "Speak soon."

I end the call. I feel a little better after speaking to Maeve, but everything still weighs on my mind. My notebook is still open in front of me on the coffee table. I pick it up, grab my pen, settle back on the sofa and wait for inspiration.

There's a part of me that is afraid I've lost my ability to write music, but I remind myself that it would only be music for me. I've written plenty of songs recently, songs for other people to sing and perform. I was number one in the charts when a song I wrote for another artist knocked me off the top position. Usually, the songs I write for other artists are more upbeat to my own style of songs, but this was a love song I wrote and passed on. I just can't work out why I'm so stuck in my own head—why everything I write with the idea of me singing it feels terrible.

It can't be being back in my hometown because I had the same issue at the end of my tour, where the idea of writing another song for me to sing seemed like an impossible task. All I know is that I need to get a grip and push through it. Something tells me my label won't be impressed if I turn up empty handed when we finally meet to discuss a third album.

Come on, Blake. I try to coax myself to write. I've an unexpected day where I can write because I'm not taking my dad for appointments. I tap my pen on the notepad, drumming myself a little rhythm, hoping it'll lead me somewhere other than just being stuck.

Chapter Five

Rose

NOW

I watch Annabeth as she dishes up fish and chips. The smell of the food is amazing, and my mouth is watering like crazy. I'm pretty sure I'm on the verge of looking like a salivating dog waiting for their master to give them some scraps off their plate.

Annabeth appears to have purchased two portions of fish and chips, a tub of mushy peas, and gravy. She smiles at me as she takes two smaller plates from the cupboard and unwraps another package from the bag, adding onion rings and a large gherkin to each of the small plates.

"Sorry, I couldn't resist the extras. I reckon I could have eaten their whole menu tonight and still gone back for seconds. You're lucky I didn't get us a pickled egg." She laughs and she moves the plates to the table.

"I definitely draw the line at a pickled egg," I reply, trying not to wrinkle my nose. Everything else on the plate looks amazing.

Annabeth laughs again and takes a seat at the table. "Relax, I'm joking. I think they're disgusting but Nathaniel weirdly likes them. He's the only one, though. Willow joins me with judging him every time he has one."

I take a seat in front of her. "This is amazing. I don't remember the last time I had fish and chips from an actual takeaway."

"I'm guessing it was so long ago that you don't actually remember how good they are." Annabeth grins. She stabs a chip with her fork and pops it into her mouth, an exaggerated look on her face like it is the best thing she has ever eaten.

I cut off a piece of the fish, listening to the crunch as my knife goes through the batter. I take a bite. The batter is crispy, the fish is flaky and soft, and it's probably the best thing I've eaten.

"My, this is so good." I grin.

"It's a good chip shop. They deliver, too, if you don't fancy going out or getting spotted," Annabeth says, giving me another one of her wide smiles. I sense she's trying to give me an opportunity to open up to her, between the encouraging smiles and the slightly probing sentences.

"So, tell me more about the kids," I suggest and her face lights up.

"Gosh, they're just amazing. Are you sure, I'll chatter for hours and bore you," she warns.

"No, I want to hear all about them."

"Okay, well don't say I didn't warn you." She laughs. "Willow is such a smart cookie; she keeps us on our toes every day. She's so funny and sweet, she has the whole family wrapped around her little finger. Nathaniel's parents live nearby—so do mine—so we have a good support network, something we feel is important with what happened to her parents."

"How long ago did she lose her parents?" I ask.

"She was five when it happened. She's handling it well, bless her. We will talk a lot about her parents, and she says she's lucky to have had two families. She calls Faith her sister. She started calling me 'Mummy' a couple of weeks ago, and Nathaniel 'Daddy,' and I swear, the minute she was out of the room, we were both crying like babies," Annabeth explains.

"She sounds like a great kid," I reply.

"The best. Faith is a sweetheart, too. She's walking and very independent, always trying to keep up with her big sister. I love listening to her babbling, whether it's to me, Nathaniel, to Willow, or just to herself. Her first word was Dada, obviously, because she is such a daddy's girl." She grins.

"You said she was just over one, and you and Nathaniel have been together for two years?" I ponder. There's a little flush on her cheeks.

"Yeah, for want of a better terminology, he knocked me up, right off the bat. Maybe not the first official date, but in the first week we were together. It was a huge shock to start, but we went all in, and every day I thank my lucky stars we did, even if it was from zero to one hundred almost overnight. I know it's unusual, and I'm sure a lot of people assumed it would be a disaster, but it just worked for us," she explains as she cuts her fish. "Best thing I ever did, accepting to go on a hike with him."

"Your first date was hiking?" I focus on a piece of innocuous information.

"Yeah, there are some beautiful walks around here. I can give you the locations if you like. There are some secluded routes, but most of the places around here are secluded this time of year."

"I'm looking for seclusion," I agree.

I eat some more of my chips. They're covered with salt and vinegar, and they taste fantastic. Annabeth follows suit, falling quiet as she eats her food. It's quiet between us while we both finish our meals. She finishes her last onion ring, licks her fingers and then sits back in the chair.

"My, that was amazing," she sighs with a satisfied smile on her face. "I'm stuffed."

"I think that has been my best meal in a long time," I admit.

"You're telling me that this fish and chips meal compares to eating at those super fancy restaurants you're photographed in?" She is clearly teasing me.

"Half of the stuff in the gossip magazines is made up, elaborated nonsense. Besides, if I've been in those fancy restaurants, it is likely that I'm there for a business meeting, where I don't get to eat because somebody on my management team is reminding me that I need to remain 'in good condition' ahead of some sort of event. Usually those types of meals, I'm the one picking up the bill, too—for everybody around the table—so I end up paying a small fortune *not* to eat."

I know I sound snippy and probably look sarcastic by using air quotes when I say in good condition, but it is something that has always upset me. I'm not stick thin. Even as a little kid, I was on the slightly larger size to the rest of my friends. Now, I'm made to work hard so I keep a figure acceptable by my management teams standards. It isn't like they recommend I starve myself, but there are definite looks they give me if I'm eating and not making the choices they'd like.

I'm reminded constantly if my weight has gone up by the press if I haven't already been lectured by my label and team.

"Sounds like that is a terrible way to live your life," Annabeth muses.

"Well, it's what I've known since I was a teenager. Literally, the day I signed my record deal, I was assigned a personal trainer and a dietician. According to the management team, it was to help me stay fit and strong ahead of what was coming, but really, they just wanted to make sure I looked good in outfits," I reply.

"Are you going to get into any trouble for eating fish and chips?" Annabeth sounds curious.

"Given I'm on the lam, to coin a phrase, I think a chip shop tea is the least of my worries."

"How far off the grid are you?"

"The only person who knows where I'm staying is my stylist, who is also a good friend. She arranged everything for me. Even my parents don't know, and I want to keep it like that as long as possible," I admit.

"There probably isn't a better place to hide this time of year. Whistlethorpe is quiet in the autumn and winter. The weather can get bad, particularly around this side given it is so close to the coast, so that keeps people indoors."

"Nathaniel mentioned you used to live in this house."

"I did, briefly. It was Willow's parents' place, so she'd lived here since she was a baby. Nathaniel moved in after they died, and the house passed to Willow. I moved in here when I found out I was pregnant. We were here until about six months ago because it felt like we were always tripping over one another, so took the leap to move to a slightly bigger place. It's still in the village though because we love the area."

"It's very quiet here," I comment. It's a tiny little cul-de-sac, with only the four cottages, nothing on the opposite side of the road, and only the gardens and the beach behind them.

"It was a lovely street. Families owned the other three houses, too, but they were put up for sale and they were snapped up by a developer. Next year, he's apparently coming back to ask us to sell the house to them because he has plans for the cottages and wants all four."

"Are you going to sell?"

"We're considering it. We were worried us moving would upset Willow, this was her family home after all, but she loves the new house. We originally thought we would rent this house out for holiday stays, but we're not sure how that will work with the other three homes if the developer's plans go ahead."

"The developer won't be around any time soon?"

Annabeth laughs. "He is off sunning himself in warmer climates. You're fine."

"Thanks. The last thing I need is somebody to turn up and see through my apparently poor disguise."

"Well, I promise that I won't say anything about who you are. You'll probably be fine around the village, too. Usually it's full of nosy neighbours, but that's typically reserved for people who live around here. It's quieter in the winter, too, so I'm sure you'll be okay to fly under the radar. Though, before you leave the village, I would love it if you could sign something for Willow, if that would be okay with you."

"I'd love to," I say with a smile. "I need to keep her as a fan," I add.

I feel a little pinch of panic when I talk about losing fans because I know that the secrets I have are things that can evolve into genuine scandal. It'll be repercussions and accusations in the media, judgement from the nation, and my whole life in ruins.

I fiddle with the fork in my hand, trying to keep the panic from overwhelming me.

Annabeth smiles at me. "Can I maybe overstep?"

I nod. "Of course. Seems like a small price to pay for a delicious plate of food."

"Before I met Nathaniel, I was engaged. Sam broke it off a couple of months before the wedding."

"That sounds rough," I reply, surprised by her start of this topic. It wasn't what I was expecting.

"It was tough, to start with. I practically hid in the garden for a few weeks because I couldn't face anybody, not even friends. I felt like the world had given me a good kicking. But, after a few weeks, I got some clarity. I started to see that Sam wasn't what I really wanted, and I'm so grateful for how my life turned out. I guess, what I'm trying to say, is that sometimes, life can seem bleak and rubbish, but you'll find your way through. Not only that, sometimes what you end up with is more wonderful than what you had. I know that's what happened to me, anyway. Whatever it is you need to get through, you'll get through it."

Her words hit me in a way I didn't expect. Mostly because I've spent the last few weeks feeling like the world has been dark, oppressive. I haven't seen even a pinprick of light in the darkness that has been engulfing me. When you're so far in the darkness, it's easy to imagine that nothing will ever get better.

"Did you ever think you wouldn't get through something?" I manage to get the words out and keep my voice steady.

I brace myself for her to roll her eyes and remind me how privileged I am or ask what it is that I could possibly have to moan about. I know people could look at my life and assume I must be upset about something petty, because I have money to solve my problems, something people assume is the magic fix for every issue. Not this though, and I can't explain it to her if she asks, nor justify what I'm so fearful about.

Instead of asking me anything I fear, she gives me a serene smile.

"You will. I'm sure you're way stronger than you give yourself credit for."

"Thanks," I reply, my throat tight. Annabeth leans over to squeeze my hand.

"Right, I've taken up far too much of your time tonight. Thanks for indulging me by joining me for fish and chips. I'm going to head off, but if you need anything, just get in touch." She smiles warmly. She stands up and puts the plates and cutlery into the dishwasher, then she grabs the bag of wrappings from the countertop as she walks out of the kitchen.

"Annabeth?" I call out. She stops as she reaches the doorway.

"Yes?"

"Thank you, for everything."

"No problem." She smiles, and with that she is gone, and I'm back to being alone.

The radio is still playing in the background, providing enough background noise that I don't feel like I'm being suffocated by silence. There is a Blake Daniels track playing. I've always loved his music, but I roll my eyes a little as I think of the mindless scrolling that I did earlier, reading articles about him and reading his social media statements. That guy could literally fall into a vat of horse shit and come off smelling like sunshine and rainbows. I'm sure if the situations were reversed—if I were being discussed in the trashy gossip sites—no amount of me asking for the sites to "do better" would result in anybody doing anything better.

When Blake, however, chooses to speak, he appears to be able to bring the media to their knees. His social media page had been inundated by messages of support, from members of the public as well as a whole host of celebrities. Despite him insisting he didn't need an apology from the sites who published photographs and inaccurate news about him, all sites have issued an apology. Every gossip site I've read over today is filled with comments from the public about how wonderful he is, how awful it was for the stories to have been run in the first place.

With a simple statement, he's back to being a media sweetheart who can do no wrong. I bet his statement took all of five minutes, and then his life was perfect again.

I'd still be being hauled over hot coals, I'm sure. I'm confident that what Blake had reported is true; he's truthful when he says the alluding of domestic violence was incorrect and underhand. I know of Blake through people, though we have never met in person. Everybody always talks about him with warm regards and affection. Though, for women in the public eye, even if there is no truth, it's attached to them forever. When people write about Blake in the future, there won't be reminders; lines like "Blake was once embroiled in a dispute when he was accused of domestic violence" won't appear. Not like how they do with women. Find any female celebrity and there will be an article linking them to something they'd rather forget. The media has a long memory when it comes to the villainy of women.

Curious, I pick up my phone and refresh Blake's social media page. Since Saturday when he posted, there are thousands of comments, double the amount from when I had last looked at his page. I skim through the comments. They are all positive. There isn't even one single response that looks like they believe the presentation of pictures and innuendo in the original article.

The woman who had provided the picture to the news site in the first place had commented on Blake's page, defending her actions. She claimed Blake had been cheated on and that they had both been wronged by Blake's ex, but she was quickly dismissed as being a jealous ex-girlfriend by Blake's fans—somebody looking for their moment of fame—and the threads on the story she concocted had unravelled quickly, everything from "a close source" discredited, the photograph confirmed as being misconstrued.

As I skim through the comments, I scroll up to the best rated. There is a comment from FitzOliveSaunders2299, whom I assume to be the woman who the article had been about. It's a heartfelt thank you to Blake, finishing with "*you're such a good guy, Blake, I'm so happy to see your success*," which has been liked thousands of times. She may be an ex of his, but there doesn't look to be any bad feelings, just genuine warmth.

Another top liked comment appears to be from somebody claiming to be the person Blake had mentioned, the driver of the car. It's a humble brag about how he attempted to flirt with a pop star's girlfriend, wishing he'd known at the time so he could have told his friends all about it. It strikes me as being slimy, but it's had so many likes it is ridiculous.

An anti–knife crime charity has commented, thanking Blake for highlighting their cause, commenting that they're grateful for the increase in donations they've received. Several charities that support people who experienced domestic violence have written similar messages of thanks.

Nearly all celebrities who have posted comments on Blake's statement have reshared his post, reshared the charities' posts, highlighted their causes to their own millions of followers, and made their own generous donations.

All the comments from the charities have been replied to hundreds of times, people from the public saying they're donating.

Blake has remained silent since his initial post, but based on the comments, the fans are loving it—more in love with him than ever.

Honestly, you'd think he was Jesus reincarnated.

I chide myself. It isn't his fault that I have my own issues with the way I'm treated in the media. I remind myself that I've heard nothing but good things about Blake. If he has been mentioned in my presence, it has always been in a positive light. The most negative thing I heard about him was when he first started on the music scene, there was some bad blood with the band that he had originally been in. They didn't take kindly to him going solo, but Blake handled it with grace and dignity, refusing to attack them back. Either he really is a good guy, or he has an excellent media team.

As I scroll, an idea starts to form in my head. It might be verging on crazy, but it might also be the best idea I've ever had.

I call Libby. She answers on the fifth ring.

"I'm so sorry to interrupt your holiday, I swear this is the only time I'm going to call you like a needy child—" I start, but her laugh cuts me off.

"What do you need?"

"Blake Daniels," I blurt out. "That's what I need."

"In what capacity? I thought you were sworn off men."

"Still true. I know it is a huge ask, I know you're both on holiday, I know I'm out of line, but can you maybe ask Maeve to ask Blake how he would feel about making music together?" I almost shout out my request.

I can't believe I didn't think about this before. Even before my life went to shit, I never collaborated with anybody, but if I did, he'd have been the top of my list for choices. I've always loved Blake's music. A couple of his songs on his first album had me crying the first time I listened to them. One of his songs I played on repeat, blown away by the beauty of the lyrics, the emotion in his voice, and slightly envious that I wasn't the one who had created the song because it was absolute perfection.

He's the perfect choice to collaborate with. Like me, he writes all his own music. Every lyric is his. He's passionate about singing live and playing his own instruments—mostly guitar—and I know he's also just finished touring. He's basically the male version of me.

"I thought you were going to chill and recover." Libby sighs, all teasing in her voice gone.

"Come on, you sound like you'd have said yes if I told you I wanted him in my bed."

"I would not! I'd say the same thing. You're supposed to be getting better."

"This is me getting better."

"No, this is you panicking about something that isn't going to happen, trying to come up with something as a distraction. You don't need it."

"I do. Libby, please. Besides, it isn't about need. It's a want. I really want this. I want to make an album with him."

There is a long silence between us. I hear her sigh.

"Let me talk to Maeve. Blake's supposed to be writing music for a new album, but Maeve mentioned he hadn't really focused. Like you, he's rented somewhere to be out of the way, but I'm sure you saw how his last week went."

"I did. I was reading his page earlier."

"Yeah, well, the media found out where he was staying. He's had photographers camped outside the rented place since Saturday afternoon. Then all the stuff with his dad..."

"His dad?" I frown to myself. I don't remember seeing anything about his father. Maybe I missed it in the hundreds of messages he had from fans.

"Blake spoke to Maeve today. He didn't have a good relationship with his father when he was younger, but they have been trying to make peace with it.

His dad was recently diagnosed with cancer. Blake was going to spend some of his downtime taking his dad to appointments, but apparently his dad has said he doesn't want him to be around. I believe his dad has been convinced to do a tell all story about his relationship with his son. From what I can gather, he's having a really bad day today."

"Oh, that's terrible." I bite my lip. "Forget I asked. It's not the right time. Forget it."

I know what it is like to be disappointed in your father. My relationship with my father is so rocky it is unbelievable. I can't remember the last time we spoke. I know our last words face to face were in anger—a vicious argument. We then argued over text and neither of us have tried to make amends.

"No, it might be just what Blake needs. Let me talk to Maeve. Leave it with me, but don't get your hopes up, not just yet."

"I feel bad that you're both on your holiday and it seems like you're firefighting for us annoying clients."

Libby laughs. "You know I'd do anything for you, sweetie, and Maeve feels the same about Blake. Leave it with me. I'll be in touch. In the meantime, try to enjoy your downtime."

The phone clicks, signalling she has gone.

Despite it still being early, I switch everything off and head upstairs for bed, locking the door as I pass it on my way up the stairs.

I head to the yellow bedroom again so I can get myself changed for bed. I'm just pulling my pyjama top on when my phone rings. There are two people who have this number, Libby and Annabeth, given I had texted her earlier. I know it will be Libby.

"Hey, everything okay?" I ask as I answer.

"He's in," she replies.

"You're kidding me? That was fast!"

"Well, speaking of fast, he'll be arriving tomorrow, in the afternoon," Libby says. I feel my heart skip a beat. I can't believe she's managed to pull this off and so quickly.

"You are amazing, Libby."

"You're welcome. If there are any problems, let me know."

"Good to know I can call you, but I will do my best not to. Say hi to Maeve for me," I add.

Libby hangs up again and I finish getting ready for bed, putting my phone on charge. I get into bed, wrapping the covers around me, and despite it being early, I fall quickly asleep.

***

I wake with a cold sweat. My heart is pounding in my chest. It has been two weeks since I last woke up like this, and I was hoping that it had been the end of the nightmares, the dreams gripping me in the middle of the night. I crossed my fingers when Libby told me her plan to get me out of the battlefield for a while, praying that the spark of hope I had in my chest would last, but it appears I'm back to where I was.

I sit up in bed. I reach for my phone and launch the gossip websites, scrolling and searching for my name. Even though there is no notification on any of the alerts I've set up, it doesn't stop me scrolling to check. This is the nightmare that woke me up, the fear that the news is out there, that people have found out.

I scroll every site I can think of, but there is nothing there. No scandal. No accusations. No revelations. It still takes me a while to get my heart to stop racing, to stop the adrenaline running through my body. It's ridiculous how much even the perception of the news being out in the light affects me. I've never felt fear like this before. Even before my first concert, when I was going to be performing in front of a massive crowd for the first time, I never felt a drop of fear—just excitement and anticipation. The media has never bothered me, the press has typically been kind about me, but suddenly everything feels so scary.

I navigate to the main paper I tend to read, and in the entertainment section there is an article about him—the man who could destroy me. My gasp of surprise seems to echo around the bedroom. The picture of him doesn't do him full justice; it doesn't capture his charisma, the way his personality makes him appear larger than life.

I zoom into the image, looking at his eyes. They're the colour of the sky on a clear summer day.

I think of the first time I met him. How he looked at me with those beautiful eyes of his, how I had felt like he was staring into my very soul. He glanced over at me over his coffee cup, then he lowered his cup and gave me a beaming smile, flashing his perfect teeth. He put down his coffee cup, crossed the table to where I was sitting, handing me a pastry from the selection in the middle of the impromptu breakfast buffet that had been set up. His fingers traced against my hand as he gave me the pastry, smiling at me again, and the curve of his lips made me wonder what it would be like to kiss him. I was shaken to my core because I'd never been affected by a man like that before. I put it down to excitement about the morning, the project we could be working on. I assumed it was a one-off reaction.

As it turned out, he affected me time and time again. There were hundreds of times I felt my heart flutter again like that first time, hundreds of times when I felt like I was falling from a great height. Hundreds of times when I felt like the world was spinning too fast.

Until the day he broke me. Left me broken and alone, and terrified that everybody would know what had happened. Fearful that every decision, every mistake, every touch, every conversation—everything I would love to take back—could be splashed for the world to see.

I look back at the article. I shrink the picture back to the normal size, skimming the headline. I read the tag line under the photograph.

Hunter Greenway and wife, Isla, arriving for the restaurant opening.

I drop my phone onto the bed and run in the direction of the bathroom. I'm grateful I manage to kneel down before I'm violently sick.

Chapter Six

Blake

NOW

I pull my car into the driveway, parking next to a little Fiat. The street is deserted. The only sign of life is the twitching of the curtains from the front room of the house bearing the number I've been told.

Whistlethorpe is picturesque, and the house in front of me is quaint. It is nothing I imagined an artist like Briar Rose staying in, but Maeve had explained she was having some downtime, time out of the gaze of the media. It was what I was aiming for when I had taken my rented flat, but my chance meeting with Olive and then the spectacular actions of Dad had set that dream on fire.

I hope she is having a better go of it than me.

It's late afternoon, almost evening. I was later setting off than I anticipated. The drive over had me slightly paranoid that somebody was following me, but I know it was because Maeve warned me to be careful as Briar Rose doesn't want anybody to know where she is. She told me on the phone yesterday—when she had called with the offer—that nobody was to know what was happening. The only four people who know are me, Briar Rose, Libby, and Maeve.

Maeve's warnings left me so paranoid this morning that I drove a criss-cross route, convinced that I was being followed until I eventually accepted that the blue car following me was actually just a car with a family in it, rather than one of the crazy photographers or reporters who had been camped outside my flat for the last few days.

The last half hour of my journey was on quiet country lanes—where I was the only car on the road—so I feel more relaxed now I'm here. I take a deep breath, get out of the car, and stretch before heading to the front door. I'm about to knock when the door opens.

The woman standing in front of me looks so different to how I know her. I haven't met her before, but everybody in the UK knows who she is. I'd bet the majority of people overseas could pick her out of a line-up, too. She's been on the cover of magazines, in TV shows, advertisements, dominated awards shows, and has sold out concerts for the last decade. Her rise to fame is always noted as being stratospheric, the type that others can only wish for in their wildest dreams.

There is no denying the difference to her usual image though, and it takes me by surprise. This is not the look of somebody who is trying to have some downtime from the image they usually have to project.

This is the look of somebody who is hiding.

Her hair—which has always hung to her waist in a honey-blonde colour—is cut in a long bob and dyed dark. She is wearing a big jumper-style dress over a pair of leggings. Despite the changed look, there is no hiding her features. I haven't seen her up close before, but her wide eyes, high cheekbones, and bee-stung lips are world famous.

"Thanks for coming," she says, skipping the need for awkward introductions. She opens the door, and I swear her face falls. "You're not staying? Came to let me down face to face? I guess that's decent of you, but—"

"No, that's not the case. What makes you think I've come to say no?" I laugh at her assumption.

"You don't have a suitcase," she explains with a slight shrug.

When she shrugs, it makes the stance she has appear more noticeable. She is definitely standing with her shoulders hunched, almost like she is afraid of taking up space, or trying to make herself as small as she can to avoid attention.

"My stuff is in the car. Clothes and my guitar. I will bring it all in later," I reply, and I try to keep myself from looking surprised when I see the relief on her face. Maeve wasn't kidding when she said she needed some help. I thought Maeve might have been trying to make me feel sympathetic to get me on board with this joint-album idea, but I should know better than to doubt her. Not that I really needed convincing. If there was ever an artist I'd have begged to collaborate with, it would be Briar Rose. She is an amazing singer and lyricist with a vocal range that is unparalleled.

"Okay. Come through." She starts to walk further into the house. I kick off my trainers, leaving them by the door, then I take off my baseball cap and put it on the little table in the hallway before I follow her.

"Nice place. I didn't expect this would be somewhere you'd stay." I look around the kitchen as we enter it. It's more function than style, but it's still nice. Small though. I would have thought somebody who was used to fame from such an early age would default to stays in mansions and more lavish locations.

"Libby rented it for me. It's rented until the start of the new season."

"Libby and Maeve are a pair of diamonds, aren't they?" I comment.

"Yes, I don't know where I would be without her."

"It's odd that the two of us have never met before, given they play such a big part in our lives," I muse.

"Our tours have usually overlapped, then we all want our rest afterwards." She shrugs and she flicks on the kettle. I take a seat at the little table.

"So, what's your plan here, Briar Rose?" I ask.

"Don't call me that," she snaps. She takes a deep breath. "Briar Rose is a stage name. A stupid moniker I made up when I was twelve and mucking around making home videos. It's something the music execs jumped on and decided sounded perfect. I'm convinced I'll never be able to shake it."

"What's your real name?" I ask.

"Rose Elodie Dalton," she replies, her tone a little calmer. I stand up and step in front of her. I offer her my hand.

"Nice to meet you, Rose Elodie Dalton. Blake Indiana Daniels," I say.

For the first time since I arrived, her smile looks genuine, and she shakes my hand.

"Indiana? Seriously? How have I never read that before?"

I laugh. "Mum was a big fan of the films. I owe it to my grandma that it is only Indiana as a middle name because I think she'd have gone for the full name if she could. I've never published my full name because I like holding some things back, keeping some things private. The media takes enough."

"Yes, it does," she mutters.

"See, we can all have secrets," I add as I take a seat back at the table.

She glances in my direction, her expression guarded. "What did Maeve tell you?"

"Well, she didn't warn me not to call you by your stage name, so I'm sorry about that. What she did tell me was that you wanted to make an album with me, and to come here, so here I am."

"Okay." She nods, looking thoughtful. A small silence falls between us. The only noise is that of the kettle humming up to a boil. I clear my throat when the silence feels like it is going to move from awkward to painful.

"Unless you have a recording studio hidden away, this isn't the usual set-up," I point out.

"You used to write your songs in your bedroom, didn't you?" Rose's chin juts out as she talks. I recognise she is being defensive, although I don't know why.

"Oh, Ms. Dalton has been reading fact files and articles about me," I tease.

She rolls her eyes. "It's hard to avoid articles about you since you came onto the scene. Everybody knows how you used to write your music."

"It's how you write your music, too, right? I suppose I imagined you'd have moved on to the big studio work since you became a mega star." I shrug.

"Perhaps we should both stop making assumptions about one another."

"I'm fine with that," I agree.

"Tea or coffee?"

"Coffee, one sugar, milk, please," I reply. She busies herself making the drinks and when done, she sits down at the table with me, putting my coffee in front of me.

"Look, I know it is an unconventional set-up, but it isn't different to what we are used to. I read you used to write your lyrics and play music on your guitar when you composed songs before you got your record deal. I used to do the same—write my lyrics and sing along with the guitar or keyboard. I don't have my keyboard here, but I can get some, I guess. You have your guitar. We can work together to write lyrics and the base of the music."

"Are you planning on rounding up a few locals to play the tambourine?" I grin at her. I watch her expression fall, and I feel guilty for teasing. "I'm only joking. It sounds nice. We can get into the recording studio later."

"So, you'll do it?"

"I'm here, aren't I, Red?" I smile and I take a sip of coffee.

"I went dark, not red," she points out, touching her hair and looking self-conscious.

"Your initials, not your hair." I laugh. "Code names for our secret album making. You can be Red, I'll be Bid. Or maybe not, if we released under those names, you know the media would end up combining. What bullshit nickname would we end up with? Bed?" I suggest but she reacts like I've scalded her. I hold my hands up in a mock surrender. "I was joking."

"Music making only, Indiana."

"You know the 'heartthrob Lothario lover' and 'string of broken hearts' stories are fabricated bullshit, right?"

"Most stuff is. I'm sure the media played the 'virginal pop princess' story far longer than necessary with me." Rose shrugs.

"Why don't we agree to cast aside the media assumptions, as well as our own assumptions, and judge each other on how we are?" I suggest and she nods.

"Libby tells me your dad might be doing a tell-all story." She switches the subject.

Now it is my turn to feel bristled and under attack. I sigh before I respond.

"Yeah. It is supposed to be out over the weekend. That'll be my second fun weekend in the news."

"Do you want to talk about it?"

"Do you want to talk about whatever it is you're running from?" I stare at her.

Despite the pose she has adopted, with her squared shoulders, straight back, and blank expression, it is her watery eyes that give her away. That and the small bite of her lip.

"So, we're agreed, making music, and no questions about the heavy stuff," she replies eventually.

"Deal." I lift my coffee cup and hold it in front of her in the offer of a toast. She rolls her eyes slightly but lifts her cup to clink against mine.

We drink our coffee in silence. When I'm done with mine and my cup is in the dishwasher, I start towards the front door so I can get my things from the car. I've travelled relatively light, one holdall bag with clothes and toiletries, plus my laptop and my guitar.

The street is still deserted when I go out to my car. I look around for longer than I did when I arrived, convincing myself that the other three houses are empty. It looks like Rose has somehow managed to find a getaway location where nobody is going to notice her coming or going. I wonder if it was intentional or pure serendipity.

"Do you need any help?" Rose asks as I come back into the house with my things.

"Just show me where you want me to dump my stuff." I gesture at my bag and guitar case.

"Come on up."

Rose walks up the stairs and I follow her. Upstairs, there are four doors, so I assume it is a three-bedroom property and a shared bathroom. One of the doors is open; it looks like a small bedroom, and I can see there are some clothes on the bed.

"Stole the third bedroom as a dressing room?" I tease.

She shakes her head. "I'm staying in there. So you have a choice, you can have either room at the back of the property."

I start to walk to the door that is diagonally on the opposite side of the house to the room she is apparently staying in. I'm here to work, but I know it is a weird set-up, to be staying in a holiday house with a woman I don't know, a woman who is clearly hiding from something. Sharing a bedroom wall feels like it would be an additionally weird step.

I step into the bedroom and look around. It's neat, nicely decorated. There is a comfortable looking double bed in the centre of the side wall, a thick-looking mattress that looks like it's going to be comfortable to sleep on. The curtains are open, and I can see the view through the window is overlooking the back garden. There are a few rows of tall trees at the back of the garden. I squint to get a better view between the trees.

"Is that the sea?" I look at Rose who is standing at the bedroom door.

"Yeah, it's really quiet on the beach, or it was when I went out on Monday evening."

"Are you up to see what it's like on a Wednesday evening?" I ask, and I can't help but feel a little excited.

I knew this was a coastal village, but I hadn't expected the sea to be right there, almost like it is in the back garden. It isn't like I haven't been on some fantastic beaches since I had my record deal, and I've been near the seaside at various stages through my last tour, but to have the beach right there, when I have nothing else that I need to be doing, nothing preventing me sinking my feet in the sand, swimming in the sea, it's exciting.

There's something about the beach that I have always loved. On the very rare occasions I went to the beach as a kid—usually on day trips with my grandma—the vastness of the area, the roar of the waves up the sand, I found it exceptionally grounding. I'd have a bad day as a kid and remind myself, the sun will set, the sun will rise, the tide will come in, and the tide will go out, no matter what else is happening.

I smile at Rose, hoping I don't look too much like I can't control my excitement at being so close to the sea and sand. She gives me a small smile in return and shrugs her shoulders.

"Sure, sounds good. The woman who owns this place said there were some good hiking locations around here, if we need any downtime. Maybe we could check one of the locations out."

"I feel like I'm getting way too much out of this deal." I laugh as I put my bag onto the bed.

"I'll let you unpack. I'll see you downstairs."

"Sure, I won't be long." I start to unzip my bag, and I hear her footsteps as she retreats down the hallway and then down the stairs.

I open my bag and take the clothes out, hanging them in the wardrobe. I put my toiletries onto the bedside table, then put my laptop in the drawer. I plug in my phone charger and then put my guitar case next to the wardrobe. I take my phone from my pocket and send a message to Maeve, telling her that I've arrived. I remind her that she and Libby are now under strict instructions from both me and Rose to enjoy their holiday, that I'm sure between us, we can solve each other's problems to try to avoid bothering them again.

I walk back downstairs and find Rose sitting in the living room, her legs curled underneath her as she sits in the armchair. I walk into the kitchen and check the contents of the fridge and cupboards. There is barely anything inside, just some butter, cheese, milk, bread, a few tins of soup, and a box of cereal. The state of the fridge and cupboards looks even less than what I have in when I'm staying by myself.

I walk back to the living room. Rose looks up at me.

"All settled?" she asks.

"Yeah, just thinking about some food. What have you been eating?"

"Cheese sandwiches or soup mostly so far. Though I had fish and chips last night, they were amazing." She gives me a grin and my stomach rumbles. Fish and chips by the seaside are second to none. At some point, I'm convincing her to have fish and chips together.

"Are you hungry?" I ask.

"I haven't been to the shops, I'm a little disorganised at the moment," she apologises. I'm already on my phone, looking for local takeaways that do a delivery.

"Chinese? Indian? Chip shop? Pizza?" I fire suggestions at her.

"Oh, pizza sounds amazing."

I update my profile on the food ordering app to the address we are staying in. It isn't often I order my own food, but there are several old addresses from when I have been between gigs when I have had the urge for hot food being delivered. It's under a fake profile name, not that delivery people tend to notice too much. For the most part, I've found if I tip in advance, I can get my food handed to me without a second glance.

I input my order preference and then hand my phone to Rose. She glances at the menu, smiles, taps away on the screen and then hands me the phone back. I complete the order and pay, then sit on the sofa. I search for local shops that do a delivery, finding a large supermarket in a nearby town with a delivery slot for tomorrow morning.

"I'm going to order some food from the supermarket. Any food aversions or allergies I need to know?"

She shakes her head. "I eat most things."

I make a rough plan of meals we could eat, adding items to the basket. I add more toiletries, more cupboard staples, snack items, fruits, and treats.

"The pizza will be here in twenty minutes. The food shopping will be here tomorrow at nine. That'll give us the whole day to then start writing, what do you think?"

"Sounds amazing. How much was the shopping? I have cash upstairs I can give you," she offers.

"I don't think either of us are hard up for cash, are we? Besides, you've paid for this place, how about I cover the food and entertainment costs?"

"By entertainment cost, are you springing for some decent TV because the daytime offerings here are terrible and the TV is pretty basic, I hope you weren't expecting anything other than dire shows." She grins at me, and I think it's nice to see her looking relaxed.

"You leave the entertainment to me." I grin back at her. A minute later, I've connected my phone to the TV, showing the menu of films from one of the streaming services I subscribe to, something that has felt like a necessity since I started touring. "What do you fancy? Any films you've been waiting to watch?"

"Not really, but a terrible disaster film sounds great." Her response is automatic, like she doesn't need to even think about it.

"When you say terrible, do you mean the type where everybody dies, or the type where the acting is questionable, the stunts and special effects are low budget, and the heroes are almost defeated before one final rallying speech from some random character?"

She laughs. "The second type, but I'll give you top marks if you can find a film that suits both examples."

I nod and scroll through the film categories. I pick one and she settles further into her chair as I make myself more comfortable on the sofa.

We don't talk as the film starts, both of us focused on the action on the screen. The film starts with a large explosion and disaster, no lead-up to the story, and when I glance over at Rose, she seems engrossed in what is happening on the screen. The little pinched expression she had when I arrived is gone. We keep watching until the doorbell rings, the food delivery arriving. I pause the film and go to the front door. I requested doorstop delivery so as I get to the front door, I hear the motorbike heading away. I open the door to grab the food.

"In here or the kitchen?" I ask from the doorway. Rose scoots off the sofa and sits on the floor.

"This film is too entertaining to take a break to eat. I'm happy to eat in here if you are," she replies.

I step into the room and hand her the box containing her pizza. I follow her lead and sit on the floor, opening my own pizza box. She has sausage meat and mushrooms on hers. Mine was described on the menu as fiery hot, and it's covered with chilli sauce, jalapeños, and spiced meats. I restart the film, and we eat as it continues.

"Do you want to swap a slice?" I offer, nudging my box towards her once I'm halfway through my pizza. She nods and offers me her own box so I can take one of her slices.

The film seems to take ages to finish, one of those with twisting plotlines and additional disasters being thrown in the way. Almost every character that seemed halfway nice dies a horrific but noble death, and only two of the plucky crew remain after the disaster is averted, saving everybody on Earth. It's cheesy as hell, the dialogue terrible, but it seems to have thrilled Rose.

When the film eventually finishes, I put the remaining slices of pizza into one box and put them in the fridge.

Rose follows me. "Do you still want to see the beach?" she asks as I put the pizza away. I look at the clock. It's late and dark outside, but I really do want to see the beach.

"If you're up to it, otherwise I can go by myself."

"Let me just grab a pair of shoes," she says.

I get my trainers from the hallway and by the time I have them on Rose is back downstairs, wearing her own trainers. She locks the front door and walks back towards the kitchen, so I assume we are going out the back garden. I follow her and it isn't long until we are on the sand. The tide is high, but it looks like it is on the way out again.

"Okay, I don't care what else is planned, I'm coming out here every night," I proclaim, and she shakes her head wryly.

"You look like a little kid who has just seen the sea for the first time."

"Always loved the seaside, Rose."

"Yeah, me, too."

"Besides, before you came here, when was the last time you stood on a beach and didn't have to worry about anything?"

She laughs and shakes her head. "The last beach I went to looked very different to this."

"Okay, so it's maybe missing the crystal-clear, warm, blue water you're used to, and I doubt we're going to see a ray of sunshine now we're in September, but look!" I stop walking, stand still, throw my arms wide. "There is nobody here!"

"That's because it is freezing cold and it's just going to get colder. Nobody else is going to be mad enough to be on the beach this time of night." Rose grins.

"Then this beach is ours. I'm claiming it. Tomorrow, I think I'll brave a dip in the water, if you're up for it. We can be tougher than the cold North Sea."

Her expression falters. "I might leave the swimming for you."

"Are you scared of cold water?" I tease.

"No, it isn't that."

"Why then?"

"I can't swim that well."

"Seriously?" I drop my arms and look at her.

"Can't swim properly, can't ride a bike, can barely cook, and there are about a million other things I'm terrible at." She shrugs.

"How is that possible?"

"I've been busy working since I was a kid, so a load of things I should have learnt as I became an adult, I didn't."

"Swimming and bike riding are little kid stuff, what age did you start working?" I cock my head to the side as I look at her. I was sure she was a teenager when she released her first album, but maybe she was working to break into the industry for a long time before she finally did.

"My parents were both busy when I was little. They insisted that they only had the time and the money for one hobby. I chose music. So instead of learning to ride a bike, I was learning the guitar. Instead of learning to swim, I was mastering the keyboard. Then, as I got older, instead of learning how to cook, I was recording and touring. The only adult thing I learnt was how to drive, and that was because some nice guy on my staff insisted that I needed to know how to drive in case of an emergency."

She gives another shrug, but then she blinks faster than usual, and I sense that while she has a matter-of-fact tone, this is something that bothers her.

"Okay, forget the music for a bit. We are going to rectify this situation."

"What bit, particularly?"

"All of it," I suggest.

"I'm going to magically learn how to do things?" she scoffs.

"Yes. Well, not magically learn. I'll teach you. We'll start tomorrow and cook together."

"You can cook?"

"Wow, the scepticism is strong." I laugh. I start walking down the beach again and she falls in line with my stride.

"I wasn't suggesting that you can't cook because you're a man," she protests.

"Well, of course, a penis is clearly a blocker when it comes to working an oven or hob. We just can't get close enough." I laugh.

"I meant," she starts with a mocking sigh, "I assumed you were too busy getting rock star famous to know the best way around a sauté pan."

"Hey, I'm talking more roast dinners and good steaks, not anything fancy, don't get too excited. I'm not going to be making soufflé or anything like that."

"It is probably best to start small," she says with a small smile. It's nice to see her smile; she looks more relaxed. The troubled expression she's been wearing seems to leave her face.

"Well, to go back to your scepticism, I was taking care of myself until I got my break. I was twenty-eight when my first album came out. Twenty-nine for my second. I lived by myself since I was eighteen, so I knew how to cook, clean," I tell her.

"No special lady who was looking after you?"

I think about my life before my record deal. I left home as soon as I was able, my relationship with my mother slightly less fractious than the one I had with my father but still not great. The only person in my life who had ever truly looked after me was my grandma, but she died when I was fifteen.

After I left my mother's house, I lived by myself in a run-down, cheap flat because it was the only thing I could afford. It was damp and tiny, but it was mine, a place where I could feel like I could be comfortable and not an inconvenience to somebody. I had a series of brief relationships before I met Olive when I was twenty-five, when I was starting to think about a serious future. I thought if I could crack through her walls, we might have been able to make a go of it, but she wasn't ready, and I wasn't mature enough to prove I was a worthy shot. After that, there was nobody serious. I landed my record deal when I was twenty-seven, and it was full on from then. No time for serious dating, not when days were crammed fill of promotions and touring.

Instead of answering her question, I deflect it.

"So, you're in agreement, cooking tomorrow?"

"Why would you do that for me?" She sounds quizzical. I stop walking again.

"Look, I know you think I'm doing you a favour by coming here to write an album with you, but really, you're the one doing me a favour. I've been in a slump. I had planned to get an album out next year, but I don't think I'm going to get over the slump, rehashing the same thing I've done before. I didn't realise it, but I needed something different. Making music with you is going to be different. Maybe it will be the kick to get me back on track, or a different track, a better track. Who knows? Maybe I'll be able to write a record-breaking album after writing one with you."

"Or maybe our collaboration could be record breaking itself." Rose gives me a wry smile.

"Now wouldn't that be amazing." I grin. "So, some cooking first?"

"Yeah, okay, but I'm not taking the song writing off the table for tomorrow. We can do some writing and then I'll let you humiliate me with a frying pan."

"How exactly do you think I'm going to humiliate you with a frying pan?" I snort.

She flushes, her cheeks scarlet. "I meant that I would be burning food!"

"I'm only teasing, I'm sorry. Just so you know, I'm as likely to burn food as you. Maeve takes the piss out of me all the time because I tend to eat things like chocolate spread sandwiches, but it is mostly because cooking for one is a pain."

"Come on; we should get this walk sorted before the cold wind kills us off," she suggests. Her cheeks look like they're returning to her usual colour. I nod and follow her as we walk along the sand with only the sound of the roaring waves between us.

Chapter Seven

Rose

NOW

The sound of somebody banging around downstairs wakes me in the morning. For a second, I'm startled by the noise given the house has been so quiet, but then I remember my mad plan of inviting Blake to stay with me.

I groan and open my eyes, checking the time and see that it is just gone nine. I remember Blake telling me yesterday that he arranged for the shopping to arrive at nine and I assume that is why there is so much noise.

I've never shared a home with anybody but my parents before, but now I wonder if there are some social rules that both Blake and I missed out on yesterday, like stating whether either of us were noisy early risers.

I didn't mean to sleep in so late this morning, but I think the fresh air from the long walk on the beach last night made me sleepy. By the time we got back from the beach, the only energy I had in me was to say good night to Blake before I headed up the stairs and to bed. I assumed an early night might have led to an early morning for me, but clearly not.

I get up and pull a cardigan over my pyjamas, belting it around my waist. I head to the bathroom first to freshen up and then go downstairs to help with the shopping. I'm halfway down the stairs before I wonder if I should have got dressed properly. I barely know Blake. Wandering around in my pyjamas might be a sight he is not expecting.

I'm fully covered up, so I carry on downstairs and walk towards the kitchen. Any concerns I had about being underdressed this morning is removed when I see him in the kitchen.

Blake is wearing only a pair of grey jogging bottoms. He's bare-chested, and his feet are bare, too. He doesn't look like he has been up long, as his hair ruffled from sleep. I try not to stare at him, but it's difficult. He's certainly a sight to look at and it is easy to see why he seems to have women constantly falling at his feet. He's got the body of a man who could easily be selling aftershave in big advertising campaigns, coupled with a face that most movie stars would be envious of.

I think of something my mother used to say, about how God sometimes gives all the gifts to one person. Blake's got a good body, a handsome face, and a voice that sounds amazing. It seems unfair to have all that wrapped in one package.

I clear my throat and force myself to stop staring at him. He's unpacking one of the shopping bags and he looks at me as he pulls out a jar of chocolate spread.

"I had a dream last night that they didn't include this in the delivery, I'm fucking relieved to see it," he says, his grin wide.

His enthusiasm makes me smile. He looks like a kid opening his Christmas presents, finding out that everything on the list is under the tree.

"Morning. I'm glad you got your precious chocolate spread," I reply.

"It makes up for the fact that I woke up late. I meant to get up earlier, shower, and dress before the shopping arrived, but I slept through my alarm clock. It's a good job that I signed up for doorstop delivery, otherwise some delivery person was going to get the sight of sleepy me behind the door." He laughs. He doesn't comment that I also slept through his alarm clock, and I wonder how long it had been blaring out without either of us noticing it.

"You don't sound particularly sleepy," I comment.

I start to unpack one of the other bags. I pull out what appears to be the meat order. There are beef steaks, a pack of mince, a leg of lamb, some tasty looking salmon, bacon, chunks of beef, and what looks like kidneys. I'm ignoring the kidneys. I've no idea what he has planned for them, but I'm not on board, at all. They sound disgusting.

"I'm fine once I get up, but getting up is the problem. Once I've convinced myself to put my feet on the floor, that's fine, I'm wide awake, but sometimes I'll spend an hour or so convincing myself to do it," he explains.

"Yeah, I know what those mornings are like," I reply.

I put the meat into the fridge and then go back to the bags. I start unpacking the vegetables. He looks like he's got a variety, covering all colours and bases. Bags of potatoes and carrots, a large swede, green beans, asparagus, broccoli, cabbage, red onions. I put most of them away in the drawer in the fridge, some in the cupboard when I get a vague memory of my mum putting potatoes and onions in a dark cupboard when I was a kid, before life got hectic.

"At least you're not going to judge me for my inability to be a morning person," Blake says.

There is a warmth to his tone that I didn't expect, but I'm thankful he doesn't ask me any questions about my mention of struggling to get out of bed, especially given I'm so late getting up today. I used to be up at the crack of dawn, eager for the day to start, and I've given interviews stating the same. In one of my first-ever interviews, I bragged about how I was always up early, wanting to squeeze every possible second of the day. It was something that other interviewers would ask me, whether I was still an early bird. I always laughed and answered with a yes.

The last few weeks, though, have been a complete change to my usual patterns. It isn't unusual for me to be awake late at night or sleeping in late. I've had days of being wrapped in the blanket, feeling like an invisible force was holding me against the mattress, where nothing could make me force my way out of the bed.

I shake my head to clear my thoughts. I need to stay focused, otherwise he's going to think more about my occasional silence and ask questions. Being questioned is not something I want, from anybody.

"That isn't what I would be teasing you about, if anything, it would be about that giant jar of chocolate spread you have got there." I break the small silence between us.

"Hey, shots at the chocolate spread are below the belt," he argues, a small smile on his face, like the little silence hadn't happened.

"Then it's a good job I'm not going to tease. I wouldn't, not when I know you are doing me a huge favour being here."

"Hey, come on, I told you last night, I'm getting enough out of this deal. You do not need to feel like you are in my debt, at all, Red." Blake's tone is firm, and I shake my head at him.

"If you think I'm going to be calling you Bid, you have another thing coming, Indiana," I throw back and he smirks.

"Sharpening those claws, I see."

"No, just being clear on the boundaries," I reply as I look in another bag and find it full of fruit. "How much did you spend on shopping?"

"Hardly anything, in the grand scheme of things. I just thought I'd cover all bases so we can focus instead of having to keep ordering food." Blake shrugs. He opens the bag in front of him and pulls out pints of milk and cartons of juices. It looks like he has opted for every flavour, apple, orange, cranberry, breakfast, tropical, pineapple. There's even a carton of tomato juice.

"Well, you certainly covered all bases." I smile at him as I take the fruit out of the bag. The grapes look amazing, and the green apples look like they're going to be sharp and juicy.

I put the harder fruits into the bowl and the softer fruits into the fridge, which is now fully stocked with the things I've put away as well as the things he must have put away before I came downstairs, things like tubs of yoghurts and more cheese.

"Do you want any breakfast?" he asks after he puts the final items away.

"What do we have?" I ask, half teasing because he appears to have ordered a bunch of breakfast options.

"Granola and yoghurt? Eggs on toast? Bacon sandwich? Sausage baguette? Bananas on toast? Good old-fashioned Rice Krispies?" He fires off some options.

"I think I'll have some granola, yoghurt and fruit, and some tea. You?"

"You handle the tea," he suggests. I nod and head to the kettle, flicking it on to boil.

I grab two cups from the cupboard. I focus on the tea as he puts granola and yoghurt into two bowls. He produces a tub of honey and puts it onto the table along with the bowls. He starts pulling some fruit together and takes a seat at the table, waiting for me as I finish making the tea.

"So, do you know any more about your dad and his tell-all story?" I ask as I take my seat.

He grimaces a little. "I thought you said no heavy topics?"

"Yeah, but I can't help being curious." I open the honey and dip the teaspoon in before drizzling it over my yoghurt, making swirling patterns in the yoghurt. I reach over and take a handful of berries, scattering them across the bowl.

"How about we exchange one sad story each this morning, and talk with honesty, and no judgement?" he suggests.

"Deal," I say, taking a spoonful of my breakfast.

As soon as I finish talking, I can feel my heart rate increase slightly because he could ask me any question. What will I say to him if he asks me what I'm running away from. He asked yesterday on the beach, and I had felt sick when he did. To talk honestly and answer that question would feel like torture.

Blake takes a breath before he speaks.

"My dad split from my mum before I was a teenager. He ultimately decided that he didn't want the responsibilities that came with being a husband and father, and he wasn't much of a father before then. I didn't see him much through my teenage years. If I did see him, he was distant and uninterested. It was shitty behaviour, and I learnt from an early age to rely on myself, accepting that a strong relationship with my father wasn't going to happen. A little while after the record company took an interest in me, I thought it would be good to clear the air with him. I was a little selfish when I think about it, but I thought it would be better to close any potential loose cannons in my life. I had enough to deal with, what with the former bandmates," he explains.

"Sounds sensible, not selfish," I comment when he pauses for a moment.

"Yeah, so, I reached out to Dad. I didn't think anything would come of it, but I was surprised when we started to build some bridges. We kept in touch over the last couple of years. I guess it's been easier to build something as adult to adult, not father to son, even if we weren't seeing one another often. A few months ago, he told me he was sick. He thought originally it was a problem with his kidney. I did all the tests to see if I was able to donate, sneaking off to doctor appointments between concerts, ready to donate after the tour finished."

He pauses again.

"That sounds incredibly selfless of you," I say. I can't decide if I would be so selfless to offer to undergo major surgery and a long recovery period for somebody who had treated me the way Blake's father appears to have treated him.

"Well, there was a twist of medical fate, so I still have my kidneys. Dad told me just before my last concert that the doctors had changed their assessment. He didn't need a kidney, but he had been diagnosed with cancer. I offered to pay for private treatment, and he told me no. He told me he didn't want to take my money. Then, the recent media stirrings into my past put me on some front pages, and somebody tracked down Dad. Apparently, they were looking for confirmation that I was violent, wondering what I was like as a child. When he told them I wasn't violent, they touted him up for a tell-all story."

"What is he getting out of telling a story?" I wonder.

"I don't know. Dad seems to have his eye on the money, selling his story and using money to pay for private medical treatment. He doesn't want to accept that he's making money off me, that it would be less painful all around if I just paid for his treatment or other expenses directly like I had offered. He just doesn't see it the same way. There will be a story about my childhood, our messy relationship, and I will grin and bear it."

Blake pokes at his granola as he talks. His voice is even the whole time, but his pose is defensive.

I think of him as a young kid, his father walking out. How that must have made him feel. My relationship with my father might be rocky right now, but at least my childhood was blissful, and through my teenage years we never had the argumentative relationship that is so often expected between teenage girls and their father. He doted on me, and he gave me everything that I wanted. I knew my mother and my father loved me dearly.

I'm not sure that is still true. Even if we were able to mend the cracks that appeared after he left my mother, I know he won't forgive me if he finds out what I did in the last few months. I don't think my father is as gracious and forgiving as Blake appears to be.

"You drew the short straw with the father allocation," I comment.

"I'm aware that not everybody gets the great parents and loving childhood. I used to think it was normal that my parents were never around, that I was letting myself into the house and fending for myself. Then I started to see people with a different home life to me. Don't get me wrong, I know there are lots of other people who had it much worse than me. They just weren't really cut out to be parents." Blake shrugs. "How about you? What was your family life like?"

"Idyllic, I guess, when I was growing up. I certainly had a different type of relationship with my own dad than you did. Everything was great until last year. I genuinely think he had a mid-life crisis. He got a sports car and hair implants. Then about eight months ago, he left my mother. He currently lives with somebody he met on one of the shoots for one of my music videos last year. I don't know how long he was with her while he was with my mother, but I'm pretty sure there was some overlap. He was already in love with her when he left my mother, that was one of the things he told her when he announced he was leaving for another woman. He said he couldn't stay with her as another woman had his heart."

"That's bullshit," Blake comments.

"His new girlfriend, she is twenty-five. He paid for her boob job, a fancy car, keeps her in designer outfits, and pays for her place. Her social media page is full of pictures of him with his arms around her, or her sitting on his knee by a swimming pool, wearing a skimpy bikini to display those perky new boobs to the best of their ability. She posts photographs of him, tagging him and calling him Daddy, and I want to bleach my eyes out every time I see it."

"How old are you?" Blake asks.

"Twenty-four. So, yes, miss-perky-boobs who could be my stepmother is only a few months older than me."

"Oh, wow, that's rough. Do you speak to either of them?"

"Him, not for a while. Her, no, never," I reply. I take another spoonful of my breakfast.

"What's her name?"

"Krystal. With a K. That's how she introduced herself to me."

"Well, sounds like we are strong out of the gate with our first heavy story," Blake muses.

"First?"

"Yeah, that situation with your dad is shitty, but I'm fairly sure that you're not hiding away here because of him."

I poke at my granola. "Do you need to know why I'm hiding?" I ask after a moment of quiet between us.

"No, not at all," he replies. He leans a little forward. "But, Red, if you want to talk, about anything, I'm a good listener, and I know how to keep my mouth shut."

"Thanks, Blake," I say after another full minute of silence because I can feel my throat is too tight to talk immediately.

"Come on, eat up, then we can get ready and started with this amazing album of ours," he suggests. I smile at him and then turn my focus back to the breakfast.

***

I finish breakfast then tell Blake that I'm stealing the bathroom first. He doesn't object, sitting at the table with a second cup of tea and one of the green apples. I head upstairs, lock the bathroom door, and strip out of my clothes. I look at myself in the mirror, my dark hair still taking me by surprise. I gave up on the coloured contacts. All they were giving me was sore eyes, and not really necessary when Blake knows who I am, and I'm not venturing outdoors.

I step into the shower, turning the water on, wincing a little because it takes a while for the water to heat up, and even when it does, it's more lukewarm rather than hot. I should be used to it by now, given the showers have all been in lukewarm water. I soak my hair under the water and then shampoo and condition it, wash my body with the shower gel, and get out of the shower as quickly as I can so I don't use all the hot water. Despite what Blake said about me not owing him anything, I at least owe him some hot water for his shower.

I wrap myself in the big towel and then head to the little bedroom I'm staying in. I can still hear Blake downstairs, clattering around in the kitchen, and it sounds like he's singing to himself. I shut my bedroom door, get myself dry, and then pick out an outfit to wear. I opt for an oversized shirt and a pair of leggings, thick socks on my feet. I scrub at my wet hair with the towel to take most of the moisture out and then clip it up out of the way. The idea of drying it with the hairdryer feels like too much energy to exert, and I'm keen to get downstairs and make a start trying to make some music.

I hear Blake in the bathroom so I hang my towels over the radiator in my bedroom so they can dry, then I grab my laptop, my notebook, and pen before heading downstairs. I go into the kitchen first, intending to clean the kitchen after breakfast, but Blake has already done it all. Everything looks neat and tidy, everything put away, the countertops wiped clean.

With nothing else to do, I go sit in the living room and wait for Blake to come downstairs. He comes into the living room, dressed in a pair of black jeans and a tee. It's his trademark look. If I've ever seen him at a music event or in the papers, he's always in this type of outfit. Only the guitar case in his hands makes him look different to how he's usually photographed, off stage at least.

"I hope you don't mind, but I turned the heat up on the shower," he says as he takes a seat on the sofa.

"What? You mean I've been taking lukewarm showers and didn't have to?"

"Yeah, sorry, there's a setting on the boiler for the water. I just turned it up," he says, shrugging.

"Is there anything you can't do?" I tease. He flashes me a grin, and I half expect some sarcastic or innuendo-laden remark.

"Write songs for myself, apparently," he says instead.

"How bad is your block?" I ask, feeling nothing but sympathy for him. Writer's block isn't anything I have suffered from, but I know it can be agony to go through it.

"I've written for other people and that's been fine, but sitting down to write for my own album has been hard going. I'm sure it'll work out, though," he says. "So, how do you want to do this?"

"I have no idea," I admit. "I'm not sure how to mesh our usual sounds together."

I'd compared our albums as soon as Libby had confirmed Blake would be coming, listening to each track on a loop, looking for the similarities. My older albums are very pop based, no offensive lyrics, the typical bubble-gum, sugar-style pop aimed at younger kids, especially as I was so young. At fourteen, they wanted me to sing about fun, fluffy topics, and I didn't have the life experiences or the depth to write much more, and my label steered me away from singing anything written by somebody else that could have been considered risqué. My record label preferred to play the girl-next-girl vibe, the sweet and innocent girl.

My latest albums are more comparable to Blake's albums given they're more mature, except they're typically the exact opposite of his. On his albums, most of the songs are love songs, or slow ones with lyrics about heartbreak, with one or two more upbeat tracks. Mine are still classically poppy songs, with more ballads creeping in. The pop songs are for my younger fan base. The more melodic stuff is an appeasement from my label to let me release tracks more fitting to my style now I've grown. Blake's albums have songs that contain explicit lyrics. My management team would have a fit. The only thing our albums have in common is that they are released by the same label.

"Maybe we just wing it and see what we come up with," Blake suggests when it is clear I'm still pondering his question. His attitude makes me laugh.

"I'm not sure any award-winning albums are made like that, but sure."

“Have you got any lyrics you want to start with?” Blake takes his guitar out of the case.

He holds his guitar in a way that makes me think of somebody holding a loved one, somebody they’ve been separated from for years and just been reunited. He looks completely at peace and serene. Again, it is easy to see why everybody seems to melt at his feet.

He looks at me, expectantly. I wrinkle my nose. The lyrics I’ve written since my life imploded have been terrible, dark and depressing.

“Nothing that I think is worthy of turning into a song.”

“How are you at making stuff up on the go? I have some music, but I haven’t been able to put any lyrics to it, but maybe you’ll have better luck than me.” Blake strums a few chords on his guitar.

“I haven’t made stuff up on the fly for a while, but I’m willing to give it a go.” I look over at him and catch the small smile on his face.

“I think we should record this, then if you have any amazing lyrics, at least we’ll remember what you came up with.” Blake pulls out his mobile phone and taps away, then leans to place it on the side of the sofa. He starts playing some chords. I stand up, pace the room as I listen to the music he is making. His music makes me think of longing, despair. It tugs on my heartstrings and makes me feel melancholy.

I hum to start with, joining in on the notes. He keeps playing as I think sentences in my head. He starts playing the music again, and this time I’m ready. When I start to sing, it’s tentative, but then I feel bolder, getting louder, feeling more confident.

“You said, ‘I can’t breathe without you,’ and I thought, ‘this is love.’ But look at you, still breathing, and I’m the one trying to catch my breath. You said, ‘I’d die without you,’ and I thought, ‘this is forever.’ But look at you, smiling to the world, and I’m the one waiting for revival. If I could go back, I’d tell myself, walk away, walk away, walk away. Get up, get out. Don’t you dare stay,” I sing.

I run out of words, and Blake stops playing the guitar as I stop singing. I look over at him and he whistles.

"Damn, Red, who hurt you?"

"Nobody," I say quickly, sinking back into the armchair. "Was that any good, or was I singing a load of rubbish?" I bite the skin of my little finger.

"Here, listen," Blake says, and he clicks on his phone to start the recording. I listen to the long introduction of his music playing and then my voice, my lyrics. He clicks the recording off after the recording catches up to the point where he'd stopped playing. "You need to write that down, Rose because that was amazing."

"The start of a song, I guess."

"If that is what you can come up with on the fly, I'm looking forward to what you can do when you're putting your mind to it."

"Says the guy who wrote 'Freefall' and 'Reputation.' Actually, my favourite of yours is 'The Things I Did,'" I say, and he smiles, almost shyly.

"Thanks. Nobody ever mentions that track."

"They should, it's beautiful. I cried like a baby listening to your second album. I played that track on repeat for ages."

"You did not," he protests, laughing.

"I did. It's an awesome album."

"Says the woman with so many more albums than me, and the collector of song of the year awards," he scoffs. "Your latest album, those last three tracks, if they don't win a host of awards, there is something wrong with people. They're sensational."

I roll my eyes at him and reach for my notebook and pen.

"So, shall we write down what we have so far?" I ask.

"Let me replay it so you can write it down. Do you think you have another couple of verses? Do you want me to try to draft the bridge?"

"Maybe we can play around with the second verse together," I suggest.

He nods and replays the recording so I can write down the words I'd sung. When I finish, I get up from the armchair I'm sat in and go sit next to him on the sofa.

"Do you want to continue in the same style, or maybe the third and fourth verses could be the response to you, I could sing it?" Blake asks.

I offer him the notebook. He frowns for a moment, concentrating, and then he scribbles down some sentences. His handwriting is neat, small, precise.

"I thought you said you were rehashing, or in a slump," I comment as I cock my head and read his sentences.

He shrugs. "I have been."

"If this is you in a slump, no wonder your albums have been so successful."

"It's sometimes easier to write about something when my emotions aren't tied into it."

"I hear you," I reply with a small sigh.

"Come on, I think we can play around with this track for a bit, and then I thought maybe it would be a good idea if we took one of our existing tracks, and each played around with it? Or even tried to mash up two of our tracks," he suggests.

"That sounds like a good idea."

"I'm full of them, Red." Blake winks and grins at me.

I would remind him that the idea of us joining up to write an album was my idea, that I'll take the credit for the good idea, but I know it's the only sensible decision I've made in the last six months, so I sit quietly, grab my notebook, and focus on the lyrics like my life depends on it, not just my career.

Chapter Eight

Rose

THEN

My mother looks at me across the dining table in my hotel suite. Her lips are set in a firm, thin line and as she holds her phone in front of her, I know she's about to launch into her current hot topic.

"Can you believe the audacity of that man?" she snaps.

By that man, I know she is referring to my father.

By audacity, that could be anything. Everything he has done recently feels audacious.

I take a deep breath. There's no avoiding this, I can't pretend I didn't hear her. I'm stuck with this, no matter how much I wish we could talk about anything else in the world.

"What has he done now?" I ask as I fork a piece of melon from my breakfast bowl, trying not to scowl.

I wish I was having something else to eat this morning, but given fruit was the only thing on the menu, per the nutritionist, I'm stuck with it.

Mum turns the phone towards me. On the screen there is a picture of my father and on his knee is Krystal. Dad's arms are wrapped around her bare waist, his fingers inched upwards towards the bottom edge of her bikini top. She has the selfie stick held high, so the angle of the photograph displays her new breasts to their full impact. They're far too large for her frame in my opinion, but she seems pleased with them. I guess some people like the giant watermelon stuck-on look. It certainly looks like my dad enjoys them. She's tagged his profile with the comment "*thank you, Daddy, for my new boobs. I can't wait for you to try them out.*"

The melon slips down my throat, making me want to vomit.

"Careful," Mum chides as I cough uncontrollably.

Part of me wants to defend my dad, to point out that this is on Krystal's social media page, they are Krystal's words, not Dad's, but it won't make much difference. There is no reasoning with my mother when it comes to my dad. She's paranoid that somebody is going to find out what has happened and publish a story about it, and I know I'll have to listen to her ranting about how this could be the key to somebody publishing the news, and she'd be right. Dad's profile is fairly locked down and private, but Krystal's is wide open. It won't take long for somebody to realise my father is... what... acting like a sugar daddy to his new girlfriend? The only saving grace is that I know that isn't how they met, because I'm the idiot that introduced them, but I know how it will look to other people. They'll look at Dad's relationship with her, compare the two of them, and come up with two assessments: That he's too old and she's too young.

Will they call him a dirty sleaze? Will they call her a gold-digger?

Will they point out that she is literally young enough to be his daughter?

Will they point out that she looks like a younger, surgically enhanced version of my mother?

"You shouldn't keep torturing yourself by looking at their pages. You should block them. Especially hers. You probably lose several brain cells every time you read her posts." I push my bowl away. All my thoughts of breakfast have disappeared. Maybe that should be the trick a nutritionist tries when they think I've put on weight, show me pictures of Dad feeling up Krystal instead of limiting my calorie intake.

"It is better to know the enemy you want to destroy," Mum says, darkly.

I'm not sure how she plans to destroy either of them, or what her end goal is. If she wants my dad back, attempting to sleep with any guy that even glances in her direction is probably not the best bet. It makes me wonder if she wants to have a list of young, hot men she's managed to have fun with so that if Dad ever does come to his senses, she'll show she didn't just curl up without him.

"It upsets you every time you read a post, so don't do it," I snap.

I sound more forceful than I intended, but I can't stop myself. I know it hasn't been long since Dad announced he fell in love with another woman. I know it probably kills my mum every time she thinks about it. But I also know the way we feel changes nothing. Dad told me as he moved out, he's never felt like this before. I assume he means a reckless teenager who has no regard for anybody else, because it seems laughable to suggest he's never been in love before. He seems to have forgotten that, forgotten everything he thought was important. Aside from Krystal, that is. She is apparently important. Anything that she wants, she seems to get.

I get up from the table.

"Where are you going, Briar Rose? Come finish your breakfast." Mum's voice is just as snappy as mine was.

I stop walking, turn to look at her.

"Why do you insist on calling me that?" I ask. It isn't my name, but it may as well be. Until I was fourteen, she called me Rose. Dad used to call me Princess Rosie Posie. I was the one who came up with Briar Rose as a stage name, but I never expected my parents would start to use it more than my own name.

"Everybody calls you it, you never mind when it is somebody else. Why can I never seem to do right by you? No matter what I do or say, you're always so cross with me. I bet you think it's right that your father left me. You probably think it's my fault he left."

Mum's voice is shrill. I close my eyes for a moment as I count to ten in my head before I speak. I can't criticise her; I haven't been able to since Dad left. Any criticism, she weaponizes it, turns it back to me and makes me feel guilty for having an opinion. She always asks the same question, about whether I think she deserves being left by her husband.

"Of course I don't think that, Mum. I've never thought that. Dad's a dick, clearly. I just hate being called my stage name by family," I reply once I've composed myself.

I've told her this before, I've told her how much I've come to dislike having a stage persona, that I can't even use my own name. I'm fairly sure that if I used my real name, people wouldn't know who I was. I'm twenty-four with a record label who wants me to hold on to the fan base of teenage girls, as if I am still a teenage girl. If I'm forced to do that, the least they can do is let me drop the moniker I gave myself before I was even a teenager.

"I'm sorry, I'm just all over the place, you know that." Mum's bottom lip wobbles and the ball of guilt is back in my stomach. She's always like this in the mornings. The mood swings are shocking. I can't decide if this version of my mother is preferable to the one that she presents in the evening, the one that is half dressed as she heads out on dates or to social events where she has her eye out for single, often younger men.

Apparently, whatever my dad can do, my mother wants to do better.

"Mum, I'm going to be late if I'm not careful," I cut in with a sigh.

I don't have time this morning for her emotional outbursts. The last time she started like this, it was an hour of crying and cursing my father under her breath, cumulating in her threatening to hunt Krystal down to punish her. At least with Dad sunning himself in Cyprus with Krystal, I don't have to worry too much. Mum would have run out of steam before finding her way to the airport.

"You're leaving me here alone?" Mum asks. She almost looks wounded.

"I told you; I have a meeting with the casting director this morning. I'll be back in a couple of hours. We can go do some shopping afterwards, remember?"

"I don't know why you are putting yourself through this acting business. You're successful as a singer, why do you want to do something else?" Mum's expression has changed. She no longer looks wounded, tragic. She's back to boss mode. Back to ignoring me and what I want, thinking she knows best for me and my career, not caring about what I really want.

I've acted before. I enjoyed it, and, surprisingly, I was good at it. While it had only been for cameos or brief stints on UK soaps, I started to think that acting could be something I seriously get into, something I could do on my own terms. It wasn't just the directors and other actors who had told me I was good; I had been boosted by the reviews in the tabloids, thrilled that they had been complimentary, printing reviews like "genuine emotion" and "like she's been doing it all her life," calling me a complete natural.

Now, to know that there is a director who wants to cast me as the lead in a major drama, it's the first exciting thing to happen to me in a long time, the first thing that has left me with a fizzle of excitement in my stomach. Usually, pop stars seem to end up as minor parts in movies or within teen comedies, but this is a lead in a franchise of a book adaptation and a massive opportunity at a big break.

The main character is what every actress dreams of. She's feisty, independent, and is more important than the main male character, dominating the story on the page, and as such will command the screen. It's a role I want desperately and have since the moment I heard whispering about the film being made. I bumped into the director by chance at an award night and he casually asked if I would be interested. I've been counting down the days to this meeting.

"Mum, I will see you later, okay?" I turn to cross the suite, grabbing my mobile phone and my bag as I walk past them. I slip in the hotel key and then I'm out of the door before she can say another word.

I haven't told my mother that the meeting is in the same hotel, and she's too much in a haze or fury about my dad to insist I need a chaperone. When the director's assistant had contacted me to discuss the opportunity in more detail, I asked for the meeting to be based near the hotel I was staying in, and I was thrilled when they accommodated me in the same hotel. My time is scarce, so being in the same location to where I'm staying, and not far from where I'm supposed to perform tonight, feels like serendipity.

I access the lift, and when it arrives, I click the button for the second floor. I'm staying on the top floor of the hotel, in their fanciest suite, per my mother's usual demands. She always insists on it with the management team. I feel like I live in hotels, even when I'm not touring. When there is a break in touring, my parents used to holiday in warmer climates, staying in one of the many houses they purchased through the years since my record deal. I spend my time on a what feels like an extended holiday, swapping hotels for holiday homes or spacious villas, never really feeling grounded or connected to one particular place.

The conference rooms I need to get to are on the second floor. I know the lift I'm in is not far from the location of the room I need to be in. It's early morning so I'm unlikely to bump into any fans or anybody who recognises me. When I was a teenager, my parents insisted on security for me whenever I went anywhere, but the last year or so, I've pushed back on the constant supervision, even if Mum would prefer me to be with somebody all the time. Now I only have security when I'm performing.

When I reach the conference room, I take a deep breath and then knock, waiting until a woman opens the door.

"Hi, Briar Rose, so nice to meet you," she exclaims.

"You're Etta?" I ask.

"Yes, Etta Price, assistant to Mr Wise. Please, come in, we have been expecting you."

Etta opens the door wider for me and so I step inside. The conference room is modest, but it is still probably more than what is needed. There's only me, Etta, and Mr Wise, the director who is supposed to be here. As I look around the room, I spot somebody else, somebody I wasn't expecting.

Hunter Greenway. The man rumoured to be in the running to play the male lead. I assume he has the part, and now it's for me to prove I'll play well opposite him.

I square my shoulders. I can do this. I don't care how experienced Hunter is with TV shows and being a film lead. I want this. I will not let him intimidate me.

The room has been set out with a large, oval-shaped table in a dark walnut colour. There are eight large leather seats pushed up against the table. Hunter sits in one of the chairs, on the opposite side to Mr Wise. Etta takes a seat next to Mr Wise. In the centre of the table there are various pastries, including the little raspberry ones that are my favourite. Due to my abandoned breakfast of only fruit, I really want to eat one.

Given that Mr Wise sits in the centre of his side of the oval table, I take a seat almost opposite him, a few seats down from where Hunter is sitting. My attention should be on the director.

"Thank you for meeting with me," I say, giving a big smile.

"She doesn't look like she's ready to save the universe in that outfit." Mr Wise addresses this to Etta, and I can't help but feel a little stung. As if he realises that he's just said this out loud, he laughs and looks at me. "So sorry, I sometimes forget to engage my brain before my mouth."

"I didn't realise you expected me to be in a costume, Mr Wise." I stare at him.

It's March, it's cold in the hotel, and my outfit is suited for the weather. If I had known he was expecting me to turn up looking like any interpretation of the character, I would have happily dressed accordingly. I'm sure I'll do anything he asks. If he wants me to sing and dance right now, I'll do it. I'll climb onto the tabletop and tap dance as I belt out a song and then give him one of the monologues from the book that I've been practicing. I want this part more than I've wanted anything since I got my record deal.

"I didn't, don't worry. This is mostly so we can introduce you to Hunter. Have you met before?" Mr Wise gestures towards Hunter.

I'm sure everybody in the country knows Hunter Greenway, even if he seems to guard his personal life as well as a superhero manages to protect their alter-ego identity. Hunter had seemed to burst onto the scene almost two years ago, and he went from being a nobody to being everywhere almost overnight. It helps that he's exceptionally attractive but also seems to be a humble, grounded guy. He seems incredibly bashful when interviewed, painfully shy. He's the same age as me and he is always listed in the articles about people to watch—people who are going to set the world on fire.

"We haven't met before," I say.

I look across at him and he stares back at me with eyes that remind me of the skies on a perfect summer day. He has a coffee cup in his hands, staring over the cup at me, and he looks like a little kid who has been caught with his hand in the cookie jar. Hunter lowers the cup and gives me a beaming smile. I watch as he stands, and he reaches for one of the pastries from the plate in the middle. He walks towards me, past the spare chairs I left between us when I sat down. He hands me the pastry, his fingers grazing against mine. His lips are curved into a soft smile.

"Well, that's such a shame, something we must rectify immediately," he says, his voice deep and teasing. "I'm Hunter Greenway. It is very nice to meet you, Briar Rose."

I don't correct the use of my name. It barely even registers with me. I'm too busy looking at his lips, wondering what it would be like to kiss him.

"I do believe we have our leads," Mr Wise says from across the table to Etta, and I wonder why he seems so far away, like Hunter and I have been swept into a sphere that nobody else seems to be able to penetrate.

"Perfect," Hunter says, still looking at me, still with that dazzling smile.

"Perfect," I echo, and I'm not sure I'm talking about the film role.

It feels like the world has shifted and I'm the only one who realises. I imagine this is what it would feel like to wake up in an alternate reality, being the only one who knows the world is different to how it should be, but it doesn't feel scary. Instead, it's an exhilarating sensation. It suddenly feels like there is a promise of something fun in the future, something other than returning to my hotel suite and listening to my mother either venting to me or flirting with any man who passes her gaze for the rest of the day.

Hunter takes a seat back at the table, sitting next to me rather than his first seat. He turns his attention back to Mr Wise, so I mirror his behaviour, focussing on what is being discussed, though all the while my body feels conscious that Hunter is right next to me. I can feel the warmth of his skin close to mine, and I'm sure he can hear how my breathing is slightly hitched. I swear his breathing is also slightly hitched. As I wonder if he can tell how much he seems to be affecting me, he moves slightly in his seat, his knee knocking against mine, and I feel like I've been electrocuted. He gives me a small, almost bashful smile.

"Briar Rose?" Etta says, getting my attention. I wonder how much I've zoned out during this meeting. "We'll courier over a contract for the film today, but we are delighted to have you on board."

"Thank you, I'm honoured," I reply, and I look at them across the table. At some point, they appear to have gathered all their paperwork together and I realise they're leaving.

Hunter leans closer to me. "Briar Rose," he whispers. I jolt again and he smiles. "What are you doing for the rest of the day?"

I think of my promise to go out with my mother. I think about the concert that I'm performing tonight.

"Nothing until the afternoon, why?"

"Are you up for a little fun?" he asks, a mischievous twinkle in his eye.

I think of my father, abandoning the family. I think of the past ten years of my life, so carefully managed and everything vetted twice before I'm allowed to do something, say something, be somewhere, be with somebody.

I think about how tired I've felt about the control, the micromanaging, the judgement, the million things I have to do because somebody insists on it.

I think of how tired everything seems to make me feel these days, how much joy seems to have gone from everything I used to love.

More than anything, I think about how I want to be free.

"Yes, I am," I reply, and when he smiles at me again, I feel like I'm jumping off a cliff, knowing there is no parachute, wondering if I'll catch my breath.

Chapter Nine

Blake

NOW

The sound of somebody screaming "no" in the middle of the night scares the life out of me. I'm up, out of bed, and out on the hallway before my brain engages enough for me to realise where I am, who it is shouting.

I cross the hallway towards the room Rose is staying in, knocking a couple of times in quick succession on the door.

"Rose, are you okay?" I ask.

I can only think of two reasons that somebody is shouting out in the middle of the night, especially in that type of distressed tone. Either they're having a nightmare, or they're not alone and in trouble. As Rose hasn't given me any indication that she wants anybody to know where she is, the probability of her inviting somebody into the house seems low, so anybody in her room would be an unwelcome guest.

I hop from foot to foot as I wait for an answer, feeling more awake and now anxious. What if some crazy fan has found out where she has been staying and broken into the house? Has she been hiding because she has a stalker, and they've managed to find her? Why didn't I ask her more questions about why she's hiding away? Why isn't she answering me? How long am I supposed to wait until I decide she's clearly under duress and go into her room to tackle the person who is here?

My hand reaches for her door handle.

"I'm fine," she calls before my hand connects. It feels like an eternity has passed since she shouted out no, and she sure as fuck does not sound fine.

"You sound a million miles away from fine," I call back to her through the closed door. My hand is still halfway out to the door handle because this doesn't feel right. She still sounds like she's under duress.

"Go back to bed."

"There's nobody in there with you, is there? I swear, if I go back to bed only to wake up tomorrow to you having been mauled in your sleep, that's going to be a ball ache to explain to the police. I've got 'wrongful conviction' vibes going on right now," I call back.

I'm surprised to hear her laugh. Then there is the sound of her footsteps on the floor, coming closer to me. The door opens wide. She stands in front of me wearing what looks like a pair of thermal pyjamas, a pair with long trousers and a long-sleeved top. She has a wry smile on her face.

"You are such an idiot. However, feel free to look around, if you want to be reassured there is no monster in the room," Rose teases, and she opens the door wide for me.

I take a quick look into her room. It's a small room so there isn't much for me to scan over. Everything looks in its place. The bed is a divan so at least nobody could be hiding under there. I glance at her wardrobe.

"Nobody hiding in there, is there?" I ask.

"Nope," she says, grinning.

She crosses to the wardrobe, opens the door and gestures at it. It reminds me of how a magician's assistant demonstrates a box is empty. Rose closes the wardrobe door.

"Okay, thank fuck for that, because I really don't think I'd do well in a fight," I joke. She steps closer towards me, back to where she'd been when she'd answered the door. I wave my hands in front of her. "Got to protect these bad boys, for making our sweet tunes."

"Perhaps if somebody is in the house and I need defending, you could knee them in the balls." She offers a solution, and I can't help but grin again.

"Oh, come on, no man knees another in the balls."

"I would bet they do."

"Nope. Never. It's like an unwritten man code."

"Then you'll need to decide if you're going to risk those magic fingers of yours or break the man code. Should I need you to rescue me, of course, if I am too much of a damsel in distress to deal with something by myself." She leans against the doorframe, her arms folded across her chest. She looks like she's having fun, but she still has that air around her, the air that makes her seem smaller than she actually is.

"Well, if there is no monster to rescue you from, what had you crying out?" I ask, and the smile is gone from her face.

"Just a bad dream." She says this and then takes a deep breath before exhaling loudly. Whatever dream she's had, it seems personal and upsetting. I'm sure I run the risk of upsetting her if I push her to talk to me about it.

"Don't tell me you were reliving the kitchen disaster?" I ask, teasing her instead of pushing for the truth.

Last night, we had steak, asparagus, and poached eggs for tea. The fact that Rose had never cracked an egg before was something she hadn't told me, and the first attempt had ended up with one egg dripping down the kitchen cupboard door. Rose had looked at me with surprise on her face and then she collapsed into a fit of giggles. Her giggling had taken me by surprise and started my own chuckles. It had taken us both a while to stop laughing. Even after we cleared up and served tea, she occasionally giggled and shook her head.

"No, though I understand the concept of being as fragile as an egg much more now," she says, grimacing.

"Maybe we'll avoid eggs for tea for the time being."

"Dinner," she counters.

"Ah, you southerner. You'll find it is breakfast, dinner, and tea," I tease.

"No, you northerner. It is breakfast, lunch, and dinner," she reminds me. We had this discussion yesterday when we cooked. I suggested we started making tea and she replied that she wasn't thirsty, sparking a discussion on correct naming terms.

"I think you'll find the person who can actually crack eggs is the one who gets to decide the labels for food times," I joke.

"I can crack eggs, just not well, or maybe too well as I proved last night," she says with a laugh. When she laughs, she seems at ease, but I can tell there is something bothering her.

"Do you want to talk about whatever it was that upset you?"

"Nothing is bothering me," she counters.

"Well, something clearly interrupted your sleep."

"Go back to bed, Blake. I'm fine. I promise."

"Okay. Good night, Red." I turn to walk back towards my room.

"Hey, Blake?" she calls.

"Yeah?"

"Thanks for checking on me, even if it was just so you could avoid a potential wrongful conviction."

"You're welcome," I reply.

Rose shuts her bedroom door, and I go back to my room. I fall back into bed, wrap myself in the quilt, wondering what it is she is holding back. There is clearly something, but it doesn't look like she's going to talk to me about it. As I slip back into sleep, the last thought in my head is that I'm going to do my best to take her mind off whatever it is that is causing her nightmares and provide a little bit of fun in her life. Hopefully the things I put into place last night will go someway to helping take her mind off things; hopefully it'll make her smile.

***

When I wake in the morning, I do my best not to make a lot of noise. If Rose has been waking up having nightmares, I assume she'll appreciate some additional rest.

I shower and dress before heading downstairs. I make breakfast and a cup of coffee, sitting at the table to try to write some lyrics.

It's just before midday when she comes downstairs. She's dressed in another oversized jumper and a pair of leggings.

"Why didn't you wake me?" she asks. I get up from the table so I can put the kettle on for her.

"I wasn't sure you would want me to, and I wasn't sure what time you'd actually got back to sleep, but I thought it would be good for you to sleep," I reply as I grab a cup for her drink.

"I'm sorry for disturbing you last night," she says.

"No, it's okay, I slept like a baby once I got back into bed."

"I feel like I wasted your morning." She bites her lip. I gesture at my notebooks, trying not to beam at her because I'm happy I've had some inspiration to write something. Not just that, but something that isn't shit.

"I was writing. Take a look, if you like," I offer.

She takes a seat at the table. I wait for the kettle to finish boiling so I can make her a mug of tea. When I finish, I take a seat opposite her.

"These are really beautiful, Blake," she says as she reads what I've been writing. She runs her fingers across one of the verses.

"I hope you don't mind what I've been attempting here," I say, leaning over to tap one of the pages where I've taken two of our most famous songs, playing around with them, mixing the lyrics.

"'Repercussions,' you wrote that about the woman you dated, the one who was in those articles?" She looks at me. I nod.

"Yeah, the day she broke up with me, which I completely deserved, but it still stung. I went home, wrote the song. I thought it would mix well with this one of yours. I thought we could change a few lyrics, switch it so you sing what was mine, and I sing what was yours," I suggest.

She reads back over the lyrics I've jotted down. It starts with a line from my track—"*despite what you say, I've only myself to blame*"—followed by a line from hers—"*are you haunted by the ghost of my smile.*" Back to my lyrics with *"thought I was losing, but fuck, was I even in the game,"* and then another line from her song, *"does your soul ache with the absence of my touch."*

"It works. I can hear how it would sound," she replies. She reaches for the mug of tea I've placed on the table for her.

"Feel free to kick around with it while I make us something to eat," I offer. I already have things ready to make us toasties.

"You don't have to make us food," she protests.

"You focus on the song I've started on the next page, see if you can find a suitable ending for it," I suggest.

I start to assemble the items to make the toasties and put the pan on to heat. I hear her turning the pages of the notebook, then the sound of her scribbling notes on the paper, adding lines to the song I've started. I'm nearly finished the toasties when I hear her put the notebook down. I look at her. I'm about to ask her what is wrong, but she cuts me off.

"Tell me about your old band. Why was there so much bad blood between you?" she asks.

"Is this the sad story for today?"

"Yep," she replies.

I don't reply immediately. I finish making the toasties and switch off the pan, then put a plate with her toastie in front of her. I sit down opposite her. She takes a bite of her food, eating while she waits for me to speak. I like that she's calm and doesn't push for an answer.

"Jay was somebody I met through work. We got friendly and he told me he was in a band. He told me they were looking for a new guitar player, and I thought it was an amazing step of fate, that this was going to be my big break, our big break. I auditioned for the band, and they asked me to join. Jay was the lead singer. Lucas and Vic, they are brothers, were the drummer and keyboardist. Their cousin, Marcus, played bass. Marcus and Jay had known each other since they were kids, so I was the odd one out. I was twenty-four when I joined, and I genuinely thought we were going to go big."

"I take it you were successful as a band?"

"Yeah, nothing huge but enough for us to feel like we could make it. We had a following in the city, loyal fans who would follow us and turn up for our shows. We started playing for bigger audiences. Then, Jay tells me that he has this friend who knows a guy who was a talent scout, and he thinks we can perform for the friend and then he'll convince the talent scout to come see us. Sounded like a dream, right?"

"Did you meet them?"

"The friend came to watch us rehearse one night. We were on fire, honestly, it was an amazing night. We wrapped up, and the rest of the guys wanted to celebrate. They were getting their shit together to go out and party, and I didn't want to go because I just felt like I was in the zone, do you know what I mean, the times where you just want to carry on performing, like your life depends on you singing another song. So, they left, and I just stayed, mucking around on the guitar. I was singing one of my own tracks. I was singing 'Freefall.'"

"You didn't sing that with the band?" she asks, her expression curious.

"No, it was my song. I wrote it and composed it. It was all mine, and I just wanted to sing it, for myself. I thought the guy had gone with the band, but he was still there. He asked me why we weren't doing music like that, instead of what we were doing. I'd proposed my tracks before to the guys, but they were happy to stick to the vibe they had going."

"I checked out their social media after you hit the scene, I was curious about your former band. You're right, their vibe is totally different to what you have now," she comments.

"Yeah, a bit like chalk and cheese, I guess. Anyway, the guy asked me for my details. He called the following week and asked me to meet him, and the talent guy, in London. I should have been loyal to the band. I know I should have said no, but I didn't. I went and performed. They asked me to sing 'Freefall.' They asked me to sing something else, so I sang some other tracks of mine for them. It was all my music, only lyrics I wrote and music I composed. Me, my songs, my guitar. By the end of the meeting, they wanted to offer me a record deal. Just me. Not the band. That was non-negotiable. I tried, I swear."

"What did the band have to say?"

"It wasn't pleasant. There were accusations that I stole their opportunity. I get it, I do, but I didn't really have any option other than turning down the deal. I thought they'd be fine without me, anyway, given I was only their guitar player. It wasn't like I couldn't be replaced easily. They just didn't see it the same way and it turned nasty, but I understood, and I know I deserve it," I explain.

I take a bite of my toastie, more for an opportunity to pause talking. I sometimes hate the way I treated the band. When I was in the band, I tried to fit in. I changed my style, just to fit in and have an opportunity to play music, to do something more than busking in the street.

Olive kept telling me that I should sing solo, but I liked the idea of having bandmates, people who cared about me, people who wanted me around. I'm sure, if I saw any type of therapist, they may have pointed out that I was looking for people who wanted me around because I didn't have that when I was a kid, but I didn't recognise that at the time. I just felt like I'd found a place where I belonged.

The day the record company had offered me a deal, it felt like winning the magic prize; I could see everything there, being held out for me on a plate. Mine for the taking, if I was willing to sacrifice four other people to get what I wanted. I did at least try, and I hesitated to accept until the label told me I had to decide or lose their offer. So, I accepted.

There had been some acrimonious postings on social media sites after I released my album, the band doing some interviews with some negative comments about me. They kept up that rhetoric because they benefited from the publicity, enjoying their own burst of fame and exposure. It took a while for that to die down. I never responded in public apart from positively talking about my former bandmates, but regardless of what went down, I still feel guilty about it.

"Some people wouldn't have even bothered to ask for anything for their bandmates. At least you tried," she says after a silence between us.

"I still feel like shit about it, like my success is not really mine, like I don't deserve it." I shrug as I speak.

"If the tables were turned, if the offer was for the band but not you as the guitar player, what do you think they would have done?"

"Oh, they'd have totally taken it. I was always the odd one out there." I laugh.

"Then why do you feel so guilty?"

"It's hard to know your happiness comes at the expense of somebody else."

"I doubt my father or Krystal give a shit about how their happiness comes at the expense of my mother, but never mind. At least you care, though I don't think you really need to beat yourself up about it. It isn't like you took their songs or even took anything that you'd performed with them."

"Yeah, I know."

"Your success is down to your talent. You're an insanely talented songwriter, Blake, and you sing beautifully." She stares at me intently as she talks. I can't help but feel flustered. She isn't the first person to tell me that I'm talented, but she's one of the few who I feel are saying it out of nothing but genuine feelings, rather than benefiting from stroking my ego.

"So that's my heavy story for today. How about you tell me who you wrote this song about."

I tap the page with the song I've been looking at today. For a moment she looks surprised at my question. I assume she expected me to ask her more questions about whatever it was that woke her last night.

I pick up my toastie and take another bite, waiting for her response.

"I wrote it about an ex-boyfriend."

"Care to elaborate?" I ask with a smile. I've never seen a single thing written in the papers about Rose and any romantic partner.

"I was twenty-one. He went to the same church as my family," she adds, and then she is quiet again.

"Your family is quite religious, right?" I ask. This is something I have read about her.

"What about you?" she asks, deflecting my question.

"I think the most appropriate description is agonistic, but that's getting off track. Tell me about this boyfriend," I coax.

"He was a nice guy. My parents and his parents did what they could to get us together. My mother was very vocal about him, telling me he was wonderful. I guess he was, on paper. He was kind, good-looking, smart, ambitious. He was just starting a proper career, as my mother called it. We dated, quietly, for about six months." Her voice trails off again.

"Six months is a bloody miracle, to keep something secret." I smile.

She laughs quietly. "Yeah, well, he signed a non-disclosure agreement when we started dating, per the standard practice of my management team and parents. God forbid I'm seen by anybody as an adult. He never batted an eyelid at signing the NDA, he was fine with us having dates out of sight, keeping everything quiet. I thought it was because he liked me, and I thought we were falling in love. Then I found out that he was fooling around with some other woman, or rather, women."

"Oh, Rose, I'm sorry. Cheaters are the worst," I say, and I know I've touched a nerve as her eyes well up with tears. "You must have really loved him."

"I didn't really know him," she replies, her voice coming out slightly strangled.

"Maybe you should ask me a tougher deep question tomorrow, as I feel like you've let me off easy with mine today, if you're crying over yours."

She's quiet for a second as she composes herself.

"Perhaps no more questions about men."

"How about, if I ever meet this two-timing ex-boyfriend, I kick him in the balls for you?" I joke, and she giggles.

"I'm fine about him now. I think it's better to learn what people are really like before hearts get totally mangled."

"I still made you cry, I'm sorry."

"I was just thinking, don't worry about it."

"Well, I'll still kick him in the balls for you, if you like, even if men don't usually break that bro code."

"You are such an idiot." She rolls her eyes.

"Yeah, I know, but I make a great toastie, right? Eat up. We have some work to do this afternoon." I gesture at her half-eaten toastie. She smiles and picks up her food, and we fall into a comfortable silence.

***

"When you said we had some work to do this afternoon, I thought you meant singing." Rose sounds apprehensive.

"Come on, we can do this," I coax, holding the tandem bike.

"Where the hell did you even get this?" She eyes the bike like it's a crocodile lurking in the water, waiting to bite her. The bike had arrived earlier this morning when she was still in bed, along with a keyboard I arranged for her, both things I ordered the night I arrived, after our conversation about learning things.

The keyboard is set up in the third bedroom, I've promised we'll be using it tomorrow, but the bike, I don't want to wait. I hid it in the back garden when it arrived, and this is the first time she has seen it. She doesn't have the same expression of happiness at seeing the bike as she did the keyboard.

"I ordered it, along with the keyboard. It's second hand but it should fit us well, according to the specifications on the website."

"Do you even know how to ride this?"

"I'm not going to lie to you, Rose, I've never been on a tandem bike before, but I've been reading up on this since the day I got here. We'll be fine, and if worse comes to worst, we have helmets," I tease, tapping the helmet I've got on. She has hers on, too.

"We're going to attract a lot of attention on that." Rose frowns.

"For the bike, yes. For us, no. Trust me, you look nothing like your normal self. Besides, the place is deserted. It's a weekday, everybody is at work or at school. We can ride around for a bit, and nobody will know it is us. I've mapped a route; once we are off this road, we take a right, at the end of the road, another right, then we are on the country roads. It'll be quiet, I promise. It was quiet when I drove in, so I expect it'll be the same today."

"I thought you were joking about the bike riding," she mutters.

"Was I joking about the cooking?"

"Oh, my, do not tell me you're planning on trying to get me to swim?" She glances at me, a horrified look on her face.

"Not today," I reply with a grin. I don't think I can convince her to swim properly, and I wouldn't push her if she didn't feel comfortable, but I think she will be brave enough to at least go knee-deep in the sea with me.

"This is incredibly dangerous, you know that, right?" she exclaims.

"Red, do you trust me?" I ask. She pulls a face, looking like she is seriously mulling over my question.

"I trust you," she says, but only after I feel like she's looked me up and down several times and assessed me.

"Good! Right, so, we're going to do this. I read up a bit about this. I'm going to be at the front. I'm the captain."

She smirks. "If you think I'm going to start calling you Captain Daniels, you would be wrong."

"Captain Indiana will do just fine, thanks. Being the captain means I do all the hard work. I'm navigating, steering, providing the balance, the gears, and all that fun. You, you're the stoker. Your main job is to trust me. Okay?"

"Okay," she replies, this time sounding more certain.

"Good." I give her a smile.

I eye the bike and remember what I had read online about getting on. I can't swing my leg behind me like I would on a usual bike, as behind my seat is the handlebars that she'll be using. Instead, I lean the bike towards me and then swing my leg over the front handlebars. I put my foot on the other side of the bike, then right the frame. I look behind me towards her.

"That looked painful," she comments, and I laugh because she's right.

"Yeah, I think maybe we should try some yoga before I do that again. Right, it's easier for you to get on, you can swing your leg behind you. I'll hold the bike in place. Sit on the seat, feet on the pedals, hands on the handlebars. I won't let you fall. I promise."

She steps closer to the frame and after a moment of hesitation, she is in position. I can feel the frame moving slightly as she gets into position. I hold tightly onto the brakes, keeping the frame upright.

"Oh my," she murmurs. I laugh, turn my head slightly.

"Right, now you need to pedal backwards a little, so the pedals are in a position on my right where the pedal is at the top."

I can see that she is gripping the handlebars tightly as her knuckles look drained of colour.

"Okay," she says.

"Relax," I call to her, though I'm starting to feel nervous myself. I have no idea how well this is going to go. There is a good chance we both end up falling off and end up with bumps and scrapes. I take a breath and then take my first foot off the ground, putting it onto the higher pedal and then I start to pedal. I steer us down the road towards the end of the street. Fortunately, it's a long, curved corner, so easier to navigate.

"This is crazy." Rose giggles from behind me once we've taken the second turn and are on the longer country road.

"Fun though, right?" I call back to her.

"Amazing."

I grin to myself, carry on pedalling with her, picking up some speed on the straight road we're on. She doesn't seem to mind the speed we're going at, more confident now she's settled into what we're doing. There is nothing ahead of us but the wide, open road.

I can't remember the last time I did something so fun.

I hear her start to sing as we cycle, and although her lyrics are lost on the wind behind me, I get the feeling she's singing songs of joy.

Chapter Ten

Rose

THEN

"Briar Rose, wake up," he whispers against my forehead, kissing me awake.

"I'm not asleep," I murmur back.

"You totally are. Come on, you know we can't stay like this."

I stretch in his arms.

"Why not?" I ask. "What would be so bad if we spent the night together? Think about how nice it would be to wake up together in the morning. Think about the fun we could have."

"You know I would love nothing more than that, but we're not supposed to be dating. We agreed to keep this a secret." Hunter smooths down my hair and kisses against my eyelids.

I laugh. "I'm not sure this constitutes as dating."

I sit up in bed. I don't bother to pull the sheets up around me. Hunter and I have been together for a month, right from the day we met in the hotel. He's seen everything and there is no need for any type of modesty, but I enjoy the fact he blushes slightly whenever I sit naked. I tease him all the time that he's a classic upper-class British man, bumbling along with a Victorian attitude, though he didn't seem too prudish when we left that meeting and went straight to his hotel suite. It had taken less than thirty minutes for us to be naked together on his hotel bed, and I stayed there until the point I had to get ready for my performance, ignoring all the calls on my mobile from people desperate to know where I was.

As I walked back to my hotel room—slightly sore and smelling of sex—I was smiling from ear to ear. Jumping into bed with somebody was something completely new for me. All my other sexual experiences happened after I really knew the other person, but Hunter was mesmerising. He told me we should keep everything quiet, and I managed to sneak back into my hotel room for a proper shower before facing up to lectures about my absence.

Since that day, Hunter has checked into rooms near to where I've been performing. Mostly, it's the same hotel. Sometimes, it's a hotel across the street as he wants to avoid suspicion. A couple of times, he's rented a place in the town, a whole cottage or house just for us to spend a few hours in. Each night, I've waited until my mother has fallen into her drink or pill-induced sleep, then tiptoed out of my hotel suite for a few hours. Every day, when I have a break in rehearsal in preparation for the concert and in gaps between interviews, I find my way to him.

Tonight, he's rented a cottage on the outskirts of town. I prefer it like this to when we're in hotel rooms. There's something that feels so special about having a whole house to ourselves, almost like a vision of what life could be like when we get past the secrecy required until the filming is complete.

Tonight, I was driven to the cottage by my driver under the guise of meeting a friend. If I wasn't on tour, I'd have driven myself, but my lack of car had left me no option but being driven, and a taxi would have been out of the question given it would have led to speculation neither of us want. I let myself into the house without knocking so Hunter could avoid being seen opening the door for me. As far as my driver knows, I'm catching up with a female friend who is in town, enjoying a glass of wine and some food, not falling into Hunter's arms the moment I arrived, the two of us barely making it up the stairs so we could be undressed and with one another.

A few hours may be all we have, but the hours are precious and special. I'd do anything to extend them if we could.

"You know the production company has a clause to forbid relationships between the cast members. Too much drama," Hunter reminds me.

I personally think it is a ridiculous rule. We don't start filming until after my tour finishes. I don't understand why the news the lead cast are dating would do anything other but generate positive press for the production. So many film franchises have benefited by even the rumour and innuendo of the main characters falling in love in real life. I don't understand why this would be anything different. If our relationship as our characters transpires on screen even half as hot as it feels between Hunter and me in real life, the movie is going to be amazing.

"That contract is turning out to be a pain in my backside," I grumble.

I'm regularly reminded by my manager that I went against the rules and advice when I accepted the role, getting scolded more than once for accepting the role without having the required people on my team doing their due diligence and counter negotiations. The only reason anything is continuing is because my signature is on the contract, and they can't backtrack from that without financial repercussions.

So, as pissed as everybody is about it, it's all going ahead, though I'm still in the doghouse about it. Even though Harry gets his required percentage as my manager, he seems pissed that this is something I worked for on my own. I keep reminding him how much I've told him I want to move into acting, that he promised to make it happen, and I'm sure he's just annoyed that I did this alone, something I don't have to express gratitude to him or my parents on a regular basis.

"Such a cute backside you have, too, a good handful for me to grab. Maybe something you'll need to focus on before filming starts. I'm not sure dystopian heroines have a fat ass," Hunter teases and I swat his arm.

As I reach for him, he grabs my wrist, and I feel the jolt through me. It's the same jolt I feel every time he touches me. He looks at me with that same expression, the one that makes me think he wants to devour me, the one that ultimately has me wanting to promise him everything and give him anything he wants.

The air seems thick around us. I can see the hunger in those clear eyes of his in the glow from the light on the bedside table. He leans closer towards me, and I know what is coming next.

"I thought you said I had to leave?" I tease.

"We have time before you have to go," he murmurs, then his mouth is on mine. "We just need to keep this a secret, my beautiful Briar Rose. Nobody can know about this, not yet."

"I'll never tell a soul," I murmur back, and then I'm lost in his kisses, on fire from his touch, desperate for more.

***

After, I shower and re-dress. After the first time together, I always shower before I leave to go home, scrubbing the evidence of him from my skin. I wish I could stay, but I know what Hunter says is logical. I know it is a risk; not just because of the clause in our film contract, but because this is the first time I've been with somebody without my team insisting on a non-disclosure agreement being signed. I've never even been for a meal with a man without jumping through various hoops and negotiations, though as they have always been private dates—in that respect—keeping things quiet with Hunter is no different to my other relationships.

"Will I see you tomorrow?" Hunter asks. Tomorrow I'm performing my final night on a set of three nights of concerts in the same city. Last night and tonight, we have been together at the cottage.

"Will you be here?" I ask. I sit down on the bed next to him. He is still naked, the sheet covering up to his waist. He's a beautiful man to look at.

"Yes, I'm here until the end of the week."

"I move on to the next city on my tour after tomorrow," I remind him.

"Maybe I will hurry up my business in this town so I can follow you." His lips curve into a smile. "You don't know what hold you have over me, my beautiful Briar Rose."

"I feel the same way about you, Hunter."

"This isn't just sex for me," he vows. I feel my heart seemingly skip a beat, something I thought only ever happened in romance novels.

"Me, either," I tell him.

"I feel like there is something more going on, something special."

"I feel exactly the same way," I reply.

He pulls me towards him. Our lips meet and he guides my hand to his lap. I can feel under the sheet that he is hard, despite us being together a couple of times tonight, but I guess this is what the first throes of a relationship is like—insatiable and desperate.

"Please?" He stares at me.

I'm mesmerised by the colour of his eyes, the smell of his skin, the heat of his body, the pleading on his lips. I know what he wants, so I sink to my knees on the floor, pull the sheet from him, and proceed to give him everything he wants.

***

"Did you have a good evening, ma'am?"

"Seriously, Pete, ma'am? How long have you been driving me?" I scold.

Pete's been driving me for as long as Harry's been managing me, both things that have probably been happening for as long as Dad was off fucking around with Krystal. I like Pete; he's a nice guy. He even taught me to drive, insisting to my parents it was ridiculous that I didn't know how, telling them that I should at least know how to get away in a car in case of an emergency.

"Did you have a nice time with your friend?" Pete asks.

He glances at me through the rearview mirror. I wonder if he can tell from the flush on my cheeks or the smile on my face that there is no way I was meeting a friend this evening, no way I was catching up on gossip and having a laugh. He doesn't look like he's judging me though, and I'm grateful.

"I had a great time, thanks. She and I had a lot to catch up on. You know how it is when you haven't seen somebody in some time."

"Even with all the talking yesterday?" he teases. I'm sure he knows something is going on.

"Yep, and we'll probably be doing more talking tomorrow, if you're available to drive me," I reply.

"I will be. Your mother called me while you were busy. She was worried when she woke up and you were not in your room."

I wasn't expecting my mother to be awake. On the nights where she isn't out with friends, looking for the attention from a younger man—something to bolster her confidence—she's usually asleep until morning.

"I hope she didn't keep you on the phone for long," I reply as diplomatically as I can, trying to think of an excuse to tell her when I get back. I know she will be waiting for me. There is no way she'll be asleep until she's seen me and, no doubt, given me a lecture.

"I told her I was driving you to get some fast food. It wasn't long ago that she called, so that should hold." Pete glances at me again through the rearview mirror.

"Pete, you are an angel."

He drives the rest of the way in silence, and after he pulls the car into the garage and parking space, he hands me a cup. It's a takeaway cup from a local fast-food restaurant, their branding on the side. It feels like there is a small amount of drink left in the cup.

"To appease your mother," he says with a smile.

"I've always liked you, Pete." I grin at him as I get out of the car.

I walk across the car park to the lift, Pete walking behind me. He doesn't have to do this, but I'm sure he's just cautious because I know he will be taking the car home now he has dropped me back at the hotel. I appreciate him and what he has done, so I give him a little wave goodbye before the lift door closes.

The lift takes me to the top floor, and I cross the hallway to the suite I'm staying in, pulling my hotel card from my bag. I step inside, praying that I'm lucky and my mother has fallen asleep, but I know I'm going to be out of luck.

"Briar Rose." My mother's voice is stern. It makes me jump, given she's sitting in the dark. I flick the light on.

"Mum, what are you still doing up?"

"Where have you been?"

"I was hungry, so I went to get something to eat," I reply, holding my cup up to show her the takeaway cup. She frowns.

"You know that is no good for you."

"First, you're upset that I went out, then you're upset because I wasn't getting salad and water?" I scoff.

"You need to take care of your body," Mum scolds. If it weren't for the lecture that I'd get from her, I would tell her that I was out having sex rather than eating burgers and fries. She may find that more preferable. Maybe my nutritionist can tell her how many calories I burnt during sex, just to shut everybody up.

"I do take care of myself, Mum. You see me exercise. You know what I eat." I put the cup down. "I'm sorry you were worried about me. I'm going to go to bed now. I need to get my beauty sleep."

I reach the door to my room before I hear her give a big sigh. The sound of it makes me stop walking.

"Your father has asked for a divorce," Mum says. I knew it was likely to be coming, but it still makes me feel sick.

"I'm sorry."

"He's a real piece of shit," she snarls.

"I took your side, Mum," I remind her. I had a row with my father when I tried to talk some sense with him. It had turned vicious and ugly between us, and we haven't spoken directly since. Sparse, angry text messages have been sufficient instead.

"I gave my whole life to him, and what do I have to show for it?" Mum carries on like I never spoke.

I take a seat on the sofa next to her.

"Mum, your life is not over. You're still young. There's plenty of things you can do with your life."

"I have nothing to show from my marriage."

"Not one to brag, but I'm something to show from your marriage, and when you get over what he's done to you, you'll look back and remember the good years. You had many good years together."

"Mark my words, Briar Rose, men will walk all over you if you let them. You can give them everything, and they'll still say it is not enough. Don't ever play recklessly with your heart. If I could go back and do my time again, I'd do everything differently."

"Not all men are like that," I protest, but she waves away my sentence.

"They're all like that. You'll see. Make better choices than me."

"Mum." I sigh.

Mum gets up from the sofa. She looks me up and down.

"You're so young and naïve. Don't make the same stupid mistakes I did."

"I won't, Mum, I promise," I reply, though I'm not entirely sure what mistakes she thinks she made. Her marriage to my dad had seemed perfect, right until the moment he blindsided us all. The sentences and questions form in my head, but I'm not brave enough to ask Mum. She heads to her room, shutting the door behind her, leaving me alone and in silence.

I pull my mobile phone from my bag. I open my last texts with my dad. They've been infrequent recently, even less regular than before we'd argued. I've given up contacting him, mostly because I was tired of getting no responses, or worse, dismissing responses, but more recently, because I've been distracted by Hunter.

I fire off a message, telling him I've heard from Mum that he wants a divorce.

Despite the late time I'm messaging, and the time zone between us, I get a response back. His message is stern, telling me to stay out of things I don't understand.

I fire a message back, telling him I understand perfectly, and, if that is how he feels, he can stay the hell out of my life as well.

I get up and head to my room. I push thoughts of my parents out of my mind. I want to dream of only Hunter tonight, of something much brighter than the stress between my parents. I strip off my clothes, getting into the covers, allowing my mind to go over the night. I think of how his hands had felt on my body, how he smiled at me from above me on the bed before his lips had found mine.

I fall asleep with him in my mind and a smile on my face, grateful that there is something in my life that can be a distraction from everything else that seems to cause me so much pain and heartache.

Chapter Eleven

Rose

NOW

Sunday morning, I'm awake before Blake. I lie awake for a while, feeling like I'm twiddling my thumbs until I give in and get up. I head to the shower, spending time under the gloriously hot water, thankful for Blake turning the heat up. Even if we don't manage to make a stellar album, at least I'll have had hot showers for the rest of my stay.

As I dress, I listen for any signs from Blake's room that he's awake, but there is nothing. I think about how he let me sleep in, so I keep as quiet as I can, deciding to return the favour and let him rest. He probably needs it given I woke him up in the middle of the night again.

I go downstairs when I'm showered and dressed. I sit at the kitchen table with my laptop and launch the internet page so I can open the online Sunday papers. Today is when Blake's father is supposed to be in the papers. I'm hoping that his father has reconsidered. I don't want to see him hurt.

Since he arrived, Blake and I have formed a friendly relationship, something I didn't expect when I asked Libby to help organise this. I thought we would spend a couple of days writing some lyrics, playing around with some music and for him to leave and not see me again until we got some time in the recording studio. What's unfolding is something entirely different, but something that I'm so grateful for. Blake's been a cheerful presence, somebody who has boundless energy and nothing but positive vibes to give me. I hadn't expected that we would laugh so much together. Before he arrived, I wasn't sure I was ever going to laugh properly again.

Our tandem bike ride was the most fun I've had in a long while. We managed to ride successfully through country lanes for an hour, not seeing another living soul the whole time. It felt like the world belonged to us. He joined me with singing as we cycled, taking it in turns to sing the first verse from a random song and for the other to then sing the chorus. His song choices had ranged from disco to pop, rock to indie, almost like he had a catalogue of song lyrics in a database in his head. He even started a couple of my songs, and I smiled in the seat behind him as I listened to him.

Despite the shaky start on the bike and my initial apprehension that it would end in a disaster, it had been fun, and surprisingly, we kept upright the whole time. We cycled until my legs were sore from the effort and I had to give in and suggest we went home.

When we got home, we made a spaghetti dinner together. We ate in the kitchen and then Blake had produced a pack of cards, insisting we play gin rummy. I beat him nine hands in a row, and he settled his debts with a pack of cookies, accusing me of counting cards while I told him he was a sore loser. As I climbed the stairs for bed, he shouted after me that he expected a rematch.

Yesterday we spent a few hours writing together. He made a steak and kidney pie, and I categorically refused to entertain the idea of helping cut up the kidneys. I have my limits in this cooking adventure he's insisting on taking me on. Though the kidneys looked disgusting, the pie ended up tasting amazing. Later in the evening, we went for a run on the beach together. At one point, we stopped running for exercise and started to run for fun. We ran like a pair of children, arms stretched wide, like we were hoping the blowing winds could lift us up and let us fly. We arrived home sandy and tired. We chatted over hot chocolate and a couple of games of gin rummy before bed. I had a poor night of sleep, dreaming of Hunter again, waking with a cold sweat.

Like the night earlier in the week, when I woke up shouting, Blake arrived at my bedroom door to check I was okay, joking with me until the dream was a distant memory.

I sent him back to bed, but not before telling him I appreciated him checking on me, thanking him for being a friend. Friendship wasn't something I expected when I came up with this plan, but I'm glad to have this with him.

Our fledgling friendship is what makes me anxious knowing that the article is printed today. The idea that his life might be on display in the front pages gives me an unsettled feeling in my stomach. I know what it is like to live under this type of scrutiny, but to know the secrets being spilled are coming from a family member, that's got to hurt.

The online Sunday paper loads on my laptop, and I don't even need to search the articles for it because it's the main headline in the entertainment section. It practically screams out at me. I open the article to read it, my heart sinking, feeling pain on behalf of Blake. The article is bad—really awful. It's bad by most celebrity standards, but for Blake—somebody who has always appeared to conduct himself in an impressive way and tried to keep his private life from being in the papers—it's terrible. Blake told me he was trying to rebuild his relationship with his father, but this feels like a torpedo.

I've just finished reading the article when I hear Blake's footsteps coming into the kitchen. Part of me wants to close the web page as fast as I can—before he sees it—but I'm sure he'll know I'm looking at it, so I leave the website up. I turn to look at him.

"It's bad, isn't it?" he asks before I have chance to say anything.

"Haven't you read it?"

"Yeah, I read it upstairs, but I was hoping I dreamt it," he replies. However flippant he wants to sound, there is hurt etched in his expression. I feel terrible for him.

"Do you think it's true?" I ask.

"Which bit? The bit where my father might not be my father, the bit where my mother had multiple affairs, or the bit where he talks about what a mistake it was to have me?"

"I'm so sorry, Blake." I feel guilty that I haven't got any better words to say to him. What could I possibly say that could make him feel better?

"Neither of them has ever said anything about this to me before. I'm not talking about me being a mistake–" he starts.

"No matter what that article says, or what your parents may have thought, there is no way in the world that you are a mistake," I argue, cutting him off.

"It probably explains why my parents were so neglectful when I was young, I guess." He shrugs.

"They clearly weren't prepared to be parents, but that's on them, not you."

"I just wish they'd spoken to me, about any of it, because everything they told me now feels like a lie. My mother always said that my father left her. He never said anything on the contrary. Nobody has *ever* said there was a possibility he wasn't my father. But, hey, more fool me. I thought we'd been making amends in our relationship, but what the hell do I know? What's the point in me even trying when they never wanted me in the first place?" He sounds bitter, and I think back to the article I read.

One of the photographs in the article was Blake's dad, holding a photograph of a young Blake, with a quote of *"Blake may not be my son, but he'll always be my boy, and I'm devastated we're estranged."*

His quote doesn't align or reconcile to everything else he said in the article. I don't know how he can proclaim he hates their strained relationship by bringing up everything else.

From the look on Blake's face, it looks like he's lost any hope that he could have a good relationship with his father. He looks like a little kid who has had everything taken from him—lost, upset, and alone. He runs a hand through his dark hair, and I can't take it for another second.

I get up from the seat and stand in front of him, putting my arms around his neck, pulling him close for a tight hug.

"Your father is a piece of shit, Blake. He should have spoken to you about this in private. There is no justification that he did it like this. There's no justification for the papers to even run the story. This is just salacious reporting, and everybody involved ought to feel ashamed of themselves. I'm so sorry," I whisper against him.

"I think this maybe covers the heavy story for today, don't you?" he asks. He doesn't pull away from my embrace. Instead, he holds me tightly, his arms slipping around my waist, holding me closer.

"For the whole week, I think," I murmur against his chest.

"That doesn't get you off seven stories, Red."

"Fine," I grumble. I step back from him. "Do you want seven of my heavy stories right now?"

"No, right now, I think we should go out and do something fun," he says.

The way he says it reminds me of the way I end our conversations after I wake from a bad dream—appreciative of the support, but not willing to talk further. The way he respects my boundaries on the nights I wake up makes me want to do the same for him, so I won't push him for more conversation. Instead, I'll go along with his plan to do something fun, even if I have no idea what he thinks constitutes as being fun around here. From what I've seen and heard, the village is exceptionally quiet.

"What do you have in mind?" I ask. I grab the packet of bread from the countertop so I can make us some toast.

"You leave the plans to me. We'll have breakfast and then get going. I think trainers would be best, unless you have walking boots." Blake smiles and then puts the kettle on.

We eat breakfast together, chatting about anything other than the article in the paper. As soon as we have cleared away the breakfast pots, it is clear Blake wants to get out of the house. He looks like he is going to burst out of his skin.

I hurry to get ready, going up stairs to get my things. I pick up my baseball cap. It's too overcast to get away with sunglasses. Summer is truly over. Instead, I add a hoodie to my outfit as it looks cold outside. By the time I'm back downstairs, Blake is ready to go. He stands at the front door, a rucksack at his feet. Along with his dark jeans and trainers, he is also wearing a dark hoodie and his own baseball cap.

I grab my set of car keys. He picks up his rucksack and we step outside together. I lock the front door behind us. We head to my car and I get into the driver's seat.

"So, Indiana, where are we off to?" I ask as I start the car.

He smiles when he sees the satnav in the car dashboard. He starts the satnav and puts in some information then settles back in his seat.

"I didn't know you had satnav in here, I thought I was going to have to wing it as I left my phone behind," he explains.

"Well, I hope we don't get lost wherever you plan on going, given I've also left my phone behind." I laugh.

"Why are you leaving your phone behind?"

"Not much point taking it anywhere, only Libby has the number. She organised the phone for me. Oh, and the owner of the house has my number, but I doubt she needs to call me," I tell him as I drive down the street, following the directions of the satnav.

"What about your parents?" He sounds curious.

"Absolutely not." I laugh.

"Aren't they going to be worried about you?"

"I doubt my father will stop his activities with Krystal long enough to remember he has a daughter. We haven't spoken since the day he told my mother he wanted a divorce. Well, we fought before then, and only really communicated through text at that point. I messaged him and he told me to stay out of things I didn't understand. I told him to stay out of my life, and, hey, for once, he listened," I joke.

"When do you think we get our badges to the 'we have a shitty dad' club?"

"I think they send them out annually, on the first of January, so a couple of months to wait. I'm going to take a photograph of mine and create a new social media page just so I can post a picture of it." I grin. I turn the car down another road when instructed.

"Why do you need a new social media page?"

"Oh, I don't get control of my own social media pages. My team does that. I haven't even got access. I guess I'm an outlier, given I've never really had my own social media, aside from the account I used to post my singing on, but my mother controlled that anyway."

"You weren't ever tempted to open a secret account just for friends?" Blake asks.

"What friends?"

"Come on, you must have friends?" he scoffs.

"Not really. I found it hard to keep up friendships when I left school to start touring. I met a few people in my late teens who I felt were friends, but they were other singers, and you know how the media likes to play off women against one another. Jealousy and careers got in the way of those friendships. I thought I made new friends as an adult, but then I realised they were either people on my payroll, or they were people looking for their own minute of fame, and nothing was really genuine." I shrug. "So, if I'm counting friends, there is Libby, and you, I guess."

"I'm honoured." Blake laughs.

"I'm a little jealous that you have your own pages. The statement you released recently, that was amazing."

"I don't often, if ever, post a response to anything in the media, but I couldn't let it stand when it was something hurting somebody innocent. I hadn't seen Olive in years, and the idea her life was being picked apart in the papers was horrible."

"I'm sorry you had to write it, but it was beautifully written." I shrug. "I wish, sometimes, I could do something like that."

"You should take control back, Rose."

"I'm trying," I sigh.

There is a pause between us. I focus on the driving.

"So, that explains you not being worried about your dad trying to get in touch, but what about your mum?"

"She is at a wellness retreat. She's been there for a while, and she feels that, and I quote, my presence is a reminder of my father and his betrayal, that I'm the consequences of her life choices, and currently it is too painful to see me."

"She said all that?" Blake twists in his seat to look at me. I keep my eyes on the road.

"Yep. When she told me about Dad divorcing her, she told me she wished she'd made different choices in her past. I'm sure she meant me."

"She's probably just hurt and too stunned to think about what she is saying. I'm not condoning her, at all, but it is easy to not think clearly about what is being said," Blake soothes.

"Well, whatever. Either way, she is out of contact. She won't be trying to contact me, but I don't want to be contacted, either. I don't have the bandwidth to deal with my parents' shit."

"I'm counting this as two of your heavy stories for this week. You're down to five."

"Maybe I should tell you about my dead childhood pets to even the score." I grin.

"I'd only offset by telling you that I was never allowed a childhood pet," he says, but I hear the teasing tone to his voice. I glance at him quickly, sticking my tongue out at him, and he laughs.

The satnav tells me to take another turn and that we have then reached our destination. I pull the car into a parking space. There are no other cars in the area. It's probably not surprising given the weather. We both get out of the car and Blake picks up the rucksack, slinging it over his shoulder.

"This looks interesting," I comment, looking around. Beyond the car parking area looks to be mostly trees, pathways paved between them as walking areas, nothing around us but the sound of the wildlife. It feels tranquil.

"You said the woman who rents out the house mentioned hikes in the area. I looked it up earlier in the week. There are some nice walks around here. There's even a lake, should you want to swim."

"For a start, I'll remind you that I can't swim well. Secondly, are you freaking kidding me? It's freezing!" I laugh.

"It's good for the circulation, or so they say. I'm totally taking a dip in the sea before we finish writing. I'm game if you are." He grins at me.

"I'll pass." I shake my head wryly. I'm surprised he doesn't want to suggest something extreme like parachuting, but I get the sense he's only pushing for things he mentioned when we first met. His focus still seems to be around the things he joked about rectifying.

"Come on, a light walk. Some chatting. Back home in the afternoon for some writing. We're making salmon for tea tonight."

"Sounds good," I reply. He starts walking and I follow him down the path he's chosen. We walk in silence for a while; the place is deserted and peaceful.

"I can't remember the last time I was somewhere so quiet," Blake comments.

"Not down the beach?" I ask.

"I meant this place in general. All week has been quiet. It's been nice."

"Well, I'm glad you're enjoying it." I smile.

"I've been thinking about the album. You're due to deliver an album to the label, right?"

"Yeah, you, too?"

"Yep. Well, I thought, with the songs we have been writing, if we stay on track, we could have enough for two albums. The songs we have written, to me it feels like they're falling into two vibes. I thought we could do one album with me featuring you, and then one with you featuring me on some tracks. I think a few of the songs we have so far, some seem like they're question songs, and some seem like answers. Am I rambling?" Blake trails off. I smile at him because he seems so passionate when he is talking music.

"Not rambling. I do get what you mean about the idea that some are questions and some are answers. The one we wrote yesterday, if feels like it is a questioning track, asking why, full of longing and despair. The one before that, that was more answers, love, happiness."

"Maybe we could call one Questions and one Answers. Or, I don't know, one Longing and one Love? Maybe work to release them at the same time."

"You're just full of bright ideas, aren't you? Are you going to tell me your plans for the album designs?" I tease.

"I'm sorry if I've overstepped. I know this is all your project and idea." Blake sounds so apologetic I feel guilty for my teasing. I reach and grab his wrist to pull him to a stop. He looks at me, a curious expression on his face.

"Blake, I was teasing. You could tell me you had an idea to have, I don't know, sphynx cats on the covers, and I would go for it. I've really enjoyed the last week. Writing with you feels special. I cannot thank you enough for doing this with me."

"I keep telling you, you do not have to thank me. This has been a great distraction for me, too. I feel like I have my groove back for writing, and I'm enjoying what we're creating." He smiles, and it lights up his whole face. We carry on walking. "So, for the album covers. Sphynx cats, right?"

"Don't, I feel the same way about them as I do the kidneys before they were cooked."

"You're lucky I'm not suggesting liver and onions."

"Absolutely not." I laugh.

"It was a staple in my house when I was growing up," Blake teases and I scowl.

"I'll remind you that nobody knows you're here, I could push you off a ledge and leave you to die, you know," I joke.

"Maeve knows I'm here."

"Hmm, but Maeve's wife is Libby, and Libby is the closest to a real friend I have, so do you want to bank on where the loyalty lies?" I grin.

"I thought *I* was almost a real friend." Blake smiles.

I pretend to mull this over for a minute before smiling back at him.

"You are. I'm not cooking liver though. You'd have to get another friend for that."

"I hated liver, actually. My mum always overcooked it. When she did cook, I mean." Blake shrugs and then falls silent.

"Are you going to talk to her?" I ask. He gazes at the floor as he walks, his face partially obscured by his baseball cap. He's hunched over a little, shoulders drawn together. I recognise the pose because it's a pose I've adopted a lot over the past couple of weeks.

"I don't know. I don't know what to say to her."

"What about your dad, are you going to talk to him?"

"I don't think it would really change anything."

"Your dad said in the article that it doesn't matter to him, that he still considers you his," I remind him. I don't know if he read the whole article, or whether he did but everything has become a blur.

"I know it doesn't really change anything, but it leaves me with questions. Who is he, that potential biological father of mine? Does she know? The article didn't particularly paint my mum in a positive light, but maybe she knows who he was."

"You're only going to know if you ask her. She's the only one who can confirm and give you the information your dad can't," I point out.

"I might sound like a judgy asshole, but I've never liked people who lie, and it turns out both my parents have lied to me my whole life."

"It isn't judgy to dislike people who don't tell you the truth." I feel a wave of heat over my body.

I understand exactly where he is coming from. Nobody likes being lied to, especially when you are the one who gets hurt in the process. People are far too easy to say they hid the truth to protect you, but it's never really your protection they're interested in, but their own self-preservation.

"I don't really have an easy relationship with either of my parents, the whole loving-family thing is a bit of a myth to me. I'd see friends growing up with these amazing parents, telling me stories that made them sound like superheroes. I didn't have anything close to that."

"It's all an illusion, I'm sure. I had what seems like an idyllic childhood, but it sure as hell got toxic in the last couple of years."

"I thought I was getting to a good state with them both. Mum and I, we have done better over the last five years or so. I thought we established some good foundations, but now, knowing she's kept something from me for my whole life, I don't really know what to say to her. I know it shouldn't make a difference, but I feel let down."

"I think that seems like a normal reaction. Especially how your dad decided to announce it. That's unforgivable."

"The worst thing is that I don't even feel like I can say anything to him because he has cancer. You can't shout at the man who has cancer, you can't call them out on their bullshit, no matter how much I want to." Blake kicks at a little rock that is on the path, like it was positioned there just for his frustration.

"So, yell it out here," I suggest.

"Send it out into the universe?" he says, a small smile on his face.

"Get it off your chest before you explode under the things you haven't said."

"Okay, well, only if you join in," Blake counters.

"You want me to walk and shout out things about your family?" I laugh.

"No, your own. Or whoever else it is that has screwed you over. Get it all off your chest."

I snort, because, while the list of names is short, I'm not sure if I would be able to stop shouting things if I start.

"So long as there are no follow-up questions to what get said," I agree after a moment of consideration.

"Promise."

"You go first," I suggest.

"Okay," he says, clearing his throat. "Fuck you for spilling your guts in the Sunday fucking tabloids without giving me any fucking warning about what you were going to say!" Blake shouts out. When he finishes, he looks at me. I take a deep breath.

"Fuck you for telling me I was too naïve to understand your reasons for screwing around on your wife!"

"Fuck you for selling your soul when I'd already told you I'd pay for whatever you wanted or needed!"

"Fuck you for telling me my feelings were irrelevant!"

"Fuck you for letting me believe a lie my whole life!"

"Fuck you for telling me I deserved it!"

"Fuck you for never being there for me in the way a parent should be!"

"Fuck you for every tear you made me shed!"

"Fuck you both for being such shitty adults that it affected my whole childhood!"

"Fuck you for telling me I was fat!"

"Fuck you for making everything so public!"

"Fuck you for breaking me!"

"Fuck you for making me feel unlovable!"

We're walking together, staring straight ahead as we take turns to shout out the sentences, but his last sentence stops me in my tracks. Blake stops next to me and takes a deep breath and then looks at me, expectantly.

"I'm sorry," I say, biting my lip and wondering if I should continue. I was the one who had said no follow-up questions, but I can't let that last one rest. "I'm telling you now, you are lovable, Blake. Fuck all the people who ever made you feel like you weren't."

"Well, you...." he starts, but I shake my head.

"I don't need you to say anything about what I shouted out, and I can't fix the way your parents treated you in the past, but I can tell you that you are lovable. One hundred percent. Take that into your future, Blake, don't ever forget it."

He looks like he doesn't know what to say. He opens his mouth, almost like he wants to protest, but I know I won't let him. How anybody has made him feel unlovable is beyond me. He's the sweetest person I think I've ever met—generous, giving, and unselfishly genuine.

We stand together for a couple of minutes, until he shakes his head and smiles.

"So, Red, are we cracking on with this walk of ours or not?"

He doesn't address what I've said, so I won't, either. Instead, I give him a big smile.

"Lead the way, Captain Indiana."

Chapter Twelve

Blake

NOW

"Thank you for today, I really needed it," I say to Rose as we get back to the house in the late afternoon.

"I don't think I really did anything, but I'm glad you had a nice time." She smiles at me.

This morning, after I read the article in bed, there had been a small part of me that didn't want to get out of the covers. It felt surreal, reading the words of my father but not really comprehending anything, until it had all sunk in with a bang.

I eventually gave in and got ready, mostly because I didn't want Rose to worry about how I was dealing with it all. Even before I stepped into the kitchen and saw the website on her laptop, I knew she had read the article, if only to support me.

The article still makes me feel like shit when I think about it, but Rose has made me feel better, whether she realises that or not.

"I did have a nice time, surprisingly. I think a change of scenery and a bit of shouting out to the universe was the perfect antidote to a shitty morning," I reply.

"I had a nice time, too. I was worried you were going to suggest something mad, like parachuting, but I think after this morning, I'd have been willing, if only to help cheer you up."

"Good to know. Maybe I can convince you to swim this evening?" I tease.

"Absolutely not," she says with a laugh.

She pulls her hoodie off over her head, and it pulls her T-shirt out of the waistband to her jeans along with it, rising slightly up her stomach.

"You rebel," I comment, and although her head is still inside her hoodie, she automatically puts a hand on her stomach to cover the tattoo she has there.

"Don't judge me," she half protests, sounding muffled from inside the hoodie. I wait for her to wrestle herself out of it.

"I'm not judging. Just teasing. I didn't know you had any tattoos. Any others?"

"No," she replies, but the flush on her face makes me think that she's lying.

"It's a good tattoo." I gesture to where she still has her hand clamped over hers, like she's stemming bleeding from a bullet wound.

She slowly removes her hand, keeping her gaze on me like she's afraid I'm about to tease her about her design choice. She has a dragonfly and lotus flower design. It's in black ink and there is just a splash of purple, like a watercolour wash, through the wings of the dragonfly. The very bottom of the dragonfly looks slightly unfinished but then I realise the bottom has been turned into a semicolon rather than two final circles. I know a semicolon tattoo is often used to represent when somebody has chosen to carry on through adversity. I wonder how long she's had her tattoo.

"It's always covered up. I sometimes forget it is there," she explains as she tucks her top back in.

We walk through to the kitchen together. I'm planning a hot coffee to help warm my bones after the cold walk back to the car.

"So, what is your other tattoo?" I ask. The pink is back on her cheeks.

"Do you have any tattoos?" She deflects my question.

"Let me guess, you have a cartoon character on your backside," I tease.

"No!" She's laughing as she picks up the kettle to fill it with water. "Come on, tell me."

"You've already seen the only tattoo I have," I tell her. I have a dragon tattoo that climbs up and around my arm, curling across my shoulder and finishing at my chest. I got it after the sales for my first album went wild.

"So, given you were so quick to jump to conclusions, I'm assuming you have an embarrassing one on your backside? A little cartoon bird, or something?" she asks.

"Nope."

"Some character from another language which you thought was something profound, but probably translates to something terrible instead? Instead of Strength, you've got Garden Furniture?"

"Nope, nothing on my ass. You're welcome to check if you don't believe me." I smirk. "Stop deflecting, Red."

She rolls her eyes at me. "Oh, yes, I forgot, I've a giant 'I heart Blake Daniels' tattooed across my butt."

"I'm flattered." I laugh as I take the cups out of the cupboard.

She puts the kettle on to boil.

"Remind me, what are we making for dinner tonight?"

"Salmon and salad for tea, with some boiled eggs and little potatoes. Nice and straightforward."

"You remember I haven't cooked fish before? I'm likely to give us food poisoning," she jokes.

"Come on, Rose, I'm not going to let you down. I'm the king of fish." I grin at her. I enjoy cooking with her. She seems to enjoy it, too, though she often protests before we start.

"Are you going to tell me who taught you to cook, I'm not sure I buy the 'teaching yourself' explanation." Rose looks at me as she puts the coffee granules into the cups.

"I would cook a little with my grandma when I was younger, but, truthfully, I worked in a few kitchens. I started washing pots, switched over to the prep team when I was old enough, then moved to the cook line. I preferred it to being a waiter. I considered becoming a chef at one point, but then I got a more stable day job to let me be able to go to gigs at night."

"Oh, my, you are such a liar," she exclaims.

"Not a lie, more an omission," I argue.

"Just as bad in my opinion. You made it sound like you just knew how to cook because you're an adult, and I thought I was defective." Rose pouts, and she pushes me slightly.

"Loads of adults can't cook. My mum is terrible at it." I laugh, and then I try to ignore the pang I get in my stomach. Laughing with Rose, I almost forgot the whole debacle of my parents, my father's revelations, and the shitty news article.

"You should go see her." Rose sighs. She steps around me to get her phone.

"I'll phone her later."

"I don't think it is the type of thing you should talk about over the phone. Your dad was shitty to do it in the papers. Don't make it worse by having this conversation with her over the phone."

For somebody who jokes she's not an adult, she's sage with the advice when she wants to be.

"Coffee, then we'll start tea." I deflect her comments.

"Actually, you need to speak to Maeve. I've had a load of messages from Libby." Rose looks up from her phone. I sigh. She smiles gently. "I'll finish the coffee. You go get your phone and speak to Maeve."

"I'm not looking forward to switching my phone back on," I admit. I switched it off earlier and have no intention of turning it back on any time soon.

"Then use mine to speak to them." She hands me her phone.

It's the most basic-looking phone I've seen in years. The only things she has on the phone are messages, the camera app, contacts, a radio station, the option to go online, and the call options. Everything else seems disabled or missing. There are no social apps or even games on her phone.

"Do you mind?"

"Nope." She shrugs.

As she'd told me earlier, the only contacts in her phone are Libby, and the contact named "homeowner." I click to connect to Libby.

"Rose, where the hell have you been? Maeve's been trying to get hold of Blake all day. She's absolutely frantic. Is he still with you?" Libby doesn't give me the opportunity to interrupt so I let her finish.

"Hey, Libby, it's Blake. May I speak to Maeve?" I ask. I haven't spoken much to Libby in the past, mostly the occasional shout to say hello whenever I've been on the phone to Maeve, or when she's called Maeve when we've been on tour.

"One second," Libby replies, then I hear the scuffle of the phone being passed between people. I brace myself. Maeve is formidable even in her most relaxed state, but when she's angry, she's like a firecracker.

"Blake, you cannot go radio silent on me. You've aged me twenty years. I'm on the cusp of sending you some shitty red apples," Maeve scolds.

"I'm sorry, Maeve. I did message to say I was switching my phone off. I didn't mean to worry you. I feel awful this is happening when you're supposed to be on holiday."

"My holiday isn't important. Are you okay?" Maeve sounds highly strung, and I feel guilty for not having phoned her earlier. I glance over at Rose and gesture with my head towards the living room so I can take the rest of the call in private. She nods and busies herself making the coffee as I walk out of the room.

"I'm okay. Rose and I went for a walk today and it helped clear my head for a bit," I reply to Maeve as I step into the living room.

I'm tempted to add that now I'm back at the house I no longer feel like my head is clear. Thinking about my phone upstairs—switched off but probably full of a million messages—makes me feel worse. Did my mum message? My dad? I can't decide if it is worse if they have, or if they haven't.

"Sounds like you and Rose are getting along well," Maeve comments. The stress in her tone appears to have given way to intrigue.

"Not like that. We're both just kicking back for a bit and getting on with some writing."

"Okay," she says, but she sounds unconvinced by my reply. "Look, I had a few places contact me for a quote or response from you in relation to your dad's article."

"First, why are those calls coming to you, there's a team who gets paid for that, and as I keep reminding you, you are on holiday!"

"You might have a whole team, but you decided to go off-grid today," Maeve reminds me, and I feel guilty.

"Remind me to give you a substantial raise."

"Like you even know what you pay me."

"Whatever it is, it isn't enough."

"How about, instead, you let me know if there is any response you want to give?"

"The response should be 'fuck off,' but how about 'no comment'?" I suggest.

"Okay," she replies. "No comment it is. Though, between us, how are you doing, really?"

"I'm fine. It's just one of those things. I can't change it, can't do anything about it. It is what it is." I sigh. I pace around the living room as I talk.

"It feels like your life has gone crazy these last couple of weeks," Maeve muses.

"Maybe I shouldn't let you have any more holidays," I joke.

"I'll be home before you know it. I'll help you get your life back on track, though it sounds like you're doing okay. It sounds like Rose is taking care of you."

"Maeve Olsen, are you fishing for information?"

"Well, Rose has told Libby you two are making some lovely music together."

"Shocking, for two musicians." I laugh.

"Shall I let you get back to this music making?"

"How about, instead, I let you get back to your holiday, again."

"Okay, but I'll tell you again, anything you need, any time, you know where I am."

"Speak to you soon," I say and then I end the call. I walk back into the kitchen where Rose is now sitting at the table, her fingers wrapped around her cup of coffee, like she's warming her fingers on the heat. A second mug is placed at the seat opposite her.

"Are you okay?" she asks. I nod and sit down. I take a sip of the coffee she's made for me; it's hot and strong, and I feel like it hits the right spot.

"Yep, ready to make some salmon."

"Are you going to face up to your phone first? No time like the present," Rose prods.

I get the feeling she won't let this drop, so I get up, walk upstairs to get my phone, and go back to the kitchen. I sit back at the table, switching my phone back on. I unlock it once it's powered up and then slide it across to her. For a moment, the room is filled with the sound of multiple updates coming through my phone.

"Feel free to do the honours," I say.

"Seriously?"

"Go for it."

She picks up the phone and looks at me, sceptically. "I'm not going to find a load of nude pictures, am I?"

"Mine, or others?" I grin. She rolls her eyes. "Neither, Red, come on, what kind of person do you take me for?"

"Somebody who lots of people would like to send a nude picture to, or receive one from," she replies.

"I'm flattered, but no. I have my socials switched to no direct messages, so you're fine."

"Fine," she replies, shaking her head. She busies herself with the phone for a moment, her brow furrowed as she reads. "Shall I delete anything that looks media-shit related?"

"Yep."

She's quiet again for another minute, her fingers swiftly moving over the phone screen. She looks up at me again.

"You have a message from your contact, *Olive Who Inspired Repercussions Saunders*," she comments.

"What does it say?"

"You don't mind me reading it?"

"Nope, you can read them all."

"She says she's sorry for the recent media intrusion in your life, and she and Ty apparently still look forward to welcoming you for tea." Rose reads out. "Ah, she's a northern girl, otherwise it would be dinner, right?" she adds with a smile.

"Yeah, she lives back home."

"Would you like me to reply?"

"Just tell her thanks, and I'll be in touch at some point."

I watch as she types away on my phone.

"How do you want me to sign off the message? 'All my love, Blake'? Or shall I sign off with something like 'love you forever, Blake'?"

"How about just 'thanks, Blake.'"

"Who is Ty?"

"Olive's husband," I explain.

"Probably a good job I didn't sign off with a comment that you think of her every time you see the tattoo of her name on your ass."

"I do not have her name tattooed on my ass, or anywhere else, thank you very much." I laugh. Rose grins at me, like she's won a prize.

"Relax, I'm joking. I was being nosy. I know who she is. I've seen her social media page."

"Seriously?"

"Yeah, I had a look at it when you posted your statement the other week. She's very pretty. Her husband is hot as hell. I just didn't connect the name."

"He's a nice guy, though I don't think he likes me much. We are civil, though," I reply.

"Why wouldn't he like you?"

"Tyler and I didn't gel, mostly because I was an idiot when I dated Olive, and because he intimidated the hell out of me. All her friends did, to be fair. They all seemed so grown up and put together, and I felt like I was the opposite. I saw

Tyler and Olive before my album was released though, and it was civil, so maybe it's just my opinion of things." I shrug.

"Sounds like you're too hard on yourself, Blake, something for you to work on," she scolds.

"Well, if I ever get to tea at theirs, I'll tell them that the lovely Rose Dalton thinks Tyler is as hot as hell."

"Oh, don't, I wouldn't want to cause trouble. I was only trying to tease you to get you laughing."

"I'm just teasing you, too. Though, knowing Olive, she'd find it hilarious. Especially the idea that I had her name tattooed on me."

Rose smiles at me and then she returns to the phone, tapping away again.

"You have a message from your mum. She says please could you get in touch. You have a couple of missed calls from her, too."

This hits me harder than I thought it would, and any lightness I gained from laughing with her is gone again and it's just the heavy feeling in my stomach.

"Anything from my dad?" I wonder, clearing my throat.

"No, I'm sorry."

She hands me my phone back, tidied up, all messages read through; it looks like she's deleted all the crap that would have been on there.

"Thanks."

"I'd let you return the favour with my phone, but I only get messages from Libby."

"Where is your actual phone?" I wonder, finishing my coffee.

"With Libby."

"Is she fending and vetting your calls and messages on your behalf?"

"Perhaps." Rose shrugs, and then she clams up.

I can tell I've hit a nerve for her because she adopts the pose she does sometimes, her shoulders squared back. I don't know what makes her defensive, and I'm not going to push her if she doesn't want to talk about it.

I get up from the table and start to gather the things out of the fridge so we can cook tea.

"Do you want to put two saucepans on with some water to boil?" I ask. Rose gets up and I hear her giggle. It's lovely to hear after I dampened her mood.

"Starting me off with the basics, I see."

"At least we don't have to debone and take the head off the salmon," I tease, and she shudders. I don't think she's forgiven me for the kidneys yet.

She puts two pans on the hob, one for the eggs and one for the potatoes. She joins me to cut the salad items. She's a slow and cautious cutter, but every night when we have prepared food together, she has gotten more confident.

I turn on the oven to preheat so we can cook the salmon. We work together in a comfortable silence, and I know the both of us have things on our mind.

***

"You really are the king of fish," Rose comments as she finishes her food.

"There's no way for me to answer that without it sounding like I'm bragging, but I did tell you so." I grin at her.

"It's a lot less scary than I thought fish would be."

"Next time, you can make it for me."

"No, I think it is just because you make everything look simple."

"If I'm actually making the effort to cook at home for myself, I tend to do a salad and cook salmon one day and some chicken the next."

"Then substitute with chocolate spread sandwiches." She grins.

"Don't knock them until you've tried them." I laugh as I start to clear the plates away.

"Have you decided if you're going to see your mum?" Rose asks as she loads the dishwasher with the glasses.

"I think I might head out there tomorrow," I reply, stepping around her and slotting the plates into the dishwasher.

I don't particularly want to go see my mother, to have the conversations with her, but I should get ahead of any further news, if there is any. It wouldn't be out of the realm of possibility that the reporters are hounding my mum for her version of the story, especially if I remain silent on the article from my dad.

The last thing I need is to be in the papers again. I can almost imagine the feature next Sunday—pictures of my mum holding my childhood photographs, even if they're few and far between.

"Are you going to let her know?"

"I'll message her. She works evenings so she'll be around in the day."

I put the rest of the pots in the dishwasher while my mind wanders to my mother. We started rebuilding our rocky relationship when I was in my mid-twenties, before I got my record deal. After I started making some real money, I paid off her mortgage. I took her on a holiday. It was the first overseas trip we had ever taken together. I thought I helped fix any damaged bridges with her, likewise with my father. Seeing the article has set fire to any idea of that with my father, and who knows what my mum thinks.

"How long do you think you'll be at your mum's? Do you need a few days?" Rose asks, and I hear a hitch in her voice.

I look at her, trying to keep the surprise off my face. It sounds like she's anxious. I'm not sure why she would feel anxious. We're having fun and have a couple of songs under our belt already. Our combined writing abilities are proving to be a great combination. I'm committed to finishing the albums we have planned. When I agreed to write music with Rose, I hoped it would knock down my writer's block, but it's already done more than that. For the first time in ages, I actually feel inspired to write a song for me to sing. I'm invested in these songs. I believe in what we're doing. Of course I'm coming back.

"Just for the day. I'll set off in the morning, and I'll be back in the evening."

"Okay," she says, failing to sound nonchalant. I don't want to upset her or make her feel embarrassed, so I put the salad back into the fridge and tidy everything else away without saying anything about her reaction.

"I know we usually have a walk on the beach after tea, but I guess after the long hike today, you're not fussed if we skip it?" I ask.

"I think we've completed our required exercise and health benefits today." She grins at me.

"I know you said no follow-up questions from our shouting into the void, but who the fuck told you that you were fat?"

She shakes her head, a frown on her face. "Somebody who has already taken too much time of my life and too much space in my head."

"Somebody I need to add to the 'kick in the balls' list? Do they have balls?"

She giggles. "Why is it, when I think I'm about to fall into a spiral of upset, you make me laugh instead?"

"What else are friends for?" I smile. It's met with a shy smile back. "Right, I'm going to have an early night, I'll be setting off early in the morning, so I'll lock the door and post the key through the letterbox. Is that okay?"

"Sure. Good night, Blake. I hope everything goes well with your mum. I'll see you soon," Rose says. She starts to walk out of the kitchen.

"I'll see you tomorrow, Red," I call to her. She gives a small wave, and then she's off to bed, in that little room she insists on staying in.

I stay in the kitchen for a few minutes before I head upstairs, to my own room, hoping I can sleep without worrying about what I'm going to say to my mother.

***

"Blake, I'm so glad you could come," Mum exclaims when I arrive at her house early Monday morning. I'm still not ready for this conversation.

I tossed and turned most of the night, imagining the different things she could say to me, wondering if she would even avoid talking to me about the topic I want to discuss. From the noises coming from Rose's room, it didn't sound like she was faring any better for a restful night. There was no sound that she was having any of her nightmares, so I resisted the urge to get up and check on her. Her room was quiet at six in the morning when I eventually gave up the idea of sleep, getting myself out of bed and ready to start the drive towards my mum's house.

"Hi, Mum. I'm glad you have time to talk," I say.

"What do you want to talk about?" she asks, opening the front door so I can step inside the house. She walks through to the living room. I follow, shutting the door behind me. I take a seat on the chair while she sits on the sofa. I can't bring myself to sit on the sofa next to her.

"Did you read the article, the interview Dad gave?"

"Yes, but I don't know why Brandon thought it needed to be discussed." Mum wrinkles her nose.

"It certainly didn't need to be discussed in the paper, but it is something that needs to be discussed." I find myself looking at my feet instead of at her directly.

"You know that what he said was crap, right? You were a wanted child," she states.

I still can't bring myself to look at her. I didn't feel like a wanted child, not from my parents, that's for sure. I spent most of my childhood feeling like an inconvenience, and when I was old enough to fend for myself, I spent a lot of time alone. Of all the things in the article, that is what cut the deepest, but it isn't anything I want to bring up with her.

"I'm not here to talk about whether I was a wanted child. I want to talk about whether Dad is my biological father or not," I explain.

"Why does it need to be talked about, Blake?"

"How about I should be able to know my proper medical history, for a start? How about I should know whether I have any half-siblings out there?"

"I don't know what you want me to say." Mum gives a big sigh.

I feel guilty, like I'm asking for something unreasonable, but my whole life feels like it has shifted. I used to be able to say my mother is called Chloe, and my father is called Brandon. I have no siblings. I have no other living relatives. Only one of these statements I can say for sure is still true.

"Dad said you told him there was a chance I wasn't his. Is that true?" I force myself to look at her.

Is that why Dad was always so distant with me? If there had been no doubt, would he have been better, or was he always going to be a shitty father? Did

Mum's admission that I might not be his fracture their relationship and change her ability to love me like a mother should?

Or would none of it matter anyway? Maybe they were always destined to be terrible parents—unequipped to show a child love and make them feel it, too.

"I shouldn't have to have this conversation with my son," she mutters.

"Well, Dad put it on the table, and he doesn't seem to know the answers, so that only leaves you," I snap, a little more forcefully than I intended. I take a breath and look at her. She's no longer looking in my direction. Instead she is leaning back on the sofa, looking up at the ceiling, pinching the bridge of her nose.

"Goddamn Brandon. He makes a mess and leaves me to clean everything up," she growls.

"I'm just looking for answers," I mutter. I'm not sure why I feel guilty for wanting answers to my questions.

She doesn't answer me straight away. The silence goes on longer than I thought could ever be possible. Eventually she looks up at me.

"Well, fine, if you want answers, I'll give them to you, if I must," she replies, sighing as she gets up. "Just, don't blame me if I tell you something that you don't really want to know."

Despite her warning, I get up and follow her into the kitchen. In the kitchen, I flick the kettle on. I get the cups from the cupboard and grab the milk from the fridge. I'm more comfortable at my mum's house than my dad's. It doesn't feel like I'm an unwelcome visitor here. Mum leans against the countertop as she watches me work, that frown still on her face.

"Here you go," I say as I pass her the cup of tea I've made. She takes a sip and then puts her cup to the side, sighing as she looks at me.

"Where do you want me to start?" she asks.

"At the start is always a good option," I reply. She pinches the bridge of her nose and then drops her hands, staring at me.

"Last chance," she warns.

"Just tell me," I say.

I've come this far. There is no point falling at the final hurdle, no matter how much it might hurt. It's going to be several shades of awkwardness between us, but it may give me some of the answers to questions and emotions that have plagued me since I was a child. Maybe I'll come away from this all with a better understanding of my parents, and an acknowledgement that the abandonment I felt as a child wasn't imagined—and wasn't my fault.

I square my shoulders and wait.

Chapter Thirteen

Rose

NOW

Monday morning, I wake to silence. I check my watch for the time, seeing that it is ten thirty. I'm not surprised that it's late morning that I'm waking up; the night wasn't an easy one.

I tossed and turned a lot of the night, unable to get comfortable or settled enough to fall asleep. From the muffled sounds of tossing and turning coming from his room, it sounded like Blake had a similar experience. At one point, I was tempted to get up, knock on his door and suggest we give up on the idea of sleep and play cards in the living room instead, but I knew he had a long drive to his mother's and letting him get some sleep seemed like something I should do.

I wonder how he's getting on.

I wonder if he'll be back this evening. He had said he would, but anything could happen today. It might not be a conversation that can be wrapped up with a flying visit.

I stretch and get out of bed. I head to the bathroom and brush my teeth. I look around the bathroom and my gaze settles on the bathtub. The slipper bath looks so inviting. I haven't treated myself to a bath for a long time. Since I've been here, all I have had has been quick showers. Some of the showers were under protest when I just didn't have the energy for them. Now, the idea of getting in a hot bubble bath seems like the best idea I've ever had, especially since Blake changed the boiler settings and the water gets lovely and hot.

I lean over to start the water running, adding some of the bubble bath that sits in a little box of toiletries on the windowsill. It appears to be another of Annabeth's gifts for people staying in the house. The day I arrived, I saw the bubble bath, shower gel, moisturisers, and scented candle with a note in her handwriting saying "enjoy."

As the water is running and a slight, steamy mist starts to fill the bathroom, I go downstairs to get a few items to help make my bath feel magical. There are a few books in the living room, so I select one from the pile, skimming the back for the content. It's billed as a romantic thriller, and I think I can stomach that, hoping it leans more towards the crime investigation that is depicted in the book rather than the main characters getting it on. The cover looks like it's aiming more towards crime.

I head to the kitchen to find the matches so I can light the candle, and I pour a glass of water. I walk back upstairs to the bathroom, stripping off and pulling my hair into a high ponytail so I can keep it out of the water while I'm reading.

I pick out the candle from the box of Annabeth's treats, lighting the wick and watching the flame dance around. The scent of vanilla wafts towards me, making me smile. It's always been such a homely and grounding scent. I take a sip of my water and place it on the windowsill for later.

Once the bath is filled and the mist clears slightly, I get into the water. A little groan escapes when I feel the heat of the water and the heavenly scent of the sandalwood bubble bath hits me. It complements the vanilla so well, and I wonder if this was just a lucky pairing or something Annabeth put care and consideration into, trying to create a beautiful combination for guests.

I slide further into the water, the bubbles lapping around my body, groaning out loud again because this is perfection.

I open the book to read, hoping the story is good and doesn't ruin my bath. I read a couple of pages, trying to keep my focus on the storyline, trying not to let myself get distracted. It's harder than I want it to be.

I wonder if I will ever truly be able to focus again without getting distracted. It sometimes seems like an impossible task, trying to stop my mind wandering into dark places. The fears I have—the thoughts that keep me up at night, wake me from sleep and give me a cold sweat—they seem never-ending. The fear that my life will be upended, that my secrets will be laid bare for the world to see, is that ever going to go away? The idea that this level of anxiety can hang over me for the rest of my life makes me want to cry.

I close my eyes for a moment, counting to one hundred in my head. I tell myself that I'm safe, okay, that the thoughts in my head are only thoughts. They are not reality. I count again to one hundred until I feel the anxiety recede a little. It doesn't go away entirely, but it's enough to eventually allow me to refocus on the story I'm reading.

I read a little longer, up until it becomes clear the main characters relationship is going to become the focus instead of the mystery. I throw the book onto the floor. I pull the hair tie out of my hair and then slip down the bath so I can slide under the water, getting my hair wet. I wash and condition my hair then lie back, my ears and hair under the water, so that just my nose, mouth, and eyes are above the surface. I lie like this, listening to the sound of my breathing until the water cools around me, getting too cold to stay in the bath.

After my bath, I get dressed. I take the time to properly dry my hair before I go downstairs, ready for my day. The clock in the kitchen reads one o'clock so I make myself a cheese sandwich before getting my notepad and pen, planning to write some lyrics to keep myself occupied while Blake is away. If I can write some lyrics, I can probably put some music to it before the day is done.

Blake arranged for a keyboard to be delivered when the tandem bike arrived, something I was grateful for. The day after the keyboard arrived, I spent an hour in the morning playing some music, my fingers feeling at home on the keys. I want to arrange for a guitar because I miss the feel of mine in my arms, and the idea of playing guitar with Blake feels like it will be an amazing experience, but for now, I can put the lyrics to the keyboard. There's a little part of me that feels excited about producing something to show Blake when he gets back.

I scribble ideas in my notepad, getting engrossed in the process, forcing my mind to stay on track but then it wanders again—to Hunter and what happened between us. I grip the pen harder, my writing almost gouging into the paper and the words turning from sweet lyrics to venom as I try to carry on writing, until I throw the pen down in disgust. I leave the notebook on the coffee table and switch on the television instead. Daytime television is potentially mind-numbing enough to stop me thinking, and I cross my fingers that I can calm myself enough to finish the song. I really want to show something to Blake.

There is nothing to interest me on the television, and again, I find myself missing Blake's presence in the house. He has a host of films that he connects for us to watch on the television. We've watched a couple of what he says are classic nineties movies together, as well as some terrible action films with questionable dialogue and almost laughable special effects. Blake tends to find something amusing in anything we watch, laughing at something, which starts me laughing. I can't remember the last time I had so much fun watching films with somebody.

Bored with the television and feeling listless, I get up from the chair and go to find my phone. There are no messages from Libby, not that I was expecting any. Blake doesn't have my number, mostly because we have been at the house together since he arrived and there hasn't been a need. Now though, I wish I had his number just to text and ask him how he is. I hope he's okay, I hope he's getting the answers he wants and not being dismissed by his mother. Even without the interview given by his father, I feel awful about Blake's detached parents and the way he describes his childhood. Mostly, he sounds like he's trying not to be bothered by what happened, but to me it sounds like neglect and abandonment.

No child deserves to be treated like that.

I put my phone down on the sofa. The house is way too quiet without Blake. I hope he'll be back tonight like he said, because I'm not sure what I'll do if he doesn't arrive.

***

At five, I give up trying to distract myself and head to the kitchen so I can start making dinner. I unlock the front door as I pass it so that Blake can let himself in when he gets back. He didn't say what time he would be back, other than evening, but I figure I can make something to eat and if he does arrive home tonight, he can reheat it. There is salad in the fridge from yesterday. I can make some pasta, and I can put some chicken pieces from the freezer to cook.

I switch on the oven and then grab a pan to fill with water and put on the boil. I potter around the kitchen as the water heats so I can put the pasta on. I start singing as I put the pasta into the saucepan, the words to one of the songs we wrote earlier in the week. The melody echoes around the kitchen.

The lyrics are filled with pain, the verses laced with my heartache and complemented by a beautiful chorus Blake created. I can hear the emotion in my tone, and I wonder if it'll always sound like this when I sing it. More than that—will I always *feel* like this when I sing it? Will I ever be able to perform this song live at a future concert? Can I sing this song live and force myself to relive the emotions on stage? I remember hearing an artist perform live at a concert, where her voice had broken with the emotions. That performance was recorded and the hitch in her voice—the overcoming of emotion—was forever immortalised. What if that happens to me, being so lost in the emotion that I break down on stage?

Maybe it is one of the songs that Blake should sing on his album, instead of me putting it on my mine when we split the songs. I wonder if Blake feels the echo of emotion when he performs his own songs. His songs are so beautiful, and I know he wrote them based on his own experiences. When he sings "Repercussions," does he always think of the breakup that inspired it? Does his heart ache with the reminder of the loss?

I wonder how much—if anything—he feels for his ex. I know it's been years since they broke up, but every time he performs the songs inspired by her, she must cross his mind. Do you truly move on if every time you sing, it takes you back to that emotional state? I've written songs about heartbreak, but when I'm performing in concerts, it is mostly my upbeat tracks, aimed at the younger audience. I rarely sing my emotional songs on stage, so it's never anything I have had to consider before.

Maybe Blake doesn't get the same emotions when he sings. He doesn't seem hung up over his ex. He speaks of her with affection and warmth. Since he's been here, I've taken a couple of looks at Olive's social media sites, wondering what she is like, curiosity making me check in the spare minutes when Blake's in the shower and doesn't see my snooping and can't tease me for my curiosity.

Olive is a beautiful woman. She is the opposite of me in physical attributes. She's short and has a slight frame, even in her pregnancy pictures. Whereas my eyes have always made me look a little like I'm constantly surprised, and my lips are like I've been stung by a bee, her eyes are often crinkled in laughter, and her smile is bright with an evenly shaped mouth. Even our colouring is different; she has dark hair, and I am usually blonde. We have nothing in common.

I've never really compared myself much to other women—only to the vision of the woman everybody expects me to be—so for the first time, I've felt a pinch of envy. I'm slightly envious at her physique, given my hips and curves, the thighs a stylist had called "thunderous" and the ass that Hunter told me was fat.

I know, logically, I'm a healthy weight, but it is something I have to work to maintain, under the strict instruction and supervision by those close to me. Being called fat by Hunter—especially now I've seen pictures of him with the supermodel-worthy Isla—hurt, but I don't think it really matters how she looked; it was always going to hurt to see them together.

I shake my head to clear my thoughts. I'm sick of going down that path. I stop singing given my mind has been wandering and it has made me lose my place. Instead, I hum for a minute, a new tune, and then I play around with some lyrics.

As I sing, I grab the tub of salt so I can put some into the pasta water.

"I like the shape of your lips when my name is on them. I like how my heart beats when you make me laugh. You're lighting me up like bonfire night, tell me, baby, has anything ever felt so right?" I sing.

"You sound cheerful." Blake's voice from behind me scares the life out of me. I jump in shock, dropping the salt-shaker. It lands in the saucepan with a large plop, splashing hot water upwards and onto my hands.

"Shit," I exclaim, not entirely sure if I'm cursing being caught singing something so stupid, the fact that all the salt is dissolving into the pasta water, or that my skin hurts.

"I'm so sorry." Blake drops the box he is holding onto the table. He rushes forward, guiding me to the sink and putting the cold tap on. He holds my hands under the flow of water.

"You're here." I sound a little dazed.

"I did knock on the door, a few times. I'm so sorry I startled you."

"I wasn't sure you were coming back," I say.

"I told you I would be back. We have music to make." Blake smiles. "Why do you look so surprised?"

"Because aside from Libby, I can't remember the last time somebody in my life told me something and then actually delivered," I admit.

He frowns. "Well, that's pretty depressing, Red."

"How was it with your mum?"

"I'll tell you over tea."

"I'm not sure we should trust that pasta. It probably tastes like the sea now. Even I know, that was far too much salt in the water." I laugh.

"Well, lucky for us, I got us some takeaway chicken to go with the salad from yesterday."

"Oh, my, you really are pushing the boat out." I grin.

"How are the hands?"

"They'll survive."

"Well, keep them under the cold water while I get the plates sorted."

Blake leaves me at the sink. My hands feel freezing under the water now, so I turn the tap off, shaking my hands in the sink to get the excess water off.

"Do you want any help?" I ask.

"You're so stubborn. Why don't you sit down?" he suggests.

I sit as instructed and watch as he sorts out the pan of water then finishes making plates of salad, two glasses of juice and grabbing knives and forks. He puts everything on the table and then opens the box that he came into the house with. The smell wafts out of the box and my mouth waters.

"Oh, that smells so good," I exclaim. The box contains several pieces of heavily seasoned, battered chicken that look deep fried.

"Hot off the press, and by press, I mean the doorstep as I ordered it for my arrival back," he replies, putting some pieces onto the plate in front of me and the rest onto his own plate. I stab my first piece with my fork, cutting a piece to eat. It's hot and tasty. I let the flavours settle on my tongue.

"Oh, my, that is the best thing I've ever had in my mouth," I groan after I've swallowed.

Blake snickers and then coughs like he's trying to cover it up. He looks at me, a grin on his face as I roll my eyes.

"Sorry," he says.

"Tell me about your mum," I suggest.

"She doesn't know for sure that Dad is my biological father, but she believes he is. The other options are two other men, one who was married, the other who died when I was one." Blake shrugs. He takes a bite of his piece of chicken, and I study his expression, wondering how he is really feeling.

"Are you going to talk to your dad?"

"I swung by his house on my way back. He says he doesn't want a DNA test. He says he is my dad, regardless. Honestly, I'm wondering if he's hit his head, I'm not sure how you can pivot from telling the Sunday papers that I'm possibly not his child biologically and then tell me the following day that I'm his son. I know he's my dad in the sense he's the one that raised me, even if not in the best way."

"So, have you any idea what you want to do?" I wonder.

"I don't really have much of an option. If my dad doesn't want to do a DNA test, there isn't much I can do. Nothing logical, anyway. I could turn up on the doorstep of the guy who was married, is still married, to say, 'hey, I could be your son, fancy spitting in a tube so I can check,' and then I could track down some relative of the guy who died to see if we have any shared DNA to rule them out."

"You don't have any other relatives on your dad's side to ask them to do a DNA test?"

"Nope. I'm out of relatives on both sides, just me and my parents."

"Did you end things on a good note with your mum?" I ask.

"It seemed okay. I can't say it was enjoyable to listen to my mum telling me about her wild sex life and how I was potentially conceived, but hey, just another Monday, I guess."

"I'm sure if you talk to your dad again, after the dust has settled, he might change his mind. He might come to his senses and apologise for the way he handled it and he'll give you the answers you want."

"Do you think it is selfish of me to keep picking at this topic?" Blake wonders.

I put my knife and fork down and reach across the table to put my hand over his. We have spent days where we have consoled and cajoled each other but we seem to have progressed to an easy, natural physical comfort since the article was released. It's nice.

"I don't think you're being selfish. He lit the fuse, Blake, and it is perfectly reasonable that you want to know your biological history, even if that is all you want to know."

"I don't think I'd be ready for anything else if that was the result. I've enough drama with my two parents, the idea of adding a third is crazy." Blake shrugs. I take my hand from his and pick up my knife and fork again.

"I don't have the same kind of drama as you do, but I see what you mean. A third parent is a scary prospect."

I stare at him as I talk, trying to gauge how he is really feeling. I don't have anything else I can say. If he proceeds with trying to find out who his biological father is, there is the possibility that his biological father has died, or the possibility his inquiry destroys a marriage with the information of infidelity three decades ago.

Blake takes a deep breath and then looks at me with a grin. "Well, I guess you have it potentially worse with your potential third parent."

"Well, if both my parents remarry, I end up with four parents, but you could end up with six, should your mother remarry, your dad remarry, and there be a surprise biological father with a wife," I shoot back, and I can't keep the grin from my face, too.

"Touché, Red, well played. How about I apologise for joking about Krystal being your stepmother?"

"I'll let you off, for two reasons. First, because of this amazing chicken," I start.

"Yeah, what's the second?" he asks, picking his glass from the table.

"For coming back like you said you would," I add, and I catch the wide smile he has before he can disguise it by taking a sip of his drink.

"Film after tea, then a walk on the beach?" he asks.

"Sounds perfect." I smile.

***

I wake in the morning to the sound of Blake in the bathroom. He's whistling, and it makes me smile because he sounds much happier. I feel happier because I feel like I slept well, much better than the night before. No tossing and turning, no dreams.

I stay in bed, listening to the sounds of Blake in the bathroom, waiting until it is free. I feel a grip of pain in my stomach, and it makes me sit upright in bed, clutching my stomach. There's a second pinch of pain, almost like somebody is squeezing my insides. I get out of bed, pulling my cardigan on to cover my pyjamas, and then I walk down the hallway towards the bathroom.

"Blake, are you going to be long?" I ask from outside the bathroom door.

"I'm just finishing shaving, what's up?"

"I feel sick," I call.

Another grip of pain and a wave of nausea washes over me. I know I'm going to be sick; the only outstanding question is whether it will be in the hallway or if I get into the bathroom in time.

Blake opens the door. He stands in front of me, a towel wrapped around his waist, half his face shaved, the other half still covered in shaving foam. He opens the door wider.

"Damn, Red, you're pale as a ghost," he comments. I open my mouth to reply but then I push past him, kneeling in front of the toilet and retching. Blake pulls my hair out of the way, holding it back as I throw up, twice in quick succession.

"I'm sorry," I choke out, but I throw up again before I have the opportunity to say anything else.

"Better out than in, I guess," Blake replies. He's still holding my hair as I remain hunched over the toilet.

"I'm sorry, this is gross." I lift my head, pulling some tissue from the roll of toilet paper. I wipe my mouth. The smell of sick hangs in the air, turning my stomach again.

"All done?" he asks. I want to tell him yes, but instead I throw up again. "I'll take that as a no." Blake chuckles as he holds my hair back again.

"Not funny. This is disgusting," I mutter between bouts of being sick.

"No, this is the most amazing way to spend a Tuesday morning." His tone is teasing, clearly unbothered by me being sick. I don't know how he does it. Whenever somebody throws up in front of me, I'm always sick as well. I spit into the toilet. I sit back down and wipe my mouth again, and then I wipe the sweat from my brow.

I close the lid to the toilet and reach to flush, but Blake beats me to it.

"I'm sorry," I murmur.

"Why are you apologising for being sick?"

"I'm apologising for throwing up in front of you when you're trying to shave." I manage a small, wry smile.

"The great Rose Elodie Dalton throwing up in front of me while wearing pyjamas and I'm half shaved with only a towel to protect my modesty, highlight of my life. Going in my autobiography, for sure."

"People will read way more into that than is actually happening." I roll my eyes.

Blake smiles and then he reaches for my toothbrush. He adds toothpaste before passing it to me.

"Here you go," he says. I take it from him and start to brush my teeth. The action makes me gag but I manage to finish brushing them. Blake helps me up from the floor so I can spit out my toothpaste.

"Finish shaving. I might go back to bed." I rinse my toothbrush and start to make a move towards the door, holding my stomach when I get another pain, swaying slightly when the pain and a wave of dizziness washes through my body.

"Nope, you sit here." Blake pulls me by my elbow to sit me on the toilet.

He returns to the sink, picking up his razor and finishing shaving. I watch him as he glides the razor across the rest of his face, repeating until his five-o'clock shadow is gone, then rinses off the traces of shaving foam. He puts his razor away and wipes his face with a towel. He reaches over and touches my forehead.

"You should go back to bed. You have a temperature," Blake comments.

"I'm not sure that's the proper methodology for confirming an actual temperature."

"Well, you should rest. You must have picked up a bug somewhere. Either that or you had a dodgy piece of chicken."

"Please don't mention food," I grumble.

He laughs. "Come on, back to bed." He helps me get up from the toilet. He walks me back to the bedroom I'm staying in. "Why is it so cold in here?"

"It's always like that in here."

"Well, you need a warm room. I'll go put the heating on again. It shouldn't take long to warm back up. I don't want you to get worse."

"Stop fussing, I'm fine." I laugh, but then another wave of sickness washes over me. I pull away from his grasp and sprint back to the bathroom where I throw up again, proving I'm not actually fine.

"I was just going to suggest breakfast, but I'll take that as a no," Blake calls from the other side of the door.

"Firm no," I call back. I get up to brush my teeth again.

"Let me know later if you want something. Maybe some dry toast?"

"I think I can survive without the food. Might be good for my fat ass," I joke as I step out of the bathroom.

He frowns at me. "Not that it would matter if you did, but you do not have a fat ass, nor is any other part of you fat. Seriously, who the fuck was it who told you that?"

"We'll start with my mother, raise that by several stylists before Libby, then top off with the last guy I slept with."

"We have already agreed your mother is a piece of work, and your ex deserves a kick in the balls. As for the stylists, I'd put it down to jealousy. You have an amazing figure and you're strong. You need to be strong to perform and tour like we do. It takes a toll, and your body needs the fuel," Blake reasons.

"Thanks, Blake," I reply with a smile.

"Now, bed! Rest up. We have an album to finish when you're better."

He pauses at my bedroom door. I give him a smile before I step inside, but then I stumble under another wave of dizziness. Blake catches me by my elbow. He guides me to the bed and then he tucks the covers around me.

"Thank you," I murmur, suddenly sleepy.

"Get some sleep. I'll check on you later, if that's okay with you."

"Yeah, that's fine," I reply. I snuggle further under the covers as he retreats out of the room.

I don't think it'll take long until I'm asleep again. I cross my fingers for some dreamless, uninterrupted sleep, and that whatever sickness bug I've picked up is gone after some more rest, so I can get back to making music with Blake.

Chapter Fourteen

Rose

THEN

"Oh, God, Briar Rose. This is my favourite place to be, ever," he pants above me. I stare up at him, watching as his expression changes. He looks like he's seeing stars for the first time in his life.

"Right there, don't stop," I pant back. I feel like I'm at the very top of a clifftop, about to go flying off, if he just gives another little nudge.

"You're so fucking sexy," he growls.

His hands move, grabbing at my wrists, pinning me onto the bed. He continues to thrust into me, clutching hard on both wrists. He holds tightly, and the weight of him above me keeps my wrists pinned to the mattress. The mattress that had felt so soft underneath me now feels like a brick wall—firm and unyielding.

Along with the change in position, his expression has also changed. Instead of looking mesmerised and enthralled, now he looks determined and fierce.

"Hunter," I whisper, trying to get his attention. I need him to loosen his grip on my wrists, but he doesn't pay me any attention.

My wrists start to ache as he carries on. The feeling I had before—the one of impending euphoria—is gone. I feel like everything in my body has gone tense, but he doesn't react to the change, like he's oblivious to it all.

Nothing feels good anymore. Not the way he's moving above me. Not the way he's touching me. Not the weight of him against me. Not the way he seems lost, like I'm not even here. It doesn't feel like something we're doing together anymore.

"Oh, God, this feels so good," he groans. Unbelievably, he squeezes harder on my wrists. I feel the tips of my fingers start to tingle.

"Hunter, stop," I say, louder and more firmly this time. It doesn't seem to penetrate the focus he has.

Again, I try to push my arms and wrists upwards, but I'm insignificant against his strength. It does nothing to loosen the grip he has on me. The only thing I can do is move my legs. I unwrap them from around his waist. I use my feet to push me a little underneath him, trying to get his attention so he can realise he's hurting me.

"Oh, God, yes!" He growls. He slams harder into me, and it doesn't seem to matter how much I try to move. I can't get away from him. His head bows and I think he's going to kiss my chest, but instead, he bites hard on the swell of my breast.

I yelp and cry out—a mix of pain and surprise—but then all I feel is the shudder of his body against mine, the heat as he seems to explode all around me, and all I hear is his deep grunt and guttural groan.

"Hunter," I gasp.

"That was amazing," he pants against me. "Every single time with you just gets more amazing."

Hunter lifts his head. He unwraps his fingers from around my wrists. The pain shoots up my arms as the blood flow seems to restore. I look at my fingers, seeing them return to their usual colour. He rolls off me, lying back on the bed, an expression of triumph on his face.

"I'll be back in a minute," I say, trying to keep my voice steady.

I get up from the hotel bed and head to the bathroom. I switch on the shower and step inside, under the hot water. It takes me a second to realise that my hands are shaking. My body gives an involuntary shudder.

I don't understand what just happened. Hunter has never been like that. It's been three months since that first day. Three months of us sneaking out and around to be with one another, of hotel rooms and secret escapes. Three months of sweet messages and bouquets of flowers delivered to my hotel rooms. Three months of hot, passionate sex, but never anything that has hurt me, frightened me. I can't deny that what just happened frightened me.

My hands continue to shake as I shampoo and condition my hair. As I wash my body, my hand moves across my breast. It feels tender and sore where he bit me. I look down and see the teeth marks on my chest, little white indents in my skin within the red swelling.

Despite the fact the water is streaming down me, when I wash my face, I realise that I'm not just shaking, but I'm crying, too. My stomach is in tight knots, and for the first time ever after being in bed with somebody, I feel used and dirty, unsettled and afraid. I've never felt like this before. Even the first time I had sex wasn't filled with the sense of being used for somebody's pleasure, like I wasn't even present.

I finish the shower, dry myself off with the towels, and then wrap myself in the hotel dressing gown. I check my face for any evidence of the tears, to make sure my skin isn't blotchy, and my eyes aren't red. I wait until my skin looks normal before I head back into the bedroom.

Hunter smiles at me from his position on the bed. I sit down next to him.

"That was amazing. You were so good. I mean, you're always good, but that was sensational." He moves on the bed to sit next to me, slipping an arm around me.

"Please don't hold my wrists that tightly again, it hurt me." I blurt the words out. I look at my wrists. They still look a little red.

"You didn't enjoy that?"

"It hurt," I repeat.

"I thought you were enjoying it."

"I was enjoying things until you grabbed my wrists," I explain. I want to add that I didn't like how I felt like he'd pinned me down, how he seemed to *enjoy* it—almost relish in it—but something about that sentence makes me feel ashamed, so I don't say it.

"I was just swept up with the passion of it all. You drive me wild, Briar Rose." He kisses my neck.

"I get lost in the passion, too, but that hurt me."

"You are making me feel guilty, my beautiful Princess," Hunter says, and the tone of his voice makes me feel like he is scolding me, like he's disappointed in me.

"I'm sorry," I reply quickly. I rub my wrists, one at a time. "It's okay. Forget about it."

"What time am I seeing you tomorrow?" Hunter gets up from the bed and heads to the bathroom.

"I can be free at eleven, until three," I call to him.

"What time do you need to go?" Hunter pops his head around the door to look at me. I glance at the time.

"I have to go in about twenty minutes, otherwise I'll be late."

"Do you really have to go to this stupid thing?" he asks.

"Yes, I'm presenting an award," I remind him. It's a rare night off from performing, but I'm expected at the show tonight. People are expecting me to be dazzling and charming on stage as I hand out an award. I'm already cutting it fine to meet Libby and get ready.

"Such a shame to waste a potential night together." He shrugs.

"You could always come with me," I offer. I get up from the bed and walk towards the bathroom. I step into the room with him.

"You know we can't be seen together," Hunter chides.

"We could just be there as friends," I point out.

"The way I look at you, my beautiful Briar Rose, it would be obvious what we are doing. As if I can sit next to you, dressed up, without me looking like I'm already undressing you in my head." Hunter grins at me as he gets into the shower.

"How on earth are you going to survive filming when we start?" I laugh.

"Come in the shower with me." Hunter's mouth curves in a cheeky-looking smile.

"You heard me say I need to go in twenty minutes?" I grin.

"I think we can get a lot done in twenty minutes," he growls at me, and I shrug off my dressing gown and join him, trying to banish the feelings I felt earlier, trying not to remind myself that he didn't exactly apologise for getting carried away.

***

"Are you trying to give me a heart attack?" Libby scolds when I finally walk into my hotel room.

I knew I was going to face her wrath. I'm later than I said I would be. My mother is out on a date. It's with a younger guy who she met on a dating app, something she gushed about non-stop over breakfast. As Mum is out, there is only Libby waiting for me, so I'm confident I can calm her down. It's easier when there is only one person disappointed in me—just Libby to appease. There is nobody else to scold me for being late, for arriving back with damp hair, for pushing the time I need to be ready and leaving so I can show up on time.

"I'm sorry, Libby. I didn't do it on purpose. I won't do it again, I'm sorry."

"Sit down now so I can sort out that hair of yours." She rolls her eyes a little at my over-enthusiastic apologies but then smiles affectionately.

"I love you, Libby." I smile, taking a seat. She stands behind me, plugging in the hairdryer so she can dry my hair. I sit quietly as she dries and then straightens my hair. When she finishes, she positions herself in front of me with the makeup bag.

"So, where were you?" she asks, a small smile on her face.

"Nowhere."

"Original," she says with a laugh. "Come on, spill the tea."

"You always tell me off for talking when you're doing my makeup," I remind her.

"True," she agrees, sweeping the silver eye shadow across my lids. "Did you at least have a good time?"

"In my visit to nowhere? Yes," I confirm. She takes the lipstick from the makeup bag and slicks it across my lips.

"Right, let's get you dressed. Come on."

Libby nods in the direction of where my dress is hanging on the door to my room. She was so excited when she showed me the dress last week and I was swept up in her enthusiasm. It is more daring than anything I've worn before, with a strapless bodice and a full skirt. It's in a shimmering silver, and I'm excited to wear it.

"You did a great job picking this dress," I comment. I step into my room to strip out of my clothes and change into a strapless bra. I pull my bra a little higher because the bite mark from Hunter is still there, the skin looking red.

I step back into the main room. Libby is pulling the dress out of the protective wrapping, unzipping it.

"Here you go," Libby says, holding the dress so I can step into it. She pulls the dress up from behind me and zips me up. She walks around to the front of me, looking at me, a frown on her face.

"What's wrong?" I wonder.

"What's this?" She points at my chest. I look down and bite my lip as I can see what she's referring to. The mottled skin is just above the edge of the dress, on display for the world to see, pushed up over the bodice.

"I...." I start but then stop talking because I've no idea what she's expecting me to say.

"Jesus, Rose. I don't have anything else for you to wear. You should have warned me," Libby exclaims.

"I didn't intend for it to happen, and it just happened!"

"Yeah, on your little trip to nowhere," she mutters. She presses her fingers to her temples, like she's trying to think. She knows that I'd be torn apart in the media if I turn up with a visible mark like this, especially where it is. "Wait. I know."

She steps away from me and over to where she has left the makeup bag. She digs around and returns to me with a pot of foundation. I know the foundation is the one that she sometimes uses to cover my tattoo when I'm expected to wear something that flashes my stomach, given nobody seemed impressed when I got my tattoo and so it isn't allowed to be displayed.

"You're a lifesaver, Libby," I whisper as she unzips my dress so she can put the foundation on without getting it on the fabric. She waits for it to dry before putting the dress back in place and zipping it up again.

"It should be fine," Libby murmurs, and I'm not sure whether she's talking to herself or to me.

"Thank you." I smile. She reaches to get my shoes so she can help me put them on. As she kneels on the floor, she looks up at me.

"I'll let this slide tonight, but you and I are going to talk at some point about that."

"Fair enough, Libby."

She helps me into my shoes and passes me the clutch bag that she's stuffed my things into. As a final touch, she puts an expensive-looking bangle on my wrist.

"Speak to you soon, Rose." She gives me a pointed look. I just nod a reply and then square my shoulders. My driver will be waiting and the evening should be filled with fun, but the only thing on my mind is Hunter.

***

"You looked so beautiful at the awards last night. I wish you could have come to mine afterwards. I think I would have enjoyed unzipping you out of that dress. I thought about it every time I saw you on the screen." Hunter's voice is husky as he stands behind me. It's just gone eleven and we're in his hotel room again.

"Well, you could have come with me," I remind him.

"Hmm, but we agreed to keep this secret."

"I know, but don't you think it's just silly, filming is going to take ages. If we can't be seen publicly until everything wraps up, that's a lot of sneaking around," I point out. He slips a hand down my top, into my bra.

"You're not having fun?"

"I'm having fun." I smile to myself. His fingers stroke across my breast. He's always so intense. There is no delay with Hunter. I always know exactly what he wants and what he expects.

“I’m having a lot of fun,” he murmurs.

He pulls my top up over my head and unclips my bra, throwing it on the floor. He moves his hands to his jeans, unbuttoning and unzipping, pulling them down his body, freeing himself. He pushes on my shoulders, and I know he wants me to kneel in front of him. I do as he wants, feeling slightly like I’ve had a couple of drinks, my head cloudy.

I look at him from my position on the floor.

“I believe we can make it more fun,” I tease.

I know what he wants so I take him in my mouth, listening to the hiss of desire that escapes between his teeth.

“Oh, God, that feels so good. You’re so good at this. Those bee-stung lips around my dick look so good. Fuck.”

Hunter sounds lost in what we are doing. He grips my hair with one hand, bunching it together, tightly pulling and clutching. I glance up at him; he looks completely absorbed. I carry on, but suddenly Hunter’s palm cracks across my cheek. The sound of it seems to echo around the room. I blink in surprise and move my head as if to pull away, but Hunter pushes on the back of my head, keeping me in position, urging me to carry on. He lifts his hand again and I flinch, but instead of his hand landing on my face again, he lets his hand fall to my throat, gripping it.

His grip is tight. Too tight. My eyes water. A tear escapes one of my eyes, rolling down my cheek.

Hunter lets go, pushes me off him, and then he pulls me up from the floor. He puts me down on the bed, his hands up my skirt to pull down my underwear. He enters me, swiftly, pushing his body against mine, groaning into my hair.

“Hunter! Wait," I gasp. We always use a condom, and he seems to have lost his senses.

Hunter groans again, louder this time. He clamps a hand against my mouth, the other hand against my throat. Again, his grip is tight. I grab his arms, my nails digging into his skin, but he just tightens his grip, his breath hot against my skin as he keeps telling me how good this feels, how much he wants me, how I’m driving him wild. His hand is so tight against my mouth that any noise of protest I want to make about the condom is lost.

"Oh, baby, you're so good. You know the only thing better? When you cry. Fuck, Princess, it turns me on. Cry for me, Princess, watch what it does to me," he growls.

No. No. No.

I panic, try to push him away, tears in my eyes again. This is too much. His passion for me is too much, but I can't get him to stop, and I can't breathe. Hunter carries on until he climaxes, then he lets go of my throat, takes his hand away from my mouth. I take a deep breath, feeling like I was close to suffocating, gulping in the air that had been denied to me. There is a metallic taste in my mouth. Hunter murmurs words of adoration against my ear between kisses against my skin. It's more words about how good I feel, how hard I make him, how hard he comes when he's with me. He doesn't say anything about the tears that now roll down my face. He wipes them away and then rolls off me, lying on the bed, a satisfied smile on his face.

"Back in a minute," I say, my voice steadier than I feel. I get up and walk to the bathroom, amazed when I manage to walk with my shaking legs. I shut the door behind me, flicking the little lock on the door so I can have some privacy and time to myself.

I stand in front of the sink, grabbing hold of it to keep me steady. I look at myself in the mirror on the wall above the sink. The inside of my lip is bleeding from where my teeth had pushed into it. The skin around my throat is red, the rest of my skin looks like a mix of blotchy red and pale white spots. My cheek stings.

I look at my reflection, wondering what just happened, trying to process everything.

He just got carried away. There's just so much passion. It gets intense.

My reflection in the mirror looks back at me, cynically, so I turn away and clean myself up so I can get back to Hunter. I quickly wipe my eyes, then rinse my mouth to get rid of the taste of blood. I realise my hands are shaking, and that my breathing is too fast. I take a deep breath and count to ten, telling myself to calm down, to relax.

"Princess?" Hunter calls to me. It makes me jump.

"I'm nearly done," I shout back, working faster so I can go back to him. Once I'm done, I take another deep breath as I reach for the doorknob to open the door, my hand still shaking slightly.

It's at that moment I realise, I'm afraid of what he will say when I tell him again, I didn't like what he did, that I don't ever want him to do that to me again.

Chapter Fifteen

Blake

NOW

Thursday signals eight days since I arrived at Rose's hideaway and her third day of being ill. I've been keeping an eye on her each day, checking if she needs food or water, but she's mostly been sleeping. She spent all day Tuesday in bed, not eating anything, and occasionally running to the bathroom to be sick.

Tuesday night was awful. I woke up several times, hearing her shout out and clearly distressed by something. I checked on her the first time, knocking on her door to ask if she was okay. She called out to me from bed, giving permission to open the door to talk to her as she didn't want to get out of bed. She looked exhausted, pale, and surprisingly lost under the covers of her single bed, and she promised that she just needed to have a bit more sleep. She added it was fine for me to check on her, telling me she hated the idea that I was going to worry about a mythical intruder. We agreed to leave her door open for the rest of the night.

Yesterday, she ate some toast for tea and managed to keep that down. Sleep seemed easier, and she spent most of her time in bed—with fewer times of her shouting out—but she still isn't well.

Initially, I put her illness down to a twenty-four-hour bug. Yesterday, a forty-eight-hour one. I expected to hear her up this morning, but so far, nothing.

Is there such a thing as a seventy-two-hour bug?

It's gone eleven, so I knock on Rose's bedroom door. She doesn't answer. I push the door open to check on her. She's fast asleep, and her facial features are relaxed. The covers are curled around her, making her look like she's wrapped up like a burrito. I made her take the extra quilt from the spare bedroom. Why she keeps insisting on sleeping on a small single bed is beyond me.

I step quietly into her room and put the glass of fresh water onto the table, touching her forehead to check her temperature is okay. It feels better than the first day. I take away the empty glass from last night and head back downstairs.

In the kitchen, I sit at the table. Rose's notepad is on the table, still open from when she left it on Monday evening. I haven't looked at any of her lyrics because I know how I feel about people looking at things I've created before I think they're finished. It always makes me uncomfortable, like they're seeing me half undressed. I wouldn't want her to feel embarrassed by glimpsing at her lyrics. She seemed embarrassed enough when I came home on Monday to find her singing in the kitchen. I didn't mean to startle her. When I came in, she was initially singing one of the songs we wrote together, but then she stopped and changed to something I haven't heard before. The line about how it feels in the heart at the sound of laughter had stuck with me all night, because there is something about the way Rose laughs that makes me feel like a fire has been lit inside me. Somehow, it makes me feel warm and happy myself.

I wonder who she was singing about. I assume it wasn't about the guy she was last in a relationship with, or at least I hope it isn't because he sounds like a dickhead. All I know about this guy is that he called her fat and has taken up too much space in her head. I wonder if he's the reason she's hiding away here, or whether it's everything with her parents that drove her to hide. Aside from Libby, there doesn't seem to be anybody in her life who has her needs in mind, and I find it sad. I know Rose—like me—will usually be surrounded by people. There will be publicists, managers, stylists, makeup artists, agents, drivers, security, personal assistants, nutritionists, fitness instructors, often a hub of people. The starkest reality check when you're famous is realising you're surrounded by people but they're only there for the pay packet. Sometimes, friendships become genuine—like I have with Maeve, and Rose appears to have with Libby—but the rest are often people with their own desires. They're there for the pay packet rather than genuine care and concern.

Guiltily, I feel blessed that my fame isn't on Rose's level and not from such an early age. Her whole growing up seems to have been done on stage and on camera, under parents and management who have controlled everything about her image and her life. I might complain about wearing baseball caps or needing to keep my head down to avoid people looking at me properly so they don't truly notice who I am, but at least I can say what I want, if I choose. I can change my image without critique. I can write and release whatever songs I want without being reminded about a fan base I had ten years ago. I did all my growing up outside of the media speculation. Rose has lived in a fishbowl of scrutiny and seems stuck by people who want to perpetuate the artist and person she was, not who she wants to be now.

Rose's upbeat songs are great—they're catchy, fun, and popular as hell—but the songs she's been allowed to release that are more melodic, they're amazing, and the stuff she has been writing since I got here, they're on another level. I don't think I've ever been in the presence of anybody who can do what she does—pluck those beautiful sentences and find the perfect sound to match with them. One of the mornings when she was on the keyboard, I sat, enthralled by her process, watching her fingers quickly finding a new sound to go with some lyrics I had given her.

I'm determined to finish these planned two albums with her and to help her release music she wants to make. I just need her to get better first, and I'm wondering how long I should let her stay sleeping without getting her checked out. I've never looked after anybody when they've been sick before. Am I doing the wrong thing by assuming she just needs to sleep this bug off? What if she is sicker than I think and needs a doctor?

I take my phone from my pocket and search "how long does a stomach bug last," trawling through the answers, varying from one to two days, up to five.

None of the other symptoms listed seem to fit with Rose. She only had a slight temperature and the vomiting. I search for food poisoning. Again, the results vary from a couple of days to a week, and the symptoms don't seem to fit, either.

I scroll my contact lists, wondering if there is anybody that I can call to double-check I'm doing the right thing, or whether I should be calling a doctor. It makes me feel oddly anxious that I'm potentially making an error when looking after somebody, and I need somebody to put my mind at rest. I scroll past Maeve because—although she is the first person I turn to—I've disturbed her enough already. The next contact in my list is Olive. Without giving it too much thought, I send a text.

Hey, in exchange for more university fee money for Mia, how long does a stomach bug typically last?

Almost straight away, my phone rings. I connect the call.

"I didn't expect you to call." I smile to myself as I talk. It's nice to reconnect with somebody who knew me before life went wild.

"You're lucky because I'm currently on my way to a surprise baby shower brunch. I could do with the distraction."

"Not much of a surprise," I comment.

"Well, I'll fake being surprised. It's just with some people from work. Ty was supposed to come but he's poorly, that's why I thought I'd call you. Have you been struck down by the same thing? There must be something going around."

"I'm not ill, but you should go enjoy your not-so-surprise brunch," I reply, feeling guilty for bothering her.

"I don't like the attention being on me, so I'm gearing up to go in the building."

"You should bask in the attention." I laugh.

"That's so not my style. I'd suggest you join me, so you can have all the attention instead, but turning up with you and not my husband would be stirring the pot, and I'm glad it's settled. I'm not going to kick that nest again, if I can avoid it. Anyway, who is ill?"

"Just a friend that I'm staying with. They started being sick on Tuesday morning, they were sick all day. They've been in bed since Tuesday, mostly asleep."

"That sounds different to Ty. He's been sick, but he's been up and about, just with a raging headache. The idiot got up this morning to take Mia to nursery. I told him off and sent him back to bed, but you know Ty, he'll push himself for other people." Olive sounds wry and affectionate. I should correct her, that Tyler will push himself not for other people, but for her.

"Why aren't you at work today?" I ask instead.

"Ty and I booked the week off to have some time to get some stuff ready ahead of the due date, so I'm back at work next week, but I will be starting my maternity leave early anyway. Mia arrived early, so I don't want to take any chances. This week is a chill week though. Just this brunch to get through, then I'll be back at home with Ty and Mia. Anyway, this friend of yours, make sure they're hydrated. Try juice instead of just water, especially if they're not eating. The doctor recommended that to me when I had terrible morning sickness."

"So, I don't need to call a doctor?"

"I'm assuming when they are awake, they're coherent?" Olive asks. I think back to last night when I took some water into Rose's room, how she opened her eyes, smiled at me, and whispered words to thank me.

"Yeah, they're coherent."

"Well, keep them hydrated, see if they want to eat later, and see how they are then. You can always call a doctor if you're not sure."

"Thanks. I think I was just having a moment and freaking out."

"Adulthood will do that for you." Olive laughs.

"Expecting to unlock a new achievement point in November, given it's my birthday."

"Oh, yes, it's the big thirty, isn't it? Are you doing anything special? Big party with all your celebrity friends?"

I remember Olive's thirtieth birthday. Tyler and her friends arranged a night out, and I left halfway through the night, jumping to the beck and call of my bandmates who insisted I get myself across the town to check out what they felt was a bit opportunity for the band. It wasn't the first time I abandoned her, and it makes me feel ashamed that it wasn't the last time, either.

"Probably a quiet night in."

"Have you given up your party lifestyle?" she teases.

"I never had a party lifestyle," I protest.

"Okay, I retract my comment. You're right. I know you loved the stage, but you were never comfortable in a crowd when you weren't performing," she muses.

"Exactly. Right, get into that surprise baby shower. Speak soon?" I suggest.

"Sure, speak later, Blake."

Olive ends the call.

"When is your birthday?" Rose's voice behind me scares the life out of me. I drop my phone onto the table.

"Fucking hell, that just aged me ten years," I joke.

She takes a seat opposite me. "Now you know what it feels like."

"Maybe we should start wearing bells around our necks, otherwise one of us might have a heart attack," I suggest. I get up so I can put the kettle on for her, and I pop some bread into the toaster so I can make her some toast.

"Stop deflecting, when is your birthday?"

"November fifth."

"You're kidding me, right?" Rose looks at me with a bemused smile.

"No, I mean, you can check my driver's licence if you like."

"November fifth is my birthday."

"No way," I reply, laughing.

"I can get you my driver's licence if you like," she repeats my words in a teasing tone.

"You'll be twenty-five, right?"

"Yeah, you?"

"Thirty."

"So, did you have plans for your birthday?" she wonders. I look at her. She still looks tired, but somehow, she looks so much better than the day I arrived.

"No, Red. I planned to be here, unless you had plans to go out to celebrate your birthday."

"Absolutely not. I'm just going to be here."

"Well, then we'll celebrate here together. I'll order us a cake when I do the shopping for that week." I smile. The toast pops up. "What do you want on this?"

"Maybe just some jam if we have any. Ease me back into the food world with gentle flavours."

I check the cupboards but I'm sure I didn't order any jam. I make a mental note to order some for the next delivery.

"Chocolate spread?" I offer instead.

"Okay, I'll risk it."

I finish making her toast and a cup of coffee, putting it in front of her. I take a seat opposite her and pick up my phone. I scroll the entertainment papers. The papers appear to have stopped doing updates about me, which is a relief. I scroll past the captions for the articles. There is one about a singer I know who is pregnant, the article mini headlines promising lots of pictures of their baby bump. There is another about Hunter Greenway spending the day with his wife and two young children while he takes a break from filming. Underneath that, there is an article that makes me pause. The headline reads: *The Shocking Reason Briar Rose Is in Rehab.*

I look at Rose. She's eating her second piece of toast, slowly chewing and looking thoughtful. I could hide the article and pretend it isn't there and pretend I didn't see it. What kind of man would that make me, especially when she was so kind on Sunday when the articles were about me. She made sure to read the whole article before I saw her and knew how to support me. I'd be a terrible person if I ignored this and let her stumble across it herself, and I refuse to let her be surprised by this article.

"There's an article here, claiming to know why you're in rehab," I say. She looks up at me, swallowing her toast and frowning.

"Seriously? I guess it shouldn't be a surprise."

"Yeah, sorry, it's there, though you're not top billing. You're behind pictures of Jessica Hope, apparently flaunting her pregnant belly in Mexico, and Hunter Greenway playing with his children at an amusement park." I summarise the articles. I look back at the headlines and where the one about her lands. "You are ahead of the breakup of some reality TV show contestants I've never heard of."

Rose looks pale. "Seriously?"

"Yeah, do you want to read it?"

"How about you read it and give me the highlights?" she suggests, no longer looking at me. Her eyes are focused on the table.

I open the article on my phone, skimming down. There are pictures of Rose's dad with Krystal. They look like they're lifted from social media. It includes a picture of him proposing to her and another photograph of her flashing her engagement ring. The article comments that their announcement was not acknowledged by Briar Rose, apparently due to her stint in rehab and being unable to access her social media. The article notes that—according to a close source—Briar Rose turned to drink after her father met Krystal, upset at no longer being the centre of his world.

It makes me frustrated that her team hasn't posted something as a response. She told me she doesn't control her own social media pages, but it would have taken two seconds for somebody on her team to make a post to offer a simple congratulations. It would have gone someway to stop the speculation that she wasn't replying because of rehab.

"Well, looks like you're getting to that three-parent family before me," I comment.

She snorts, and despite the news being about her family, she looks almost relieved.

"Oh, my mother or my father, which one is winning the race down the aisle?"

"Your father," I say, closing the article. I open my social media app and type in Krystal's name. Her page is wide open. The same photographs are there. Under the picture where she is flashing her engagement ring, there is the caption: *I can't wait for my big day. Daddy's going to spoil me rotten.*

"What?" Rose asks when I laugh.

"Oh, that won't last. She's all me-me-me, isn't she?"

I turn the phone to show her what I'm looking at. Rose takes the phone from me, looks at it and smiles.

"Don't be talking shit about my stepmum. I'm sure she'll be telling people at some point how she saved me from rehab."

"I don't get why your team won't respond to stop the speculation you're in rehab," I admit.

"Oh, well, they only ever post about brand-related things. When my parents split, I made it very clear that no social media posts could be made about them. I guess I should be grateful that they've listened."

"Except they're not protecting you. You're not in rehab. People shouldn't be reporting that you are," I argue.

"It's not the worst thing they could write about me," she mutters. Before I can ask her what she means, she shakes her head. "It's fine."

"Create your own social media profile now and tell everybody what you think," I suggest.

"Not worth my time. Besides, I think that me getting ready and us writing some music together would be a much better use of my time."

"Do you know what a better use of our time would be?" I ask.

"Enlighten me, o wise Indiana."

"A day off."

"I don't feel up to hiking or even walking today," she warns.

"Exactly. If you don't feel up to walking, then I vote we bring down the quilts, get on the sofa, watch some films, and eat some popcorn. For medicinal reasons, obviously."

"Obviously." She laughs. "Do we even have popcorn?"

"You seem to forget you can get anything delivered these days. Go get the quilts and leave the popcorn to me."

I take my phone back from her and look for a shop that does swift delivery as she leaves the room. I order popcorn, tortilla crisps, dip, a load of chocolate, some ice cream, and some premade sandwiches as something more substantial. I opt for doorstop delivery again. I love contactless delivery. Everything I've had delivered here has all been contactless, meaning I'm able to protect Rose's secret. I'm delighted that the notification says it'll be here within fifteen minutes.

Rose comes back with the quilts, huffing as she puts them onto the sofa. I feel bad that I asked her to get them instead of me, as she looks worn out now, but it reassures me that my suggestion of a relaxing day is the right one.

I put the television on, passing her my phone so she can search for a film for us to watch. We lapse into a comfortable silence, and I'm pretty sure she'll be asleep before we're halfway through.

***

"I really needed that," Rose comments. She gets up from the sofa and stretches, looking like a lithe cat. She groans a little as she stretches.

We spent most of the day on the sofa, so it's unsurprising that she seems stiff. We watched a franchise of films, back-to-back. We'd taken a break in the afternoon so Rose could have a shower before we ate tea and went back to the films. It's late evening, and though I've done nothing all day, I'm looking forward to an early night.

"You're welcome. We can get back to the music tomorrow. If you don't feel up to singing, we can just work on the music or the lyrics, what do you think?"

"I think you're an incredibly nice guy, Blake. I'm going to head up. I'll see you in the morning."

"Good night, Rose," I reply.

She gives me one last smile and then she heads upstairs. Both double quilts are on the sofa. I assume she's back to using the single quilt on her bed, but I carry both quilts upstairs just in case she wants one later. Her bedroom door is shut, so I fold the spare quilt up and leave it in the hallway in case she wants it in the night. I take my own quilt to my room and then go to the bathroom, getting myself ready for bed. It always surprises me how a day where I do nothing makes me more exhausted than a day where I've been energetic.

I crash on my bed, pulling the quilt around me. I pick up my phone and refresh the news site I read earlier. The article about Rose is still there, but now there are thousands of comments. I open the comments section, scrolling through them, skim reading and wincing.

There is so much judgement from the public. The general consensus is that it was inevitable Rose would end up in rehab. Somebody proclaims they believe Rose is addicted to cocaine, not alcohol. Another announces they're adamant it is heroin. Loads of people have commented that her dad is terrible for getting with somebody the same age as his daughter but still condemn her for being immature in how she's dealt with the situation. There are only a handful of comments supporting her, and this fact gives me an unsettled feeling in my stomach.

I care for Rose. Watching strangers tear her apart in the papers—almost relishing this supposed downfall she's having—is disgusting. I'm tempted to create a profile and set the record straight. I'm even at the point of saying fuck it and creating a statement on my own social media profile and my website in her defence, announcing to the world that we're making music together. I want to tell them she isn't in rehab, and that everybody should shut the fuck up. The only reason I don't is because I know it's a dangerous game to play with the media, and she doesn't want to tell anybody what we are doing. Though she won't tell me why, she wants to hide away from the world for a bit before coming back with a bang and our albums. Even though it's frustrating to watch the rumours about her circle around, I'll respect her wishes and keep quiet.

I shut down the site I was reading. The only thing I'm achieving by reading is making myself annoyed. They're never worth the paper they're printed on. I told my mother the same assessment when she chose to read a few comments to me when I saw her after my dad's article. I told her the comments should be ignored, but she insisted on calling my dad names as she read out people's judgement of our so-called fucked-up family.

Frustrated and looking for a distraction, I open my emails and look through them, trying to forget the papers. There are a few emails Maeve has forwarded to me. I'm going to have a stern word with her when she gets back from her holiday. She clearly doesn't know the meaning of the word downtime. Though when I read the last email—one sent this morning—I reject the notion of having a word with her about relaxing.

She's forwarded me information of a house being sold. It's in my hometown, in a gated community. It's set back from the other properties, and it looks spectacular. She's added a note that the house doesn't go for sale until February, but the seller is willing to negotiate directly if I'm interested rather than going on the open market. She's signed off the email with a comment that it's about time I put down roots, given I'm turning thirty. It seems perfect so I reply to tell her I'm interested, and that we'll sort it out closer to the time. She's right. I should have a home to call my own.

I switch to scrolling on the internet to find a present for Maeve for Christmas. I've already got her a gift, but she deserves something more, something extra special. I'm scrolling through the websites when there is a little knock on my bedroom door.

"Blake?" Rose sounds like she's been crying. I'm instantly alert.

"What's the matter?"

"Are you decent? Can I come in?"

"Yeah, sure," I call back to her, frowning as I wonder what has upset her. She opens the door and steps inside.

"I just...." she starts, standing awkwardly for a moment before she seems to dissolve into a noisy batch of tears.

I get out of bed, grateful that I'd put some pyjama bottoms on rather than sleeping naked, like I would at home. I cross the room to her and stand in front of her.

"What's happened? What's wrong?" I ask.

"Nothing. You'll think I'm a loser," she says, hiccupping.

"Never. Tell me what's wrong."

"I know it sounds lame, but I just wondered if it would be okay to have a hug. I didn't want to be alone." She looks at me with watery eyes and a pained expression.

"Oh, Red, you're not alone," I soothe.

I pull her into my arms, hugging her tightly as she weeps. She gives little silent sobs against me, her body shaking as she cries. It makes me feel like somebody has just punched me in the gut. I wish I could take all the pain away from her. She feels so small and fragile in my arms.

"Can I stay for a while?" she asks, her voice muffled against my chest.

"Of course," I reply, ignoring the voice in my head that reminds me I didn't want to complicate things, that at the start, I thought it would be weird to share a bedroom wall with her. I ignore it because right now, I know she needs somebody to be there for her, and I want to do that for her. Things have changed. We've gone from strangers to something more—people who care about one another.

"Thank you," she whispers. She steps around me, getting into my bed. I get in beside her and she turns to lie against my chest. Her cheeks are still damp.

"What upset you?" I coax.

"Nothing."

"I'm not an expert at anything, Red, but I'm pretty sure if you shared what is going on in your head, it'll go someway to helping you feel better," I murmur.

"No, I can't."

"You can tell me. I won't judge, I'll just listen, I promise."

"I can't. I'm sorry. I'm sorry." She starts to cry again. I hold her tightly. Again, her body shakes with the silent tears, tears that spill from her cheeks and onto my chest.

"It's okay, Red, it's okay. Whatever it is, it'll be okay, I promise," I soothe, and then as I don't know the best thing to say next, I start to sing to her. I sing some of my later music, song after song until she goes slack in my arms, falling asleep with tears still stained on her cheeks.

Chapter Sixteen

Rose

NOW

I wake up in Blake's bedroom, alone.

The first thought in my head is: *oh shit.*

Last night when I went to bed, I stupidly opened the online papers to read through the article about me. I couldn't stop reading the comments. One comment had struck me hard in the chest, like the words jumped from the page and thumped me. Some woman announced she would not allow her children to listen to my songs given I was a bad influence having landed in rehab. I'm not in rehab—and I've a lot of respect for people who are doing it to get their life back on track—but being judged in the media for something that isn't true is hard.

It's worse knowing that if my secrets get out, they're worse than rehab. The comments won't be about me suffering and needing help. It'll be carnage. I'll be over. Any plans I have for my career, I'll have torpedoed them out of the water. Endorsement deals will disappear. Acting roles will vanish. My concert sales will dwindle.

You can come back from rehab.

It's hard for a woman to come back from being an adulterer. Even if they were one unwittingly stupid and naïvely.

After reading the article and comments about me, I was in a low mood and stupidly decided to make it worse by reading the article Blake mentioned, the one about Hunter being at an amusement park with his children. There was a series of photographs of them all together. Hunter and Isla, pushing little Finlay in the pushchair, with Amelia holding on to Hunter's hand. Hunter, holding Finlay, giving his wife a break. Hunter, helping Amelia with her ice cream. Hunter and Isla, kissing passionately. Picture after picture with captions of Hunter being a doting father, a loving husband.

Caption after caption that I know are lies.

Can you claim innocence if you weren't aware the people you were hurting even existed? I didn't know about Isla. I sure as hell didn't know about their two children. Finlay is only four months old. Isla was pregnant when Hunter was busy sneaking across the country to be with me. I didn't have a clue. He wore no wedding ring. There was never even the merest hint from anybody—ever—that he was married, let alone with children.

They look so perfect in the papers. He's cultivated this new image of a perfect family man, but I know what he is really like. Being the only person in the world who truly knows who he really is makes me feel full of bitterness. He's a liar who hid everything about his real life, claiming what he wanted under a veil of deception.

How many times did he tell me he couldn't imagine being with another woman when he had a wife at home? A wife I had no idea about.

When the news broke about his family, he gave an interview to say Isla suffered from periods of anxiety and they agreed to keep her existence a secret for her mental health and to give their children some privacy. Now, she is apparently better and wants to support her husband as his stardom rises, far beyond any height they imagined. He even said the secrecy of her existence gave him so much comfort when he started to get more famous, knowing he could go home to her and live like things were normal. A normal, loving husband and father.

A normal, loving husband and father who had a mistress.

If anything between us becomes public, it will still be me who is assassinated in print, not him. He might face a little bit of heat at the start, but it won't last. He'll bounce back. They'll bounce back as a couple. They'll put on some united show together in the pictures. There will be some speculation if she went out without her wedding ring on, but then they will give interviews about how everything between them is so much stronger. The headlines would quote them that nobody could ever break their bond.

It will be a completely different experience for me.

I will be painted as the homewrecker who tried to break them apart. I'll be the one mentioned whenever they're pictured together and always painted in a bad light. If they did separate—if Isla couldn't forgive him—he'll still be eligible. He'll be portrayed a wounded bachelor that women want to heal, and I'll still be the homewrecker.

It'll always be my fault, because society has always judged women involved in affairs more harshly than they ever treat the men. A man is portrayed as weak, unable to resist the temptation. A woman is portrayed as the manipulative whore.

Nobody will care about what he did to me. They won't care about the lying, the deceit, the way he got rough, the way he spoke to me. These things are just the tip of the iceberg. I can't even allow myself to think about what else lies under the surface—the things I've tried to bury so far down but keep bubbling back up. They come to me in my dreams, pulling me from peaceless slumber, making me shake and cry out.

After reading the article, I spiralled—completely lost it. I just needed somebody to keep me grounded. Somebody to hold me in place when everything felt so uneasy. I tiptoed to Blake's room, got in his bed, let him hold me and sing to me. I've heard him sing hundreds of times, but last night, quietly singing me to sleep in a voice like warm honey and love song after love song on his lips, it felt different.

Now I'm alone in his bed, wondering if I've just ruined the best thing I have in my life.

I get out of Blake's bed. I head to the bathroom to shower, trying not to overreact. As I get dressed in my room, I think again about the choices I made last night, reprimanding myself. I didn't have to go to his room. I could have called Libby. She's the one who knows everything about Hunter. She told me to call her if I ever feel like I'm falling down a dark hole. Except it was Blake that I wanted. I wanted to feel his strong arms around me, feel the heat of his skin, hear his soothing voice.

More than wanted. It felt like I *needed* it.

There is part of me that maybe wanted more than comfort, and the idea terrifies me. We could ruin everything. *I* could ruin everything, if I haven't already. I have no idea how Blake is going to be with me today. He might feel so weird about what happened and decide to leave.

That idea terrifies me more.

I muster the courage to head downstairs. With every step down the stairs, my stomach twists further with apprehension. At the bottom step, I take a deep, steadying breath and then force myself to find him.

Blake is in the kitchen, so I sit at the table. He's making breakfast and the kitchen countertop is messy, with the half empty packets of sausage and bacon scattered on top, and the hob is filled with pans that are sizzling away.

"Morning," he says.

"Morning," I reply.

"I thought a mini fry-up would be good for breakfast. Do you want to make the coffee?"

I don't answer him. I just get up and start to make the coffee. Maybe he doesn't want to talk about last night and he's just going to pretend it didn't happen. Maybe he feels awkward. Maybe he never expected me to ask to get in his bed last night.

I put the coffee onto the table then grab the knives and forks from the drawer before sitting back down. I listen to him whistle. He sounds so cheerful and *normal*. Did I dream last night? I woke briefly in the middle of the night and his arms had still been around me, him sleeping soundly and his strong, firm body against mine. At some point, he woke up and left me in the bed.

I half expected—when I got into bed with him—that his soothing would have turned into something more between us. I thought he might smooth down my hair, kiss away my tears, let his hands wander across my body, under my clothes, and tell me he just wanted to make me feel better. I thought he might suggest we could be friends with benefits or just have one night of passion to help me feel better.

He did nothing. He didn't even skirt against the line.

I know as well as the next famous person that the reports in the media are often more elaborated than what has happened. Blake had even said it himself, that his lover-boy image is far from the truth. Maybe the reason he didn't do anything last night is because I'm not the type of person he wants to be with.

I look at him as he finishes making breakfast.

"Are you attracted to women?" I ask.

"What?" He turns to look at me. His expression is bemused. "Yes, I'm attracted to women."

"Do you have a girlfriend I don't know about?"

"Nope." He still looks bemused.

"Are you hung up on another woman? Is it Olive?" I wonder. She's the type of woman I can imagine Blake pining over.

"No." He laughs. "Any other questions? Or, rather, are you going to tell me the reason for these questions?" he asks, and I feel a little awkward.

"You didn't take a chance last night," I point out.

"Yeah, because I assumed you needed comfort, not because you needed somebody pressing their dick against you."

"I did. I mean.... No, I did need that, but...." My voice trails off. "Are you not attracted to me?"

"How come I feel like nothing I say is going to be the right answer?" he grumbles as he turns away from me and starts to put things onto the plates. "If

I say yes, then I'm the dick who is only here to take advantage of you, faking friendship and trying to work my way into your pants, right?"

"No. Just forget it. It was stupid of me to ask. It is fine if you're not attracted to me."

"I'm attracted to you, Red," he cuts in, turning to look at me again. I blink a couple of times in surprise.

"You are?"

"Yeah, I mean, you're an outrageously talented woman who is also beautiful, smart, sweet, and funny. You've the most beautiful eyes and smile I've ever seen, and my goodness, I love the sound of your laugh."

"So, what is the problem?"

"I'm just not going to be the guy who takes advantage of you."

Well, that was an answer I did not expect. I think of the five-year age gap between us. That's nothing for a couple of celebrities. In fact, it's more normal to have wider age gaps.

"If you're worried about the age gap, I did the math. It's acceptable." I grin at him.

"Acceptable math? Do tell." His tone is teasing.

"Half your age, plus seven. If they're over eighteen, per the math, it is acceptable."

"Well, I'm glad the math is on our side, but I meant your vulnerability. I've been with somebody before when they were trying to heal from something. It doesn't work out well for either party. I don't know what's got you rattled, but we should only consider something when you feel better."

"Sounds logical, I guess," I reply, and I can't help but feel a little disappointed.

"Unless I've misunderstood the situation, and you don't find me attractive, given you climbed into *my* bed, and *you* didn't do anything. If this is just a theoretical conversation...." Blake says, grinning even wider at me.

"Come on, Blake. You know you're like sex on a stick. You must know how attractive you are."

"In the same way you know you're attractive, sure. But not whether you, specifically, find me attractive." Blake shrugs.

"I do," I admit.

I'm not sure when these feelings snuck up on me, but it seems like they're here to stay and they're intense. The more I look at him, the more I wish he would wrap his strong arms around me again. I'm surprised my thoughts about him aren't written all over my face.

"So then," he says, putting a plate in front of me and one in front of his chair. He takes a seat and smiles at me. "Here's to you getting better and let us thank fuck the math is on our side."

"Can't argue with the numbers." I laugh.

"Do you want to talk about what upset you last night?" he asks. He cuts a sausage. He eats and doesn't seem to mind the silence while I think.

I know Blake doesn't like people who cheat or people who lie. I would never have looked twice at Hunter if I knew he was married. I sure as hell wouldn't have been anything but friendly with Hunter if I knew about his wife and children. That day in the hotel—when he asked me to do something fun with him—I would have politely declined and gone to find my mother. I certainly wouldn't have ended up in his hotel room, stripping out of my clothes.

I could tell Blake some of the story, that I was, unwittingly, with a married man, or I could keep it a secret. If I do that, I'm no better than what I teased him about, or what Hunter did. It would be an omission rather than a lie, but it would weigh on my heart. I just don't know if I can tell him everything. There are things I've only told Libby, and that was bad enough. Confessing things to Libby felt like I was spewing acid with every word I spoke, and I don't think I'm strong enough to do that again.

I clear my throat. "Can I maybe tell you tonight?"

"You don't have to tell me anything, if you don't want to," Blake replies easily.

"Can I tell you the things I like about you instead, given I didn't say it earlier?" I ask after another short silence.

"Sure," Blake says. He sounds like he doesn't mind either way, but I can see the small smile on his face.

"I like how you're so easy-going about everything. I like how true you are, how principled you are, how kind you are. You're incredibly gifted at song writing, no matter what you say. You have the most beautiful voice; I could listen to you for hours. I love the look you get on your face when you are holding your guitar. It's like you know you're in the exact right place in the universe. I like how I feel when you make me laugh, and how you look so happy that you were the one to make me laugh in the first place."

I stare at him when I finish talking, and for a moment he's quiet. I can tell he's trying to fight back a bigger smile.

"Well, Rose, you sure know how to flatter a guy."

"You know what else I like?" I ask.

"Go on."

"I like how well you cook." I grin as I cut a piece of my sausage.

"Eat up, Red." Blake laughs.

We eat our breakfast, and I can't help but feel the bubble of warmth in me now that I realise that I didn't throw everything away by going into his room last night. I ignore the pinch of panic and instead focus on the hope that the same is true, and he won't be disgusted when I tell him some of the things that led me here in the first place, seeking sanctuary from the storm.

***

"Blake?" I knock on his door. It's just gone eleven, we've been upstairs for the last twenty minutes, and I've been pacing my room, panicking.

The day was perfect. We worked on some songs, walked on the beach, and then cooked together. Although everything today has been things we've done since he arrived, now there have been added stolen glances and shy smiles between us. We haven't spoken about being attracted to each other since breakfast, but the lyrics we have played around with today have done the speaking for us.

Blake didn't ask me any questions about why I was upset the night before. He never pushed me to tell him anything given I had said I would tell him later. As I changed in my room and paced around for a while, I decided that now is that later. It is now or never. I owe him the truth. Some of it, at least.

"You can come in, I'm decent," Blake calls back.

I open his bedroom door. He looks anything but decent. I wonder if he has any idea how he looks. He's sat in bed, the covers over his legs. I can see he's wearing pyjama bottoms, but like last night, his chest is bare. I try not to get distracted by his firm muscles. Instead, I stare at the tattoo he has on his arm, the dragon that curls around and finishes on his chest. He looks amazing, and I'd quite happily get into his arms right now and never leave.

I force myself to focus my attention on what I've planned to say.

"Can we talk?"

"Of course."

I step into his room and make my way towards the bed. He doesn't bat an eyelid when I pull back the covers and get into the bed, sitting next to him. The bed is warm. I know it's because he probably has the electric blanket on to heat the bed before he goes to sleep, but part of me thinks it's just from his heat. He always feels a few degrees warmer than I am, or maybe just touching him affects me more than I've really realised.

"I'm afraid," I blurt out. I keep looking straight ahead of me rather than looking at him.

"What are you afraid of, Red?"

"I'm afraid if I tell you some things, you won't like what you hear. I'm afraid you'll leave. I'm afraid of ruining everything. I'm afraid to speak things I've kept hidden. But I'm afraid to keep it in." I take a deep breath between each sentence.

"Rose," Blake says, sighing and reaching for my hand to hold. "I don't think there is a single thing you could say that would make me leave."

I highly doubt that.

"Can I tell you things, without you asking for names?"

"Okay, but believe me when I tell you that you can tell me anything."

I take a deep breath. "It's about the person I was last involved with."

I feel the reassuring squeeze he gives me.

"Okay. What do you want to tell me?"

"It wasn't a good relationship. We weren't supposed to be together." I force the words out. I take a deep breath. "He was already involved with somebody else."

"He had a girlfriend?" Blake guesses. Oh, if only it were that simple. I shake my head. I look at him.

"Worse," I whisper.

"He was married?" Blake's eyes turn darker as he speaks.

"Yes, but it was worse than that."

"Tell me he didn't have kids." Blake sounds almost pleading.

"I didn't know about them, I swear," I gasp, fighting for breath as it feels like I'm going to pass out. This is much harder to talk about than I imagined it would be. I'm not sure if it is just because I'm talking about something I've kept hidden, or if I'm telling Blake. "I didn't know about any of them until it was too late. He kept them all a secret from me, I didn't know, I swear. I'd never have even looked twice at him if I had known, I swear. I didn't know."

"When did you find out?" Blake asks, his voice is gentle.

"Not until after it was over, and I've lived with the shame of it since," I cry.

I turn away from him because I can't bear to look at him now. I brace myself for him letting go of my hand, for him to walk out of the bedroom and leave our little hideaway. I'm prepared for the condemnation, the accusations, and the disappointment.

I'm prepared for everything I think I deserve.

Blake sighs. "This is the big secret you have been keeping. This is what has you hiding away from the world?"

"Yes." I sniffle, though it isn't everything. There's more, but I can't bring myself to say everything, not yet.

"Why are you the one feeling ashamed?" Blake asks softly. He squeezes my hand. "He was the one who was married. He is the one who lied to you."

"It doesn't make me feel any better. I feel used, dirty and ashamed."

"Okay, right," Blake starts. He shifts his body to angle himself, facing me directly. I wipe my eyes. "You need to put a stop to that, right now. He's the dick. He's the one who lied. He's the one who deserves the kick in the balls. You shouldn't feel dirty, at all."

"I could have destroyed their marriage."

"He is the one who stepped out on his wife. He is the one who lied, to her and to you. This is on him, Red."

"Maybe, but I'll be the one the media wants to lynch." I sniffle.

"If it ever came out, then I can be the one to be vocal about why they're full of shit."

"Nobody would believe if I said I didn't know."

"I believe you. This is who you shouted about, wasn't it, on the hike? When you shouted that sentence about somebody cheating?"

"Yes," I admit.

"I thought it was about your dad, but it makes sense now."

"I hate that I let it happen."

"You didn't know, Rose. You didn't walk into an affair with your eyes wide open and knowing about the other people. He lied to you."

"I still feel ashamed."

"This is the secret you're afraid of, isn't it, afraid that everything could become public?"

"I don't want to have to defend myself or talk about it in the media. It's not like it was a loving relationship. I was going through some stuff in life and felt reckless. I fell for the first man who seemed to be offering me some fun, somebody who seemed to see me as me for the first time in my life. I didn't see through it all, didn't realise that all he was really offering was sex. I misunderstood everything. For the first couple of months, it was a nice distraction from life and what was going on, then things changed, and it wasn't... normal. He didn't treat me well, and it took me a while to wise up and for it to be over."

"Do you want to tell me what you mean by 'not normal'?" Blake asks, voice quiet.

It's like there's a movie reel in my mind of the times Hunter went too far. The times his hands were on me, and he didn't recognise I was trying to stop him. The times it felt like my struggling was something that spurred him on rather than made him stop in his tracks. The times I'd dig my nails into his skin in a desperate attempt to get his attention, but he only grabbed me harder. The times he held his hand over my mouth so I couldn't protest. The time I thought *"you're going to die"* when he had used his forearm across my throat, leaving me gasping afterwards.

The disastrous way it finally ended.

The things he said to me after the hospital.

I shake my head to get the images to stop. I look again at Blake.

"I don't think I'm ready to talk about that yet. Is that okay?"

"Of course it is okay. Whenever you want to talk about it, I'm here," Blake promises.

"I want to tell you, but I'm not ready, I'm sorry."

"There's no rush, Rose, but whenever you want to talk, I'm here. I promise."

"Can I stay in here again tonight?" I ask.

"Sure." Blake smiles.

He leans over to switch the electric blanket off. I'm grateful because I'm wearing thermal pyjamas and starting to feel like toast, though that could be partly because I've been talking about some of my secrets. Blake lies on the bed, holding an arm out for me. I lie against his chest. I trace my fingers up and around his dragon tattoo, down the dragon face that finishes on his chest.

"I love this tattoo," I murmur. "They symbolise protection, right?"

"Among other things," he replies.

"Did it take long to complete?"

"A couple of sessions. I keep meaning to get another one."

"Why haven't you?"

"Time just seemed to fly by, I was always on the go, you know what I mean?"

"Yeah, I know. This is the first time in a long time that I've stood still. Running away from everything was my only option, and it was scary at first, but it's been good, being away from the pressure. I know it's all waiting for me when I choose to go back out there, but for now, I'm just enjoying being free to do what I want with the day, not being micromanaged."

"Nobody dragging us off for interview after interview, nobody driving us from arena to arena," Blake comments.

"Nobody telling us to watch what we eat," I murmur. He squeezes me tighter.

"Nobody telling us we're not good enough."

"Nobody talking at us, rather than to us."

"Maybe we should just hide away here forever," Blake suggests.

"That sounds nice." I sigh. I don't think there is anywhere else in the world I would rather be than right here, wrapped in his arms in this little hideaway cottage.

"It sounds perfect," Blake echoes.

I fall quiet. I keep my fingers tracing over the face of the dragon, and he sighs contentedly. After a while—like last night—he starts to sing quietly, and it isn't long until I'm falling asleep, feeling protected in his arms, listening to the sound of love songs on his lips.

Chapter Seventeen

Blake

NOW

"October is really flying by, don't you think?" Rose comments over breakfast. I smile at her.

"Time flies when you're having fun," I joke.

She nudges against me and calls me an idiot, making me smile because I love when she's like this. She seems completely at ease with me, and she seems much happier than the day I first arrived. It makes me feel weirdly happy to know she is.

It's been a couple of weeks since the first night Rose came into my room. She's slept in my bed ever since. She always goes to her room first for a bit, but then she knocks on my bedroom door, smiling as she gets into my bed.

Nothing has happened between us. We just lie together, hold one another, and talk before we fall asleep. Nothing else.

Nothing, yet.

I'm sure she wonders why I haven't tried anything with her or wonders how long I can keep up my assertion that I'm not going to push her for anything. It wouldn't surprise me if she thinks I'm only saying it. Based on the past experiences she's told me about, the measuring stick she has for men isn't high. She probably assumes bad behaviour is the norm. I want to show her that they were the exceptions, not the norm. I want her to see how she should be treated by men in the future, so that no man can ever claim their actions towards her are normal, something that all men would do.

I told her that first morning that I wasn't going to take advantage of her, and I meant it. I don't think there is anything in the world I want to protect more than her. If I had to make a list of the top things I'd defend, Rose's name would take every slot.

She hasn't said much more about the person she was with—the guy who lied to her—and I haven't asked her questions. I get the sense that he didn't treat her well, the lying and betrayal aside. It's clear he hurt her. It's clear something happened that she doesn't want to tell me, yet.

I'll give her all the time she needs. Stepping forward with Rose, that is something I want to do right. I know she hasn't been in the right frame of mind to do anything further than the cuddles in bed before sleep. If all she can do is find comfort in my embrace at nighttime, then I'll give her that. I'll help her heal and feel safe. More than feel it—I want her to know she is safe. With every night that passes, I feel like she is healing. I'm sure it's driven by the peace she's had, being out of the spotlight, but I like to think our shared nights are helping, too.

She doesn't cry at night now. When she lies in my arms, she traces her fingers across my tattoo. She whispers things into the darkness and tells me she feels content.

We still talk about everything together, both in the day between other activities and long into the night. She tells me more about her parents, her upbringing, her hopes for the future. She asked me about my regrets in life, and I told her I regret the times I was immature, when I should have made better choices. She asked me one morning about why I said I deserved it when Olive broke up with me, so I told her that I made a stupid choice and wasn't there when she needed me. She almost seemed relieved that it was my immaturity that led to it and smiled affectionately when I told her I hope I've changed.

"Are you going to let me into the secret for today?" she asks, distracting me from my thinking.

Every day, between creating new songs, we have spent time doing something fun. We have had more time on the bike, more hikes, more running and messing around on the beach. There have been play fights and jokes, hysterical laughter and smiles, competitive card games, and shared bottles of wine before bed. We have watched a long list of films, popular ones she missed out on when starting out in the business, as well as those cheesy disaster movies that she loves to watch.

Today I've organised a surprise that will keep us busy for the day. I've been keeping quiet about what it is, and she's been trying to get the information out of me all morning.

"Nope." I laugh. I glance at the clock. "Only an hour to wait."

"I'm not used to having to wait," she grumbles.

"There is something to say about delayed gratification, no?" I joke. Her cheeks flush scarlet and she looks at me, a smile on her lips.

I want to kiss her.

"Unless you get wound so tightly it's like a rubber band snapping," she replies.

"Still talking about today's surprise?" I tease.

"Obviously." She somehow makes the word sound like it has twenty syllables.

"Eat up. I reckon you'll find the time goes faster if we sit and go through the songs to split them into the potential albums."

"Fine, we can start working through them now," she suggests.

I lean to grab the notebooks from the countertop, putting them on the table between us. We've written over forty songs together. For both of us, it's been like the words won't be contained. As soon as we pick up a pen, there seem to be words on the pages. At the end of last month—in my rented flat before joining Rose—I was desperate for inspiration. What I hadn't realised was that I was searching for her. Everything I write around her feels like magic, and her lyrics are stunning. Forty beautiful love songs, but I feel like we could write double.

There's something about Rose that makes me feel like I'm at the top of my game.

"Are there any you want to keep back for a later album? Even if we both released an extended album, we have too many tracks for two albums," I say.

"I love them all. It's still an even split between your classification of longing and love songs. Do you still want to split by that category?"

"Yeah, if that is okay with you."

"My biggest hurdle is getting this by my management team. They might object given it's so different to what I've been allowed to release in the past." Rose shrugs like it doesn't bother her, but there is frustration written all over her face.

"We'll go to the label together. Not to big us up, Red, but we are their biggest selling artists, and these tracks are great. I'm going to do whatever it takes to get these out there. I don't care if we have to start busking in the street, getting filmed and going viral until the fans are screaming for the album. If that is what it takes, I'll do it. We'll get your songs out," I vow.

"Well, first, let's agree who gets which song on their album, and then agree which tracks we'll feature on for the other album. We'll do our eighteen favourites, for an extended album. The remaining, we can divide up later."

"This is going to take longer than the hour."

"I've nothing better to do tomorrow, unless you have another plan you won't tell me about." She smiles.

Rose tucks her hair behind her ears then starts looking over the notebook, her brow furrowed in concentration. She changed her hair colour again last week. She ordered some hair dye remover, stripping the dark out of her hair and taking her back to her natural colour, or as close as she could get with products at home. She hadn't told me what she was doing, just that she was going to hog the bathroom for a while. When she came downstairs later—her hair back to a honey blonde—she gestured at it shyly, asking me if it looked okay.

She told me that night when we were in bed that she was feeling more like herself.

We work in silence for a while, splitting the tracks between us. Rose scribbles down potentials for the split of the songs and then she stops, frowning.

"What's up?" I ask.

"I know we earmarked this one as mine when we wrote it, but I think it suits your voice more."

She taps the pen against the title of the song she has stopped at. It's a ballad, one we have already decided sits better with one singer with no second singer to complement the main vocals. It is one of the songs I love to hear her playing around with. She sounds like an angel when she sings this. Though we have only sung it to music on the guitar, I can imagine her singing this on stage, playing the music on her piano.

"Put it in the maybe pile for now," I suggest. I'm sure once we get in the studio, we can both record a version and she'll see that it suits her perfectly, or maybe she'll convince me that it suits me.

We carry on working on the track split until there is a knock on the front door. Rose looks at me, startled.

"What the hell?" she asks.

"Relax, this is the surprise. This is a friend of a friend, who has already agreed to keep the details of our meeting confidential until a later date, at our choosing," I reassure her. She nods slowly.

"I trust you," she says.

"Good, because I wouldn't do anything to jeopardise what we have going here," I remind her.

"I know that."

I offer her a hand so we can walk together through to the living room. I push the living room door open for her so she can go sit down while I open the front door.

"Blake, it's good to see you, man," Kirsty says when I open the front door. I help her into the house with her things.

"How are you, Kirsty? Theo says you have opened a new studio?"

"Yeah, but still happy to do home sessions, for those who need it." Kirsty laughs. I walk into the living room with her.

"Rose, this is Kirsty. Kirsty, Rose." I introduce the two of them.

"Nice to meet you, Rose." Kirsty smiles. She gives no indication that she's surprised by who Rose is, but she is used to meeting celebrities in confidence.

"Nice to meet you, too," Rose replies. She looks curiously at what Kirsty is holding. Kirsty puts her kit down. She dusts her hands together and smiles.

"Right, so, who is getting tattooed first?"

I laugh at the look on Rose's face. "Relax, Red, it's me, you are optional. Kirsty is booked for all day if needed. It's up to you if you want to expand that cheesy book quote tattoo you have on your ass."

"I do not have a tattoo on my ass." Rose laughs. She looks at Kirsty. "I really don't."

"Hey, I don't judge. I'm just here to doodle." Kirsty grins.

"What are you having?" Rose turns her attention to me.

"A cartoon bird on my ass, obviously." I grin at her.

"I was *joking*."

"Usually, people are really drunk before they start the talk of tattoos on the ass, especially ones of cartoon characters." Kirsty laughs. "Where are you getting it done, Blake?"

"My arm. Still the same design we have talked about," I say to Kirsty as I take a seat on the armchair. Rose disappears for a minute then returns with a chair from the kitchen for Kirsty to sit on. Kirsty busies herself taking things out of her kit, getting everything set up.

"What design is it?" Rose asks, standing next to me.

I pull my phone from my pocket and scroll through my picture reel to find the ones I've sent to Kirsty. It's a mandala design. The plan is for it to be black ink only. Kirsty and I have agreed the tattoo will be done in sections so at each session it will still look complete, but when the next section is added, it will look cohesive.

"What do you think?" I ask.

She smiles back at me and then sits down on the sofa. "That is going to look awesome."

"Right, let's get started," Kirsty suggests. I settle back in the seat.

"I feel like I'm getting an insight into your pain threshold," Rose muses as Kirsty rummages through her things and gets everything organised.

"I have a high pain threshold," I shoot back.

"I am going to make a note of every time you wince or flinch," she teases.

"You only get to tease if you put yourself though a tattoo as well," I counter.

"Maybe. I'll have a think when you're getting yours done. I've never watched anybody get a tattoo before," Rose replies.

"Don't pass out on me. If you thud to the floor and startle Kirsty, and I end up with some dodgy line on my arm, you'll be the one I blame," I joke.

"I won't pass out." Rose laughs.

"First, I'm a professional, I can tattoo through anything," Kirsty cuts in, a big grin on her face. I know her work is excellent. "Second, I've seen people pass out before, and it always makes me laugh when it's the big, strong man who gets faint and woozy."

"I'll do my best to stay upright if Rose gets one done." I grin at them both.

"You're not watching me get tattooed if I get one," Rose protests. I glance at Kirsty.

"See, just confirming my suspicion that she has something embarrassing tattooed over her ass and wants you to do a cover-up." I look back at Rose.

"Are you just trying to get an opportunity to check out my ass, Indiana?" she says, smirking slightly. Her eyes are twinkling and she looks so relaxed.

I wink at her, and she stares back at me. She's still relaxed, but there is something else in her expression now, something that almost looks like temptation.

"So, who is going to tell me what you two are doing, holed up in the back-arse of nowhere?" Kirsty chuckles, breaking the concentration between us.

"I'll talk. That way, Blake can focus on his breathing if he feels like he'll pass out when you're working," Rose jokes.

I laugh and get comfortable. I fall silent, listening to the two of them chatter, smiling to myself at the relaxed tone Rose has when she talks.

***

"So, Rose, what are you thinking?" Kirsty asks as she finishes wrapping the bandage around the tattoo just finished on my arm.

"If you want it on your backside, I'll make myself scarce for you." I grin at Rose as I get up from the chair. I stretch slightly.

"You're so obsessed with the ass, Indiana," Rose quips.

I laugh. "I'll be in the kitchen."

I leave the two of them in the living room, going into the kitchen to put the kettle on. My arm is sore, but I love the design Kirsty has done so far. I've been meaning to get this tattoo started for months. I admire the design through the clear bandage Kirsty has put on. It's supposed to protect the skin through the initial healing of the tattoo.

I hear the buzz of the tattoo equipment from the living room. I wonder what Rose is having done. I wonder where she is having it done.

I drink a cup of coffee while I wait for them to be finished. The noises from the living room stop for a while and I assume they're done, but then the sound starts again. I wonder if Rose is having something colourful done.

When the sounds stop again and it remains silent, I boil the kettle again so I can make us all a drink. Kirsty and Rose walk into the kitchen just as the kettle finishes boiling.

"All done?" I ask.

"Done for today. I'll message you to arrange a time for the next section of your design, give it a bit of time for this part to heal first," Kirsty suggests.

"Take the cost of Rose's tattoos from my tab," I suggest, given I've paid already for the proposed artwork I'm getting, plus another that I'm planning across my chest.

"Okay, will do. I'm going to hit the road. When you're ready to debut those designs, let me know, as I'll put them on my pages." Kirsty smiles. Her socials are filled with famous people she has tattooed.

"Are you sure you don't want to stay for a coffee, or some food?" I ask. I glance at the clock. The time has flown by.

"I'm sure. I'll see you both soon, thanks for letting me loose on your skin." Kirsty grins. With that, she walks down the hall to get her things. I hear the front door shut.

"What did you go for in the end?" I ask Rose. I look at her.

"I got two small ones," she replies, and she points in turn to each of her ears. "Behind each ear," she adds.

"Damn, Red, you're hardcore. That's supposed to hurt."

"Like a son of a bitch." Rose laughs. "I didn't pass out though, so all good."

"Can I see?"

She steps closer to me. She pulls at her left earlobe with one hand, sweeping her hair out of the way with her other hand. Behind this ear, under the clear bandage, I can see that she has the phases of the moon. There are eight small tattoos with the moon at various stages.

"What do you think?"

"I love it," I reply. She straightens up and steps to the kettle.

"What about the other?" I laugh. I step closer to her and can see the top layer of the bandage hasn't been removed.

"I want to keep it a surprise, for a bit, until the bandage is ready to come off," Rose explains.

"You know I'm now curious as fuck what you've had done there." I laugh.

"As somebody said, there is something to say about delayed gratification, no?" she teases.

"Touché, Red, touché."

She laughs with me as she finishes making us both a coffee. She asks me what we're making for tea together and I run through the options, still curious about what she's had tattooed onto her skin.

***

"Are you ready?" Rose asks.

She sits in front of me, her fingers poised at the edge of the bandage over my tattoo. It's been days since I had the tattoo done, so the bandage needs to come off.

"Go for it."

"Shall I do it gently or just whip it off."

"Maybe don't talk about whipping stuff off, Red." I laugh.

Last night, she ditched the thermal pyjamas when coming into the bedroom, instead sleeping in a pair of shorts and a vest top. She told me it was too warm in my room for thermals, but her feet had been cold when they had pressed against me, so I'm not entirely convinced.

"Okay, for that...." Rose starts, and she whips the clear bandage from my skin.

"Fuck, that feels like you've just waxed my arm," I complain.

"You're such a baby," she says. She takes the washcloth from one of the bowls she'd set on the table between us. She washes across my tattoo. "It's a great tattoo, Blake."

"I'm pleased with it. I can't wait for it to be finished."

"I don't think I'll have another when you add to this one. I think my manager will have a fit when he sees these two new ones." Rose shrugs.

"You don't regret them, do you?"

"No, of course not. I should be allowed to have a tattoo without being made to feel like it is a crime, which is exactly how they reacted when they saw I had the tattoo on my stomach. I'm not sure who went more apocalyptic, my mother or my manager," Rose explains.

"Your dragonfly," I start. She looks at me, expectantly.

"Yeah?"

"The semicolon," I say. She seems to understand what I'm wondering without me having to ask.

"I had a brief time where I felt like I wanted to give up on everything. I didn't. The tattoo reminds me I'm strong, even if I sometimes don't feel like it."

"You are strong. Much stronger than you think you are," I reply.

"Maybe," she says, shrugging. I've learnt this is the way she indicates she wants the topic of conversation to change direction.

"Are you ready for me to take the plasters from yours?" I ask, pivoting the conversation slightly because she doesn't look like she's enjoying the route the conversation is going in.

"Yep." Rose switches around in her seat so I can get to behind her left ear, the tattoo she has of the phases of the moon. I remove the plaster carefully then take the cloth from the second bowl to clean the skin behind her ear.

"Perfect," I say. She twists in her seat again so I can get to the cover behind her right ear. This one makes me curious. I've been wondering what it is for days.

"I hope you aren't offended by this one," Rose says, and she sounds nervous.

"Why would I be offended? You haven't got a gang tattoo, have you?"

"No." She giggles. I focus on what we are talking about, not how her giggle makes me react. I've always liked her laugh, but now when she giggles, I feel like it comes from genuine joy and happiness rather than nervousness like it had felt in the beginning.

"A string of swear words?" I guess.

"Nope." Another giggled response.

"Lyrics from Luka Haycox?" I suggest, naming the up-and-coming artist who has been bandied around in the papers as my replacement in the popularity contests.

"Absolutely not. He doesn't even write his own music." She sounds scandalised.

"I know, I wrote a couple of his songs." I laugh. At this, she twists her head to look at me better.

"Seriously?"

"Yep, he knocked me off the number one spot with a song I wrote for him." I smile at her.

"Well, maybe I'd consider getting some of the lyrics tattooed on me now." She smiles back.

"Come on, Red, you're putting this off now."

"Okay, well, I'm still going to hope you aren't offended." Rose shrugs, and she turns herself around again.

I put my fingertips against the bandage. All I can see through the outer layer that Rose had kept on is that the tattoo is in black ink. I pull gently at the bandage to remove it, and then I stare. Curved around the back of her right ear, starting at the highest point, twisting down around the ear and finishing at her lobe, is a miniature version of the dragon tattoo I have on my arm.

"Wow." I breathe out the word. She sits, almost rigid, in the chair and doesn't look at me.

"I know it's your tattoo, but I've spent so long looking at it, tracing my fingers over it, and I just wanted to replicate it on me, even if it is only a small one. Do you mind?" she asks.

I take the cloth and gently wipe at the skin behind her ear. Some of the water rolls down her neck. I dab at the skin with a dry cloth.

I clear my throat. "I don't mind," I say.

My voice sounds a lot hoarser than I was aiming for. I reach out to touch the skin near the tattoo, careful not to touch where the skin is healing. I let my finger follow the curve behind her ear and down the side of her neck. I hear the intake of her breath. I lean forward.

"Do you like it?" Rose whispers. She remains completely still on her chair.

I know my tattoo isn't unique, but there is something about Rose's choice to have it replicated on her skin that makes me feel fuzzy and warm. To me, it feels almost as intimate as if she chose to tattoo my name on her skin.

The awed feeling overwhelms me. I'm so close to her that I can smell her shampoo. I can't stop myself from leaning closer still and letting my lips graze across the side of her neck.

"Yes, Rose, I like it," I say between kisses, still feeling awed.

"I like it, too."

Rose moves slightly in her seat now, and I'm not sure she is still talking about the tattoo. She leans closer towards me, and everything else in the world seems to melt away. It's just me, Rose, the thick air between us, the thump of my heart.

Her lips are parted slightly. I don't think I've ever wanted to kiss anybody more than Rose in this moment right now.

Rose is the one to bridge the gap between us, but the second our lips meet, it's like we've been doing this forever, like we're designed to be together. I don't know which of us moves first, but one moment we are on separate chairs, then she's on my knee. One second my hands were by my side, the next they're cupping her face. One second there is air in the world, the next, it's just heat and fire and the feel of her tongue on mine.

Her fingers curl into my hair, clutching at the strands, and, oh fuck, it feels so good. Our kiss deepens and she lets go of my hair, her hands dropping to around my back, her fingernails trailing lightly across my skin. If I thought that her fingers in my hair felt good, this is a new, next-level sensation.

It is Rose that pulls away. She still has her arms around me, remains sitting in my lap. She looks at me, and her eyes look like they're shining with excitement.

"Oh my," she says, sounding slightly dazed.

"Oh my," I repeat, because I am too damn stunned to think of anything else.

"I think I want to do that all day."

"I can't think of anything better," I murmur, feeling like I've got a little bit of control back over my words. My thumb strokes across her cheek.

"In the living room, where we can get more comfortable," she suggests.

She gets up, holding out a hand for me. I get up and we walk to the living room, hand in hand. She pulls me towards the sofa, where we fall together, a tangle of limbs and lips, heat and hope.

Chapter Eighteen

Rose

NOW

I pace around my bedroom, mustering up the courage. It's the eve before our shared birthday. Blake and I have kissed what feels like a million times since we first kissed in the kitchen. That day, spending the whole afternoon kissing on the sofa, was absolute bliss. We kissed until my lips felt swollen. The whole time we kissed, his hands had been on my face, or in my hair, or lightly trailing down my arms. Heavenly touches, but still letting me take charge with how far things could progress.

I love his kisses. They're like divine gifts. He somehow kisses me in a way that is hungry but slow, in a way that screams we have all the time in the world to enjoy this, laced with a desperation of how much he enjoys them. When Blake kisses me, it doesn't feel like a cursory step to take until pushing onto a more intimate moment. Instead, the kisses feel like he's arrived at a destination he wants to set up camp in.

Sometimes, he kisses me against the countertop when we cook dinner. He'll walk past me, smile, and then wrap his arms around me to pull me closer and then kiss me slowly until I feel like I don't know how to breathe. Sometimes, I pull myself up onto the kitchen counter so I can sit down when I pull him closer to me. Kiss after kiss until the oven timer beeps, dinner cooked, but not the thing I'm hungry for anymore.

I feel so comfortable with him, so at ease, so happy. When he touches me, I feel electrified, full of energy, full of joy. When he kisses me, I understand what those cheesy romance books mean about melting into a puddle. Everything is so wonderful, so perfect, but I want more. I want him. I want all of him.

Blake told me he didn't want to take advantage of my vulnerability, and I think he needs me to show him I'm not vulnerable. I may have been a mess when he arrived here, but I'm not that same person anymore. I feel stronger, and I know that being around him has gone a long way to making me feel like that. Not only do I feel stronger, but I feel I'm ready to be intimate with a man again.

After everything happened with Hunter, the idea of having another man touch me made me want to vomit. Not because I craved Hunter's touch instead, but because I hated the idea another man could deceive me or treat me the way he did. After everything blew up, I spent some time trying to understand why I kept going back into his bed. I would lie in bed, unable to sleep, tormenting myself with the way I acted, scared that I could fall into the same situation with another man.

I know in my heart—Blake is *nothing* like Hunter.

I'm ready to take that step with him.

If Blake needs me to show him it's okay for us to take the next step, then tonight is when I'm going to make that move.

I don't know about him, but I might explode if I don't.

I glance down at my chosen outfit again. The clothes Libby had packed in my "hide away from the world" suitcase don't exactly scream "I'm trying to seduce you," and walking into his bedroom with no clothes on felt like it would be too brazen. Feeling stuck in a predicament, I ordered some things earlier in the week. I used the prepaid credit card Libby gave me. I'm sure that splurging on sexy underwear wasn't exactly how she imagined me using the card, but I was grateful to have it.

After trying on what felt like a million pieces, I've settled on a black silk slip with a lacy pattern on it. I abandoned the idea of the stockings and suspenders. I've stuffed back into the box the elaborate bras and corsets. I like this, I like how I feel in it, and I'm sure all Blake really needs from me is the confirmation that I want to take this step with him.

It's cold as anything tonight so I grab the silk robe that I added to my order. In the pocket of the robe is a box of condoms. You really can get anything delivered to you. I haven't discussed preferences with Blake. I'm covered by the contraceptive shot I had before I got here, but I want to give him the option. I know I'm okay because I got tested after Hunter. When you realise the man that you're having sex with is having sex with you outside his marriage, it isn't too far of a stretch in the imagination to understand there are likely other women, too.

I force thoughts of Hunter out of my mind. There is a part of me that wishes I could set fire to every memory of him, of what he did to me, of what happened at the end. I don't want to think of him a second more, certainly not tonight. I'm determined not to let thoughts of him taint my night with Blake.

I slip the robe on, leaving it unfastened so my slip is on display. I take a deep breath and walk down the hallway to Blake's bedroom. The door is open. He's on the bed, chest bare. He's reading the book that I started reading the day he went to see his mum. I haven't finished reading it, but sometimes he reads pages to me when I tell him I'm too tired to read. The book is boring as hell, but I'd probably listen to Blake read an instruction manual and find his voice beautiful.

"Hey," I say from his bedroom door. I let the robe fall a little down my shoulders and watch his expression as he looks me up and down. He seems to have forgotten he was holding a book, as it falls to the floor with a clatter.

"Smooth, Blake," he mutters, and somehow it makes my whole body warm, how endearing he is.

"Good to know I can be a distraction." I laugh.

He smiles. "Red, you've been my distraction for weeks."

I step into the bedroom. I want to rush into the covers, into his arms, but I force myself to take it slowly because I want him to know I'm not rushing into this. I make my way to the bed, on his side. Usually, I get into the bed on the opposite side. I slip the robe from my arms, shivering slightly as the silk moves across the bare skin of my arms. I put the robe onto the bedside table and then pull the covers from his lap. I get into the bed, straddling his lap. He gives a sharp intake of breath. I lean forward to kiss him.

"Thank you for being patient. I'm better," I whisper to him when I pull away. "I want you."

"Are you sure?" he murmurs. He kisses me again and my brain screams yes, now. I could ignore his comment and just let my hands wander to demonstrate what I feel, but I know I need to answer properly. I'm not leaving this to misinterpretations or for him to not know exactly what I feel. I look at him.

"I'm covered by the hormone shot, and I got tested after my last relationship, but I have condoms in my pocket if you prefer to use them. If you want me, if you want this, I'm ready, Blake," I murmur.

"Oh, Rose." His voice is almost a growl as he answers.

He kisses me deeply in that luxurious way he kisses, leaving me feeling heady and punch-drunk when he pulls away. I can feel his arousal under me. He lifts my hips then we're twisted together, and he settles me onto the mattress. He leans on one arm, staring down at me with a fierce expression on his face, like he thinks I'm made of spun sugar and it's his job to protect me.

Not just that, but that he *wants* to protect me.

Blake's other hand falls on my hip, skimming upwards, taking the slip with it. His hand touches against my bare hip, and his eyes seem to darken when it is clear I don't have underwear on. His fingers travel further up, tickling me slightly where his fingertips are calloused from guitar playing. He skims over the silk of the slip, caressing my waist before going further up. The pad of his thumb grazes my nipple, then his hand skims up the side of my neck before resting on the side of my face, gently caressing my cheek. His lips return to mine, kissing me until I want to beg him for more. His lips move across my face, following my jawbone, down my throat, then my body. He kisses down my stomach, then I feel the silk of my slip as he pushes it upwards. He kisses from hip to hip, then down to the top of my thigh. I let my legs relax, giving him better access, and then his mouth slants over my clitoris. The sound I make is undignified but impossible to stop. It's been a long time since anybody did this to me and longer still since anybody did it so gently, seemingly only intent on giving me pleasure.

It feels like heaven, and I don't feel like I'm in control of my body anymore. He's gentle but relentless, taking little cues from the way I react so he knows when to move slightly, when to apply a bit more pressure. My hands reach for him, blindly, just because I cannot stand the idea of not touching him somewhere. It's his hand that connects to mine, fingers linking with mine as he carries on. His tongue teases in a series of sinful sucks and luxurious licks until I feel the familiar stirrings building up inside me. I realise I'm clutching his fingers like they're my life ring, but I can't stop. I grip him tightly as I climax, and for a second, I'm sure I lose my vision.

"Wow," I whisper once I've caught my breath. Blake kisses his way back up my body, chuckling slightly.

"I'll take a wow."

"How about I give you your own wow instead?" I shift my position on the bed, planning on reciprocating, but he reaches for my hand instead.

"If you do that, this is going to be over way too soon, and you won't be saying wow."

"You're skipping your starter for the main course?" I tease.

"I've been imagining this since the first time we kissed, Red, I've skipped nothing." Blake smiles.

"I want to be on top," I say as I push gently against his chest so that he lies on the bed. I'm not ready to give him that control yet, to feel his weight above me, to make myself feel completely vulnerable. I trust Blake—with my life—but I want to do this without any flicker of a reminder of how things had been in the past. I want this to feel special and new, without my mind wandering to previous experiences.

"I had a full check-up when getting tested for my kidney, and I haven't been with anybody since, but if you prefer to open those condoms, that's fine with me," Blake says.

I shake my head. If we don't need them, I don't want them. I want to feel all of him. I pull his pyjama bottoms down his legs, my hands running down his firm thighs, feeling his muscles. Once he is naked, I straddle him again. I shift my hips against him. He groans a little.

"Is this what you imagined?" I ask, moving myself up against the length of his cock, watching his expression, his eyes going darker.

"This is infinitely much better than I've imagined during my cold showers this week."

"No wonder I've always had an abundance of hot water." I giggle. I move against him again and he closes his eyes. His breathing is slightly ragged.

"Don't think I didn't notice that tattoo on your hip, Red," he says, but then I lift my body and reach to guide him into me, and all his words cease. My words disappear, too. All there is in the world are our bodies, designed to fit perfectly together, finally slotting into a space it feels like they should have always occupied.

Blake's hands fall to my hips, guiding me, but he lets me set the pace between us. I move above him, head back slightly, not sure if I want to go faster, because I want to experience the bliss again, or slower, because I never want this to end.

Blake sits upright, slipping his arms around me. He pulls my slip up and over my head, dipping his head to my right breast, his tongue grazing against the nipple, then sucking a little harder when he hears me groan. I move above him, already feeling at breaking point. My hands are around his back, feeling his muscles moving under my fingertips as he moves with me, pushing me to higher levels of bliss. I love every thrust, every touch, every kiss he gives.

I feel like magnesium being exposed to a flame, like I'm burning brightly and about to combust, setting fire to everything around me. I hold tightly to Blake, our skin slick with sweat.

"Like that," I pant out as his thumb finds its way to my clitoris. Blake doesn't break stride, doesn't do anything to change the rhythm or pressure and seconds later I'm losing control, my eyes screwed shut, not sure if the *"oh my God, oh my God, oh my God,"* is only contained in my head, or if I've shouted it out loud.

I feel the impact of Blake's orgasm, the way his muscles tense under me, the way he grips me a little tighter as he spills into me. I hear it, too, the low groan he gives slightly louder than my own ragged breathing.

I wait until I feel his thigh muscles untighten under me, then I slowly open my eyes. He's staring at me with an expression of wonder and amazement on his face. I'm sure I've the same look of awe on my own face. I thought—when I was with Hunter—that the sex had started with passion, that it was amazing, but now, with Blake, this feels like so much more.

This feels like transcendence, like our souls have fused together. I don't ever want to let go.

"There are not enough cold showers in the world that will take this out of my head, Rose. That was.... That was everything," he murmurs against my ear.

I want to reply, but I can't find any coherent words in my head to start. Instead, I stay in that position, letting him kiss me, slowly feeling my brain connecting again. It's like every kiss he gives makes another neuron fire properly. I don't care that we're both sweaty; I don't care that both of us have skin that feels heated a few degrees more than normal. All I focus on is his lips on mine, and the connection we have.

"That was perfect," I whisper when he eventually pulls away. A shy, small smile forms on his face.

"I'm glad we waited," he says.

"Are you going to say something cheesy like good things come to those who wait?" I tease.

"You are always worth the wait." He says this with such a feverish tone that it makes me feel like my heart skips a beat.

I lean to kiss him again and then I pull away, getting up from above him. I reach down the side of the bed for my robe so I can cover up while I go to the bathroom to clean up. Blake gets up from the bed and I laugh when he follows me down the hallway.

"You can think again if you think you're coming into the bathroom with me while I pee and clean up, Indiana."

"Hey, I've held your hair back when you were throwing up, we're past any level of bashfulness." Blake laughs. He stops at the top of the staircase and looks at me. "However, I was going to go downstairs and get us some juice. What do you want?"

"Whatever you put your hands on first." I smile. I watch as he walks down the stairs, trying not to be distracted by the glorious form he has. "Hey," I call to him. He stops on the stairs, turning to look at me. I'm momentarily distracted by the view.

"Yes, Red?"

"I'm glad to see you weren't lying about that bird tattoo."

"You and I are going to talk about that secret tattoo of yours when I get back upstairs." Blake grins up at me.

"It's not on my ass, I did tell you that." I laugh and I step into the bathroom, shutting the door behind me. I can hear him laughing as he walks down the stairs.

I join him back in his bedroom once I finish. The bedside table light is on, and there is a glass of orange juice on both bedside tables. I slip off my robe and get back into the bed with him. I don't bother putting my slip back on. I can wear it tomorrow for bed. Tonight, at least, I want to feel his skin against mine when he holds me before sleep.

Blake looks over at me, smiling.

"Come on, let me see that tattoo properly," he says. I lie still as he looks at the tattoo that is on my hip bone, always hidden away by underwear. He looks over at the musical notes, tattooed to look like they're on sheet music, humming the notes. He smiles when he recognises the song as "Somewhere over the Rainbow."

"It's one of my favourite songs," I explain.

"Sing it to me," he suggests. He pulls me close in the bed, kissing my temple before pulling me even closer to his body. I feel so cherished. I sing to him until his fingers stroking my arms are a distraction, and I turn to kiss him. We both get lost in the kisses, and this time, when our bodies connect, I let him be above me.

The weight of him above me no longer feels like a scary prospect. He's gentle and tender as he pushes me to higher levels of bliss, and I don't think I've ever felt anything so perfect.

***

"Happy birthday, Rose." Blake's whispers wake me in the morning. I look at him and smile.

"Happy birthday, Blake. How does it feel to be thirty?" I ask.

"Sensational. I mean, I feel pretty much the same as I did last night, but I'm sure that's your presence, rather than reaching a magical milestone." Blake grins at me.

"You are so full of shit." I laugh.

"Absolutely not. Any man waking up with a wonderful woman in their arms would feel the same. Especially a naked one," he teases.

"You are also naked," I point out.

"I usually sleep naked, or would have slept naked before I was here," he explains.

"Does that mean you'll be sleeping naked going forwards?" I ask.

"Whatever you want. I mean, I love that silky little thing you had on last night, but this is a sensational look for you, Rose," he proclaims, gesturing at my naked body.

"If you keep the heated blanket on before I get into bed, I think I can be convinced." I grin at him.

"As long as you're not complaining that I'm not quick to get out of bed in the mornings. Toasty warm bed with a naked you—I can't imagine leaving."

"I could never complain. You're always up before me." I laugh.

"So, speaking of getting up—how are we spending our joint birthday?" he asks.

"Showers first. Breakfast. You can open your presents. We can go on the beach for a bit, make sandcastles and pretend we're five years old. Cake for dinner. Cake for tea. All items punctuated by us coming back to bed," I offer.

"Sounds like the best birthday ever. I'll be nice and let you have the first shower."

"Such a birthday present." I laugh. I get out of bed and head to the bathroom. I reach for my toothbrush and spot a little wrapped box on the windowsill. My name is on the label.

"Don't get too excited, it's only small, but happy birthday, Red," Blake calls, and then I hear his footsteps as he goes downstairs. I smile to myself and open the box. Inside is a guitar pick. I take it out and instantly wish I had my guitar with me. I've missed playing it, even if I have had the keyboard to play instead. I wonder if Blake would let me play his guitar. I know how possessive musicians can be about their favourite instruments, and Blake has had his for years.

I put the pick back into the box and then hop into the shower. I shower quickly and go to my room, shouting to Blake that the bathroom is free. In my room, I find another box. This time, it is on my pillow and a little larger in size. I hear Blake's footsteps on the landing.

"What are you playing at?" I laugh, picking up the box.

"Still only small, don't get excited," Blake calls, then I hear the shut of the bathroom door. I stand, still wrapped in my towel, and open the box. Inside is a guitar strap, one that is bright and colourful, with a rose pattern stitched into it. I smile to myself.

I dry myself and dress quickly. I dry my hair and then put it up in a high ponytail, my hair up from behind my ears. Blake likes my tattoo more than I had even hoped. I dress in jeans and a jumper, given the weather is cold, and go downstairs, hoping to beat Blake to make breakfast.

Blake's in the kitchen already. He's dressed, his hair still damp from the shower. He smells fresh and manly and looks absolutely divine.

"Goddamn it, I wanted to make breakfast for you," I grumble. He looks like he's planning pancakes for breakfast. The eggs are on the countertop, ready to be cracked, and flour already in a bowl.

"You have a present." Blake smiles. He gestures over to the corner of the kitchen. I turn to look where he is pointing. In the corner, propped up and adorned with a large red bow is an acoustic guitar. It's the most beautiful looking guitar I've ever seen. The body is in a rich, inky, midnight-blue colour, reminding me of the sea outside, with a gold edge that runs around the whole body. The pickguard has a beautiful golden design on it and the tuning pegs are a shining gold.

"You got me a guitar?" I gasp. I step to pick it up, testing the weight of it in my arms, cradling it, feeling suddenly like I'm home. I look at him, a wide smile on my face, and he stares back at me with an affectionate expression.

"You told me that you like the look I get on my face when I'm playing guitar, but damn it, Red, I wish I got you one sooner because you look so happy right now."

"This is amazing, Blake, I don't know what to say."

"You don't have to say anything. I'm glad you like it."

There's a knock on the front door and we both freeze. It's clear to me from his reaction that he hasn't organised anybody to come to the house. My phone buzzes on the kitchen counter so I have a look at it, seeing a message from Annabeth, telling me she is at the front door.

"It's the homeowner." I frown. "Stay here. She knows who I am, but she might faint when she sees you," I joke. I leave him in the kitchen and answer the door.

Annabeth stands on the doorstep, holding two bags in one hand, and a wicker food basket in the other. She looks like she's dressed for work.

"Hi, I know it is early, but the woman who booked your stay arranged for me to come over with all of this for you," she explains, holding up the items.

"Do you want to come in? I have somebody in here with me, I hope that's okay," I ask. I'm sure if she faints seeing Blake, it'll be fine. She's clearly managed to keep my presence here as a secret, I'm sure she'd keep Blake's a secret, too, once over the shock.

"Oh, of course it's fine you have somebody here. I don't need to come in, I'm just dropping these off on my way to work. I don't want to keep you. It looks like you're celebrating today."

"A little." I smile. She hands me the basket and the bag.

"I'll let you get back to celebrating then. I'll see you later," Annabeth says, and she turns to walk back down the path. She stops and looks back at me. "You look happy," she comments, an affectionate smile on her face.

"I am," I reply, and I can't stop the big smile that forms on my face.

Annabeth gives a knowing, tinkling laugh before walking away, back to her car. I shut the door and walk back into the kitchen where Blake stands at the doorway.

"I thought we were rumbled." He laughs.

"No, just getting surprises, apparently."

I carry the bag and basket into the kitchen. I open the basket first and there is a selection of breakfast items, muffins, pastries, and spreads. The smell that wafts out of the basket is divine. There's also a small birthday cake, proclaiming happy twenty-fifth and thirtieth birthday. I take the items out and put them on the countertop. The other bag contains flowers and presents, from Maeve to Blake, from Libby to me. We sit at the kitchen table together and open the presents. Blake laughs loudly when he finds two of his gifts contain bags of apples and jars of chocolate spread.

"I feel so spoilt." Blake sighs after he has opened his presents.

I smile at him. "Wait, you haven't opened anything from me yet."

"I wasn't anticipating anything," Blake replies. I roll my eyes at him. As if I would let a milestone like him turning thirty go unmarked.

"I hope you're not disappointed, as they're not as fancy as a new guitar," I warn. I get up and grab the presents I'd hidden in the kitchen cupboard for him, more things that I purchased with the prepaid credit card, grateful to have it.

Blake opens the gifts and smiles at both. One box contains a watch, and the other contains an engraved ring for him to wear on his thumb. He looks at me after he pulls the ring out of the box.

"What's the etching?" he wonders. I smile at him.

"It might sound cheesy, but that's a soundwave from the clip of us singing together, the first song we sang together and recorded on the phone," I explain. He stares at it, and I can't work out his expression. "I'm sorry, I know it's cheesy, and it doesn't live up to what you got me, I just—" I start, but then I can't speak anymore because he's leans forward, kissing me.

"It's perfect, Rose. I'll treasure it forever." He makes his promise, and my heart seems to sing with happiness.

***

"Have you had a good day?" Blake asks as we get into bed together.

"It's been the best birthday I've ever had," I reply, getting settled in his arms. I rest my head against his shoulder, my hand resting on his chest, feeling the rise and fall as he breathes.

"Me, too."

He sounds so happy, even if the day has been simple. I know, if we were out in the world as usual, his birthday would probably have been entirely different. It could have been a huge celebration with a roomful of people, more than what we had today, but for me, everything was perfect.

We started the morning playing guitars together, and I can't remember the last time I had so much fun with music. Blake would start strumming a tune, waiting for me to catch on to the song and join in, before waiting for me to start the next song for him to guess and join in on. The sound of our melodies bounced and echoed on the living room walls. I played some of my music for him to sing to, and I sang some of his tracks as he played the melodies on his guitar. I strummed and sang a faster version of his "The Things I Did," and he slowed down one of my tracks, taking a catchy pop song and turning it into a slow, haunting melody.

We spent the afternoon on the beach. As usual, the beach had been deserted, and we dug a moat around some sandcastles we built. We waited as the tide came in, feeling elated when the moat filled with the water of the incoming waves, the water splashing at the bottom of our jeans. I took photographs of us, windswept, wet and slightly covered in the sand the wind was whipping up. We held hands as we walked down the beach before coming back for tea.

As we ate tea, Blake produced packets of sparklers for us to use in the garden, and we spent a while drawing elaborate shapes in the air with the lit sticks, laughing until we ran out of packets. We sat in the garden and watched some of the fireworks being set off further down the town in celebration of Bonfire Night. I almost suggested wrapping up in hats and scarves and going to the display, but I didn't want to share him with anybody else. The only time we were apart in the day was for him to call his parents, as I always give him some privacy when he talks to them.

Afterwards, he wrapped his arms around me on the sofa, and I held him close, wishing I could make that part of his life easier. We lay like that until Blake proclaimed it was time for bed.

Now, he pulls me closer. I trace my fingers across his tattoo and then idly down his body. It doesn't take long for him to catch my hand, entwine his fingers in mine, and kiss me until I feel like we could combust together. When he finally enters me, all I can think is how happy I am, how if living in this little house—hidden away from everybody—is how I spend the rest of my days, I'll have no complaints.

Chapter Nineteen

Rose

THEN

"Mum, where are you going?"

I feel sleepy and disoriented, but I was compelled to get out of bed when I heard noises coming from the main area of the hotel suite. Usually, Mum is asleep when I go to bed, and she sleeps through until morning.

I cannot comprehend what I'm seeing. She's fully dressed, her coat is on, and a suitcase rests at her heels.

I squint at the clock across the room, it reads three thirty. Mum looks at me as if she's disappointed to have been caught by me.

"Go back to bed, Briar Rose," she urges.

"Where are you going?" I ask again, and she sighs.

"I didn't want to do this like this."

"Do what? Leave in the middle of the night? Or tell me, to my face, what you are doing?"

"I wrote you a note. It says everything I want to say." Mum shrugs.

She looks at the coffee table in the living area of the hotel suite we're staying in. I switch on the table light and see the note she's referring to. I snatch it from the table and skim read the words, still bewildered about what is going on.

"You're going to a wellness retreat? What the fuck is that? Why do you need that?"

"It is a place for me to relax," she declares.

"You don't need to go to a wellness retreat to relax," I argue. She lives a life of luxury with me—the best hotels, the best of everything.

"I want to get away. I've been so stressed after your father."

"I know you've been upset, Mum, but you don't need to go to a wellness retreat."

"What exactly do you think I need to do? What advice does my child want to give me?" Mum scoffs.

"Why are you making it sound like I'm the one in the wrong? You're the one who is skipping out in the middle of the night, leaving me a letter instead of telling me to my face," I snap.

"Maybe every time I look at you, all I'm reminded about is your father and what he did to me," Mum sneers, and it feels like she has slapped me.

"Mum!"

She doesn't immediately respond. She doesn't even look at me properly. I want to hope that it's because she's ashamed of her cowardice—that she didn't have the guts to talk to me about this—but I'm sure it's because she genuinely cannot stand the sight of me. My heart cracks a little. I know things have been rocky since Dad left, but I hoped we could find our way to a better relationship. It hurts enough not talking to my dad.

Mum takes a big breath, but she still doesn't look at me properly.

"You are a living, breathing reminder of the choices I made with your father, and I need some time by myself." Mum reaches for the handle of her suitcase.

"So, what, that's it? You're skipping out on my life, like Dad did?" I spit.

"I'm surprised you'd even notice, given you're always so quick to get away from me. You cut me off when I speak, you don't pay attention to anything, and you disappear for hours because you can't stand to be around me. Maybe this will just make things so much easier on us both." Mum's tone is laced with sarcasm and disdain.

She doesn't wait for me to respond, and she doesn't look at me to see if her words have hurt me. All she does is tighten her grip on her suitcase, and within seconds, she is gone.

I stand in semi-shock, then sink to the sofa. I re-read the note she wrote until the words become blurry through my tears.

I can't believe she left. I don't think I have ever spent much time without my mother being around. She's been with me at every concert because she travelled with me on every tour. She's sat in on interviews with me, guided me through everything, even if at times I called her overbearing. I never imagined doing any of this without her. I wanted independence, I wanted to be my own person, I wanted my voice to be heard—off stage—but I didn't want this. Not for Dad to leave. Not for Mum to leave, too.

For the first time in my life, I feel completely alone.

***

"Briar Rose, have you fallen in?" Hunter's voice is teasing as he calls from the bedroom to where I'm in the bathroom, supposedly getting a shower before I sneak back to my hotel room. I snuck out at midday—a little gap of time carved so I could see him. Mum's been gone for a week, so sneaking out at night is easier—or sneaking him in—but the daytime hookups are always dependant on our schedules.

"No," I shout back to him. It's a panicked sound on my lips.

I clutch the sink, praying that the sound doesn't alert Hunter to anything. My whole body is shaking, and I can't stop it. I sit on the floor because I'm not sure I can stay upright. I pull my knees up to my chest, wrapping my arms around my legs, trying to hold myself together.

My throat is sore, and my windpipe feels bruised. It still feels like Hunter's forearm is against it, like I'm still pinned against the mattress. I can hear the echo of him panting into my ear, his moans and sentences telling me how much I turn him on, how good it feels. Except it didn't feel good. I couldn't breathe. I couldn't catch my breath. I could feel my face getting hot as I struggled and tried to get him to move. I clawed at his arms, I dug my nails into his flesh, but nothing had stopped him.

The tears roll down my face and I feel so stupid for putting myself in that position again. Hunter is passionate and sometimes everything feels great, and then, like today, he goes too far, does things I don't want, don't ask for, don't consent to. Today, I'm not upset—that's not the right word for what I'm feeling. I'm *terrified*. Just before he climaxed and relaxed his hold against me, the only thought in my head was that I was going to die.

Once I feel a little in control of my body, I stand. I'm still shaky, but I know I can't hide in the bathroom forever. I need to shower. I need to look in control when I get out of the bathroom and leave Hunter. I cannot look blotchy, bruised, or shaky when I go back to my own room.

The knock on the bathroom door scares me, making me yelp.

"Are you going to be long?" Hunter asks.

"No, just getting in the shower now," I call back. I hear his footsteps retreating. I get into the shower, turning the hot water on so I can clean myself up.

I shower slowly. I scrub the evidence of him from my skin. I try to ignore that some areas feel tender and sore from where he held me. I let the hot water wash my tears away. I get out and dry myself, pulling on the hotel robe and then joining him in the bedroom.

Hunter looks at me from the bed.

"There's my beautiful Briar Rose," he says, smiling at me. He says everything so evenly and brightly, like I didn't just claw my nails into his skin in a desperate attempt to get him to stop.

"I can't stay." I force myself to smile. I grab my clothes and pull them on, putting on the baseball cap and my sunglasses. "I have to be back before people notice I'm gone. I have a packed schedule this afternoon."

"I was hoping we could have gotten a second round in, but that was so good, don't you think?"

"I will be here tomorrow." I gather my things.

I hear him say goodbye, but I don't respond; I just head out of the room and to the lift so I can go to my own room. I manage to make it into my own bedroom before anybody sees me and I'm grateful. This afternoon I have three interviews and this evening I'm supposed to be at a movie premier, posing on the red carpet, waving and smiling like I'm on top of the world. The rest of the week, the nights are taken up with concerts in this city.

There is a knock on my door. My body jolts and then tenses. I would give anything to be by myself and not be interrupted.

"Rose, sweetie, it's me," Libby calls.

"Come in," I call back. I'm sure she's the only person I can tolerate right now, even if I would rather be alone.

The door opens and she steps inside, holding several outfits on coat hangers in one hand. She hangs the coat hangers on the wardrobe door.

"I've been shopping, my lovely, and I hope you like everything," she trills. Her enthusiasm and smiley face go someway to making me focus on her rather than getting stuck on thoughts about Hunter.

"I'm sure I will love them, you are a genius stylist, after all." I manage to grin at her. She looks at me.

"You look a little flush, are you okay?"

"I was exercising earlier, must have overdone it."

"You need to go easy on yourself, sweetie."

"Maybe tomorrow." I laugh.

"Okay, well, this is what I've picked for your interviews," Libby says, showing me the tailored wide-leg black trousers and black-and-white top. On the hanger, she's hung a chunky silver necklace and a thick silver cuff for my wrist.

"Looks perfect."

"I have two dresses here, but I think one will be better for the awards next week." Libby holds up two dresses. One is a deep purple sheath dress, something that flares from the hips. The other is white, floor length, something that will cling to my curves.

"The white dress is amazing, Lib." I cross to touch it. It is silky and looks beautiful.

"This is the one I'm thinking for the show next week."

"No, tonight," I protest. It is a beautiful dress. I don't want to wait.

"I assumed you wouldn't want to risk white this time of the month," Libby comments.

It takes me a second to register what she has said. Libby has been my closest thing to a friend, and because she dresses me, she knows the times of the month to change my outfit sizes and styles when I feel bloated and when I might prefer to wear something darker, just in case.

"Oh, yeah, of course." I laugh it off. "The purple will be great."

"Come on then, sweetie, time to get ready!"

***

"I think I might be pregnant."

The words seem unreal and unnatural on my lips. They sound it, too. Hunter looks at me like I've just told him I murdered somebody and need him to help me bury the body.

"Sorry, what?"

"My period is late."

"How is it possible that you're pregnant?" Hunter asks as he paces in front of the sofa.

"Well, I'm not on the pill and you haven't always taken the time to put on a condom," I point out. I think of the day when he pulled me from the floor and nudged my legs open.

"You didn't say you weren't on the pill."

"It's hard to say anything when you have your hand clamped over my mouth. Besides, would it have stopped you?" I shoot back, but then I shrink back into myself. Hunter sits down on the sofa next to me. He grabs my hand, giving it a quick squeeze.

"I'm sorry, my beautiful Briar Rose, I'm just in shock. Are you sure you are pregnant?"

"I said I might be pregnant. I'm late and I'm never late."

"You mean, you haven't done a test yet? This might be a theoretical panic for us?" Hunter laughs softly.

"It isn't like I can easily run off and get a pregnancy test. Besides, I thought you might want to know as soon as I thought it was a possibility," I point out.

"Well, we should get a test sorted. That will put your mind at rest. Let me arrange one for you." Hunter gets up to get his phone. He types away on the screen and then takes a seat back next to me.

"Who did you message?"

"My personal assistant. A friend. We can get this concluded in a jiffy. I'm sure it's fine. People are late all the time, right?"

"I hope so."

I bite the skin next to my little fingernail. Being pregnant seems like a terrifying prospect, especially when I'm sometimes afraid of Hunter and what he is capable of doing.

Afraid, but still coming back to him, time and time again. The voice in my head seems judgemental and snide.

"Come here, let me massage your shoulders while we wait, get some of that tension out of you," Hunter suggests, and he puts his hands on my shoulders. I flinch a little. "Oh, you're so tense."

"What will we do if the test is positive?" I whisper my question.

"I can take care of it." Hunter's response is quick. "I have some doctors I can call."

"You make it sound so simple, a simple decision." I turn to look at him. He looks at me, patiently.

"Anything else would be too difficult. We can't go public with our relationship. We're both so young, with so much to achieve. A baby would ruin everything between us, and your career would suffer. You told me you want to act, how are you going to do that when you're pregnant, or looking after a baby? You'd have to give up the film role, for a start," Hunter reasons.

I know everything he says is logical.

Hunter massages my shoulders until there is a knock on the door. I make myself scarce because I know Hunter won't want me to be seen. I slip into the bathroom to stay out of the way. It isn't long until Hunter appears at the bathroom door, a pregnancy test in his hands. He throws it towards me, and I catch the box.

"I guess we'll know in a couple of minutes." I shrug. He gives me a smile and then he leaves me in the bathroom. I take the test out of the box, looking at it like it's a nuclear bomb I'm supposed to disarm.

I read the instructions carefully, even though it's a simple process. Pee on a stick and leave it for the required time. Simple but also terrifying. I follow the instructions to the letter.

"Well?" Hunter asks from the bathroom door a little later when I've made no effort to leave the bathroom. He sounds a little frustrated.

"Pregnant," I reply. He comes into the bathroom and puts an arm around me.

"We'll get it sorted, my beautiful Briar Rose."

His promises sound firm, but I can't help but feel like I'm at the precipice of something that I'm no longer in control of, and I've never been more terrified.

Chapter Twenty

Blake

NOW

"Have you thought about what you're doing for Christmas?" Rose looks up at me from her position, curled in my arms on the bed.

"At the risk of sounding presumptuous, I assumed we were going to spend the time together, here, unless you have other plans." I smile at her.

My fingers are on the side of her head, near the back of her ear, touching across her tattoo. She closes her eyes for a moment, and an expression of bliss crosses her face.

"I love it when you do that," she murmurs.

"How about this?" I tease, my fingers moving a little further into her hairline, massaging her scalp softly.

"Yes, yes, that, too." She groans slightly.

I know how much she likes it when I touch her like this because she's told me many times before. When she does it to me, I'm grateful I'm not in charge of state secrets because I'd tell them all to her, just to feel it again.

"You still want to talk about Christmas?" I laugh at her reaction.

"Hmmm, maybe in a minute," she mumbles.

"How about I carry on doing this, and you tell me what you have planned, given it is only two weeks away."

"I hadn't really thought about it that much, but I guess I'll be here."

"Then I'll be here, too, if you want me to be." I lean a little to kiss her forehead.

"I do want that, I just wasn't sure if you maybe had plans with parents, or friends." Rose shifts a little, nestling herself further in my arms.

"Not really."

"How would you usually spend Christmas?" she asks.

"Last year I popped in to see my mum in the morning and then I had a pint with Dad, then I went back to the place I was renting. I ordered some food in, watched a few films."

"Not a traditional turkey dinner?"

"No, if I remember correctly, I had a chicken biryani. I don't think I've ever had a traditional turkey dinner." I laugh.

"You didn't have the whole big family event with a giant turkey dinner when you were a kid?"

"Nope. I'd spend Christmas day with my grandma, on my mum's side. I didn't know my grandparents on my father's side. My mum has always worked on Christmas day and so I'd take a walk to my grandma's house. She'd cook steak and chips for Christmas dinner, as that was her favourite dish."

"You didn't spend Christmas with your father?"

"My absent dad showing up for Christmas when I was a kid?" I laugh.

"Okay, stupid question I guess, based on what you have told me about him."

"Not stupid. It would be reasonable to assume a parent wants to see their kid at Christmas, but it didn't happen. Dad has always gone to the pub on Christmas day, something he still does. He is not particularly religious, so he never really celebrated it. Spent a lot of time telling me since we reconnected that it is all commercial bullshit and designed to keep the economy going."

"Is anybody in your family religious?"

"My grandma was. Not massively religious, she didn't insist on prayers before food or anything, but she believed there was something out there. I guess I lost any notion of agreeing with her after she died. It's hard to understand why a supposedly benevolent God would allow somebody as lovely as my grandma to suffer so much."

"How did she die?" Rose asks in a soft voice.

"She had Huntington's disease. It was awful. I spent a lot of time with her when she was in the hospital. I haven't stepped into a hospital since," I explain.

"I'm so sorry, Blake."

"It was a long time ago. My mum had to get tested, given it's heredity. Luckily, she was okay, but it was still hard for her to watch her own mother go through that. I guess Christmas excitement, for me, kind of retired when my grandma died."

"I thought we were done with the daily sad stories, but that has to be the saddest yet," Rose murmurs.

"I'm sorry to bring you down."

"Tell me something about your grandma," Rose coaxes.

"She was the one who taught me to play guitar."

"Well, the world has a lot to thank your grandma for," she says, smiling up at me. I smile back and kiss her forehead.

"So, I'm guessing you had the whole massive turkey and giant Christmas tree thing going on when you were a kid?"

"Of course. The perfect Dalton family wouldn't allow themselves to look like they weren't doing everything they should do."

"Do you miss them?" I wonder. Every time she talks about her parents, her voice is a mix of reverence and sadness.

"I miss who they used to be. I know that probably doesn't make much sense," she replies. Her fingers are on the tattoo on my chest, her touch is light as a feather. I reach for her hand, my fingers entwining into hers.

"Tell me how you feel," I whisper.

"I miss how things were before everything went crazy. They were such good parents when I was younger. I always felt loved. Sometimes, I wonder how my life would be if I'd never been discovered. Would my parents have changed in the way that they did? They twisted into these characters I didn't recognise, where the money and the fame seemed to mean more than anything else. Dad certainly wouldn't have met Krystal if I'd had an ordinary life. Maybe right now, I'd be thinking about going home to see my parents for Christmas," she muses.

"Maybe, but perhaps things would have still reached this point. Your dad might not have met Krystal, but he could have met somebody else instead."

"I get that, I don't think it is all about me, but life was so normal when I was a kid. Life now feels like a million miles away from that." Rose sighs. She squeezes my hand. "I'm grateful for this, though. When I lie with you like this, I feel happy, and I just imagine that everything else is resolved and better. I don't want to go back out there to face everything, not yet, but the idea of Christmas, thinking about what things used to be like, I guess it makes me feel a little nostalgic."

"You can reach out to them whenever you want," I remind her.

"I don't want to, yet. I might feel better than I did a few weeks ago, but I don't feel up to picking at that scab. I don't feel strong enough to have conversations with anybody from my team, and I certainly don't feel like I can have a conversation with my mum or my dad, to try to build any bridges."

I feel her body tighten, like the idea of speaking to her parents again causes her so much stress she cannot bear it. I always had a rocky and disjointed connection with my own parents, and I feel anxious about speaking to them again after their recent revelations. Rose had a much tighter relationship with her own parents; it must feel so more upsetting to try to fix that damaged link between them. I feel a pinch of frustration because I know there isn't a damn thing I can do to fix what she's going through.

"Are you tired?" I ask, giving her an out of the conversation.

"A little, but I'm not particularly sleepy yet. I'm just perfectly content lying here, just like this." Rose smiles up at me.

I go back to running my fingers along the back of her ear. She sighs contentedly and after a while, I feel her go slack in my arms as she gives into the sleep that she said she didn't need. She always amuses me when she does that, telling me she isn't tired and then out like a light, fast asleep until morning, especially because the nightmares appear to have stopped.

I hold her close for a while, letting her drift into a deeper sleep. Once she is fully asleep, I lean over to get my phone from the bedside table. I keep one arm around Rose, given she has fallen asleep on my arm and I'm perfectly comfortable holding her like this.

I unlock my phone and start to make some notes about how I can make Rose's Christmas a perfect day. When Maeve asked me to write some music with Rose, I never envisioned this is how we'd end up, but Rose has me transfixed; I want to do everything for her. I want to see her happy. I want to see her soar.

I want to give Rose everything she wants and needs, but there are things I know I can't fix, things I can't make better. I'm not going to be magically able to make her parents turn up, especially the version that Rose seems to miss the most, her parents from ten years ago. I'm not going to find a magic wand that fixes the hurt she's holding on to about the guy who has taken up too much space in her head, the secrets she hasn't told me about yet.

What I can do, though, is find different ways to make her feel cherished and to show her how much I adore her.

***

"What on earth have you ordered now? You're going to need a bloody moving van when you leave here." Rose laughs as she comes down the stairs, finding me hauling large boxes from the delivery I've just had. I look over at her and can't help but smile. She looks like a vision as she descends the stairs. It isn't the usual leggings, oversized jumper, and thick socks that has me smiling but the look of happiness she has on her face. She looks genuinely happy, and I love it.

"Hey, don't rain on my parade."

"You have a shopping habit," Rose teases. She reaches the bottom step and helps me pull some of the boxes from the doorstep.

"I think I can stretch to this. Anyway, did you wake up with your battery recharged, as we have some work to get done this morning," I joke as I pull the biggest box into the living room. She follows with one of the smaller boxes before we both head back to the doorstep for more boxes.

"What have you got?" Rose asks.

"I thought the living room might be a little bare." I smile. We get back into the living room and I pull open the packaging on the largest box.

"You got a Christmas tree?" Rose laughs when she sees inside the box.

"I know you probably had a real one when you were growing up, and you might not like this is an artificial one, but at least you can take this one for next year," I explain. I'm about to pull the tree out of the box when she flings her arms around me. She's so exuberant that we topple back and land in a heap on the sofa.

"I love it. This is such an amazing and thoughtful surprise." Rose smiles at me and then she dips her head to kiss me.

"This feels like we are running the risk of getting very distracted," I murmur between kisses. Her hands find their way up my T-shirt.

"Do you mind me being a distraction?" she murmurs back.

"Absolutely not," I reply between kisses.

She straightens herself up and pulls off her jumper before returning to kiss me. I roll us over on the sofa so I'm above her. My fingers trace along her side and we sink further into our kisses. I let one of my hands skim along her throat, something I think I've done a million times as I make my way to caress her face, but I feel her stiffen underneath me and her lips seem to freeze.

I pull away and look at her, surprised at the change.

"Please don't," she whispers. I'm not sure what she means by *don't*. Don't pull away? Don't carry on kissing her?

"What do you mean, Red?" I ask. I move my hand to move the strands of hair around her forehead.

"I just...." she starts, and her voice trails off. I sit up, moving off her and she scrambles to sit in the corner of the sofa, pulling her knees up to her chest. "I'm sorry."

"I'm not entirely sure what is wrong, Rose, but you don't have to say you're sorry. You can tell me what's wrong," I reply. My voice is low because I get the sense that she is thinking about something painful. She looks over at me, her blue eyes wide.

"I just had an intrusive thought, that's all. It's all me, not you. I'm sorry. It's okay. I'm okay."

Her last three sentences sound like a mantra, and I'm sure as fuck convinced that she is miles away from being okay.

"Hey." I offer her my hand. She takes it, squeezing my fingers slightly. "Do you want to see what is in the other boxes, or do you want a hug?" I ask.

Rose's laugh is shaky, but at least it is there. She moves across the sofa and settles herself in my lap.

"Maybe a hug first, and then the boxes?" she suggests, and I pull her closer, my arms around her, feeling as her breathing seems to steady out. We don't talk, I just hold her, humming a tune. After a moment, she seems to relax fully.

"Better?" I ask.

Instead of responding verbally, she leans up to kiss me. When she pulls away, I feel slightly breathless. She smiles at me in a way that makes it seem like her previous upset hadn't happened, though I can't help but wonder what the intrusive thought was.

"Come on, Indiana, show me what is in the boxes."

She gets off my lap, pulling me up with her. I pass her the first box and she opens it, smiling when she sees the decorations for the Christmas tree. There is an assorted mix, a set of plain round baubles in a bright shiny red, sets shaped like stars in a glittery silver, sets shaped like snowflakes in a bright white. There are chains of silver beads for us to thread around the tree and sets of lights.

"What do you think?" I ask her.

She grins at me. "These are going to look great on the tree. I can't wait to decorate it."

"Here you go," I say, passing her the second box.

She opens this one and smiles as she takes the angel for the top of the tree. She notices the three smaller boxes nestled under the box of the angel and takes each one out, looking at me with a curious expression on her face. Inside the first box is a tree decoration in the shape of an acoustic guitar, the second has a decoration shaped like a grand piano, and the third has a clear bauble with a hugging couple inside, filled with flakes of white that makes it look like the snow is at their feet. She shakes the bauble, watching the fake snow fall around the couple.

"These are amazing, Blake. You didn't have to do any of this."

"I know I didn't have to, but I wanted to." I smile at her, feeling like I'm ten feet tall because her reaction is so much more than I had anticipated. "Besides, if we don't have a Christmas tree, where am I going to put your presents?"

"How are you doing with your present buying? Sticking to the rules?" She grins at me.

Rose was the one to suggest we stick to themes for Christmas presents. She came up with the categories as well. One of the gifts must be something that we made. One of the gifts must be something that can be worn, and the final gift has to be something just for fun. None of the gifts are allowed to be expensive. The fact she doesn't want the gifts to be expensive has made things interesting. It would be easy to spend a fortune on something, but to find something special and inexpensive is a challenge we are both having fun with.

Both of us have spent some time hidden away in our own rooms while we make our gifts. Usually, we last for about an hour in our own rooms, working on the gifts after our usual games of cards, before she comes into my bedroom to talk and sleep.

I grin back at her. "I'm completely adhering to the rules, of course."

"I'd expect nothing less."

"Come on, Red, let's get this tree decorated. Christmas will have come and gone before you get your ass in gear."

***

"Have you any particular order you want to open the gifts in?" Rose asks on Christmas morning. We're both still in pyjamas, sitting on the floor in front of the Christmas tree, our breakfast plates stacked beside us. Christmas morning between us has been a leisurely start, and Rose looks content.

It's an entirely different approach to any Christmas that I've had before. Christmas when I was very young, I was dropped off early at my grandmother's house so my mum could go to work. When I was a little older—around nine or ten—I woke to an empty house, got ready, and then walked the short distance to my grandma's. Once she died, I woke to an empty house and spent the day alone, making my own food because Mum would eat at work and didn't want anything saved. When I left home, I was still alone on Christmas morning.

Today is the first Christmas I've woken up with somebody. The first time that somebody has kissed me and wished me a happy Christmas. The first time somebody has whispered that it's time to go downstairs to open presents.

It's the first time since my grandmother died that there has even been a tree in the house, much less one with presents for me underneath it.

"How about the funny gifts first?" I suggest. I reach for the present I wrapped with a label proclaiming "funny." Rose reaches behind her for the one for me.

"Here you go," she says. We unwrap at the same time, and when I start laughing at the lobster-claw oven gloves that she has wrapped for me, I hear her start laughing as she unwraps her own gift.

"These are amazing." I put the oven gloves on and make a motion of a lobster snapping their claws. "I'm going to use these all day for the cooking."

"I might wear these all day, too." Rose wraps the scarf around her neck. It's a novelty shaped one with a cartoonish fox head at one end and paws and tail at the other. She puts on the fox-style woolly hat, the ears sticking up from the top of her head. She slips one hand into one of the matching gloves and frowns when she touches the paper I've folded and hidden inside. She reads the paper and raises her eyebrows.

"It isn't so much a present, just a continuation of the fun. You mentioned the bonfire event. I thought we could go to the New Year celebration they have here.

We can disappear into the crowd. I'm sure people won't notice us when they're busy looking at the firework displays," I explain. The paper is the flyer that had been stuffed through the letterbox about the celebration planned on the beach, further up towards the main area of town.

"Will you buy me an incredibly unhealthy plate of cheesy chips?" Rose asks. I saw the advert on the flyer that the chip shop will have a stall, and Rose has talked about cheesy chips for days.

"Anything you desire."

"Well, don't say that. I'm pretty sure it would be obscene to give me what I want in public." Rose laughs.

"When we get home, I'm all yours," I promise.

She doesn't flinch about words like "home" and "yours," though the words make my own heart thump a little harder in my chest. We haven't known each other long, but this place feels like our home, and I feel like I'm hers. I know at some point this is all going to change. We're going to go back to our usual lives. I'm sure we'll be scheduled to perform together when some of our songs are in the charts, maybe the label will want us to be surprise guests when we both go on tour again. Is that all we will have? Is there any possibility that she wants more than that? We haven't discussed anything beyond this place, what we are doing now, and as much as I want to know what her thoughts are for the future, I don't want to push anything. I'm afraid if I push for something more, she'll either freak out, or she'll tell me she isn't interested in anything past the last time we leave this house.

"What's that frown for, Indiana?" she asks, stopping my thoughts from wandering too far.

"Nothing. What theme present next?"

"Oh, the something to wear, though I like how both of us managed to combine that theme with the fun theme." Rose smiles as she takes off her scarf and hat, and I take off the oven gloves.

"Here you go." I give her the present I'd labelled "wear me." She passes me mine and we open the paper.

"Oh, Blake, this is beautiful," Rose says with a soft sigh. I watch as she pulls out the charm bracelet that was nestled against the black velvet insert.

"You don't have to wear it, if you don't like it," I reply, hesitantly.

I've never given a woman jewellery before. I wasn't even sure of Rose's style. Relying on pictures of her on the internet would have been useless because they would have been her stylist's choices, either Libby or the ones before her. I could have called Maeve or Libby to get some suggestions, but instead, I decided to gamble by picking something I thought looked nice, and something I thought would mean something to her.

Rose rolls her eyes slightly at me as she opens the clasp on the charm bracelet and then puts it onto her right wrist. There are three charms hanging from it, a musical note, a letter R, and a little cottage. She moves her wrist when it is on, and the Christmas tree lights seem to make the bracelet and charms glisten.

"This puts my present of something for you to wear to shame." Rose carries on staring at the bracelet.

"No, not at all. I love this," I say, my thumb running over the rose design that is etched onto the leather belt she has given me. The belt is dark, and the roses themselves are in a dark blue, so it doesn't look too obvious what the design is. The same blue roses are in the lining of the blazer she has given me.

"I thought you could wear them when you are next onstage or going to some event, something of me on you." There is a hint of a blush on her cheeks as she explains, like she wasn't sure if this was something I'd like.

"I love it," I reassure her. There is part of me that wants to say that I'd like it if we were going to an event together. I can't imagine anything I want more.

"I feel like my homemade gift is going to be such a letdown now." Rose hands me the next present. It is in two sections, one large and one smaller.

"I'm sure it will be great." I smile and give her the present I've made her.

I wait as she opens her present, looking over the set of mugs I decorated for her. One mug has been painted on the words "Red's cup of positivi-tea," the second "Red's lyrics flow as strong as her coffee," and the third reads "There is always time for hot chocolate." They're all decorated with a similar design and pattern. They're cheesy and clumsy looking, distinctly homemade, but she looks delighted.

"Why did you let me have my morning drink before I opened these?"

"You can have your mid-morning coffee in one." I grin.

"Open yours," Rose urges as she puts the mugs to her side. I pick up the first present she has given me.

"I feel like this is breaking the rules, given there are two presents," I point out, but she shrugs.

"One is more a gift to me. Besides, there are three mugs here. Go on."

"I'm intrigued now." I laugh. I open the smaller of the presents and inside is a black-and-white chevron friendship bracelet. I look at her. "You made this?"

"Yep. I have about sixteen failed attempts in my room. I forgot how to do them because I haven't done them in so long. Finally got that one finished yesterday morning."

I hold my wrist out so she can tie the friendship bracelet around my wrist.

"I'm impressed," I tell her once it is on.

"Open the other one." She gestures to the bigger present.

I open it and inside is a book, proclaiming *Blake & Rose—The Lyrics*. Curious, I open the cover of the page. Inside, in silver ink against the black page, she has written a note. *Dear Blake, thank you for bringing the colour back to my life—Love, Rose.* The rest of the pages are lyric sheets where she has written up all the songs we have been writing together, collating into one book—every track beautifully handwritten. There are blank pages towards the end of the book.

"I like you've kept space for us to write more," I say after I've cleared my throat because her personal message at the front has surprised me.

"I know it's our work, I know all I've done is write them up in a book I ordered, but...." she starts, but I put the book down and lean forward so I can kiss her.

"Thank you, for igniting my world with colour," I murmur against her lips when she eventually pulls away. She can claim all the time that I've been the one helping her, but she underestimates every time just how much she has done for me.

"Merry Christmas, Blake," she murmurs back.

"Merry Christmas, my sweet," I reply, and despite my wavering belief in any religion, I find myself praying that this is the first of many Christmas mornings that I'll be by Rose's side.

Chapter Twenty-One

Rose

NOW

"Red, I've a surprise for you," Blake tells me on the first of January.

I don't answer him immediately; I'm too busy enjoying the feel of his fingers on my skin as he holds me close in his bed. Neither of us are dressed—still naked from our night together—and there is nothing between us but heat. He lies behind me, one of his arms underneath me, his hand outstretched to hold mine, the other on my arm.

It's mid-morning and I feel like my head aches slightly from the champagne we drank after getting back from the fireworks on the beach. We dressed and covered up with scarves around parts of our faces for warmth and disguise. We didn't stay for the whole event, only for the earlier firework display designed for the younger children so they could go home rather than being kept up and outside until midnight. Around ten, after we watched those fireworks, Blake suggested we go home, so we paid for our portion of hot, greasy food, leaving the crowd and eating as we walked down the beach towards the cottage.

Close to midnight, he surprised me with a bottle of champagne that he left chilling before we went out. We welcomed the new year in together, wrapped in each other's arms in his bed, making love and climaxing as the sounds and colours of fireworks lit up the skies. Everything between us felt wonderful. Every touch felt soft and full of tenderness. Blake makes me feel cherished. Aside from the morning when we unboxed the Christmas tree—when his skim of his hand against my throat made me think of Hunter and how he suddenly changed—everything with Blake has just felt like perfection. He never pushed me to explain what happened and I haven't raised the topic either, preferring to focus on us rather than my past.

"What have you been playing at?" I murmur when I remember he is waiting for a response. It sometimes takes me a moment to zone back into our conversations as he manages to distract me with his beautiful touches and exquisite little kisses.

"You're sounding very relaxed this morning," he says with a small laugh.

"Sorry for not paying attention, I'm just very comfortable. Maybe this will help me be attentive," I start, and I let go of his hand. I turn in the bed to face him instead. My breasts press against his firm chest and his leg slips over mine as he pulls me closer.

"This is certainly not going to help my concentration," Blake replies, and he kisses my forehead.

"Tell me what the surprise is." I grin, but I shift my body, pushing against him, and he groans slightly.

"Definitely not helping my concentration," he murmurs.

"I'm glad it's not just me who gets distracted," I tease. He pulls me closer and kisses across my face. They're little kisses that I know won't lead to sex, but kisses that make me feel cherished, nevertheless. They're kisses that make me feel special.

"What were we talking about again?" he jokes when he pulls away.

"Your big surprise. What is it?"

"I've got us a meeting with the record label so we can discuss these albums of ours," he says, his pace a little faster than he normally speaks.

"Are you kidding me?" I gasp, and I roll again, this time pushing him to lie on his back so I can straddle him. His hands fall to my hips.

"Yep, a week from today, we will be sitting in front of—" he starts, but I cut him off with a kiss.

He kisses me back with a hunger in his lips, the types of kisses that I know will lead to something more. It sets my heart racing. It's always like this—the craving I get to feel that beautiful connection between us.

My fingers edge along his hairline and he moans against my mouth. My stomach flips with the sheer thrill of it. There are no words to be spoken. All there is in the world are my lips on his, the feeling of our bodies against one another, and the excitement I have in my heart.

***

"Do you have everything?" Blake asks as he comes down the stairs. He holds his guitar case in his hand.

"Stop right there," I command. He stops on the stairs.

"What?" Blake laughs.

"You look so amazing." I pull my phone from my pocket. I open the camera and take a photograph of him. He is dressed in his jeans and a T-shirt, as usual, but today he is wearing the belt I gave him for Christmas. There's a feeling of pride and belonging to see that he's wearing the belt, that those blue roses I'd fallen in love with when I'd seen them are wrapped around his waist.

"Says the most beautiful woman I've ever seen," Blake teases as he comes down the stairs to me. He looks oblivious to the warm glow I suddenly have running in my body.

Blake takes the phone out of my hand, puts down his guitar case, then wraps an arm around my shoulders before taking a few photographs of us together. While I'm not in my usual style of clothes, the low-key outfit feels like it matches with his.

He hands me the phone back and I look at the photographs he took. We both have wide smiles and twinkles in our eyes. It could just be all the lighting in the hall, but I decide it's because we're both just feeling so happy about what we're about to do, and so at ease with one another.

"I'm planning on taking photographs whenever we are alone today. I'm hoping we're lucky and not surrounded by photographers as we walk around town," I joke, putting the phone into my pocket. Despite my joking around, part of me feels slightly anxious at the idea that people will be taking photographs of us. Not that I am worried about being seen with Blake, just that I'm worried about being seen at all. I haven't been seen out since September. Blake hasn't, either. The two of us have never been seen in public together, not by anybody who knows who we are.

"We will keep this low key, like I promised. We're arriving at separate times. We're booked in different hotel rooms. Tomorrow, we meet the label. We can come back here until we get booked into the studio. There's no pressure on us. If you want to get together and order room service, that's fine. If you want to go out and paint the town red, we can do that instead." Blake kisses my forehead.

I love how he has worked everything out, made all the plans but left things open to different opportunities. While he has booked us into separate rooms, I know we'll end up in the same room tonight. I can't imagine falling asleep without being wrapped in his arms. Two rooms might be unnecessary, but I appreciate his planning. I also know he is giving me the option of not making our relationship become public yet. Even if I said we could go out tonight for food, I know he would graciously accept if I suggested we act like friends instead of lovers.

"Painting the town red might have to wait until I manage to find something worthy of an official date with you." I pull out of his arms and grab my bag from the floor. There is nothing glamourous in the clothes Libby arranged for me. It never crossed my mind that I would even need anything remotely worthy of a fancy restaurant.

"If you do want to go out, we can paint the town red by going to a greasy spoon for all I care. The main thing I care about is your company."

"Has anybody told you that you are full of shit?"

"Yes, you." He laughs as he reminds me. He looks at me like he is trying to gauge how I'm feeling. "Are you nervous?"

"A little," I admit.

"About being seen with me?"

"No, you idiot." I laugh.

Although I know I have the option of us not going public with our relationship, I'm not worried about being seen with him. I'm worried about the gossip that might start about where I have been. What if reporters start digging around into the time before I decided to leave the limelight? What if somebody starts working out where I had been in the months before, discovering that it links up with where Hunter had been for the same times. The smoke will make them believe there must be flames, and they'll fan those flames until it is an inferno.

"Being seen in general?" Blake pulls me back from my spiral.

"Does it make me a terrible person to be a little nervous?"

"No, Red, it's natural. I'm a little nervous myself. They're going to publish articles about why somebody like you is with an idiot like me."

I laugh again and shake my head. "You are crazy."

"Only for things related to you." He grins over at me, and I feel the heat on my cheeks. He always sounds so flippant when he says things like this, but I can't help but tuck these sentences away into my heart. "Now, do you have everything?"

"Yep, I'm ready to go." I grab my car keys. Blake takes his own keys from the sideboard.

We head out to the cars, and he kisses me before I get into mine.

"Drive safely," he murmurs.

He gets into his own car and waits as I programme the satnav for the hotel we're booked into. It's a familiar hotel for me. It prides itself on a high-end clientele and the discretion it offers. I assume Blake has stayed there before, too, given it is close to the large arena we have both performed in. It is not a hotel I ever met Hunter in, something I'm grateful for. I've no idea how I'm going to cope in the future if I'm touring and end up in one of the rooms where I had seen Hunter.

I shake my head so I can focus. Once I'm happy I have the right route programmed in, I wave at Blake as I pull out of the drive. Blake blows me a kiss and then he sets off behind me. I have the radio on and one of his songs comes on. I smile to myself, wishing I had a collection of his albums on CD to play in the car instead of the radio, so his voice could stay with me the whole way.

***

Hours later, I pull my car into the parking spot in the hotel parking. I reach for my bag. I pull out the thin scarf I have and wrap it around my neck to hide my face a little, and add the baseball cap. I take my bag and then head in the direction of the hotel lobby so I can check in.

Blake has prepaid for the rooms, and the woman on the check-in desk gives no indication that she knows who I am when I pick up my key. There is no curiosity on her face when she sees my identification, no surprise in her tone when she welcomes me to their hotel. Clearly, they're worth their weight in gold for promised discretion.

I head in the direction of the lift that will take me up to the floor my room is on. I walk through the large lobby, down the corridor where their spacious conference rooms are set, past the staircase that leads to their basement gym and spa. I follow the corridor around and see the lifts, a smile on my face as I wonder if Blake is already here and checked in, or if I'm here first. I know we're booked on the same floor, and despite it only being a few hours since I saw him, I feel a flutter of anticipation about seeing him again.

My hand reaches for the button of the lift, but before I can touch the button, somebody takes hold of my wrist. My first thought is that it is Blake so as I turn to look at the owner of the hand, there is a smile on my face, but then I notice the hand isn't wearing the ring I got him, and the wrist doesn't have the friendship bracelet I made him.

"I thought it was you," Hunter whispers. "What the fuck are you doing here?"

"What are you doing here?" I echo. I pull my wrist free from him and jab at the button for the lift.

"I've just finished some interviews, me and Bess," Hunter explains. I jab at the lift button again.

"Fucked her yet? Or have you lost the ability to hoodwink women now the news is out there about your wife and perfect family?" I snarl.

"Keep your voice down," Hunter hisses, looking around.

"If you didn't want me making a scene, you should have left me the hell alone. You should have pretended you hadn't seen me," I snap.

I jab at the lift button again and I'm relieved to hear the lift ping, the doors opening. I step inside and press the button for the floor my room is on, but Hunter steps into the lift before the door closes.

"Briar Rose—" he starts, but I hold my hand up.

"Do not call me that! You shouldn't even be here, Hunter. I want nothing to do with you." I press the lift buttons for my floor and stare at the display to show the change of the floors, waiting for my freedom.

"Fine, but...."

"Does your wife know what you get up to behind her back? Or is she still in the dark, thinking you're a wonderful husband and the best father? You make me sick."

"I wasn't making you sick when you were on your knees before me, or have you forgotten how we were when we were together?" Hunter steps closer towards me and I take a step back, backing into the corner of the lift.

"Get the fuck away from me," I shout. It's loud, but the shaking of my voice betrays how weak I feel.

"I know you remember how we were, I bet you feel it in your bones and miss me since I left," he taunts.

"What I feel is shame, which is what you ought to feel. We were fucked-up, Hunter."

"How can you say that?" His eyes narrow as he glares at me.

"It should never have happened," I snap.

The lift pings to announce the arrival of my floor, and the doors open, but Hunter's still in my way.

"We should talk. Come on, Princess, let me into your room and we can talk about everything," Hunter pleads.

I push past him to get out of the lift. I don't want to go into my room because I don't want him to know where I'm staying. The alternative is arguing with him in a hallway. Neither is a good option, but us two being in a room together where nobody else can see terrifies me. All I can hope is I can get into my room and leave him in the hallway.

"I don't want to talk to you, ever again. You should go back downstairs before somebody misses you. Maybe that precious wife of yours?" I snap at him. I see my room so I step towards it, desperate to get inside so I can shut the door and lock him out. Hunter follows me.

"We need to talk. I hate how we left things."

"What you mean is you hate I'm a loose end. I'm somebody who could ruin that perfect life of yours," I throw back, but again, I sound a lot less brave than I want to sound. Hunter seems to know that I'm not confident in my words because he smirks.

"Like you have forgotten, my beautiful Briar Rose, that I'm the one who could totally fuck up your wonderful life. How many things could I ruin for you? Your record deals. Endorsement deals. I've already ruined your film career dreams."

He takes a step towards me. My breath quickens.

"Stay away from me," I cry.

"What are you going to do if I don't?" he taunts.

"I'll scream," I warn, though I'm still on the verge of tears and shaking from the fear.

"You never screamed before, and I know it's because you never wanted to, no matter what you say now." Hunter takes another step towards me.

"No!"

"Rose?"

This voice—the one that makes me think of warm honey—comes from behind me. I didn't hear his footsteps behind me, and I don't know how long he's been there, hearing this exchange between me and Hunter. I take a step backwards towards him and I feel Blake reach for my hand. He takes the hotel key card from my hand, and then once my hand is free, he holds it.

"Hunter was just leaving," I say. Blake's squeeze of my hand is reassuring, and I sound much stronger. My heart, which had been pounding in my chest in an erratic rhythm, seems to realise it's been working overtime, slowing slightly.

"We still have things to talk about, Briar Rose." Hunter stares at me, refusing to look at Blake.

"Actually, Rose and I are due in a meeting. Maybe you two can catch up another time, at Rose's convenience," Blake suggests. The way he stresses my name each time makes me think he knows how much I do not want to be around Hunter.

"I'm sorry, this is nothing to do with you." Hunter still doesn't look at Blake. He keeps his attention on me. His eyes—the ones that had always reminded me of clear blue skies on a summer day—look cloudy and frustrated. I never realised before how cold they are.

Hunter reaches out to me.

"Leave me alone," I warn, but my hand is shaking in Blake's, and I feel like my legs are on the verge of giving way. The next thing I know—before I'm even aware of what is happening—Blake has opened the door to the hotel room and swept me inside.

"Leave her the fuck alone," Blake snaps at Hunter before slamming the door shut.

Blake takes one look at me, then sweeps me off my feet and puts me down on the sofa in the suite. It takes me a second to realise that I've dropped my bag next to the hotel door.

"I'm sorry, I'm sorry," I cry. Blake sits and pulls me onto his lap. His arms are wrapped tightly around me, but I'm still shaking.

"That's him, isn't it?" he murmurs.

"Yes."

"You're okay, Rose, you don't have to see him. We can go check in to another hotel."

"I'm sorry," I repeat as I try to get a handle on my emotions.

"You've nothing to be sorry for. He's a piece of shit. He's a dick."

"He's the dick that can ruin everything." My heart pounds in my chest.

"I know he's married, but it wouldn't be the end of the world, Red. You didn't know about his wife. Nobody did," he says, soothingly.

"It isn't just about him being married and having children."

"So, tell me," Blake implores. I shake my head against his chest.

"I can't."

"You can tell me anything." Blake moves his head to look at me. "You can trust me."

I sit still in his lap for a moment. I know I should have told him—weeks ago—but the idea of saying these secrets aloud is terrifying. I'm scared that this will change everything between us. Everything between Blake and I has felt so precious. He's never pushed me to tell him everything, but if I leave this it might fester between us.

God knows it's already festered enough in my heart.

I shift off Blake's lap and sit on the other side of the sofa to him, pulling my knees up to my chest and wrapping my arms around my legs.

"I should have ended things with Hunter myself. I let things go on much longer than I should have. I should have walked away the first moment he hurt me," I say. Blake looks at me with an expression on his face that is a mix between fury and comprehension.

"He was violent?"

"He hurt me when we were together, sexually." I stumble over the last word. "The first time, it was just him pinning me down on the bed. Then he'd hit me in the face when we were intimate. He liked to grab my face, hold my chin so he could ejaculate on me. He liked to choke me. Sometimes with his hand, sometimes it was his forearm. Every time I struggled, it would spur him on. He said he liked it when I cried. Sometimes, when we had sex, he would get rough, put his hand over my mouth, and pin me down. I couldn't talk; I couldn't move. I told him afterwards I didn't like it, and then he'd be gentle, but it would happen again."

The words spill out of my mouth, tasting bitter. My stomach turns over and I feel the bile rise. Blake looks shell-shocked.

"He...." he starts, but I don't think he knows how to finish.

"I should have ended it the first time he did it, but I was stupid, reckless. It wasn't all the time, he would be soft and affectionate, and when he was, I convinced myself it was a one-off. When I told him I didn't like something, he made me feel like it was my fault I didn't like it. He said he was full of passion for me and made me feel like I should be grateful that he couldn't control himself around me. I can't let this secret come out because it would ruin me." The sentences bubble over my lips and everything feels disjointed.

"Rose, if he ever tried to tell this to anybody, he's the one going to be ruined. You're the innocent party in this." Blake clears his throat. He stands and paces a little.

"Hunter told me if I ever said anything publicly, he would tell everyone that I begged him for rough sex, that I knew about Isla, but I still chased him," I explain. I'm still on the sofa, still frozen in that same position of trying to hold myself together.

"People would believe you, Rose." Blake continues to pace, and I can't read the expression on his face. I stare at him. There's one final secret to spill.

"He'll tell everybody I had an abortion."

Blake stops pacing.

"What?" He sounds like he can't comprehend what I said. I wipe the tears from my cheeks.

"Hunter got me pregnant. When I told him, he told me he would sort it. Sorting it was getting me lined up with two doctors so I could be given pills for an abortion. He told me it was for the best, that we were too young, had too much to do together. He made it sound so simple, so logical. Then, the day after I had the abortion, he went out with his wife and his two children to a film premier. That's how I found out. About her, about them. I found out about them along with the rest of the world."

"Rose," he whispers. He sounds shell-shocked, but I can't stop the words from spilling over my lips.

"He ghosted me, as if announcing Isla and the existence of his children wasn't enough of a statement that I shouldn't talk to him again. I had a complication after the abortion, some retained tissue, and I had to go to a private clinic. Hunter wouldn't even answer my calls. I only saw him once after the abortion, the day he told me he would ruin me if I dared speak out about anything."

Blake starts pacing again, his brow furrowed and a look of fury on his face. I don't speak. I just wait for him to look at me. When he does, I still can't read his expression. It's jarring, as I've always thought he had such an expressive face, but I have no idea what he's thinking.

He clears his throat. "I need some fresh air," he says, his voice catching on the last word.

"Okay," I murmur. I expect him to head out to the balcony of the suite, but instead he opens the door to the suite and steps out into the corridor, shutting the door behind him.

I sit quietly for a minute. I don't know how I'd expected him to react but walking out without saying anything wasn't anything I'd considered. I think about how Blake had reacted when the newspaper article had been published about his father, how he'd gone quiet for a while. Maybe he needs a minute to process what I've told him, to accept the secrets I'd been hiding.

I sit and watch the time on my watch, counting the minute hands ticking by. Time slows, minutes starting to feel like an hour. After fifteen minutes, I'm convinced. Blake doesn't need a few minutes to process. He's upset at what I did, that I wasn't truthful with him, and it feels clear that he's disgusted about how I let things happen with Hunter.

I uncurl myself from the position I'm in on the sofa. I cross the room to my bag, picking it up from the floor. I open the door, look down the corridor. Nobody is around so I head down the corridor to the lift, trying not to cry as I flee to my car.

Judgement from people had been my biggest fear, but judgement from Blake feels like a dagger to the chest, and I can't stand it.

Chapter Twenty-Two

Rose

THEN

"You know this is for the best, don't you, my beautiful Briar Rose?"

Hunter sits beside me in the hotel room. One of his hands holds mine and in the other hand, he holds the pill that I need to take.

"I know," I whisper.

"The doctor said—"

"I know what the doctor said." I cut him off.

I've been running the doctor's words in my head for days. Hunter arranged for me to meet the doctor a couple of days after the positive pregnancy test. I had the required appointments, was asked a million times if I was sure I was making the right decision. I know I am. Two days ago, I took the first tablet. Today is the second.

"Why are you hesitating?" Hunter asks. I look at him and his face shows his frustration, but he quickly smiles.

"I'm not hesitating," I reply, taking the tablet from him. He's already placed a glass of water on the table, so I pick it up and take the tablet before I can change my mind.

"Good girl," Hunter murmurs and he leans to kiss me. I pull away.

"I think I'm going to lie down for a bit."

I stand up and head to my room. I don't want him to follow me, and I don't expect him to, either. We haven't been intimate since we took the pregnancy test. As I get to the bed, I hear the door to my hotel suite shutting, and I know he has left. I get into bed, pulling the covers around me, letting the tears run freely down my face until the pillow is damp.

***

"You seemed off tonight, Briar Rose," Harry comments as we arrive back at the hotel after the concert. I can't wait to get back to my room so I can go to bed.

Harry looks at me expectantly as we get into the lift.

"I'll do better tomorrow." I force a bright smile. The cramps I've been ignoring all night as I've performed are getting more painful. I was expecting cramps, but yesterday, after the tablets, it hadn't felt so bad. I hadn't expected them today.

"Rest up, I don't want a repeat performance of tonight when you're on-stage tomorrow." Harry's voice carries on to me when he stops at his hotel room. I carry on towards mine.

"Will do, Harry," I call back. I get to my room and let myself in, shutting the door behind me and then I rush to the bathroom, grabbing my mobile phone as I pass the cabinet it was on. I sit on the floor in the bathroom, bringing my knees to my chest, which seems to help with the pain.

I bring up my messages, expecting to see something from Hunter. He usually messages me with a location to meet, either confirmation that he'll come to me, or an address for me to go to. There are no messages.

I send a message to him to ask what the plan is. As I wait for a reply, I open one of the news sites I like to read, a mix of news and celebrities. The top story in entertainment has a headline about Hunter. I click to open it.

HUNTER GREENWAY BREAKS HEARTS

Hunter Greenway broke our collective hearts today after news emerged that the hunk is off the market. Not only is he off the market, but it emerged that Hunter is married and has children, a little girl and a newborn son. See our exclusive pictures of Hunter, wife Isla, and children as they attended the film launch of Bananas, *a film featuring Hunter's voice work.*

I drop my phone in shock. This must be a mistake. I pick my phone back up again and look at the article, scrolling to the photographs. In full colour there are multiple pictures of Hunter, his arm around a tall, willowy, beautiful woman. There are pictures of him kissing a little girl, captioned as his daughter. There are pictures of him holding a small baby, a baby that can only be weeks old.

I scroll through them all, still sure this is an elaborate joke, but there is no denying this.

I text a link of the article to Hunter. I caption it asking what the hell is going on.

I get no response. My phone remains silent, all night.

***

I struggle through the rest of my concerts scheduled for the week. I fake smiles for photographers and talk of frivolous topics in interviews. I ask Harry to make sure interviewers are told not to ask me about the upcoming film role I'm supposed to have because I cannot bear the topic. I blame nerves for my reluctance to talk and Harry—who has always been pissed at me for speaking to the producers behind his back—rolled his eyes but at least followed through.

I hear nothing from Hunter.

Sunday provides a break from everything. The only thing on the schedule is Libby to go over some outfits for the next couple of weeks. This week there are no concerts until Wednesday, but then I have three more weeks of touring. After touring, I'm supposed to have a couple of weeks of break before filming starts. A couple of weeks to get myself together.

A couple of weeks for me to recover. I don't know if it is possible. Emotionally, it feels like I'm on a rollercoaster. Physically, I'm still suffering side effects. Mentally, I'm a wreck.

Libby lets herself into the hotel room.

"Sweetie, it's me," she calls. She sweeps into the bedroom, carrying a bunch of outfits on hangers.

"Hi, Libby," I reply, sitting up on the bed. I don't feel very well.

"Are you okay? You don't look great." Libby puts the clothes into the wardrobe and then sits on the bed next to me. She leans forward and puts a hand to my forehead. "You're hot, Rose. Are you sick? Do you need a doctor?"

"No, I'm okay," I say, pulling the covers off me. I'm planning on getting out of bed, to look alert and go over the outfits with her.

"Rose, you're bleeding," Libby gasps.

I was briefed by the doctor about what to expect and what to look out for as rare side effects. This amount of blood is one of the very rare side effects. I look at Libby.

"I think I need a doctor," I whisper.

"Shall I…." she starts, but I shake my head for whatever she is going to ask. Instead, I grab my phone. I have the number of the doctor that Hunter had arranged for me to see. I connect the call.

"Hi, Dr. Baker? This is Rose Dalton. I think I'm having some side effects. Would you possibly be able to meet me at my hotel?" I ask.

"What the fuck?" Libby murmurs behind me. She's holding the paperwork I'd been given, the paperwork I'd taken out to read earlier when the cramps had become painful. I focus my attention back on the call, giving the doctor my hotel information before hanging up. Libby stares at me, mouth agape.

"I don't want to talk about it," I say, then I head to the bathroom so I can get cleaned up for the doctor, leaving Libby in my room, staring after me.

***

"Why didn't you tell anybody?" Libby asks as she drives me home from the private hospital.

"I wasn't expecting any complications. It only happens to a small number of people. It was just dumb luck," I reply, staring out the window as she drives.

"I meant why didn't you tell anybody you were having an abortion? You've been touring and performing when you should have been resting."

"The show must go on, right?" I glance over to her. I see the grimace she pulls.

"That's bullshit. You could have cancelled a couple of shows, or waited until your concerts were done. I read the information pack; it clearly states to rest."

"When has anybody ever let me rest?" I snap at her. She's quiet for a minute and I sigh. She doesn't deserve my venom. "I'm sorry, Libby."

"No, I'm sorry. I'm sorry for the way you get treated. I'm sorry that you didn't have anybody to turn to."

I fall silent. I pick my phone out of my bag and send another message to Hunter. I tell him we need to talk, telling him that if he doesn't meet me tonight, I'll contact his wife. I follow up with a second message, telling him my location. I know from the news articles about him and his family that he's in the same city as me.

Libby makes sure I'm settled in the hotel room. She offers to stay, but I tell her it's okay, that I want to be alone. I'm feeling a little bit fragile, and all I want is peace and quiet. It takes a while to convince Libby to leave. By the time she leaves, it is early evening.

When there is a knock on the door half an hour later, I assume it is Libby who has come back to check on me. I get up to open the door and find Hunter. He shoves his way past me and slams the door behind him.

"Who the fuck do you think you are, making threats to me?" Hunter snaps.

I stare at him for a moment. I can't help but give a shocked laugh. Gone is the innocent and charming man he had portrayed, the man who would blush when I first took my clothes off. Gone is the man who told me he couldn't imagine being with anybody other than me. All that remains is the Hunter he would show when he got physical in bed. Somebody who wanted his own way and cared about nobody else.

"I'm the woman who you lied to." I fold my arms across my chest.

"You have got—"

"I'm the woman you convinced to have an abortion, and once you knew I'd gone through with it, you announced your family in the papers," I carry on, ignoring his interruption, glaring at him as I talk.

"If you dare speak to Isla—"

"You'll what, Hunter? I don't think there is anything you could do to me that is worse than what you've already done."

"I wouldn't try me," he snarls.

"I just want you to explain why you didn't tell me about Isla, about the kids."

"Seriously? You need me to explain that I lied to get in your pants? How fucking naïve are you, Princess?" Hunter laughs.

"What you did was cruel. Would you have even admitted you are married if I didn't get pregnant? I mean, we're supposed to be filming together in a couple of weeks, were you going to keep her a secret all through filming?"

"I'd find a way to get out of everything, if I were you."

"Why should I be the one to give everything up? I wasn't the one who lied about everything."

"Like anybody would believe you, but you could always try it and see how it goes. See how they react. They'll call you a slut. This will ruin you." Hunter's tone is threatening.

"I'll tell everyone what you did to me in bed," I snap.

"I'll tell everybody you begged me for it, that you enjoyed it." Hunter shrugs.

"I didn't!" I protest.

"You can imagine the headlines though, can't you. Hmm? Sweet, innocent Briar Rose and the dirty sex games she likes to play. Virginal pop princess and the kinky habits. I'm sure that will go down well with all the parents of your young fans. There'd be outrage. Briar Rose, the bad influence. Briar Rose, the kinky whore adulterer."

"I didn't do anything wrong," I exclaim, but I'm starting to panic.

"I can ruin you. I have the power to do that."

"You—"

"Find a way to get out of this film and stay the hell away from Isla." Hunter glares at me.

"You're going to great lengths to protect the woman you treat badly," I scoff.

"I treat her like the queen she is."

"Tell me something, do you like to choke your wife? Do you make her cry so it can make you hard? Do you whisper to her, 'cry for me, Princess, watch what is does to me' in her ear, like you did to me?" I snap, and he looks furious. I shrink back, realising how much he towers over me, how easily he can hurt me.

"I'd never do to Isla what you let me do to you. Everything I did to you, you deserved it, you're the type that needs it."

"I didn't let you do anything, Hunter. I asked you not to, more than once. You just didn't want to listen," I reply, my voice quiet. "Besides, I never asked you to cheat on your pregnant wife with me, for months! How could you do that if you love her? I feel—" I start, but he laughs.

"I don't give a shit what you feel, your feelings are irrelevant."

"What about Isla's feelings, are they irrelevant?" I ask.

"Leave Isla alone. I swear, I'll ruin you. You've nothing but your image, what people believe about you. Take your fans away and you're nothing, Briar Rose. You're a mediocre singer, a shitty songwriter, and you'll never come back from this scandal. You'll be some other washed-up, forgotten child singer who went off the rails, ruined everything and let herself go. Some dumb bitch who got pregnant and had an abortion. I'll tell everybody what you did. They'll fucking crucify you for it, you know they will. Speak a word about this to my wife, and I swear, I'll make you pay."

"You-you wouldn't," I stutter.

"I would. So quit, and stay away from Isla. That's the price of my silence."

I want to scream at him, but I can't find any words. Hunter gives me a smirk and then he stalks out of the room, leaving me alone, panting and terrified.

***

"I can't do it! I can't be in that stupid film," I scream.

Harry stands, hands on hips, looking disapproving as I pace around the room. My final concert on my tour is tonight, and I've run out of time to face up to seeing Hunter again, run out of confidence that I should remain with the project. I'm expected to stand across from him and act as his love interest. I can't do it. It will kill me.

Harry looks like he is going to kill me first, but it also looks like he is trying to keep his temper under control. I stop pacing and look at him, imploring, hoping that he'll fix this, that I won't have to see Hunter again.

"You are under contract. A stupid contract you signed without consulting anybody," Harry reminds me, his voice making it very clear he thinks this is my fault.

"I don't care. I don't care what the penalties are," I snap back.

Whatever the penalties are, they cannot be worse than me having to play Hunter's love interest. Even if I were brave enough to risk his wrath and him following through with his threat, I'm not brave enough to see him again, to work with him, day in day out, with that history between us. A financial fine would be so much easier than the emotional toll of seeing him again; I'd pay it ten times over. We haven't started filming anything yet. I can be replaced.

"They won't appreciate being made to look like you've walked away from their project. You can wave goodbye to any acting career you thought you were going to get. Your career would be dead in the water," Harry warns.

"They can say they fired me," I shoot back. "I don't care. I'm not going to do it. Tell them whatever you like."

"Oh, you think it's my job to go tell them that you're backing out, when you were grown enough to make your own bed. It isn't my job to tell them you're breaking contract."

"No, but it is your job to do as I ask, so do it, otherwise I'll find somebody else to take your place. You're not the only manager in town, you need me more than I need you," I snap, keeping my voice as stern as I can, trying not to show my desperation. It isn't fair to Harry as he is a good manager and I enjoy working with him, but I feel like I'm clutching at straws, clutching onto the last of my sanity.

"Yet you're begging me to do your dirty work, even though you don't need me." Harry stands with a mocking look on his face.

"Do your fucking job, Harry," I shout.

"One day, you're going to have to stop being a melodramatic pop princess," Harry snarls, but I don't let his words affect me. "I'll sort this fucking mess, but threaten me like that again, or go behind my back like you did in the first place, and you'll be the one who is sorry," he continues, his voice raised, and then he storms out of the room, slamming the door behind him.

My heart is racing in my chest, and I can feel the tears coming. The whole world feels like it is shifting, and I don't feel like I'm on solid ground. I desperately want somebody to tell me that things will be okay, but I don't see how it will ever be okay. My life is in tatters.

"Who was it, Rose?" Libby asks. Her voice makes me jump. I forgot she was still here. She made herself scarce in the other room when it was clear Harry and I were on the verge of a disagreement.

"What?" I look at her. She has a concerned expression on her face.

"I didn't ask you before because it wasn't my business, but I'm making it my business now. Who got you pregnant, Rose? I know you don't want to tell me, but I'm pretty sure based on how you're acting that it is only one of two guys who could have been the father. So, who was it? Martin Wise or Hunter Greenway?" Libby keeps her gaze on me, and she knows from my reaction who it was. As soon as she says Hunter's name, I feel my legs go weak.

"I didn't know he was married," I whisper as she walks towards me. She puts her arms around me and wraps me into a warm hug.

"Oh, sweetie," she soothes as I sob against her.

"I didn't know, I swear. Not until he went public with her and their kids. I'm an awful person, Libby, there is a special place in hell for people like me." I can't stop the tears.

"No, that's not true. He kept his wife and his family from everybody. He kept that secret from everybody in the business for two and a half years. If nobody else knew, and he didn't tell you, how were you supposed to know?"

"I should have behaved better than I did."

"You are not the one at fault here! He led you on, he didn't tell you about his wife. You can't make an informed decision if he wasn't giving you all the facts. You didn't choose to be the other woman, Rose, he didn't give you the opportunity to walk away."

"I would have walked away," I cry. "I should have walked away before I got pregnant. He..." I start, but then the words seem to stick in my throat. Libby pulls away from the embrace she has me in. She guides me to sit on the sofa.

"Tell me. I know you have something you're keeping from me, and I know you need to get it off your chest before you explode," she coaxes.

"He would get rough," I admit.

She sucks in her breath and looks furious. "He got physical?"

"Not like you're imagining. He was rough, in bed. Sometimes he slapped my face, sometimes he grabbed my throat. A couple of times, I was really frightened because I couldn't breathe. He had a hand over my mouth, his arm against my throat, and I always told him afterwards I didn't like it, but then he'd do it again. I should have stopped everything then, but I didn't because I'm weak. I'm a terrible person."

"Hunter Greenway is a piece of shit!" Libby gets up from the sofa and paces the room. "You should tell the production company. You should tell somebody other than me."

"I can't tell anybody."

"You can! You could even go to the police."

"I can't," I scoff.

"If you told him no, and he kept doing it, that's sexual assault, Rose." Libby's voice is soft and gentle. She sits next to me and takes my hand. "You understand that, right?"

"I consented to sex." I frown.

"You told him not to choke you, and he kept doing it. That's sexual assault." She repeats her earlier sentence, still in a gentle tone.

"Nobody will believe me." I wipe my eyes. I can feel the headache brewing in my head. I feel like I've had nothing but headaches and heartache for months.

"People will believe you, not him," Libby vows, but I know for every person like Libby who believes me, there will be a hundred people who believe him, believe that I deserve everything. I'm the homewrecker. I'm the slut. I'm the one who slept with a married man.

"I can't talk about this, I can't! I'm going to get persecuted for this, I won't survive it. I can't do this. I can't! I can't! I can't do it anymore! I'm supposed to get on stage in a bit, sing and perform, then it'll be publicity and people shoving cameras in my face trying to find out why I'm not taking the role, I can't do it," I cry. The tears are back and I'm shaking. She holds me close for a moment.

"I'll help you," she soothes.

"How? Do you have a time machine so I can go back in time and erase the day I ever met him?" I pull away and dry my eyes again. "I'm falling to pieces, Libby, nothing can help me."

"I can help you get away," Libby offers. "I can get you some breathing space. How does that sound?"

I hold on to her hand like she is my lifeline.

"Please, Libby, please help me," I plead, and I tell her every single secret, bleeding myself dry.

***

I get through the concert. I smile and wave at fans. I get taken back to my hotel for the night and say goodbye to my driver, insisting he goes home to his family, shoving some autographs and gifts to him to give to his children. Instead of going to my hotel room, I get into the back of Libby's car. I lie on the backseat as she drives me out of the underground parking. She's already packed my bags and cleared my hotel room for me.

Libby doesn't force me to talk. She drives for hours to her house. Her wife is away—still on tour—so there will be nobody else I need to make small talk to. The two of them are supposed to be going on their holiday this weekend, Libby travelling to meet Maeve before they fly away together.

It's long past midnight when we arrive at her house. Libby ushers me into the house and shows me to the spare bedroom, telling me she'll sort things out. I give her my bank details, telling her to do what she needs to do, and she tells me to go to bed.

I do as I'm told and get into the comfortable looking bed, pulling the covers around me. Aside from going to the bathroom, I don't leave the bedroom for two days, until Libby knocks on my door and tells me I need to come downstairs. Despite sleeping a lot, I feel so tired, right down to my bones.

I meet her in the living room.

"I've made some plans for you, providing you still want to go through with what we talked about."

"I do."

"Everything is sorted for you, sweetie, but you don't have to do anything if you don't want to," she says, looking at me carefully.

"I want to. I need to." My voice cracks as I speak.

"I've booked you a place to stay. It's available until the end of January so you can stay there for a while and get your head sorted. It's in a small coastal village. I know the owner from some work they did for me. It's quiet and secluded and you stay there from Monday next week. It was the earliest I could get a long rental place sorted in a location that seemed suitable."

"You didn't have to do that."

"I said I would help. Besides, you can help me, too. You can stay here and housesit for me next week."

"I'm so grateful for everything, especially when you're going to be going on your holiday."

"It's fine. I need to set off to meet Maeve later today. I'll take your mobile phone with me, so you can avoid temptation of contacting people when you don't want to. Or you can leave it here, whatever you want. I got you a new phone to use, it is on the table, I've put my number in it for you," Libby explains.

"You have done so much for me, I appreciate everything," I say, and my voice cracks a little as I talk.

"The owners of the house don't know who you are. I think if you keep your head down, you'll be fine. It's a really tiny village."

"I'm a little worried that my anonymity will last all of two minutes." I sigh.

"Well, I've a plan to help with that, too." Libby smiles and she gestures towards the table where there are a couple boxes of hair dye and a pair of hairdresser scissors.

"You've thought of a lot."

"Yes, trying to make it easy for you to get some peace. I've packed you a suitcase in the car. There's a car on the drive, it's second hand, I didn't want to go too crazy," Libby explains.

I feel a fizzle of hope in me that this could work, that I can really get away from everything. The idea of being away from Hunter, being away from his face being plastered in every single paper, being by myself, away from the media intrusion, away from the hurt from my mother and father, it sounds like heaven.

I lean forward in my seat, holding Libby.

"Thank you," I whisper.

"It'll all be okay, I promise."

I clutch on to her promise for the rest of the day, desperate that this will be the relief I need, desperate for something in my life to change, praying it will be for the better.

Chapter Twenty-Three

Blake

NOW

I leave Rose in the hotel room, desperate for some fresh air because I feel sick, struggling with the surging hot rage within me.

I knew Rose was holding on to something but hearing her talk about how much Hunter had hurt her, knowing how badly he treated her, nothing had prepared me for it.

In my whole life, I've never felt this angry. I've never wanted to hurt anybody before—not like this. I want to harm Hunter. I want to put my hands around his throat and choke him so he can have a taste of his own medicine. I want him to be the one who feels like all the air is gone, to know he's powerless. Fucking sadist.

The way I feel scares the goddamn life out of me. I've spent most of my life being the bigger person, forgiving things, trying to focus on the light, but this is a darkness that threatens to consume me. My head is filled with images of Hunter's limp body and my bloodied fists. It feels like a poison coursing through my veins.

I storm down the corridor, trying to get away from the desire to find Hunter and make him pay for what he did to Rose. I know that finding Hunter isn't what I should be doing; I know I need a minute by myself to sort myself out and to stop myself from shaking.

I want to go outside for some air and calm myself down, then I want to get back to Rose, to hold her, to tell her I'm sorry for what happened to her. I want to tell her that I'm sorry for everything, that I'm there for her, for whatever she needs.

I want to tell her that she is amazing, that she's strong.

I just need to shake off some of the thoughts I have about Hunter first.

When I hold Rose, I want it to be only with love in my heart and tenderness in my arms, not this blind fury that seems to have overtaken me.

I walk down the corridor, away from the lift and towards the stairwell on the opposite side of the hotel, storming around the curve of the building. All I can think of is getting down the stairs, getting some air, then getting back to Rose, back to the woman I...

I open the door to the stairwell and sit down on the top step, just for a minute so I can steady myself. I put my head in my hands and take a deep breath. I think of everything Rose just told me, all those secrets about the many ways he hurt her. How many times did he hurt her when they were together? Once is too many, and it kills me to think that it is more than once. Logically, I know it would be more. I know he'll have hurt her many times and taken things from her that she might feel she'll never get back. I hate him for what he's done.

I'm not sure how long I sit like an idiot in the stairwell before I come to my senses. The thoughts and misty fury about Hunter dissipate, and all that remains in my head is Rose.

I don't need fresh air. I don't need to do anything, other than hold Rose. Hold her and tell her how much I care about her. Not just care for her but... love her.

I knew I was falling for her; I was imagining what a future with her could look like, dreaming that we could be together and hoping she could feel the same about me. Right now, it hits me like a sledgehammer just how much I love her.

I've never loved anybody in the way I love Rose. I've never loved anybody this fiercely. It burns brightly in me, the kind of love that has the power to run forever.

I stand up, step back out into the hallway, my only thought being Rose, but Hunter stands directly in my path. Instantly, the blind fury is back. Every muscle is tense and I am desperate for a release.

"So, you two are together?" Hunter asks.

"Fuck all to do with you," I snarl.

Hunter leans against the wall and looks like he has been waiting patiently for me. I wonder if he saw me storm down the hallway and waited for me to come back.

"How long have you been together?"

"Again, fuck all to do with you."

"Can I give you a bit of advice?" Hunter asks.

"Nope." I push past him.

"She isn't the type of woman you have a relationship with."

"What?" I stop and stare at him.

"Rose is the type of girl you fuck. She is not the type you make long-term commitments to. Bang her, get her out of your system, then pass her on to the next man to have their time with her."

"You are fucking disgusting, you know that?" I snarl.

"I'm just being honest, mate."

"If I'm being honest, *mate*, you make me sick."

"What I do know is you won't be able to stand this, to know what she is like. The great, romantic Blake won't cope knowing the girl he's with is a whore." Hunter laughs as he steps closer to me. "Drives you mad knowing she's not the sweet innocent virginal princess you thought she was, doesn't it? I bet it's driving you mad thinking about how hard I fucked her." Hunter gives a tut of his tongue. "The sad thing is, she's such damaged goods. If I went to her, she'd be begging on her knees for me to fuck her again, because she likes it. She likes what I give her. Maybe I'll see her before I leave, because it's a beautiful sight when she's crying and choking on my dick."

Hunter is standing way too close to me. He has completely underestimated my fury. Before he can step back away from me, I bring my knee up, swiftly, and kick him in the balls.

It's way more satisfying than I thought it ever could be, watching him crumple to the floor, knees up to his chest, hands over his dick, like anything is going to provide relief from the pain. His eyes seem to roll back in his head, and his mouth is in the shape of a wide O as he lets out an agonized moan. He looks like he is sweating and on the verge of vomiting from the pain.

There's a small part of me that still demands to get down on his level, put my hands on him, choke him, kick him, and punch him as he lies writhing on the floor. The more logical part of me knows doing that wouldn't be anything good for Rose. Instead, I pull my phone out of my pocket.

"Yeah, that'll stop your dick rising for a bit, you prick," I snap. I take a couple of pictures of him. "If you go near Rose again, if you even dare speak her name, if I even catch you looking in her direction again, I'll release these pictures with a statement about what happens to men who abuse women. If there is ever any hint of you chasing after another woman like you did with Rose, I'll send these pictures to your wife and tell her all about her loving husband and how he likes to abuse women, if she isn't already aware of it."

I put my phone away and start to walk back down the hallway towards the hotel room where Rose is.

"I didn't abuse her," Hunter groans from the floor. I turn and kneel beside him.

"You put your hands on her in violence. You never asked her if she wanted you to be rough. You belittled her when she told you she didn't like it. She didn't ask for any of that shit, and you never asked for her consent. That's assault, dickhead. That's abuse. If you're still struggling to comprehend this, maybe we should go to the police and ask for their definition."

"No, I…." Hunter starts, but I ignore him.

I leave him on the floor and head back to the hotel room that I left Rose in. It's her hotel room but the key is in my pocket because I put it in there after I rushed Rose away from Hunter. I open the door and step inside.

"Rose?" I call. I don't get a response. She isn't in the living area. I check in the bedroom, calling her name again. There is still no answer. "Red?" I call as I check the bathroom. The only response is the silence.

I need to find her. I go back to the hallway, rush to the lift, stepping over Hunter in my hurry, planning on heading to the car park. If her car is here, she's still here somewhere. When I eventually make it to the parking area, her car is missing.

Rose has left, and it's all my fault.

***

I feel like a failure as I go back up to my hotel room. Thankfully, Hunter is nowhere to be seen because I don't think I could trust myself to see him.

My bag is still packed, still on the bed where I ditched it when I arrived earlier, my guitar case propped up next to the bed. I pick up my bag and guitar case, make sure I have everything, then go back to the parking area where my car is parked. I regret my decision for us to drive in separate cars. I suggested it because I thought it would make Rose more comfortable, able to control what we present to the world. If we had travelled together in one car, would she have waited for me to get back to the room? Would she have even seen Hunter? We'd have arrived together, checked in together, and we'd be laughing together right now as we talked about going to our meeting tomorrow.

I get in my car, pull up the satnav. I pick up the address for where Rose and I have been staying but I pause. What if Rose leaving is because she doesn't want to see me? What if she needs space, needs time?

I take a deep breath as that feeling of dread washes over me. I've fucked this all up. Rose doesn't want to see me; if she did, she'd have stayed. I can't go running after her, back to the place where she has found sanctuary, not if it means I could ruin the peace she has found there. I can't be the dark cloud that settles over her happy space. I don't know what to do for the best; any option I think about feels like it could be the wrong one, something that hurts Rose more than she has already been hurt. I refuse to do that, to cause her more pain.

I sit in my car for a few minutes before I realise my heart is pounding. I take a couple of deep breaths. I lean for a moment, my head on the steering wheel. My gaze falls on the keys in the ignition and I see the door key for the place I'd rented before going to stay with Rose. It's miles away, but it is an option. A place I can stay for the night so I can think. I don't want to stay in the hotel, not given Hunter is here. The meeting with the label can't happen without Rose, so there is no need for me to stay in town. I can cancel that later. Right now, I need to get out of here.

I shake my head, decided on my course of action. I update the satnav with the details of my hometown. Without giving myself an opportunity to change my mind, I put the car in gear and start driving, out of the hotel, onto the main road. I try to focus on the road rather than my racing thoughts, failing miserably.

The rented flat is cold and feels abandoned when I arrive. It's evening, I'm shattered from driving for most of the day. I throw my car keys onto the countertop and take my bag and guitar case into the bedroom. I kick off my shoes. I cancel the meeting with the record label, claiming sickness, and then switch off my mobile as I don't want to be disturbed. I climb into the bed, pull the covers around me, and I'm so exhausted that I'm quickly asleep, despite the problems weighing on my mind.

***

I wake early due to a combination of forgetting to close the blinds and a series of bad dreams plaguing my head. I sit up and switch my phone on. I curse that Rose and I never exchanged numbers, but it had never felt needed before. We spent all our time together, living together. Aside from when I went to see my parents, if we were out, we went out together. Now I've no ability to contact her. I don't even have a key to the cottage, even if I did decide to go back to Whistlethorpe.

I could contact Maeve and ask for her to contact Rose via Libby. They're home from their holiday, but I can't bring myself to call Maeve and explain what has happened. Not only do I not feel like I can bring Maeve into the topic without Rose being the one to tell her, I'm also too ashamed to admit to Maeve what a mess I made. I know she'll call me a dick for not doing what I should have done immediately—hold Rose.

I resist the urge to call Maeve. I resist the urge to beg to talk to Libby. The only person I want to speak to is Rose. I should go to the cottage. That's where she'll be; I'm sure of it. I can knock on the door and ask her to talk. I can apologise for the way I handled the situation. I can tell her how much I love her. I can get down on my knees and beg for forgiveness, if that is what she wants or needs me to do. If she wants me to go, even after I've apologised, I can do that.

I shower and dress, gathering my things and getting back in my car. I key in the address for Rose's cottage then set off on the drive. I have the radio playing in the background, and as I hit the motorway, one of Rose's songs come on. I take it as a sign that I've made the right decision. As I drive, I think of what I want to say to her, how I'm going to apologise for handling the situation so badly.

I finally turn the car down the street to the cottage. I drive to the top of the street so I can turn around. I pull up outside the house. Rose's car isn't on the driveway. Other than travelling yesterday, in all the time I've stayed with her, she's only gone out in the car when we went hiking. There's an ominous pit of dread that forms in my stomach.

I get out of my car and look through the window next to the front door. I can tell she's been here because there is a leaflet on the sideboard. I know the sideboard was clear when we left, so it must have been something delivered since that morning, something she's picked up and placed there.

I knock on the door but there is no answer. I go sit back in my car and wait until I accept that the reason her car isn't here—the reason she isn't answering—is because she has left. Rose is so hurt and angry about the way I reacted—the way I treated her—she's abandoned the place I started to think as home.

Feeling lost, I start my car. I change the satnav back to the place I left this morning. I start the drive back, losing all my optimism and hope leaving with every mile I drive, kicking myself for my actions, and cursing my stupidity.

***

I arrive back at the rental place, feeling frustrated. I'm knackered from driving again. My legs are stiff and my back aches. Mostly though, I feel frustrated with myself. I was so sure that I wasn't going to mess up the next time I found somebody I loved, yet I did it again—made the stupid choice and let everything slip through my fingers.

I ditch my bag on the floor and start my phone. On the drive back, I clung to the idea that maybe Rose wants to contact me as much as I want to contact her, and that—maybe—she asked Libby to get a message to me. When my phone restarts but remains silent, it hits harder than I thought it would. I'm used to feeling abandoned and an afterthought, but this enforced silence from Rose has the power to kill me—even if I only have myself to blame.

I sit on the sofa and scroll through my phone and updates, looking for a distraction. When I flick through my social media, I see Olive and Tyler have uploaded several new pictures of their new baby. In most of the pictures, both children are obscured because I know they value their privacy. There is one of the oldest daughter—taken from the back—leaning over to kiss the new baby. There is a picture of Tyler holding the baby, leaning over to kiss Olive. They look exhausted but serenely happy.

I want to comment on their post, but I'm wary because I don't trust for it not to be taken out of context by somebody who has too much interest in what I post. Instead, I text Olive, telling her that I saw the new photographs, offering her and Tyler my congratulations again.

My phone bleeps a few minutes later. My heart seems to skip a beat as I hope it is Rose, but then I see it is from Olive.

Olive Who Inspired Repercussions Saunders: Thanks, Blake! Starting to feel like my brain is in gear again. Next time you're in town, let me know. I owe you tea at ours.

I reply that I'm in town. She messages back with her address, in case I've forgotten, and proposes seven thirty for the next evening.

It takes me a minute but then I reply to tell her I would love to.

***

Seven thirty, I arrive at Olive and Tyler's house. It's the same house she had when we had dated, where Tyler had been her lodger.

I knock on the door, and it takes a minute for Tyler to answer. It feels like a lifetime ago since I saw him last. It was before my first album was released, when I checked Olive would be comfortable with me releasing some songs. Before that, the last time I saw him was the night Olive broke up with me. I feel like I'm an entirely different person to who I was then.

Except yet again, I'm at this house, my heart mangled.

Tyler smiles. "Nice to see you, Blake."

"Not at all weird, right?" I laugh.

"Not at all." Tyler laughs jovially, opening the door wide. "Come in, Fitz is upstairs trying to convince Mia to get back to bed."

I follow Tyler through the house to the kitchen. I catch the smell of roast chicken and my mouth waters slightly. Tyler resumes what he must have been doing when I arrived, working his way around the kitchen doing various tasks like unplugging the steamer, setting our plates, grabbing a serving spoon.

"Do you need a hand with anything?" I ask.

"No, it's fine."

"Blake," Olive exclaims as she walks into the kitchen. "Give me a hug. No photographers around this time."

"Thankfully." Tyler laughs. Olive pulls me for a hug.

"You do not look like somebody who only gave birth a week ago." I smile at her when she pulls away.

"Thank God for exceptionally good genetics and some sturdy clothing," she jokes.

"You both look like the transition from one child to two has been a breeze." I smile.

"Ha, yeah, come back at three this morning when we're doing some crazy exchange of crying children and tell me it's a breeze." There is nothing but humour in Tyler's tone. I expect he wouldn't care if he was up eight times a night. I know he's got everything he ever wanted in life.

"Drink?" Olive asks.

"Just a water is fine, thanks," I reply. She steps around me so she can get to the fridge. She pulls out a jug of water and then moves across the kitchen to get some glasses. As she passes Tyler, she stops, pushing herself onto her tiptoes so she can kiss him.

"Mia promises me she is going to go to sleep in five minutes," she says.

"I love how you sound like you believe she isn't going to be standing at the stairgate in fifteen minutes and complaining so she can come downstairs," he replies, a grin on his face.

"Well, if fifteen minutes if what we have to play with tonight, hurry up dishing up," Olive jokes. She pours three glasses of water and Tyler carries on plating up the food. Olive hands me one of the glasses and she carries the other two.

"Come through to the dining room, Blake," she suggests. I let her lead me through to the next room where the table has been set for tea. In the corner of the room there is a Moses basket on a stand, and the baby is soundly asleep inside.

"I see you got your way with the name," I comment.

She laughs and takes a seat at the table. "You try disagreeing with the woman who has just pushed out a baby. Labour was long, there was no way Ty was going to disagree."

"It's not often I disagree with you anyway, Fitz," Tyler says as he comes into the room, carrying a gravy-boat and one plate of food. He puts this plate in front of Olive, the gravy in the centre of the table, and then heads back to the kitchen.

"I see you two still go by Ty and Fitz." I take a seat on the opposite side of the table to where Olive is.

"Old habits die hard, even after I took his surname." Olive laughs. She glances over at Ivy as she fusses a little in the basket.

"She's adorable, Olive." I smile as I look at Ivy.

"She looks so much like Mia. They're so sweet together. Mia's taking her big sister duties very seriously, she sings nursery rhymes to her every night." She chuckles. Tyler returns with two more plates, putting one in front of me, and then he takes a seat next to Olive with his own plate.

"This looks really nice." I pick up my knife and fork, feeling hungry.

I haven't eaten a proper meal since I last ate with Rose. I can't help but wonder—for the millionth time—where she is, what she is doing right now. She's been on my mind constantly. Last night, when I made a chocolate spread sandwich, I wondered what she was eating for her tea, hoping she was being taken care of and hoping she was doing better than me.

"Ty's been keeping me well fed since Ivy arrived. I hope you don't mind it's a roast dinner. I had a craving for good roast potatoes," Olive explains as she cuts one of her potatoes. She takes a bite and closes her eyes like she's eating the most delicious thing she's ever tasted.

"What have you been up to, Blake?" Tyler asks, an affectionate smile on his face as he watches Olive.

"Not much, really. I've been writing some new music recently."

"Have you still been in town?" Olive asks.

I shake my head. "No, I was staying on the east coast, getting away from it all."

"With the person who was poorly?" Olive prompts.

"Yeah," I reply. Olive and Tyler exchange glances.

"Sounds like there is a story there," Tyler comments.

I cut a piece of the meat on my plate. I take a bite, if only for a distraction from answering.

"Not really," I finally reply.

Tyler changes the subject. He asks a million questions about what it's like to be on tour. The light conversation carries on as we finish tea. As soon as Olive puts her knife and fork down, Ivy seems to know it is time to make a fuss. She lets out the loudest wail I've ever heard.

"At least I got to finish my food this time." Olive laughs as she gets up. "Excuse me, let me go give her a feed," she says. She scoops baby Ivy out of the Moses basket and heads out of the dining room. Tyler and I remain at the dining table.

"So, who is the woman who has you looking so perplexed?" Tyler asks, leaning back in his chair.

"It's that obvious?" I sigh.

"It might help to talk." Tyler shrugs.

It's a generous offer from him. We were never really friends when I dated Olive. Tyler tolerated me more than anything. In fairness to him, he tried to be friends when I initially started dating Olive, but I was intimidated by him and all their friends. It didn't make friendship easy, compounded by how inattentive I was to Olive.

We might not be the best of friends, but right now, I need somebody to offload to, before I implode under the weight of it all.

"I think I've ruined it all," I admit. "She was hurt by somebody, and I didn't handle it well."

"It's hard when somebody you love has been treated badly. Cuts you up inside, especially when you can't do anything about it," Tyler comments.

I feel like it's a jibe at me, about how I was when I was dating Olive.

I clear my throat. "I didn't treat Olive that awfully, did I?"

"God, no, sorry. I didn't mean you and Fitz," Tyler apologises.

"I know I was a bit of a jerk when I was with Olive, but I didn't think I was that bad."

"You weren't. You were just young. I meant Jen, my sister. She had a shitty ex-husband. I hated him anyway but so much more when she told me everything after they separated. I wanted to kill him," Tyler explains.

"She remarried, right? I'm sure Olive said something about her and her husband going to my concert recently."

"Yeah, she got remarried. Jack's a good guy. He loves Jen to pieces, and he treats her right. He shows her every day how much he loves her. Hayden hurt her badly, but she knows Jack never would. He reassures her whenever she feels the fear of being hurt again."

"I don't find it easy talking about my feelings." I sigh.

"Says the man who *sings* his feelings." He laughs.

"That's different. I know it sounds ridiculous, but it is so much easier for me to write something in a song. The words 'I love you' are so easy when they're a lyric. They don't come as easily when I have to say them," I explain.

"So, if you can't find a way to say how you feel, why don't you just sing it?" Tyler suggests.

"Sing to the woman I love and apologise for being a jerk?"

"What have you got to lose?" Tyler shrugs. "Look, I know you loved Olive back then, but I didn't realise that until after you broke up. The first time I really understood your feelings was when I heard the songs you wrote about her. Your actions didn't particularly line up with your emotions, and I didn't know how much you cared for her before then. She didn't know, either."

"Olive didn't feel it, so what I felt back then is a bit redundant." I laugh. She was never my destiny. I was never hers. She was always destined to end up with Tyler.

"How about this woman? Do you think she loves you?" Tyler prods.

I think about Rose. I think about the time we spent together. I think of every smile, every promise, every touch.

I sigh. "I don't know."

"Do you think she knows you love her?"

Now all I can think about is how badly I let her down.

"I don't know," I repeat. Did I ever give Rose any indication that I love her, when it appears to be something I've only just realised fully myself? How could she know if I didn't realise it myself until I was sitting on those stairs, feeling like a man drowning?

"Maybe she finds it as hard to say as you do. Especially if she has been hurt previously. Sometimes it takes one person to risk that first step, to be the one to be vulnerable first. If you can't say it, then at least sing it. Don't let this love slip through your fingers because you weren't brave enough to take that chance." He gets up and starts to stack the plates. "I'll be back in a minute," he adds, taking the plates out of the room and leaving me alone.

I sit and think about what he has just suggested. I find it difficult to say the words "I love you;" I can't recall it being a sentence that was said a lot in my childhood, to me, or by me to my parents. My grandma used to say, "love to you," and I'd reply with "and to you," but she knew it was how I expressed myself, that expressing my emotions with the real words was difficult, a foreign concept.

That same inability has followed me into adulthood.

"Why do I get the feeling Ty has given you something to think about?" Olive laughs as she comes back into the room, cradling Ivy who is now quiet but still awake. "Do you want to hold her?" Olive asks. I nod and she passes Ivy to me. Ivy feels far sturdier than I thought she would be given she seems so small, but she somehow feels so fragile at the same time.

"Is she bigger or smaller than Mia was at this age?" I wonder, thinking of holding Mia when I'd visited not long after she was born.

"About the same, I think. They were both six pounds when born." Olive takes her seat.

Tyler comes back into the dining room, carrying a tray which holds three bowls of sticky toffee pudding. He grins when he sees me holding Ivy. He looks at Olive as he puts the bowls in front of each of us.

"Making sure you had two hands for dessert?" Tyler teases her.

"Mummy needs two hands to eat Daddy's sticky toffee." Olive grins back.

For a second, I'm hit by a wave of envy. It isn't that I feel envious not being the one sitting opposite Olive as her husband, but the reminder that I've messed up everything with Rose. This is what we had in the little cottage—the secret smiles, the laughing, the teasing, the general feeling of contentment and the synchronicity. Everything felt so easy and wonderful between us, and I miss it. Far more than I ever knew it was possible to miss something. I miss her, and who I am when I'm with her.

"Do you want me to take her so you can eat your dessert?" Tyler offers, catching me staring, so I give him a smile and shake my head. I stare down at Ivy who is starting to look fussy.

"You guys eat," I suggest. I sing a little to Ivy and she seems to be content; at least, she doesn't go back to the wail she'd given earlier. As I sing, I think about Tyler and his suggestion, think about Rose, words and a plan forming in my mind.

***

"Thank you so much for tea, guys," I say later.

"Well, thank you for Ivy's first concert." Tyler smiles.

"I haven't forgotten about concert tickets for you both. I promise, when I next tour, I'll sort you a box. It might be nice for you to hear me singing without the accompanying little wails of a crying baby," I joke. Two songs into my singing, Ivy seemed to want to join in with me.

I reach for the handle of the front door, ready to make my exit.

"Wait, you don't get to leave that easily," Olive scolds. She holds her arms open for a hug and I duck a little so she can slip her arms around me.

"I had a nice time catching up with both of you," I say as I pull away.

"Before you dash off, I wanted to say thank you for the presents you sent for the kids, and for our flowers. You didn't have to do any of that, but it meant a lot to both of us. I meant to thank you earlier. I blame the baby brain." Olive laughs.

I smile at her, thinking to the day Rose saw the baby announcement on Olive's account, announcing the arrival with a smile and then sitting next to me as we scrolled for a suitable gift to send. Now, I wonder how difficult that was for Rose. She smiled the whole time she talked about Olive and the baby, but I wonder if I missed any pain in her eyes, thinking about what happened to her.

"You're welcome," I reply to Olive once I realise they're both waiting for an answer because I've gone quiet and probably look vacant.

"We'll do this again some time. Maybe next time, you can bring a guest," Tyler says.

"Maybe," I reply, thinking of Rose. Tyler offers me his hand to shake, and so I take it, feeling like we've reached a level of understanding between us we never had before. I'm sure there was once a time when he felt as wretched about Olive as I do about Rose.

"I look forward to meeting them," he says with a small smile.

There is another chorus of goodbyes before I get into my car. I wave at them as I leave. I drive home, and the only thing on my mind is Rose and how I plan to make things right.

Chapter Twenty-Four

Rose

NOW

The silence that exists in the house is deafening. It's Friday, but I only know this because the early morning news keeps telling me so. Every day seems to have bled into one another. The only thing I know is that it has been five days since my heart broke.

The look on Blake's face when I told him everything has haunted me.

I've slept in his bed every night, my arms wrapped around his pillow, trying to smell him on the sheets and pretend that he's still here with me. I miss him—desperately—and I'm devastated that he doesn't want to be with me. I underestimated how strongly I feel for him. How did I not see that I was falling in love with him? I didn't realise it until it was too late, and now he's gone and all I have left is a broken heart.

Maybe things could have been different if I told him how I felt, but I didn't realise it myself until he was walking out of my hotel room, and my head was screaming at me to call back the man I love. Except, I didn't call him back. I let him walk away, ashamed of my choices, leaving me alone.

My phone beeps and it makes me jump. It's a message from Annabeth, telling me that the car will be ready tomorrow. When I came back into the village, I swerved around a large pothole, hitting the curb and damaging my front wheel. I messaged Annabeth to ask if she knew a discreet mechanic, explaining what had happened to the car. She asked where I was before turning up with Nathaniel who had towed my car to his father's garage. Apparently, I called during their extended family teatime, and they invited me to join them, both sets of parents and their children, but when I declined, they dropped me home.

Since then, I've spent days alone in the house or taking solitary walks on the beach, late in the afternoon or evening. The weather has been terrible—cold and wet—so at least when I've been walking and crying on the beach, I've been completely alone in weather that has matched my mood.

The only person other than Annabeth who has contacted me has been Libby. She called at the start of the week—her usual weekly call since Blake had arrived. I told her Blake was away and she's called every evening to see how I have been. Maybe it was the hitch in my voice that gave me away, even though I tried to tell her I was fine.

Today though, I'm surprised when the phone rings early in the morning.

"Have you seen Blake's website?" Libby asks once I've said hello.

"No, I haven't. Why?" I ask. I haven't looked because it feels like I would be poking at an open wound. I think it might finish me off to see him posting a picture of him living his life as if we hadn't been hidden away doing something wonderful together. Not that he usually posts things like that, but my mind has apparently turned bitter as my heart has turned to coal.

"I think you ought to have a look. He's put something up. It's on his web page and his socials."

"What is?"

"You need to see it. It'll be easier than me trying to explain it all."

"Give me a minute."

I grab my laptop from the kitchen counter. I load his web page, and she must hear the sharp intake of breath I take.

"This is about you, isn't it? What exactly were the two of you getting up to when you were writing those songs of yours?" Libby's voice has a slight teasing tone.

"Can I call you back later? I feel like I need to read this all and process it without trying to hold a conversation."

"Sure, sweetie, but then I'm going to want all the gory details. Blake is refusing to tell Maeve anything, which is most unlike him."

"Blake spoke to Maeve?"

"All he said this morning was: *I meant every word*. Cryptic motherfucker."

"I'll call you back," I say, unable to stand it a moment longer. I need to absorb this all properly.

I hang up without any further pleasantries. I sit down, laptop in front of me.

His web page has been completely redesigned. All his old posts are gone. All his content, gone. All his details about previous concerts, gone. All his photographs of beaches and sunsets from his travels, gone. His social media pages are all the same. Everything is gone. There are no personal pictures, no tour updates, no album release alerts. Even his post about Olive and the media intrusion is gone.

It must have taken him hours to remove everything.

What remains looks beautiful, and I can't stop my heart from racing.

His web page has changed to a black background with images of red roses across the page, roses wound around one another to form a border. When I look closely at the border, I can see his name is written in small lettering, hidden in the rose petals.

At the top of the page, there is an audio track to play. There is a second audio track nestled under it. Under that, lyrics. Nothing else.

I click to play the first audio. Even though I expect his voice, it's still enough to knock the wind out of me.

His voice still reminds me of warm honey, but there is pain hanging on every word in his recording.

"They say love is blind, but you saw all of me and I saw all of you. Nothing has ever been so beautiful. Nothing has ever felt so right. You once sang, walk away, walk away, walk away, walk away. Now I sing, let me stay, let me stay, let me stay."

My breath catches in my throat as his voice dips on the last line.

I click the second audio track and at first, all I hear are the chords he is playing. I imagine him, holding his guitar, the way he'd go on to hold me. Then he starts to sing, his vocals powerful from the very first word, like the emotions are pushing him on. I close my eyes and listen to the whole track.

When it finishes, I play it again. This time I read the lyrics that are printed on the page to accompany the track. They're beautiful. Not just that, but they're personal. There is no doubt in my mind that these lyrics are for me.

You shared your secrets, and I gave you all mine,
We mended our gashes and claimed the coastline.
We were hidden together where the world couldn't see,
I watched you heal your scars and set yourself free.
We screamed into the wind on a long autumn hike,
And sang songs together as we rode that tandem bike.
Card games and laughter, with biscuits used as a wager,
How easily you became my all, no longer a stranger.
My Red Rose—if all I could give is my heart and my love,
Tell me, oh tell me, will that ever be enough?
I watched with joy as you shed the angst and the gloom,
Fascinated as you opened up and started to bloom.
Everything felt so easy, never been a love like this before.
I was waking with a smile, always wanting more.
Then I started to hope and thought "this could be our life,
I could be your husband; you could be my wife,"
Nothing would be greater than our souls linked together,
And knowing we could live in our bubble of bliss forever.
My Red Rose—if all I could give is my heart and my love,

Tell me, oh tell me, will that ever be enough?
But I made a mistake, should've held you tight,
Should've told you I'm always with you in the fight,
Should've held you so close and wiped away the tears.
Should've known how much he reignited your fears.
And for that, I'm sorry. I'll never regret anything more.
I can't go back to being the man I was before,
Because you changed me, healed me. You made me soar.
And, my Red Rose, I will love you forever more.
My Red Rose—if all I could give is my heart and my love,
Tell me, oh tell me, will that ever be enough?
I'm paying my penance and have a love I'll never forget.
I miss you desperately. Each day I'm destroyed by regret.
I dream of you singing in the little home where our love began.
Desperate to know if the woman I love can cherish this man.
My Red Rose—if all I could give is my heart and my love,
Tell me, oh tell me, will that ever be enough?

He's titled the song "Red Daze."

The comments section he used to have on the web page is disabled so I can't post my own comment, but when I check his social media pages, they're still active and the comments are going wild underneath the posts.

FutureMrsDaniels: OMG who is this song about?

IheartBlake20: This is so beautiful.

D3vilW0man: He sounds heartbroken.

Freefaller: Did you notice that Rose is capitalised?

User123: It's a nickname.

OhYesItIsMe: The r in Red is capitalised, too.

Rainbows&Sparkles: New album?

ThinkingAboutStuff: Daze as in dazed or should it be days?

TheThingsIDid: I wish somebody would write something like that for me.

Pseudonym11: It's not a nickname, I think it is her name, whoever she is.

WhatzUp: Is the person another singer?

In33df00d: Lucky bitch.

CoffeeIsMyFuel: I wish it were me.

I skim the comments until I've read enough. I pause for a moment to try to think properly, to truly understand what this all means.

We've been writing love songs together for months, but this is different. This is personal. These lyrics are for me. What he's done—it doesn't seem like the actions of somebody who is disgusted with me, with what I did and what I kept hidden. This seems like the actions of somebody who cares. Not just cares but—like the lyrics suggest—loves me. Me for who I am, inside and out, down to the bones, every little piece of me.

Not loving me *despite* the secrets and the fears but including them, too.

What if the reason he left was like I had first thought? In the hotel room, I was convinced he left because he needed space. It was only when he didn't come back quickly that I convinced myself that he left because he couldn't stand knowing what I'd done. What if he did leave because he was hurt by finally understanding what had happened to me? What if it wasn't a reaction to understanding what I did with Hunter, but what Hunter did to me.

The possibility makes me tremble slightly because if Blake didn't walk away, then it changes the reason he isn't here now. He didn't walk away. I ran away.

I'm the one who shut the door.

His song sounds like he's asking me to open it again.

I feel like I am glued to the seat as I consider what I want to do. Part of me thinks he's crazy. This is crazy. He's essentially deleted everything, made a clean slate online, and made everything so public, even if he hasn't revealed who the song is about.

Everything else between us had been so private, but this is there for the whole world to see. This is him announcing *something* to the world, a public declaration. For Blake to be so open—after he's spent most of his time refusing to be drawn into conversations or conjecture about his private life—feels significant.

I've been just as private about my life before. I've had people sign non-disclosure agreements and kept secrets about what we were doing. I know I could respond to him privately by asking Maeve or Libby to get a message to him, but it doesn't seem like it would be enough.

Sometimes, you can only respond in kind.

I get up, taking my laptop with me. I go upstairs to the bedroom where my keyboard is. I play Blake's song again, listening to the music, trying to focus on the sound instead of the words. For now, I need to know what to play. The words will have to wait.

I pick up the music quickly, and once my fingers feel like they have the song memorised, I lean over to pick up my notepad. I open the lyrics on the laptop screen. I re-read them and then reconstruct the sentences, making them fit to what I want to say. I want my own words, to support my own feelings, but I want it to be unmistakable that these lyrics, these are my response. I want it clear for the whole world to see that this is my reply, my declaration.

It takes me what feels like forever to feel like it is ready, though it is not even noon by the time I finish. Around me there are wads of paper that I've screwed up, thrown around the room in disgust, but in front of me is a final set of lyrics. Handwritten lyrics, neat and tidy. The title at the top, in larger handwriting, boasts "Indiana Knights."

I take a photograph of the lyrics. I practice singing them a few times to the music, feeling everything meld together, feeling more confident with each turn.

I set my phone up on the desk, positioning it to film the keyboard, to capture my hands rather than my face. I'm still wearing the charm bracelet he gave me for Christmas, and it shines a little under the light from the window behind me.

I press record, take a breath, then begin to play, to sing.

"*Thrown together at our worst, my life was in Freefall,*
I was shaken and broken, thought I'd never stand tall.
You arrived and teased out my secrets and fears,
Helped pick me up, made me smile through tears.

You made me so strong, helped me feel joy again.
Living an easy life, free from the bullshit and fame.
If I had been honest, would you have taken that turn?
It's all on me; I made us crash and burn.
My beautiful Indiana—if all I could give is my heart and my love,
Tell me, oh tell me, will that ever be enough?
And I told you so much, but not the whole truth,
About the man who hid a ring and destroyed my youth.
That secret I carried, weighed me down with the pain,
Afraid if you knew, you wouldn't see me the same.
What would I change? That night in your bed,
I would tell you all the things I'd left unsaid.
I'd spill all my secrets, let them sit like acid on my tongue,
I should have trusted you'd tell me my fears were wrong.
My beautiful Indiana—if all I could give is my heart and my love,
Tell me, oh tell me, will that ever be enough?
And I wished you had asked, I would have said yes,
You in your jeans, me in a white dress.
The two of us, smiling, joking about destiny,
Living in the bubble of just you and me.
A future for us, where we survive the weather.
Can you do that? Forgive me? Be my forever?
You left me with a silence, now I only hear your pain.
What wouldn't I give to be with you again?
My beautiful Indiana—if all I could give is my heart and my love,
Tell me, oh tell me, will that ever be enough?
I am paying my penance, missing the love that burned bright.
I fall asleep every night, dreaming you're here, that we reunite.
And I'm here in our little house, lost in the loneliness, unable to move on.
I can't sing without you. Come back, Indiana. Bring back our sweet song.
My beautiful Indiana—if all I could give is my heart and my love,

Tell me, oh tell me, will that ever be enough?"

As I finish, my voice cracks. I'm quick enough to stop the recording before I start to sniffle, overcome with the emotion of the morning.

I don't play back the video because I don't want to second-guess what I'm doing. I need to just run with this.

I turn the page to the notebook again. I write a note.

"Sometimes, someone walks into your life and changes everything. Their presence changes you, your outlook, your heart, your beliefs, your soul. When they leave, they take a piece of your soul and leave you with a piece of theirs. But, Indiana, I want it all. I've inked you onto my skin, you soaked into my bones, and all I can say is, forgive me, forgive me, forgive me, and please—come home."

I take a photo of the note and the lyrics. I launch a web page for the social media app Blake prefers, clicking to create a new profile. I use my real name, creating a profile as Rose Elodie Dalton. I've no idea what to put as a profile picture. I scroll through my pictures and look at the ones Blake took the day we saw Hunter. The pictures—taken before everything unravelled—are lovely, but it doesn't feel right to use pictures from that day, no matter how I felt before I ran into Hunter.

I scroll further back and find the photographs we took on the beach on our birthday. There's one of our feet, half buried in the sand, and our jeans wet from where the waves had raced up to our sandcastle moat. I smile at the memory and use that picture to upload as my profile picture.

I upload the photographs of my statement and my lyrics. Then I upload the recording of my song. I stare at the page for a minute, thinking about my next step. I could just ask Libby to ask Maeve to send this to Blake, but I feel like it isn't enough. I need to go all the way. I need to make the same declarations and let it be there for the world to see.

I go to Blake's profile on the site, navigating to the comments section. I paste in a link to my page. I've no idea how many people will be willing to click on a link from a stranger, but it's only going to take one person to check it, or one person to remember that this is my real name. I'm sure it will snowball. It just needs one person to do it.

It doesn't take long for there to be a reaction. People keep replying to my post on his page, pushing it further up his page until it is the top comment. Then, somebody tags Blake on a comment on my page. The comment section on my page goes crazy. It takes less than a minute for somebody to post "OMG this is Briar Rose!" There are then comment after comment about collaboration songs, and it is clear people assume this is a marketing ploy, that we have coordinated to release music together.

I don't care much what they think—what they are speculating—because all I care about Blake, and he's the one person who hasn't reacted or commented.

***

After an hour of refreshing and reading the comments, I force myself to get up. I cannot sit in front of the laptop all afternoon. I've done what I can. The ball is in his court.

I pick up my phone and call Libby.

"Holy shit, Rose, talk about leaving me hanging. What happened between you and Blake, or am I falling for a marketing scam? I'm sure I'm not, as neither of you are into that, but put me out of my misery. Maeve, too."

"I love him. It just got messed up," I admit.

"How did it get messed up?"

"We bumped into Hunter."

"Oh, shit."

"Yeah, you can say that again. I had told Blake some bits about Hunter, but he didn't know who it was, and then everything else I hadn't told him spilled out that day. He said he needed some air, and when he didn't come back, I ran away. We haven't spoken since. It's been torture," I explain.

"What was it that Blake didn't know?"

"He knew I had a relationship with a married man, and that he hadn't treated me nicely, but I hadn't said who it was, nor had I elaborated as to what I meant by not treating me nicely. He didn't know about the abortion, either."

"I think knowing Hunter was rough with you, that would have been something he'd need to get his head around."

"I know. I wish I had told him everything before. I wish I had told him in a better way, not under pressure, with Hunter in the same location. I really love him, Libby, and I think I hurt him by keeping things hidden." I bite my lip as I finish my sentence. "This is completely different to Hunter. With him, it was never love, never respect. I see that. I knew it, it just took me a long time to accept it. With Blake, I feel like I have everything I could ever want, and I'm so afraid that it's all messed up, and I can't fix it."

"Maeve has tried getting in touch with him, but he hasn't answered his phone yet. I assume he's just busy and hasn't seen your posts yet. He'll see it, and he'll get in touch, I'm sure. Don't cry, Rose. Don't worry, I'm sure it will be okay."

"I hope so." I sniffle, suddenly overcome with emotion.

"Do you want to come spend some time with me and Maeve?"

"No, I'm going to finish the lease here. It's peaceful. I like it. I'm okay, I promise."

"Okay, well, if we hear from Blake, I'll let you know. Somehow though, I'm sure you'll both be fine. Maeve's always telling me Blake is a good guy, and I trust Maeve. She's never wrong about a character assessment. I mentioned Hunter to her the other week—without her knowing anything about what happened between you—and she rolled her eyes and said he looked like a fuckboy."

"Maybe Maeve should vet everybody I talk to in future, if Blake decides he doesn't want to talk again," I suggest, but then I fall silent because the idea of him not responding hurts my heart.

"Just give Blake some time," Libby advises.

"I'll speak to you soon, Lib. I'm going to try to do something to take my mind off it all." I sigh. I'm not sure what, exactly, will take my mind off Blake, but I can't stay near my laptop with the urge to refresh and drive myself crazy.

Libby says her goodbyes and wishes me luck again. I'll take any offer of luck because I'm not sure what else to do.

***

As the sun sets, I sit on the beach for a while, listening to the waves as they rush across the sand. There isn't a soul around, which is unsurprising given the drizzle is threatening to turn into a downpour. I wish I had my coat with me, as it is much colder than I expected and the wind is wild, whipping up sand into my face and my hair all around me.

I sit still, watching the sun dipping on the horizon, feeling the chill of the winter air through my bones. My heart feels heavy, and my mind is full of Blake.

I stand back up because I know it is madness to stay on the beach in this weather. It may only be just gone four in the afternoon, but I feel like going back to the house and hibernating under the covers.

As I stand, that is when I see the figure walking across the sand, heading towards me.

I know it is Blake. I think I would recognise him from a mile away, even blindfolded. It's like my soul is attuned to him and his presence. He strides across the beach. He's wearing his usual dark jeans and hoodie, but his expression is unreadable. He comes to a halt in front of me, and I open my mouth to talk but realise I don't know how to string a sentence together. There is so much I want to say and there could never possibly be enough time to say it all.

As if he is in the same conundrum as me, he doesn't speak, either. Instead, his hand rises to my cheek, cupping it gently, his thumb stroking across the skin. He holds me like that for a moment.

"What on earth," he asks, leaning towards me, "do you think," he continues, his lips against my face, "could ever need my forgiveness?" he concludes, and then his lips skim against mine. It is the lightest touch in the world, but it makes me feel weak at the knees.

"You know what I meant. I had an abortion." I feel the tears welling in my eyes. "You looked so angry and upset when I told you, and then you were just gone."

"I wasn't upset because of the choices you made, Red. I was upset about how he treated you. Knowing how badly he treated you, I felt sick. I'm an idiot for leaving you in that room, but I went out to clear my head and calm myself down because I was angry with him. I've never felt rage like it before, and I didn't want you to see me like that. When I eventually made my way back, you were gone. I'm so sorry. I should have made sure you were okay. I should have put your needs first. If anybody needs to be forgiven, it's me."

"You came back?" I ask, my voice showing my surprise. How I've ever won card games against him is suddenly a mystery because how I feel must be written all over my face.

"Of course I came back. I told you, I'll always come back for you."

"You didn't come here," I point out.

"I did. I came the next morning, but your car was gone. I knocked and nobody was home."

"I took the car to the garage to get fixed."

"I thought you had hightailed out of here. I thought I'd fucked everything up."

"I thought I was the one who fucked everything up," I cry.

Holding back tears is no longer anything I can do. They spill over my eyelids in a way that makes me think of a river bursting the banks. It's uncontrollable and it's messy but cathartic as hell.

"Red, can we go back to the house? You're freezing already, and it's cold enough that those tears might freeze on your face." He steps away and starts to pull at his hoodie to take it off. It stops me crying and makes me laugh instead.

"The house is right there, you idiot. I'm not going to freeze before we get there. I don't need your chivalry."

"Hey, maybe I just want to earn some man points back given I lost a load when I kicked Hunter in the balls."

"What?" I exclaim.

"Come on, I'll tell you in the warmth," he suggests.

He reaches for my hand, taking it in his. His hand is warm and strong. We start walking towards the house and I feel lighter than I have in days.

We enter the house together and he shuts the door behind us. He wraps his arms around me, and it feels amazing—like birds should be arriving in the house any second now to sing above our heads.

"You're trembling," Blake comments.

"It's because I'm in shock that you're here. I really missed you. I didn't think my post would be enough," I reply, and the tears well back in my eyes.

"Just saying 'Blake, come back' would've been enough," he proclaims.

"Well, if I knew that, I might not have wasted a whole pad of paper trying to write my lyrics," I joke, teeth chattering slightly.

"At the risk of sounding like some dodgy hero in a terrible romance novel, I think we should get you out of these wet clothes," he suggests. I laugh, blinking back the tears because I really do not want to cry again.

"Sounds like a good idea."

Blake takes a step away from me, then he unbuttons the thick cardigan I'm wearing. Underneath, I have a vest top on, and it's also damp from the rain.

"Red, you're going to catch a cold. Come on, upstairs."

"There's an offer I cannot refuse." I kick off my shoes and he does the same.

Blake offers me his hand again and I take it, letting him lead me up the stairs. At the top of the stairs, he starts to lead me towards the bedroom I originally stayed in, but I pull him in the direction of his room.

"You stole my room?" Blake laughs and I grin.

"Not really. My stuff is still in the small room, but I've been sleeping in your bed."

"Then your room, for clothes," he suggests.

"What makes you think I have any intention of getting dressed? I'm proposing I strip out of these wet clothes, and we lie down together to talk."

We walk into his room. I take off my vest top and jeans. I throw back the covers, getting into the bed. Blake smiles at me, pulling off his hoodie, followed by his tee.

I look at his body, feeling my stomach flip. He's so beautiful to look at. His smile gets a little wider as he pulls off his jeans. I pat the bed next to me.

"Wait," he says with a little laugh. He leans down the side of the bed and I watch him turn on the electric blanket.

"Oh, and they say romance is dead." I laugh. He gets into the bed next to me and immediately pulls me into an embrace. I'm facing away from him. I lean, intending to move to face him.

"I love you," he murmurs. I stop moving. "I'm so sorry I didn't handle the situation better than I did because I should have. I should have held you then like I'm holding you now. I should have told you how sad I feel that somebody put you through that. I should have told you that the only thing I care about is how you feel about it all, because that is all that matters. I shouldn't have let you have a moment of doubt about how I feel about you. I haven't said it before—to you or to anybody—but I do. I love you. I love you, Rose. I will always love you."

I turn over on the bed so I can face him. I look up at him. His skin is warm against mine. His dark eyes hold my gaze. There is expectation and something that looks like apprehension in his eyes.

"I love you, Blake," I say. I expect a smile, but when he pulls me closer, I feel the shudder of his body against mine.

"I don't think I've ever heard anything so wonderful," he murmurs, and he kisses my forehead.

"Maybe I should say it one hundred times a day, so you get used to it," I tease.

"You might have to. Nobody has ever said that to me before."

"That cannot be true," I protest. He leans back to look at me.

"Completely true. When we were shouting stuff on that walk and I said I felt unlovable, that was real. I didn't grow up in a house where everybody talked daily about love. I've kept myself so guarded around people, and even if I felt it, I've never been brave enough to say it because I've always been convinced it wouldn't be reciprocated. I know that doesn't make it easy for somebody to say how they feel about me."

"You're brave enough to say it to me?"

"Every single day, for the rest of our lives," he vows.

"Your song—"

"I meant every word."

"I meant every word in mine," I say. "You thought about us being married?" I ask.

"I meant," he replies, and then he kisses me across my cheek, making his way down to my mouth, "every"—more kisses—"single"—more kisses—"word."

"Just so you know, I'll say yes, when you ask, in the future." I smile. "Right now, I have other things I want us to do."

"Oh, yes?" Blake gives me a small grin. I push against his chest, and he lies on the bed. I straddle him, leaning down to kiss him.

"I love you, I love you, I love you," I murmur between kisses, counting all my lucky stars that he came back, that he loves me, too. Then his hands move to places that stops me thinking of anything at all, and I clutch him, knowing I'll never want to let him go again.

Chapter Twenty-Five

Blake

NOW

"So, were you joking earlier about kneeing Hunter in the balls?" Rose asks.

She lies naked in my arms, and her fingers are on my chest, circling over my tattoo. I've missed this. Her touch is light as a feather, but it always feels like she's touching my soul.

Rose looks up at me, expectantly.

"Not joking," I reply as I come to my senses, still a little stunned by our reunion.

Everything has been overwhelming and amazing. Holding her in my arms. Feeling her heartbeat against my chest. Our declaration of love. Sex that—like always with Rose—felt like so much more.

"What happened?"

"I was coming back to the room, and he was waiting for me in the hallway. We had a few choice words. I disagreed with his opinion. My knee concluded my point."

"I'm guessing he said some awful things about me?" she whispers, and I detect a note of shame in her tone.

"He's a piece of shit, Rose. His opinion doesn't matter. I gave him something to think about, as well as the pain in his dick," I reply.

"I can't believe you kneed him in the balls."

"I have photographs if you want to see," I offer.

"You assaulted the UK golden boy and took pictures of what you did?" She almost sounds like she is scolding me.

"He got lucky as far as I'm concerned. He deserves much worse than that. The way he treats women is disgusting. I told him if he speaks to you again, I'll release the pictures, and if there is even a hint that he's doing the same to somebody else, I'll send them to his wife."

"He told me he'd never do to Isla what he did to me," Rose murmurs.

"He probably doesn't, but I don't think you're the only one he'll have cheated with and got rough with," I reply, and I feel tense as I think this. I can protect Rose from Hunter. I can help her feel safe with me, but what about the other people he meets? How many other women are going to be hurt by him? My threats against him don't mean much if he can charm his way with another woman.

"Does that just make me another dumb woman who got into his bed?" Rose whispers.

"No, it makes him the dickhead. It's all him, Rose."

"He made me think there was something wrong with me for not enjoying it. He made me feel like it was normal, and I was the freak for not doing it."

"Rose, there are a whole variety of things that people enjoy during sex, but things like that have to be discussed, agreed, and consented to. You can't do something like that without discussing boundaries, without knowing what the limits are, without agreeing that both people want it, and the second somebody says 'stop,' it must stop. He didn't do any of that with you. He just got off on your pain and when you struggled. That's not two people with a particular kink or fetishism enjoying it or safely exploring it together. That is somebody who was being abusive. He's a sadist, an abuser. There is nothing wrong with you at all."

"Is that the kind of sex you've had? Did you like it?" Rose sounds curious. I reach to take her hand from tracing my tattoo so I can hold it. I entwine my fingers with hers.

"No, I've never wanted to hurt anybody during sex. The idea of choking somebody, it just doesn't do anything for me. Don't get me wrong, I've role-played before, sure, but it has been light, fluffy stuff, like rock star and groupie, or doctor and nurse."

"So, you're not going to spring something on me?" Rose bites her lip as she speaks. I hate that Hunter has made her feel so insecure.

"No, I'd never spring something on you. When you and I make love, it's amazing, Rose. It's like I'm at the gateway to heaven." I squeeze her hand as I talk.

"I thought you didn't believe in the concept of heaven," she teases.

"You make me believe in more, my sweet."

"I feel the same way about you. Every time with you, it feels transcendent."

"Can I be really fucking soppy and say that's because we love each other?" I smile at her.

She laughs. "Only if I can be fucking soppy and say I melt a little every time you say love."

"Get used to it, Red. I'm going to say it many times a day, forever."

"I like the sound of that," she says quietly, but then her stomach rumbles and she bursts into a fit of giggles. "Sorry, that was so loud."

"Hungry? What do you want?" I ask, shifting on the bed so I can go downstairs for food.

"Don't bother, I've nothing in," she replies.

"I thought you were over your cooking aversion?" I tease.

"It wasn't a cooking issue."

"Don't tell me you forgot how to log into my account to order in ingredients." I laugh.

"No, I was too lovesick to eat." Rose shrugs and I feel a stab of guilt.

"If I could go back, I would never leave that room. I would hold you, and tell you everything you needed to hear, everything I wanted to say," I say quietly.

"It doesn't matter, Blake. What matters is everything from now."

"Just know that I'm never going to make such a stupid mistake again," I promise, and I pull her hand to me so I can kiss her across the fingers.

"I won't run away again, either. I should have stayed and given you the benefit of the doubt. I know sometimes you need a bit of time to process something, but I panicked."

"You never have to panic about me again, I promise. If you ever want to talk about it, I swear I'll sit and listen. I'll hold your hand, I won't give you any reason to worry," I vow. "If you ever want to report him for what he did to you, I'll be right by your side."

"I just.... I don't want to think about that right now."

"Just know I'm right there with you, okay," I murmur. Her stomach rumbles again and she laughs, breaking the tension. "Right, let's rectify that. Shall we order something in, or shall we go out to get something?"

"Let's go out. To the pub. I think they serve food for the next couple of hours," Rose suggests as she scrambles out of bed. "I'm just going to freshen up."

"Sure, no rush." I give her a smile as she heads out to the bathroom. I feel excited about her suggestion to go out, not because I want to be in public but because of her willingness to be seen with me.

I hear the shower water running and her singing over the noise. After a moment, I go and wait outside the bathroom so I can shower as soon as she is finished. I smile when I hear her singing the song I wrote about her, changing the lyrics.

"I love knowing this will be our life. He'll be my husband, I'll be his wife," she sings.

"I'll make it special when I ask, can't wait for her yes. I'll wear a tuxedo, to match her wedding dress." I sing my own version of her lyrics.

"You'd really wear a tuxedo?" She laughs. I hear her stepping out of the shower and then she opens the bathroom door. She's wrapped in a towel, her hair piled on her head to keep it dry in the shower. Her blue eyes are bright, and she's never looked more beautiful.

The shower is still running so I give her a kiss on the cheek as I head towards it, stepping in and letting the warm water run down my body.

"Of course I will wear a tuxedo. I can rise to the importance of the occasion. I do own clothes other than jeans, you know."

"Oh yeah, really?" She grins. She watches as I rub the shower gel over me.

"Yeah, I got a great blazer with roses in the lining. It's my favourite." I wink at her.

"I'm going to get dressed because if I keep staring at you, I'm going to get distracted, and we won't make it to the pub." Rose laughs.

She leaves me in the bathroom, so I finish showering quickly as I don't want to miss the opportunity to get her food at the pub.

When I'm dressed, I meet her downstairs. She's wearing one of my T-shirts, knotted at the waist, along with her jeans and a cardigan. Her lotus and dragonfly tattoo is slightly visible where she has knotted the top, and I smile because she seems so relaxed about who she is.

Rose smiles and reaches for her coat. I laugh when she adds the scarf and hat that I gave her for Christmas.

"Ready?" I ask as I pull on my boots. She responds by putting her hand into mine. I follow her out of the house, and she locks the door before we head down the street.

"So, where were you these last couple of days?" she asks.

"I went back to the place Maeve rented for me. I spent a couple of days there, like a bear with a sore head, cursing myself and my stupidity. The day before yesterday, I went to Olive and Tyler's. I saw on her social media that she uploaded a load of pictures of the new baby. I sent another message of congratulations, and they invited me for tea. We talked over tea—nothing in detail—but I realised, again, what a dick I was, and I was determined to try to put it right. I spent yesterday writing a million pages of lyrics for you." I squeeze her hand as I talk.

"I saw the new pictures. I had a little nosy when I was wating for your response today. The baby looks adorable." Rose smiles.

"She is. She has a great pair of lungs on her. I expect she'll be selling out thrash metal concerts when she's older." I laugh.

"Do you want kids in the future?" Rose's voice is quiet. I stop walking so I can look at her properly. She doesn't meet my gaze.

"Red," I start, and she takes a deep breath before looking at me.

"I did what I thought was right," she whispers. "I know you left because you were shocked about what I told you, but I still had an abortion. I know some people will think that is unforgivable. I just couldn't bear the idea of being tied forever to a man who frightened me."

"Rose, you did the right thing for you, I know that. Nobody should ever make you feel ashamed for what you chose. It's your right to choose. Every woman should have the right to choose and nobody, least of all a man, has the right to judge."

"I still feel guilty about it. I could have done things differently. I'm in a privileged position and I can provide for a baby. I could have found a way to keep Hunter out of our lives. I could have put the baby up for adoption. There are plenty of people who can't have kids and would have loved them. I see people with babies, and I feel so guilty, like when I saw the pictures of Olive on social media. What would she think of me? She holds her babies like they're the most precious gifts."

"Olive and Tyler are an entirely different couple with an entirely different relationship to what you had with Hunter."

"I spoke to the person who owns the cottage, and she said they fell pregnant really early in her relationship, but they chose to have the baby together, and they're such a happy family." Rose bites her lip as she finishes talking.

"I put money on the fact the father has never hurt her in the way Hunter hurt you. That's another entirely different couple and situation to you, Rose. You did what was right for you, and nothing else matters. You need to stop punishing yourself about it," I say, firmly.

"So, you don't think I'm going to burn in hell?"

"No, Rose. I know you have different views on religion to me, but I don't believe anybody could punish you for the decision you made."

She gives me a shaky smile and then she pulls me close, her lips meeting mine.

"Thank you for being so understanding," she whispers when she pulls away.

"I'll never hurt you, Rose, I promise you that," I vow.

"I'll never hurt you, either."

"As for kids, if you want them in the future, sure. We'll form our own band with our talented offspring. Maybe they can join Ivy's thrash metal band. Or maybe we'll give up all the fame and bullshit. Maybe we will just live perfectly ordinary lives together, our beautiful little family." I grin.

"So long as we're together, that all sounds good to me."

"Come on, let's get to the pub before they stop serving food." I take her hand again and we carry on the short distance to the pub.

The Whistlethorpe Tavern is a small pub, which is unsurprising given the village is small. There's a neat little pub garden that I can see to the side of the building, but it's deserted, which is not surprising given the weather and the time of year. I push the door to the pub open, wondering how this is going to unfold. I've no idea how busy the pub gets. I'm not sure what the style of the pub is, whether it's a family pub or we're going to walk into a bunch of drunken, rowdy people.

We step inside, and I'm relieved that there isn't an instant reaction to us being there. It isn't massively busy. The bartender looks up at us, gives us a welcoming smile, a double take, and then another smile. There's an old-fashioned jukebox in the corner of one side of the pub, and a pool table. The other side of the pub looks to be where food is served, mostly taken by families enjoying an evening meal.

Rose and I walk to the bar.

"Are you looking to order food?" the bartender asks.

"Yes, please," I reply. He hands me two menus.

"Take a seat wherever is free. I'll come take your order shortly." The man smiles. I turn with Rose to look for a spare table.

"Mummy! Daddy!"

The voice belongs to a little girl. She sits next to a man who holds a toddler on his knee. Beside him is a woman who smiles at Rose and me.

"Friends of yours?" I murmur to Rose because she also has a big grin on her face.

"That looks like Briar Rose," the girl exclaims. She grabs her mother's arm. Rose steps forward towards the table.

"You must be Willow," Rose says, and the girl looks like she is going to burst with excitement.

"Blake, this is Annabeth and Nathaniel, who own the cottage. This is Willow and Faith." Rose makes the introductions and then she looks at Annabeth with a sheepish smile. "This is—" she starts, but Nathaniel looks at me.

"Holy crap, Blake Daniels!"

"Way to play it cool, babe." Annabeth laughs. "He's a big fan of yours," she says to me.

"Well, I'm a big fan of your property."

"Ours for a few more months, until the developer is back. It'll be sad to see it demolished." Annabeth sighs.

"You didn't say they were going to knock it down." Rose frowns.

"If we don't sell to them, they're still going to go ahead with knocking down the other three and apply to build one house on the land. It'll make it impossible to rent our place out," Annabeth explains.

"I'll buy it," I blurt out. Rose looks at me, wide-eyed. I don't know how she feels about it, but I hate the idea of somebody destroying the place I fell in love with her. I can't stand the idea that somebody could destroy it and replace it with something soulless.

A big smile forms on Rose's face. "We'll see if we can buy the other three from the developer. They're a charming set of cottages. They should remain as they are."

"You two seem to really love the cottage," Nathaniel comments.

"We've fallen in love with the area. We've been here a couple of months, making music together. It's been a perfect getaway, especially being so close to the beach. We walk on the beach every night," I explain.

"Oh, we know you have been making music recently. We've been following the news today. You two kind of blew up the internet." Annabeth laughs.

"Well, if you're serious about the cottage, give me a call in the week," Nathaniel says, handing me a business card.

"Can I have your autograph?" Willow bounces in her seat. She only has eyes for Rose. I don't blame her. Rose just has that aura around her; it draws everybody in. Willow grabs a napkin and thrusts it at Rose.

"How about a picture together, and then I can sign something for you another day, rather than just the napkin? Maybe I could come to your house and sign something of yours?" Rose suggests. Willow is out of her seat like a shot, standing next to Rose. Annabeth takes a phone out of her bag.

"I'll take it for you," I offer, because it looks like Annabeth also wants a picture.

"Sorry, we're big fans," Annabeth explains.

I take a couple of pictures for them, including one of the whole family with Rose.

"We'll let you get back to your evening." Nathaniel smiles once he's encouraged Willow to sit back in her seat.

Rose and I head towards the corner section of the pub, taking a seat at one of the spare tables. I sit next to her and pass her a menu.

"Are you really going to buy the cottage?" Rose asks, studying her menu.

"Yes, of course. We can buy all four, like you suggested. We can keep them exactly as they are. They're perfect, aren't they?"

"I love the cottage."

"I can't have somebody knock down the place I fell in love with you." I smile. "Standing against the kitchen doorway, listening to you sing about fireworks."

"You did not fall in love with me then." Rose laughs.

"I totally did. Took me a while to realise it and even longer to say it, I know."

"That was months ago."

"I know."

"Do you want to know when I think I fell in love with you? Even if I didn't really realise it until later?" Rose turns in her seat to look at me properly.

"I'm intrigued now." I smile.

"When I had this done." She twists and pulls her hair away from behind her ear, showing me her dragon tattoo. I lean over to kiss it.

"I love this, my sweet."

"People are staring." She giggles, glancing around the pub where some of the diners have turned to stare at us. One of them has their mobile phone out, looking like they're trying to take a video of us. I couldn't care less.

"Let them stare," I murmur. I kiss her cheek and then reach for her hand. "Besides, what are they going to do? Put it on social media? We already let that cat out of the bag."

She turns again in her seat, angling her body towards me.

"Well, if the cat is out of the bag, there is no need for me to not do this." She leans forward and she gives me a soft kiss. "I don't care if the whole world knows I'm in love with you."

"Do you know how happy you make me?" I wonder and she gives me a serene smile.

"Mr Blake," a little voice calls out. Rose and I both look in the direction of Willow, standing next to the table with a big smile on her face. "Daddy was too shy to ask for your autograph. He sings your songs to Mummy all the time." Willow thrusts a napkin and a pen towards me. I take it from her so I can sign it.

"How about I sign this for now, and then I come with Rose when she visits, and I'll sign something properly as well?" I suggest.

"I think Daddy would love that."

"Does he really sing my songs?" I ask, handing the signed napkin back. She holds on to it tightly and nods enthusiastically.

"Is your daddy a good singer?" Rose asks Willow.

"No! Mummy says it's the one thing he can't do." Willow giggles. She looks at us, from Rose to me and back to Rose. "Are you two friends?" she asks.

"Blake is my boyfriend," Rose replies, her voice proud, the smile on her face wide.

"Willow, come on, it's time to see Aunt Lucy and Uncle Jack," Annabeth calls and Willow rushes back to her table. She grabs hold of Annabeth's hand. Nathaniel has the younger child balanced on his hip and they give us a wave as they leave.

"They seem like a nice family," I comment.

"They are. Annabeth has been so nice to me the whole time I've been here. I've got to pick my car up from them at some point, Nathaniel's father owns the garage."

"Why is it in the garage?" I wonder.

"The pothole in the road won due to a combination of the terrible weather and my mind being elsewhere." Rose shrugs. I squeeze her hand.

"I'm glad it was something minor. I'd never forgive myself if you were hurt."

"I think we should focus on the future, after we focus on the food, of course." Rose winks, just as the man from behind the bar arrives at our table.

"Are you ready to order?" he asks.

Rose places her order, and I follow. We sit and talk, hand in hand, until the food arrives.

***

"Are you worried that we are attracting a bit of attention?" Rose asks as she finishes her linguine.

I follow her gaze across the pub. Most of the families have left now and there now seems to be a large group of people in their late teens and early twenties crowded around the bar. A couple of them are indiscreetly taking photographs of us, nudging each other and pointing.

"Do you want a dessert?" I ask as I finish my steak. She shakes her head.

"The only dessert I want is you."

"Then let's go say hello to them all, and we can go home," I suggest.

"I like the sound of home," she replies. We stand together and walk to the group that is gathered at the bar. As we approach, I can see they're prepared for us being annoyed with them, so I smile widely.

"Evening," I say. Rose stands beside me, her hand in mine.

"I can't believe you two are here. What are you doing in our little village?" one of the young women exclaims.

"Please can I have your autograph? You're my dream woman," one of the men says to Rose and he blushes furiously. The woman standing next to him frowns.

"I thought you were in rehab," she says, curling her lip slightly.

"No, not rehab. I've been falling in love," Rose replies with a serene smile, and she signs the napkin that the blushing man thrusts at her.

I laugh and dip my head so I can kiss her on the cheek. I gesture for the bartender's attention and open a tab with my card, telling him to let the customers have any drinks they like and settle up at the end of the night. I thank him for the meal and then Rose and I slip out of the pub together, the group distracted by the opportunity of an open bar.

Rose and I walk hand in hand towards the cottage. As we get settled in the living room, my phone rings so I take it from my pocket, showing Rose the display that shows Maeve is calling. I answer and put it on loudspeaker so Rose can hear the conversation.

"Blake, I'm assuming you're having a great day, though I'm disappointed to find out via social media than from you directly." Maeve teases.

"Sorry, Maeve, I was driving across the country this afternoon, and then I was preoccupied and busy." I grin at Rose as I talk.

"Oh, I know you've been busy." Maeve laughs.

"Are you talking about mine and Rose's posts?"

"No, I'm talking about the pictures somebody has uploaded of you and Rose looking very loved up in a pub. I've already had one of the papers asking me for a comment. They want to know if you are dating, how serious the relationship is, and whether it is love. All the usual. Shall I tell them no comment?"

I look at Rose. She smiles at me.

"No, Maeve. Tell them yes, very, and yes."

"You and Rose owe me and Libby an update." Maeve laughs.

"Next week. We'll come to you, we can go out for something to eat."

"Okay, Blake, sounds good," Maeve replies. She tells me she'll speak to me in the week to organise it and then she rings off. Rose looks at me.

"Next week? You didn't want to do it this week?" she asks.

"I thought we could spend this week catching up on some lost time." I grin. She laughs as she pushes me onto the sofa. She climbs onto the sofa, pulling me close and kissing me.

"Sounds perfect," she whispers between kisses.

I couldn't agree more.

Chapter Twenty-Six

Epilogue

Interview by Jemma Smyth:

On Friday night, I was given an all-access pass to interview Blake Daniels and Rose Dalton ahead of their performance at their sold-out concert. Daniels and Dalton rarely give interviews, instead choosing to interact with fans via social media.

Daniels and Dalton have had two meteoric years. From their whirlwind romance, record-breaking albums, sold out concerts, domination at music awards, to them being announced as the new faces of fashion houses, there doesn't seem to be any stopping this sensational power couple.

Daniels and Dalton had two requests for this interview: for the bulk of questions to be submitted via their fans, and for their answers to be printed as provided.

Below is the transcript.

Interviewer: Thank you for the opportunity to interview you. You are both incredibly private, so what made you decide to give an interview?

Rose: It is true that we haven't given interviews for some time, but after this concert, we'll be taking some downtime, and it seemed like an opportunity to speak to our fans and answer any questions.

Interviewer: Were you surprised at the success of your albums *Longing*, *Loving*, and *Devotion*?

Rose: Yes. [Laughs.]

Blake: [Laughs.] She's so critical of herself.

Rose: I always get nervous ahead of an album launch, but especially so with these. We worked so hard on them, and they feel so special to me. I was so emotionally invested with them. I just hoped that people felt the same way as I did—as we did.

Blake: Originally, when we started writing music together, we were going to release an album each with our chosen tracks. I think we each planned about eighteen songs with a few featuring the other. We initially wondered if the label would like the proposed albums and when they called us in for a meeting after we posted two tracks online, we thought we were in for a grilling.

Rose: [Laughs.] I thought I was going to get dropped by the label. They sat us down and said they didn't want to release the albums we planned. I wasn't sure who was protesting first, me or Blake, but then the team laughed and told us they wanted us to release three albums under a combined name.

Blake: We were thrilled. We released *Longing* first, under the name of Red Indiana. It went crazy. The second and third album were just as popular.

Interviewer: Do you have plans to release music under Red Indiana, after the success of your three albums?

Rose: We're taking a break for a while. As well as these three albums, we each released an album. I felt like we were living in the studio at one point. We both need a breather. I'm sure we will release music together in the future, as well as our own music.

Interviewer: It is understood that Red is from Rose's initials, but where does Indiana come from?

Rose: Over to you, babe.

Blake: [Laughs.] It's a nickname Red gave me. Captain Indiana, wasn't it, Rose?

Rose: [Laughs.] Only when on the tandem bike.

Interviewer: You are both known for having several tattoos. How many do you both have now, and are there any with any special meaning?

Blake: I have five. I love all of mine. As soon as my mandala tattoo was finished, I booked the artist for my rose on my chest. When we released the first album, I had my favourite lyrics of one of her songs done. I added our wedding date to my dragon tattoo. I think the dragon is special to us both.

Rose: I have four, but my favourite is the dragon behind my ear.

Blake: That is my favourite of yours, too, but I am waiting for you to get that cartoon bird tattoo you keep promising me.

Rose: Dream on, babe.

Interviewer: What do you say to people who say this relationship is fake, for media manipulation and record sales?

Rose: People say that, still? Wow. I feel sad for them. Imagine being somebody who can't accept the genuine love and joy a couple have together.

Interviewer: What do you say to critics who say you rushed into marriage?

Rose: I think people don't understand that we were together for some time before we went public. We spent a lot of time together. For over three months it was just us two, hidden away, getting to know one another and falling in love. So, yes, when we married, people assumed it was fast, but it wasn't as fast as they thought, not really. We were together for over a year when we got married.

Blake: Ultimately, though, when you know, you know. I saw something somewhere saying you shouldn't marry somebody if you haven't lived together through all seasons. We did that, and we were with each other during highs as well as some really low times, for both of us. Whatever life throws at us, I know I want to go through any future low with Rose, and I want to celebrate the future highs with her. We make each other stronger.

Interviewer: Rose, your parents were quite vocal about your wedding to Blake. They accused you of belittling the sanctity of marriage by rushing into things.

Rose: Yes, and I will say the same thing I said to their faces, for them to keep their nose out of our marriage. I never comment on theirs and would appreciate the same from them.

Interviewer: Your father famously left his girlfriend to publicly beg for your mother's forgiveness. You don't have a comment about that?

Rose: No comment.

Interviewer: So you don't—

Blake: She said she had no comment, move it along.

Interviewer: This is supposed to be a tell-all interview.

Rose: Fine, I hope my parents are happy, whatever their decision about their future. Also, perhaps people who have a complicated history in their own marriage shouldn't throw stones. People in glass houses, and all that.

Interviewer: Can I quote you on that?

Rose: We agreed you could quote us, word for word, for this article. No edits. No cuts.

Blake: Whenever Bianca and Ethan want to talk, they know how to find us.

Interviewer: I assume things are still rocky with your relationship with your parents, Rose. How about your parents, Blake?

Blake: We see them. They're supportive. They love Rose to pieces. Rose has been a powerful force in bringing us all together, including arranging both my parents to join us for celebrations for our birthdays. Things like that are just another of the many things I love about my wife—something my parents love, too.

Interviewer: How is your father, Blake?

Blake: Luckily, he is still in remission. He had a checkup last week and was happily announcing that he's going to live for decades. [Laughs.] I'm grateful for his health and for all the care he got when he was sick.

Interviewer: Did you ever take a DNA test to establish if he is your biological father?

Blake: Nope. I decided it doesn't really matter. He's the man who raised me. He's my father. I'm not interested in anything else.

Interviewer: It is rumoured you both changed your surname when you married, is that true?

Rose: Yes, although we are still happy to be referred to as Daniels and Dalton, we merged our surnames and both changed to Danton.

Blake: I wanted the same name as my wife, but I didn't care what it was.

Rose: I said I would change to Daniels because I wanted to share a name with my husband, too, but he was the one who suggested we create our own. We considered everything, but eventually decided to merge them together. We're still part of the families we came from, but this is us being how we want our family to be going forwards.

Interviewer: You are often pictured on the east coast in the UK. Is it true you have a home there?

Blake: Yes! We decided we couldn't stand leaving the home we fell in love in, so we asked the homeowners if they would sell it to us. We ended up buying the other three homes on the road, too. They were earmarked to be demolished, and we decided we would keep them, exactly as they are. We stay in the house when we get a gap in the schedules. We feel at home there. The rest of the homes continue as holiday rentals.

Rose: We love the area. It's so peaceful. We do all the things we did when we first got together, we ride this tandem bike that Blake got for us, we cook together, we take long walks on the beach.

Interviewer: You often post on your social media sites videos and pictures of you cooking. How regularly do you cook?

Blake: She is such a good cook. I love coming home when I've had a busy day and she's cooking tea. She always sings when she cooks, it's my favourite sight and sound to come home to.

Rose: He is a much better cook than me. He doesn't sing when he cooks, but he sings when he preps. He'll be chopping carrots and singing a love song. So, yeah, when I come home and find him like that, I'll take a picture and upload it, or I film it and share it, to keep that there as a memory.

Blake: I don't think I've told this story in an interview before, but do you know the moment I realised I was falling in love with Rose? It was when I came to the house we were sharing. I walked in to find her singing when she was cooking. I'd heard her singing before, obviously, but I remember leaning against the doorway to the kitchen and listening to her for a minute. She looked and sounded like an angel, and she made my heart skip a beat. She still does.

Rose: If I remember correctly, I then spent the next day throwing up.

Blake: [Laughs.] I was saving that for my autobiography.

Interviewer: You're on social media in a much more informal way than you were a few years ago, Rose, why is that?

Rose: I feel like I have the freedom to be myself now. Before we released the albums, I sat with my management team about how I wanted to do things in the future, starting with me being more open on social media. I love my fans, and I love interacting with them on social media. I hope this continues.

Interviewer: In addition to your home on the east coast, you have a residence in Blake's hometown. Is this where you spend the bulk of your time?

Blake: Yes, that is our primary home. We love it there. It's not far for us to travel to the recording studios when we need to be there. We purchased the house before we got engaged, but initially, we didn't spend a lot of time there as we were in the recording studio so much. We were in the studio and then at the hotel, and we would be looking for furniture, trawling through sites for wallpaper, planning everything.

Rose: I know people are thinking, why didn't they just hire somebody to do it for them, but we wanted to do everything together, ourselves. Our friends Libby and Maeve kept giving us recommendations for teams who "stage" the house, but we wanted the items in our home to be the things we had picked out. We wanted the sofa we sit on to be the one I'd conceded to because he'd let me pick the dining table we eat at every night.

Interviewer: Rose, you are sometimes pictured in both towns you have residences with other women and a couple of children.

Rose: Yes. I assume there is a question there? You want to know who they are but trying to be delicate because one of the women is somebody Blake used to date? [Laughs.] Yes, when we are home, I occasionally spend time with Olive and her children. Sometimes, Blake and I go to her house to eat with her family. Sometimes Olive and Tyler come to ours. When we are at the coast, we will catch up with the former homeowner, her husband, and their two children. It's all very normal.

Interviewer: There is no jealousy between you?

Both: [Laughs.] No.

Blake: Why would there be?

Interviewer: You seem very secure.

Rose: We are.

Interviewer: Were you always secure? Shortly after your wedding, Isla Greenway accused Rose in being instrumental in the breakdown of her marriage. Were you secure then?

Blake: Yes.

Interviewer: You didn't release an immediate statement. How were you handling this revelation? Why did it take so long to respond?

Blake: We didn't know the news was out there, to be honest. We had decided to be uncontactable during our honeymoon. No phones, no internet, no news, just us two. It was beautiful, blissful.

Rose: [Laughs.] We did a lot of swimming, too.

Blake: It was an amazing honeymoon. Then we landed back in the UK, and it was just carnage. There were so many articles, multiple ones posted every day we were away. Headlines calling Rose a homewrecker, a heartbreaker. People were discussing her on gossip sites and calling her names. People who didn't know anything about us were quoted saying I had started divorce proceedings.

Rose: I'm still waiting for those papers, babe.

Blake: Never, my sweet.

Interviewer: How did you feel going through this?

Blake: Our joking aside, it made me sick, watching people tear apart the woman I love, making false statements about us but more specifically against her. For days, the papers run sleazy, disgusting statements about her. There was a lot of speculation about us, too, even discussing whether we had a prenup, saying we'd been having blazing rows. There was nothing like that going on, at all.

Interviewer: It was reported you were blindsided and devastated.

Blake: You can't be blindsided if you already know the truth. Rose and I, we know everything about each other. We spent months together, talking about everything. I knew everything. Any devastation for me was about how Rose felt having everything thrown at her. People were posting comments that we were having blazing rows when in reality, I was holding my wife and telling her how much I love her.

Interviewer: You previously have only addressed this topic once, when you issued a statement saying, and I quote, *"I know the truth about my wife, and I remain dazzled by her."*

Blake: Yes, and that statement is still true. She dazzles me, every day. She has the most beautiful soul.

Rose: Don't make me cry, Blake! We're due on stage soon. [Laughs.] Blake forgets how much he dazzles me. I'm blessed to be loved by him, and every day I wake up grateful to be with the man I love.

Interviewer: Hunter Greenway was recently dropped by his management team and has checked into rehab for sex addiction, citing an addiction to extreme pornography. How would you respond to that, Rose?

Rose: I hope he gets the help he needs.

Interviewer: Do you think rehab works?

Rose: I have no personal experience of rehab, but yes, I believe it works but only if the person puts in the work themself.

Interviewer: Did you do the work after rehab?

Blake: Rose did not go to rehab. She didn't need rehab. What was it you said?

Rose: I wasn't in rehab; I was falling in love.

Blake: I loved that statement of yours. You should work that into a song at some point.

Rose: Only if you work in your "do better" statement.

Blake: People do need to do better. The rehab rumours are complete fabrications. Any time they come up I'm going to refute them. If she had been in rehab, Rose would have been open and honest about it, if only to tell others going through a difficult time that you can make things better.

Interviewer: Hunter issued a statement that alluded to him mistreating Rose, among other women. He has vowed to make amends. Any response to that, Rose?

Rose: I have no interest in hearing any apologies. All I would say is I hope Isla and her children live happy lives, and if there are women who Hunter hurt, they are also doing well.

Interviewer: In the songs you released on social media, in response to Blake's song, you noted a man who "*destroyed my youth.*" Was that Hunter?

Rose: I'm sure the person I alluded to in that song knows who they are and what they did.

Interviewer: After Hunter issued his statement about being treated for sex addiction, the director Martin Wise gave an interview, noting he wished he had been able to continue with you in his project. He said he would love to work with you in the future. Would you, Rose?

Rose: Perhaps, in the future.

Interviewer: Would you be willing to meet with Hunter in the future?

Rose: No, I don't believe that is necessary.

Blake: I think we have wasted enough time on Hunter Greenway.

Interviewer: What do you say to those who say your relationship won't last?

Blake: I say, come back in fifty years, come see how we're still together, how much we still love each other. I know I'll still be holding her hand, wondering how I got so goddamn lucky as to spend my life with my soulmate.

Rose: Goddamn, Blake, you really are going to make me cry. But he is right. In fifty years, we will be sat together somewhere, strumming on our guitars and singing to our children, our grandchildren, and hopefully, our great-grandchildren.

At this, Rose puts a hand on her stomach. Blake holds her other hand and kisses her fingers. They both have big smiles.

Interviewer: Are you pregnant?

Rose: [Laughs.] You cannot seriously tell me a fan submitted that question. I've been so careful not to hold my stomach in public or wear anything too revealing.

Interviewer: No, that is my own question.

Blake: [Laughs.] Sneaky.

Rose: Well, yes. There's a five-month baby bump being hidden by excellent tailoring right now, like it has been for the whole tour.

Interviewer: Congratulations to you both.

Rose: Our planned downtime will be a carefree, restful third trimester, and then adjusting to life with a newborn. I can't wait. I'm sure I'm driving him mad, but I can't help dreaming about what they're going to be like. We don't know what we're having as we want it to be a surprise, but I wonder who they will take after. Will they have my eyes or his? Will they be dark haired like him, or light like me? There's this little baby that hasn't arrived yet, but I already love them so much. I'm so excited. Blake's going to be an amazing dad.

Blake: I can't wait, either. You're going to be an amazing mum, my sweet. I'm so excited about our future.

The interview is interrupted by somebody from their management team who informs them it is time to get ready for being on stage. Chanting from the audience, shouting for both Rose and Blake, echoes around the room. Before they leave, Rose stops. She has one hand on Blake, one on her stomach.

Rose: To those who say this a scam, say this isn't going to last, they're wrong. This is real. This is everything. This is our forever.

www.ingramcontent.com/pod-product-compliance
Lightning Source LLC
LaVergne TN
LVHW010051110826
845155LV00028B/295

* 9 7 8 1 9 1 8 1 7 5 0 2 8 *